'In a sense he was indeed being reborn. He had shed the accumulated responsibilities of a lifetime and set out with simply a set of rough clothes, even pounds ten shillings, and two books of rse as his passport to the new world...."

Mr. Sermon, R. F. Delderfield has written one his most delightful books—the story of a modern 'Mr. Chips' suddenly fed up with his life as schoolteacher, who leaves wife, home, and all e owns to set out on the road to freedom.

Ahead lies Mr. Sugg, the odd little man who teaches him the antiques trade, the generous hearted Olga who welcomes him into her home, and Rachel, the fascinating young girl who leads him into the springtime of love.

It would be unfair to tell more, but after many turns the road leads to an ending every bit as satisfying as the readers of R. F. Delderfield's *God Is an Englishman* and *A Horseman Riding By* have come to expect.

"Filled with real scenes, real people and real action....The characters in **Mr. Sermon** are so beautifully drawn, the settings are so exquisitely worded and there is such a basis of common sense under the whole plot that this book is delightful reading." —*Best sellers*

MR. SERMON
was originally published by
Simon and Schuster.

Other books by R. F. Delderfield

The Avenue
The Green Gauntlet
A Horseman Riding By
God Is an Englishman

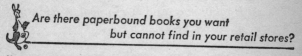

*Are there paperbound books you want
but cannot find in your retail stores?*

You can get any title in print in:
Pocket Book editions • Pocket *Cardinal* editions • Permabook editions or Washington Square Press editions. Simply send retail price, local sales tax, if any, plus 15¢ to cover mailing and handling costs for each book wanted to:

MAIL SERVICE DEPARTMENT
    POCKET BOOKS • A Division of Simon & Schuster, Inc.
    1 West 39th Street   •   New York, New York 10018
    Please send check or money order. We cannot be responsible for cash.
    Catalogue sent free on request.

Titles in these series are also available at discounts in quantity lots for industrial or sales-promotional use. For details write our Special Projects Agency: The Benjamin Company, Inc., 485 Madison Avenue, New York, N.Y. 10022.

MR. SERMON

a novel by
R. F. Delderfield

PUBLISHED BY POCKET BOOKS NEW YORK

MR. SERMON

Simon and Schuster edition published January, 1970
Pocket Book edition published April, 1971

This *Pocket Book* edition includes every word
contained in the original, higher-priced edition. It is printed
from brand-new plates made from completely reset, clear, easy-to-read
type. *Pocket Book* editions are published by Pocket Books, a division
of Simon & Schuster, Inc., 630 Fifth Avenue, New York, N.Y. 10020.
Trademarks registered in the United States and other countries.

Standard Book Number: 671-78062-X.
Library of Congress Catalog Card Number: 73-84121.

Printed in the U.S.A.

For
Guy Bavington
Who—
Always demanded a school story
and was the first I heard ask:
"How much off for the Trade?"
In friendship,
R. F. Delderfield

Contents

MR. SERMON

CHAPTER ONE

In Which
Mr. Sermon Smells Lilac
and Hits Out

It is not given to many of us to pinpoint the actual moment of our entry into a world of new beginnings. In any case, most of us don't have new beginnings but spend half our days and nights dreaming of them, of a fresh start, a setting out on a beckoning high-road to adventure and romance, a spiritual and physical rebirth. Very few of us get beyond the early stages of packing and on looking back we can recall only the trivial things, nothing really important, like being born or reborn. But Mr. Sermon can! He can recall exactly how it happened, and why it happened, and when it happened! He remembers every irrelevant detail, the season of year, the time of day, the slant of the sunbeam through the tall classroom window that invested Lane-Perkins (Satanic if unconscious midwife of the event) with a golden halo. He remembers too the battle of the smells that was being fought out under his nostrils that afternoon, the massed aromae of ink, new exercise books, dust, apple-cores, lozenges and chalky dusters all marching to vanquish the gallant smell of Spring. He remembers this and will never forget it, not even when he is an old, old man, dying in some impersonal nursing home, watched by impersonal mutes. And he remembers so well

because it was the most stupendous thing that ever happened
to him or ever would happen to him, come earthquakes,
global convulsions, nuclear wars and landings on the moon.

.   .   .   .   .

It began on the nineteenth of April, the second day of the
summer term, at precisely 3.20 p.m., a soft, warm, sweet,
nostalgic afternoon. It was quieter in class than he ever remembered, so quiet that it had crossed his mind earlier in the
period that mischief was fermenting somewhere among the
hard core of the Upper Fourth, somewhere near the tall
Gothic window under which Lane-Perkins and his cronies sat
like knots in a bulk of grained oak, knots that would resist
to the very end the efforts of educational sawyers and then,
come September, disappear only to materialise instantaneously
in the Lower Fifth, whence they had gone after the process
that ejects all dullards from familiar desks, forcing them to
adjust themselves to new syllabuses and fresh opposition.

You could almost feel the quiet. Nothing disturbed it save
an occasional scrape of shoe against the uncarpeted floor or
the soft rustle of a turned page as the odd boy ploughed
through Froude's *English Seamen of the Sixteenth Century,*
the Upper Fourth's summer-term 'author'. This was the
book that the Upper Fourth were reading that period, the
book that 'Preacher' Sermon, in his capacity as English and
History master at Napier Hall College, had chosen as a means
of attacking simultaneously on two fronts. It was good literature and it was stirring Protestant history. Mr. Sermon had
read *English Seamen of the Sixteenth Century* at least once
a year ever since he was a boy at school and continued to
enjoy its rich cadences and shameless Victorian bias.

It was very early in the term for Middle School to have a
free period, with no questions asked and no prospect of an
oral examination on the task they were set, but Mr. Sermon
had good reason for the novelty. The Reverend Victor
Hawley, owner-headmaster of Napier Hall College, had not
yet returned from his extended holiday in Lucerne and had
wired Mr. Sermon, his deputy, to prepare the school timetables, a chore that usually occupied the Head the last week
of the holidays.

Mr. Sermon had not minded the extra work. He was a

man with a neat, precise mind and he loved graphs and charts and timetables for their own sake. He was also an exceptionally concientious employee, always eager to oblige any member of the staff or any earnest scholar or even a tradesman at odds with Mrs. Fishwick, the matron-house-keeper. Like all the married masters at Napier College, Mr. Sermon lived out but he seldom caught his bus to Wyckham Rise until five-thirty, more than an hour after the end of afternoon school. Usually he remained behind to stake out pitches, supervise games, mark books, stack chairs, or carry out one or other of the innumerable duties connected with the boarding section of the school. For this, and for his painstaking tutorial work, the Reverend Hawley paid him seven hundred a year, less an insurance stamp and P.A.Y.E. deductions. It was not a big salary for a man who had only just entered his fiftieth year but neither Mr. Sermon himself nor the headmaster had ever given a thought to its inadequacy, the one because he enjoyed his work and had never been interested in money, the other because he was aware (and often boasted of the fact to parents) that his most trusted colleague had married money and, in addition, had a real vocation for teaching. Otherwise, why should Sermon have remained at Napier Hall ever since his discharge from the Ordnance Corps in 1944, and he the only man on the staff with a worthwhile degree?

The drowsy peace of the classroom persisted. Bateman Two, one of the very few boys genuinely interested in the junketings of Hawkins and Drake on the Spanish Main, turned his pages carefully and gnawed the hard skin alongside his thumbnail. Screened by the absorbed Bateman Minor, Vincent and Cooper One were sharing *Lady Chatterley's Lover* which rested on their knees four inches below desk level. Over near the window Lane-Perkins yawned, picked his nose and began to forage in his jacket pocket for the cone of French incense he had brought home from Ostend. Every now and then Mr. Sermon glanced at the class over horn-rimmed glasses and experience told him instantly that Vincent and Cooper One were not reading *English Seamen of the Sixteenth Century* but something more up to date. He said nothing, however, believing it to be space fiction.

Then, at 3.16 p.m. exactly, Mr. Sermon was conscious of the first pattering rain that was to build into the avalanche

that engulfed him and everyone connected with him. A large
bumble-bee droned in at the open window bringing with it the
rich, nostalgic scent of lilac and Lane-Perkins looked hopefully at the bee, willing it with all his might to settle on
Bateman's neck, thus varying the dreadful tedium of the
afternoon. Something like that had happened late in the
Easter term when a dying wasp had stung Dobbs-Stewart on
the mouth but today the Upper Fourth was out of luck. The
bee recoiled from the smell of ink, chalk and exercise books
and veered round, escaping out of the window as if the Devil
was behind it. Moodily Lane-Perkins continued to forage for
his incense cone.

Sebastian Sermon, 'Preacher' to everyone at Napier Hall
College Preparatory School for Boys, had watched the flight
of the bee and it had disturbed him, causing an abrupt cessa-
tion of interest in the timetables and setting up a train of
thought that had absolutely nothing to do with the filling in of
a blank period of Thursday afternoon for Lower School boys
who did not take Latin. It was almost as though the bee had
swerved in flight to buzz him a message, crying out that
Spring was outside the window and that somewhere beyond
the dusty shrubbery were rolling acres of downland stirring
with a myriad form of life pushing and pushing to break
through to the sun and, what was worse, reminding him of
the curious depression that had obsessed him throughout the
last week of the Lent holidays. It was a depression that he
had traced to the savage realisation that only a week ago he
had been a man in his forties and that now he had almost
entered upon his fifties, time was running short and that his
life stretched out behind him like a grey track across an
empty moor merging into a general pattern of drabness and
aimlessness, so that he was suddenly frightened of marching
another stride into the future. The panic had been real at the
time but he had mastered it, indeed had almost forgotten it
in the rush of preparing for the new term. He was a man who
never surrendered to panic and seldom to exasperation and
he had tried to bring to this curious birthday-morning crisis
the cool judgement that he brought to the solving of school
problems. He had taken a deep breath and looked long and
hard into his shaving-mirror where he saw a narrow, intelligent face, with receding brown hair, a long and slightly
inquisitive nose, a mouth that was neither too large nor too

small, a pair of grey, thoughtful eyes with long, boyish lashes and an Adam's apple that had always seemed to him prominent but which nobody had ever commented upon.

He had studied the face seriously, comparing it with the eager, questing expression that looked out from snapshots of the twenties and the early thirties, or the proud, challenging face of Sebastian Sermon standing beside his bride, Sybil, on their wedding day just before the war and although something had departed from the reflection in the mirror, something that might have been promise, or confidence, or a streak of determination to become something more than an assistant master at a minor Preparatory School, he had not found the face unpleasing. He did not look forty-nine. He still had a clear skin, most of his hair and what his mother had termed his 'sitting-for-examinations look', yet, there was no denying it, something had departed.

But what? That was the rub. He had never really known, never having defined a goal, or sat down and cold-bloodedly plotted a course like other men and now, with the warning of the bee buzzing in his ear and the half-finished timetables under his hand, depression swept down once more and he thought it odd and disturbing that a person who had always prided himself on possessing a tidy, departmentalised mind should have overlooked such a vital matter as this. Where was he going and why?

The shock of the question and the certainty that he could not begin to answer it caused him to shiver and at once he looked swiftly at the class to see whether any of the front row boys had noticed the shudder. To his dismay Lane-Perkins was looking straight at him, with his usual bovine and slightly insolent expression, so that Mr. Sermon flushed and then rallied, staring back so fiercely that Lane-Perkins dropped his glance and ostentatiously turned a page of his book.

Then it occurred to Mr. Sermon that he might be sickening for something, a chill or an infection, dating back to his birthday a few days ago but in his heart he knew that this was not so, that he enjoyed perfect health and hardly ever caught cold, not even in winter months when half the class was snuffling into handkerchiefs. He knew also that this spreading discomfort, this nameless depressive, seeping dread, was a mental and spiritual condition and that it had been hovering

in the background for some months but had been held in
leash by the reflection that forty-eight was not old, was hardly
middle-age and that there was therefore plenty of time,
months and months of time in which to discuss the possibility
of a change with Sybil and perhaps take Jonquil and Keith,
his daughter and son, into his confidence. The trouble was he
hardly ever conferred with his family nowadays, they were
always so deeply engrossed in their own affairs and did not
need him as an audience, much less as a confidant. Sybil was
already immersed in her Spring production for the Wyckham
Rise Operatic and Dramatic Society and the garden-room at
their home was thronged with amateurs five nights a week,
laughing, talking, trilling and flirting with Sybil his wife who
could be seen queening it over everyone.

Three-seventeen of the clock. Time was running out. Mr.
Sermon and all his world were sitting astride a rocket destined
for the outer space of experience. In quick succession he
thought of his wife, son and daughter: Sybil, dark, creamy-
skinned, buttressed from the beginning by cool good looks
and her father's money; Keith, tall and rangy, with his
mother's regular features and her powers of unlimited concentration—in his case the noisiest and dirtiest machines
available; and finally Jonquil, his seventeen-and-a-half-year-
old daughter, wide-mouthed, petulant, sought-after, with a
little girl's pout, a mature woman's figure and the arrogance
of youth perched on her hoisted bust. An impressive trio,
anyone would admit that, but what had he in common with
it or it with him? What link, what ties, now or in the past?

3.18 p.m. The scent of lilacs was so powerful that it
seemed to be whispering like spruce tops in a summer breeze
and it spoke to him of youth and laughter and triumph, the
triumph he had himself experienced when he led Sybil down
the aisle of her father's Methodist Church, treading a carpet
given by Sybil's father, past pews restored by Sybil's father,
to a car presented by Sybil's father the night before the
wedding.

Why? That was what he had been asking himself for nearly
nineteen years. How did it come about that the daughter of
a man owning thirteen suburban grocery shops had favoured
his forlorn suit from the outset? Why had Sybil's amused
contempt been converted to tolerance and then into near
eagerness in the weeks leading up to the engagement? What

had he ever had to offer apart from ardour, gratitude and the ability to provide himself with pocket money and a pound or two to spare? Yet Sybil had treated him civilly and the marriage was judged a success. There had been two children in the first three years and thereafter polite acquiescence on her part in bed and out of bed. He was still titular head of the house. She consulted him on matters such as furniture replacements, gas-bills, garden lay-out and the venue of the annual holiday. It was usually he who drove the family car. What possible excuse had he for resentment? She did not nag, she did not have tantrums. She was not extravagant and if she had been it was mostly her money. She was generous, even-tempered, very popular and in some ways far less of a snob than he was himself. If she had a fault at all it was that of giving too much of herself to social activities, like the Wyckham Rise Operatic and Dramatic Society but surely this was pardonable in a woman who had never, throughout the whole of their married life, been rude to him, defied him or ceased, even at the moment of waking, to look cool, composed and far more desirable than most women of thirty-nine.

3.19 p.m. Bateman Minor slumped forward on his elbows and turned another page. Vincent nudged Cooper impatiently, indicating that he also should turn over and penetrate deeper into the now world-famous gamekeeper's hut. Lane-Perkins sneezed into his handkerchief in order to cover the soft explosion of a safety match held between his knees. Mr. Sermon did not notice any of these trivial incidents, he was inhaling the lilac perfume in long, deep breaths and letting it carry him back to the year 1929 when he was seventeen and walking out of Selhurst Grammar School Boys' entrance for the last time, holding his three summer-term prizes under his arm and swinging his gym shoes with a carelessness that betokened freedom, youth and a confident advance into the adult world that lay waiting.

Where had it led, that sunlit, lilac-scented path? To a provincial University, a Degree and more prizes, to hours and hours of concentrated study in his bedroom in Yew Tree Road, Norwood. To eyestrain and a touch of asthma that had cost him a job at a good public school in Cumberland. To a series of frustrating, disagreeable jobs in Preparatory Schools up and down the country. To a wretchedly disappointing year as a Civil Servant and then, inexplicably, to another school in Sybil's suburb of Beckenham, eighteen minutes by electric from Charing Cross Station. Then the war and further penalties for Grade Two Vision and the youthful tussle with asthma. Rejected by the R.A.F., he had at last wriggled into the Ordnance Corps as a clerk and spent two frustrating years in the orderly-room of a depot, dividing his time between routine chores and attending to the commercial correspondence of the junior officers. On several occasions he had made strenuous efforts to get a commission and once had passed the Selection Board and entered upon the preliminary Course but the bogey ran him down in the end, laying him by the heels at the scramble net of the Commando course and hauling him, bleating out breathless excuses, before the examiners to receive the degrading Returned-to-Unit chit.

Sybil had been wonderful about that. Most wives, he imagined, would have concealed their contempt under feigned indifference but Sybil was indignant at the blindness of the military machine.

"They don't deserve you, Sebastian, dear," she had said, when he returned on leave, with his pride in ribbons; "I shall get Daddy to reclaim you to industry and we'll find you another school, a nice, better-class type of school, further out of London."

And she had done just that. She had got him out of the Services and found him the post at Napier Hall, only a three-penny bus ride from their new home and here he had remained, year after year, with the full confidence of the Headmaster (to whom staff vacancies were a permanent nightmare) and the tolerant acceptance of the boys who, on the whole, considered him a moderately sporting old buffer, a bit of a weed on the sports field but less of a bore than most of the men paid to prepare them for Common Entrance.

Ten seconds to go. Mr. Sermon took off his spectacles and wiped them carefully and as he half turned to replace his handkerchief in his jacket pocket his narrow nostrils quivered as an alien scent stole up on the lilac and drove it back through the open window. The lilac, however, made a final rally and in the last few seconds of Mr. Sermon's old life it almost drugged him with memories, the memory of quiet, inner satisfaction on gaining his Degree, of Sybil's lips and white body in the bedroom of the hotel during their Bourne-mouth honeymoon, of the ache and tug of remembered vistas seen during his solitary walking tours in North Wales, of the dazzling splendour of the rainbow of life always just out of reach but always there, glistening with the promise of Spring sunshine like the shaft now deifying Lane-Perkins' bullet-head. Then the alien scent triumphed and the lilac shambled away and the pungent smell of French incense filled the whole room, vanquishing not only Spring but the more lowly odours of ink and chalk and apple-cores and stale dust. Half the boys began coughing and all but Bateman Minor began to snigger behind spread palms.

"Stand up the boy who is making that disgusting smell!"

Mr. Sermon's voice had an edge to it that Lane-Perkins and his cronies failed to recognise, such a sharp edge indeed that nobody moved and the more discerning among them were startled by the grim expression on Preacher's face. All the easy tolerance and professionally cultivated irony were gone. It was a flushed, pitiless face, with suffering behind eyes that blinked and blinked with a kind of senseless fury. The mouth, usually relaxed, was now a savage line, and the taut cheeks twitched. The head was out-thrust, like the head of a bull on the point of charging a phalanx of tormentors.

"Christ!" murmured Vincent to himself, hastily slipping *Lady Chatterley's Lover* into his desk and jerking it under his Atlas. "What's the matter with old Preacher this afternoon? He looks as if he could murder the ruddy lot of us!"

"Stand up I said! Stand up! Come out here!"

Nobody moved and five seconds ticked by in silence. Then Mr. Sermon himself stood up, grating his chair along the dais and jumped down to the level of the classroom floor, making straight for Lane-Perkins who had paled and was reaching forward to screen his inkwell-hole with both hands.

It was a foolhardy gesture and a boy of his experience should have known better but the edge of Preacher's voice had rattled his nerves. Suddenly Preacher was towering above him and yanking at his hands so that they were dragged clear of the inkwell-hole and a blue spiral of incense crawled steadily upward.

Now that Mr. Sermon was safely anchored near the window all but Lane-Perkins relaxed and there was an involuntary titter. Mr. Sermon looked hard at the spiral, sniffing it and then, with a vicious sweep of his hand he knocked Lane-Perkins to one side and flung up the desk-lid so that the spiral became a bluish cloud, so thick and sour that the outburst of coughing was genuine and one or two of the bolder pretended to retch.

Then it happened. The taut elastic that had held Sebastian Sermon to sanity and tolerance for a quarter-century snapped and its flailing ends coiled round his brain like a whiplash. He could not have said what made him act in such an extravagant manner. Perhaps there is more truth in the old adages than we know and perhaps the final straw really does break the camel's back. Or perhaps there was something terrifyingly symbolic in the conquest of the lilac by Lane-Perkins' cone of incense, the inevitability of the overthrow of sweetness by barbarism, the terrible certainty that, sooner or later, heavy-footed oafs will trample the lilacs to a mush. Whatever it was, it converted Mr. Sermon in an instant into a reckless fiend, sweeping away his self-discipline and trumpeting berserk defiance at every canon of tutorial law. With a whimper of rage he seized the recoiling Lane-Perkins by the coat and began to beat him about the head and face with his open hand, smack after smack that rang out like a volley of pistol shots and ended in the boy tearing himself free and bolting madly for the door.

He did not get more than a yard or so. Mr. Sermon sprang in pursuit, grabbed him by the collar and threw him sideways on top of the blameless Bateman, whose face was rammed down against his own desk-lid with such violence that his spectacles snapped at the bridge and a lens flew in each direction. The classroom exploded with sound, Lane-Perkins' terrified squeals, Bateman's agonised squawk, the grinding crash of desks and the shocked protest of scholars, all scurrying this way and that in their efforts to dodge the struggling group near the window. Only Vincent, sharp for his age, realised that something was seriously wrong and that it behooved somebody to intervene. Gallantly he laid restraining hands on Mr. Sermon's left arm and hung on gamely but he was an under-sized boy and could do little to check the rhythmic jerk of Sebastian's right arm which now had Lane-Perkins in an unbreakable grip and was exploiting it by flinging his victim against the hot-water pipes. Every time Lane-Perkins' head or shoulders struck the pipes a hollow boom echoed along the system, passing across the hall and into the adjoining classroom, where Mr. Twyning, the Geography master, was explaining the nature of isotherms.

It is profitless to guess what might have happened in the end. Lane-Perkins might have collapsed with a fractured skull or Mr. Sermon might have tired and flung the boy aside like a handful of chaff, or some of the other boys might have come to the gallant Vincent's aid before murder was committed. As it was, the uproar was heard by the Reverend Victor Hawley as he mounted the steps that led from his residential quarters to his book-lined study which lay directly across the hall from the Upper Fourth. For a moment the Headmaster stood stock still a stride beyond the glass door, wondering whether there had been a head-on collision between lorries passing down the main Crowborough Road. Then, with a gasp of dismay, he realised that the cacophony came from inside the house and at once located its source as the Upper Fourth. He dithered a second or so, unwilling to believe that this could be so, and then, gathering his trailing gown, he ran across the hall and flung open the heavy door, standing on the threshold and gazing at the astounding spectacle that met his eyes.

Mr. Sermon had his back to the door and seemed to be performing some kind of Haitian ritual dance, for he was throwing his weight from side to side and putting every ounce of strength into each lunge, a movement made difficult by the dead weight of Vincent hanging on his left arm. He was holding some kind of bundle under his right armpit and the bundle seemed to be alive for it yelped and writhed in Mr. Sermon's grasp.

It was not until he was quite certain that this bundle was indeed a screaming boy that the Reverend Hawley regained the power of motion. With a cry of alarm he jumped through the cloud of bluish smoke (why blue smoke?) and grabbed Mr. Sermon by the shoulders, shouting in his ear and half enfolding master and boys in his billowing gown.

"Stop it! Stop it this instant! Are you mad? Are you insane? *Stop it I say!*"

His voice and his not inconsiderable weight had their effect almost at once. Vincent, weeping with fright, fell to the floor and Mr. Sermon braced himself, looking over his shoulder in a dazed fashion and then recoiling from the beam of the

Headmaster's eye, so that he stepped away from the window and released Lane-Perkins automatically.

The uproar subsided very suddenly and after the outcry the ensuing silence was unreal, as though what had taken place the moment before was an excerpt from a recorded jazz session on a radiogram and somebody had switched it off. The only sounds in the room were Vincent's winded gasps and the steady, gulping sobs of Lane-Perkins, now rocking himself to and fro like a boy with chronic toothache, holding his head with both hands and attempting, but with poor success, to space his gulps with protests. The pause was very welcome to the Reverend Hawley who was the first of the group to recover. He glanced briefly round the room, subduing the already subdued, gathered his gown around him and said, very crisply indeed:

"Lane-Perkins, go up to Matron and await me there! Mr. Sermon, I think perhaps you had better tell me what happened. Vincent, stop snivelling, get up off the floor and pull yourself together! You others, open all the windows and get rid of this disgusting smell. From what does it originate?"

An eager chorus answered this question—"Incense, sir!" "*French* incense, sir!" "In the desk, sir!" and so on, until the Headmaster bellowed for silence. Slowly, with limbs that seemed weighted by fetters, Mr. Sermon dragged himself across to Lane-Perkins' desk and threw up the lid that had fallen during the struggle. A cloud of incense puffed out and Bateman, always anxious to please, ran forward, picked up the glowing cone and threw it out of the window.

"Thank you, Bateman!" said the Reverend Hawley and himself lowered the desk-lid; then, to Mr. Sermon: "Come along now, Mr. Sermon, please," but at the door the Headmaster turned back, facing the class.

"If there is any more noise there will be serious trouble, you understand? Trouble for everyone! Bateman, you're in charge," and he shut the door and followed Mr. Sermon into the tiled hall. Outside the study, Mr. Sermon stood aside to allow his employer to enter first and the Reverend Hawley swept in, as though his senior master was a boy on his way to be caned. Indeed, Mr. Sermon had this impression and would not have been much surprised if the Headmaster had opened the cupboard door and foraged for his ashplant. The enormity of what he had done was beginning to steal up on him, probing the raw edges of his rage and seeking a way into his consciousness. It would be hours, however, before it found a way in, for buttressed by rage and squatting in the very centre of his brain was a malignant imp that almost rejoiced in the catastrophe, that grinned and grimaced and whispered: "There now, it's done! You've been aching to do that to Lane-Perkins for years! He won't sit there leering at you again, you can depend on that! His father will take him away tomorrow of course and probably take out a summons against you the day after, but that won't hurt you as much as it will hurt this pompous slave-driver of a Headmaster. You may get a month or so in gaol but he'll go bankrupt and serve him bloody well right!"

Mr. Sermon listened carefully to what the imp had to say, so carefully in fact that he barely heard the Headmaster's opening remark and was not really conscious of him until that exasperated man took him by the arm and shook it, repeating over and over again: "What is it, Sermon? Are you ill? Did he do something outrageous? Are you yourself, Sermon? What *happened*? Don't you see, I must know? Sit down Mr. Sermon, for pity's sake sit down, and try and pull yourself together, man!"

Mr. Sermon sat, or rather was pushed, into the spoon-backed Victorian chair reserved for parents and visiting Government Inspectors but even then he did not appear to make much effort to revert to the calm, earnest and utterly rational Sebastian Sermon who had conferred with the Head-master in this very room for the past sixteen years. He just sat there, with his hands limp on his knees, staring before him like a man who has seen somebody drown before his eyes and whose brain is still numb with shock. At last he said, almost inaudibly:

"It was the lilac, Headmaster!"

"The *what*? The . . . the *lilac* you say?"

"The scent of lilac! It was coming through the window. Then he touched off that stench, that foul, acrid stench! I don't know, I lost my temper I suppose and I gave him what he deserved! He's been asking for it for a very long time!"

The Reverend Hawley coughed and looked away but behind his dismay was a certain relief for it was now clear that Sermon had suffered some kind of brainstorm and this in itself might provide an emergency exit for the reputation of the school. The very worthiest of men had brainstorms. Wasn't nervous prostration accepted as an occupational risk for schoolmasters?

"Look here, old fellow," he said, more kindly, "I . . . er . . . I think you had better go in to Mrs. Hawley and ask her for a cup of tea. You're obviously not well, not at all well! I'll tell you what, I'll phone for a taxi and you can go home and rest. Don't come in tomorrow and I'll pop over and see you on Saturday! By that time I daresay I shall have sorted things out a little. I'll go and see Lane-Perkins now. Leave everything to me!"

Suddenly Mr. Sermon raised his head and looked hard at the Headmaster. It was as though he was seeing him for the very first time, a squarish, grey-polled old bore, a pedant who concealed his inadequacies under a threadbare gown and a smoke-screen of muscular Christianity and Kiplingesque enthusiasm, a wily old hypocrite intent upon playing the game as played by the Empire-builders of a generation ago, and Mr. Sermon suddenly decided that he had always hated the Reverend Hawley's physical and moral flabbiness, hated his flabby jowls that made him look like an old spaniel and his pursy little mouth that betrayed a weak man's obstinacy. He had, Mr. Sermon decided, flabby, flaccid, outdated mannerisms and tricks of speech. He also had a large brown mole on his receding chin and the mole, unsightly in itself, was made more so by the presence of sprouting hairs. Mr. Sermon took a good look at his Headmaster. Then, shivering slightly, he stood up and was surprised to discover that he topped the Headmaster by at least two inches. It was something he had never previously noted.

"I'm done with it all!" he announced, "I'm getting out of here!"

The Reverend Hawley began to stammer. He looked, thought Mr. Sermon, exactly like one of those idiotic stone dwarfs who smirk at passers-by from the front gardens of suburban houses, vaguely pathetic yet repulsively silly.

"Oh come now, old man . . . it's like I said . . . you're not yourself, you're run down, tho' I can't think why on the second day of the term! Has something happened at home? Have you had a . . . a shock of some sort?"

"I'm perfectly fit," said Mr. Sermon, unexpectedly, "and I never felt less repentant in my life! I don't care what happens to Lane-Perkins! I don't care a jot what his father says or does! It's like I said, Headmaster, that boy, and some of his cronies, have been asking for this ever since they came here and you can regard me as a pioneer. Sooner or later we'll all come to it, mark my words! If somebody doesn't begin handing it out the entire male population of Britain will consist of juvenile delinquents before any of us are much older and greyer!"

The Reverend Hawley swallowed deliberately, choking back a tart rejoinder that would have been expanded into a string of clichés about the sympathetic handling of boys and adult allowances for youthful high spirits. He realised, just in time, that he must forgo platitudes and concentrate on Sermon's health.

"How old are you, Sermon?"

"I was forty-nine last week, Headmaster!" said Mr. Sermon, who seemed almost to have been expecting the question.

The Reverend Hawley relaxed. "Ah, then it's The Change!" he said, gravely.

"Change?"

"Change of life, dear fellow! Physiologically, the change is supposed to be the prerogative of women but I've never believed this, not entirely. Men undergo a change in the late forties and sometimes the manifestation is more subtle than that of its feminine counterpart. It usually lasts about three or four months and takes us all different ways. Sometimes it is a barely susceptible heightening of our innermost faculties but with the highly-strung—and I think you're a case in point, Sermon—the change is very abrupt and . . . er . . . often disturbing. It needs a great deal of sympathy and understanding and I . . . er . . . I think perhaps you should take a week off and discuss it with your wife and doctor. Get some tablets. They have tablets for this kind of thing, you know, not a sedative exactly but something that aims at restoring balance and . . . er . . . mental tranquillity. Now if you'll take my advice . . ."

He stopped because Mr. Sermon was now staring at him with an expression that he could only identify as one of insolence. A little smile hovered about the corners of the man's mouth but the eyes were not smiling.

"Headmaster," said Mr. Sermon, heavily, "you are talking a lot of damned nonsense and what's more you know it!"

The Reverend Hawley's carefully mustered patience ran like liquid from an upturned jug.

"Now look here, Sermon, I've had enough of this! Hang it man, I come home from abroad a day or so late and expect to find things running smoothly and instead I find you thrashing a boy in a manner calculated to . . . to put him in hospital and yourself in front of a Magistrate! I . . ."

But the Headmaster was again interrupted, this time by a perfunctory knock on the door and the appearance of Mrs. Fishwick, the Matron, with a tear-stained Lane-Perkins in tow. Mrs. Fishwick looked very efficient in her starched coif and overalls and Mr. Sermon noticed that Lane-Perkins had a large piece of sticking-plaster on his temple. The moment he saw Mr. Sermon he shrank back, as if faced by a growling mastiff but Mrs. Fishwick took him firmly by the hand, studiously ignoring Mr. Sermon.

"I'm sending Lane-Perkins home," she announced, "and I think someone had better go with him, Headmaster. May I fetch Vincent or one of the others?"

"Certainly!" said the Reverend Hawley, still flushing from the effects of Mr. Sermon's thrust, "but since he's here we can . . . er . . . sort this matter out a little. Come in, Lane-Perkins, nobody is going to hurt you, my boy! Now then, admit to provoking Mr. Sermon beyond reasonable limits. Admit it, boy, in the presence of all of us!"

The malignant imp had now enlarged his lodging in Mr. Sermon's brain and with the cooling of his rage Sermon found that he could look at Lane-Perkins almost affectionately for the timorous urchin now standing beside Matron had been milked of his cockiness and was clearly afraid to approach a step nearer. This realisation would have distressed the original Mr. Sermon very much but now it had a reverse effect. For the first time since he had entered the world of school he felt a kind of grim pride in his achievement and pride elevated him to a position where he could look down on the Reverend Hawley and feel contempt for his entire approach to the business of educating thirteen-year-olds.

Lane-Perkins mumbled: "I had the stinkbomb, sir, I . . . I lit it, but he . . . he . . ." and his voice trailed away as he pointed an accusing finger at the erect Mr. Sermon, now regarding him with clinical interest, rather as a confident doctor confronts a detected hypochondriac.

"Mr. Sermon lost his temper and is quite prepared to admit as much," said the Reverend Hawley, briskly. "Come now, I don't like this kind of thing any more than you do. Suppose you shake hands and apologise to one another?"

The glint of triumph that showed itself in the eye of Lane-Perkins did not escape Mr. Sermon but it caused him to waver for an instant, telling him that the boy was already congratulating himself on having forged a formidable weapon against authority, something that he could use mercilessly throughout the coming term, thus winning complete immunity from punishment or close observation. Then, as by a reflex, the new Mr. Sermon reasserted himself. Turning from the boy and Matron to the hovering Headmaster he said, very deliberately:

"Lane-Perkins has always been a bad influence here. I'm not going to apologise to the insolent little rascal. I don't mind in the least shaking hands with him but I'm damned if I'll apologise for drubbing him and he can go home and tell his father as much if he cares to! If I apologised to him, nobody would be able to do anything with him for the rest of his life. That won't concern me any longer but it wouldn't be fair on the boy himself," and before the Headmaster could reply to this summarisation, Mr. Sermon nodded rather distantly and stalked from the room, ignoring the Headmaster's croak of protest and the look of astonishment that came into the sullen face of the boy.

They heard his steps echo on the tiles in the hall and then the staff-room door bang as he went in to discard his gown and collect his hat and raincoat. Only when his steps sounded again on the tiles and were passing the study door did the Headmaster make a wild grab at the reins of his authority, dismiss Matron and boy and almost run to intercept Sermon as he passed through the conservatory on his way to the path that led round the shrubbery.

"I say, look here Sermon, we simply can't leave things like this. I mean, it's outrageous! That boy's father will be round first thing in the morning. If you could get a doctor's certificate . . . anything . . ." and he trotted beside Mr. Sermon all the way to the wrought-iron gates that opened on to the Crowborough Road.

They reached the road side by side and were moving

towards the bus stop fifty yards beyond the gates when Mr. Sermon paused in his stride.

"Leave me alone!" he hissed. "Do you hear? Leave me alone, you . . . you bumbling old ass!"

Then he strode on, breaking into a run as a Number 79A passed and swung in to the stop and the Reverend Hawley, half-stupefied by mortification, stood stock-still on the edge of the pavement and watched his colleague leap on to the step of the bus with a movement that seemed strangely out of character in a man who was nearly fifty, and whose interest in organised games had been limited to marking out the white lines on the perimeter of the sports field.

"He's mad!" said the Reverend Hawley to himself, as, wretchedly, he retraced his steps to the school gates. "He's stark, staring mad and I shall have to say so! At once! On the telephone to his wife and to that wretched boy's father!"

He said this and believed it sincerely but as yet he felt no pity for his colleague. For the time being he needed all his pity for himself.

.   .   .   .   .

The 79A was not Mr. Sermon's customary bus and he had only taken it because it offered an easy escape from his Headmaster. The bus took him as far as the Westbank roundabout and here he descended and set out across the Tedington Common to Wyckham Ridge, where he could enter the new housing estate from the north and pass through it to the older residential district where he and his family occupied a detached, five-bedroomed house in a select cul-de-sac called 'Beechway'.

Sermon topped the ridge that looked down over Wyckham Rise and there he suddenly stopped and sat down on a seat, realising that before he moved another step towards Sybil and the children he must do some objective thinking about what had occurred that afternoon.

The very first thing that struck him was that perhaps he had not burned his boats after all. He remembered the desolate look in the Headmaster's eye when he announced that he was leaving and it seemed to him that this look betrayed a far deeper-rooted fear than apprehension about what Lane-Perkins' father might do when his son arrived home with

sticking-plaster on his head. Clearly the Reverend Hawley
was dismayed by the thought of losing him, and if he willed
it, what had taken place that afternoon could probably be
glossed over and forgiven, a thought that led Mr. Sermon to
ask himself, calmly and objectively, if he really did want to
break the pattern of his life.

At this point, Mr. Sermon made a desperate attempt to
concentrate and to continue to think calmly and objectively,
but he found the effort beyond him. Objective thought was
alien to a man absorbed, year after year, in helping to run a
miniature world. It could not be nourished in the soil Mr.
Sermon had been tilling for the past twenty-five years—what
had Cooper II done with his gym shoes? Would Drake House
beat Frobisher in the semi-final? Why had Truscott done so
badly in Common Entrance when he had walked away with
the History prize two years in succession? Every time Mr.
Sermon embarked upon the main stream of his own future he
drifted into an irrelevant backwater and had to find his way
out again. Then, when he was fairly launched in the current
once more, he swirled into a kind of delta studded with islands
and sandbanks representing people and problems unrelated to
one another, so that he could never determine which was the
main stream and which a mere creek.

He sat there a long time sweating with the effort of concentration and then he made what seemed to him a fortuitous
decision. He would stop drifting and study the islands one by
one, isolating them from one another and thus getting them
into their correct perspective.

The first island was Napier Hall College and its chieftain,
the Reverend Victor Hawley. This did not delay him overlong. He had quite decided what he thought about the school
and its Headmaster. The one bored him and the other irritated him to a degree that reinforced his spot decision to turn
his back on them, come what might.

The next island was Lane-Perkins and his father. Mr.
Sermon had met Lane-Perkins' father, a loud, cheerful individual reputed to have made a fortune as a bookmaker.
He neither liked nor disliked Lane-Perkins Senior. Until that
moment he had been a mere parent and as such the responsibility of the Head. But now it was necessary that he should
think seriously of Lane-Perkins Senior and what might result
if the man made an issue of the sticking-plaster. Curiously

enough the possibility did not worry Mr. Sermon very much. Surely Magistrates would understand the fearful pressures to which schoolmasters were subjected, and even if they found the charge proved, dismiss it with a caution or a trifling fine?

Having successfully isolated these two islands of thought, Mr. Sermon plunged into the mill-race of his immediate professional future. What was he chasing? What did he really want to do? Where did he want to go and at what goal, if any, was he aiming? He found the answers to these questions far more elusive. He knew that he badly wanted a change but not in the sense that a harassed man needs a holiday. In fact he decided there and then that he did not in the least want a holiday, for a holiday implied idleness and what he wanted was work, interesting but unexacting work, preferably with his hands or at some task that left him free to dream. To dream about what? Money? He was not interested in making a fortune. His needs were, and always had been, extremely simple and he had very little sense of possession. He had never collected anything, not even foreign stamps, had never owned a stock or a share and did not personally own the house he occupied. Thinking it over, Mr. Sermon decided that the only thing he did want was personal freedom, freedom not only to make the change but to live from day to day instead of from term to term, to go where he pleased when he pleased, to break out of the ring that was enclosing him and find . . . ? But here Mr. Sermon's train of thought hit the terminus buffer and went cannoning up the platform in confusion, for the truth of the matter was that Sebastian Sermon's secret heart was fully aware of what he wanted above and beyond all these generalised abstracts and Sebastian Sermon was ashamed of naming it, even to himself. The recoil headed him directly into the island represented by Sybil, his wife.

He had set out to marshal his thoughts with an express purpose and had begun this mental spring-clean with the honest intention of returning home to Sybil with a tidy mind and some kind of plan that embraced not only her and himself but the children, Jonquil and Keith, for surely all four of them were closely involved in any kind of change or move. But here was something that did not involve them, or, if it did, could certainly bring pain and distress to them and perhaps misery to Sybil, who would surely find it very difficult

to believe that a husband who, in nineteen years of married
life, had never given her a moment's anxiety regarding other
women, should in his fiftieth year admit to an almost overpowering yearning for romance.

'Romance' he called it, but was that its real name? Wasn't
it something more down-to-earth, sexual curiosity or—face it
man—middle-aged lust? He hoped not. With all his heart he
hoped not, for if it was then how thin the partition separating
him from the poor devils he read about in Sunday newspapers, men of his own age who pounced in parks and cinemas and were hauled before Magisterial Benches on far
more shameful charges than any Lane-Perkins' father could
bring.

For a moment or so he thought of the Headmaster's remarks
about the change of life and wondered if, after all, they were
as ridiculous as they seemed. Perhaps men did suffer a physical
change and perhaps the manifestation of that change included
a wild hunger for sexual adventures, for new and exciting
conquests, or weird and bizarre experiments in fields that Mr.
Sermon had glimpsed between covers in the Charing Cross
Road. As he thought about this, Sebastian was conscious of
shame and disloyalty. A man, he thought, might be forgiven
such hunger if he had married a cold, niggardly woman,
miserly with her embraces and impatient with male appetites,
but Sybil was not such a woman. She was generous and even
gracious in her duties and if gratification left him vaguely
disappointed then it was not she who was to blame but himself, for his experience in the subtleties of courtship was very
limited. Her very complaisance in these matters made him
cautious and inhibited instead of bold and boisterous and
almost masochistically he now forced himself to consider their
love-making over the last few years. He was dismayed to
discover that it fell into the same category as everything else
about which he felt so dissatisfied. It never varied. It was
like the houses and the quiet roads of the estate. It was like
the overture to one of Sybil's Gilbert and Sullivan productions, where stage business was a protocol. It began and
ended with a stealthy fumbling and was never once commented upon, either at the time or later. It was played on
a single note without the slightest variation of theme or
scale and had developed over the years into a domestic habit,
like hanging up a raincoat or putting the cat out before

locking up and going to bed. Yet, despite all this, it was never begrudged and therefore it must follow that Sybil was blameless and he alone was at fault, not only in this respect but others. The same timid approach was apparent in his relationship with the Headmaster and other members of the staff, and in his handling of money and authority. Years had gone by and he had never once asserted himself, not as a schoolmaster, a father or a husband and certainly never as a lover! Sybil had provided most of the money and Sybil, immersed in her various social activities, had thoroughly spoiled the children, and all the time he had stood in the wings, patiently but by no means unhappily wielding a titular authority. He had occupied a touchline position ready to cheer but had never entered the scrimmage. Suddenly, and with ruthless weight, the full realisation of what this implied crashed down on him and almost flattened him. If he dropped dead at this instant, he reflected, no one would miss him, for who would rush to replace something that had never really been there? He was nearly fifty and he might never have existed at all!

In the moment of his desolation, the most acute he had ever known, Mr. Sermon looked round for support and in those fleeting seconds he felt closer to his wife than he had ever felt when she lay in his arms. He wanted to run down the slope, cut through the estate, find her and lay his head on her bare bosom. He almost cried out with a yearning to be stroked and comforted, encouraged and reassured and on the crest of this tidal wave of emotion he jumped up and began to descend the downland slope at a fast trot that carried him breathless and weak at the knees through Plane Tree Road and Montgomery Close and out into Beechway to his own front gate.

And there he stopped dead. The gate was open and the twenty-yard driveway was choked with cars, all kinds of cars, from shiny new Hillmans and Wolseleys to the souped-up sports model driven by young Aubrey Marcheson, cashier at the local Midland Bank. With a loud snort of indignation, Mr. Sermon realised that it was Thursday and that Thursday was the day Sybil entertained the committee of the Wycklam Rise Operatic and Dramatic Society, and that the entire group, plus half a dozen hangers on, were now gathered in the garden room and spilling over into the conservatory and kitchen, nibbling her cucumber sandwiches and jockeying for advantage over one another. He stood at the foot of the drive for a moment almost weeping with disappointment and then, goaded by his new resolution, he threw up his head and marched stolidly up the drive and into the house via the open front door.

* * * * *

There were far more people about than he had expected. A dozen of them were standing in the garden room, listening to Aubrey Marcheson denigrate an amateur production of *The Importance of Being Earnest* over at Shute the previous evening. The women were giggling at his improvised commentary and the men stood around and grinned, enjoying the ridicule of a company that had beaten the Wyckham group in the Drama Festival the previous autumn. Aubrey fancied himself as a raconteur and was enjoying the attention his performance commanded. It was, in fact, quite a good performance, better than those he gave on the stage. Half watching, with a tolerant smile on her lips, Sybil Sermon wondered if he would do for the autumn presentation of *Arms and the Man* that she was mind-casting.

Sybil enjoyed these occasions very much. They relaxed her, giving her a sense of power and patronage that was whittled down at real rehearsals. She glided in and out of the garden-room and back and forth from the kitchen, sifting among the crop of problems that a Spring casting conference presented. Would the Bank give Aubrey the afternoon off during the final week of rehearsal? Would Diana Gordon-Scott resign if she didn't get the Presidency at the Annual meeting and if she did, who would replace her annual ten guinea sub? These queries, and a score like them, flowed into her mind like questions fed into a computer and, like a computer, her mind considered them and came up with the inherent probability. Buried a stratum deeper in her brain was the curiously abrupt phone call she had received about an hour ago from Sebastian's Headmaster, the dreary little man whom she set out to charm on Sports Days and Speech Days. The call informed her that her husband was 'not himself' and had left an hour earlier to come home. Sybil was accustomed to phone hints and she did not miss the Reverend Hawley's. He said Sebastian was 'not himself' but the Headmaster was clearly upset

about something and whatever it was it involved Sebastian.
She had evaded his implied invitation to discuss the subject
more thoroughly and had merely thanked him for ringing and
replaced the receiver. She was not a curious woman and was
not greatly interested in the school where Sebastian seemed
to have settled after so many tiresome false starts. He went
there every term-time morning and he came home every term-
time night. Sometimes he told her one or two things that
had happened during the day but more often he did not. The
school was his background. She was engrossed in her own
and as she walked away from the phone she thought, incuriously, 'Sebastian has done something the Head doesn't like
and they've had a tiff!' but then the front door bell had rung
and the first of her guests arrived. She put Sebastian into a
top-tier locker of her brain and moved into the garden-room
to arrange herself before the tall, Regency mirror before set-
tling into a deep arm-chair and picking up a script as though
she had been studying it for the past hour.

.   .   .   .   .

At thirty-nine, Sybil Sermon was a neat but comfortably
built woman who could have passed in any light for thirty.
She had soft, dark hair with a natural wave in it and good,
regular features. Her nose was short, her mouth full and her
eyes, set widely apart, grey and serious with long, dark
lashes. People could never be quite sure about her eyes. They
regarded you steadily and sympathetically when you addressed her but even her intimates had the impression that
they were not really attending to you but looking somewhere
beyond and at a considerable range. She had an exceptionally
clear complexion, pale and smooth without the waxiness
sometimes seen in fair-skinned brunettes. She had a fine bust
and broad hips but a remarkably neat waist, so that men
thought of her as what the Edwardians would have called a
fine woman rather than a pretty one. She was not pretty,
having just too much repose and dignity, particularly in the
way she walked, for when she crossed a room one never
noticed the movement of her feet and this was precisely what
she intended for her feet were large and rather clumsy. She
gave an overall impression of kindness and tolerance, even

when dealing with the dull and stupid. She was a good listener—if she was listening—but here again one could never be sure that she was for her dignity enlarged itself into a kind of polite aloofness that disconcerted the earnest and the merely talkative. Women respected her without liking her and men admired her but were seldom at ease with her. Ralph Mallow, the auctioneer who played heavy roles in her productions, was one of the few who did not like her. He called her The Ice Maiden and once said of her: "She's the kind of woman who would say, 'Die of prussic acid poisoning if you must but try not to make too much noise about it'!"

In addition to her crinoline-sway walk Sybil had a low, slightly husky voice, intimate and somehow persuasive, so that people remembered it with affection even when they had detected all her other artifices designed to establish the fact that she was not only a handsome woman but a very cultivated one. She was not, however, a conscious hypocrite, or no more so than any woman whose father had made money very quickly and whisked his only child from a flat over a shop to a somewhat pretentious but expensive boarding school and later, for a year, to a finishing establishment near Caux. Sybil Sermon, née Rudge, had suffered from this switch all her life. She could never really reconcile a world that smelled of tallow and bran and vinegar with one smelling of mink. She was not really in the mink bracket and had been young enough, when her father had expanded, to pull down the shop-blind on her natural background of cartons, stock-racks and weekly credit lists. Finding herself in this limbo she had settled for the front-rank of the *avant-garde* in suburbia and here she found her true level, for her good taste, her intelligence, her natural graciousness and her private income had soon won for her a position of undisputed leadership in the birch-tree belt a few miles south of London. She held on to this position with a desperation that was at odds with her generous and slightly indolent nature. She was not and never would be an intellectual and her obsession with the current trends of literature and drama was largely assumed, much as a tourist might pretend to a genuine interest in the customs and history of a country in which she was spending a fourteen-day holiday. Her chief asset in this field was her astonishing memory. She could swallow and regurgitate an article from *The New Statesman* in a matter of minutes and this did as much to win her social leadership of Wyckham Rise as did her carriage, her money and her soft, appealing voice. In the immediate area of her home she had no rivals. The women deferred to her as an expert who could quote critical opinion on the current production at the Royal Court Theatre verbatim, and men of all ages flirted with her because she was a striking woman and because she encouraged them to flirt. Sometimes she reproved them with her serious eyes but she allowed them to retain her hand for a few extra seconds when a prompt script was exchanged. In the handling of men she was remarkably skilful, promising much but yielding very little. She would have described her marriage as a quiet success for she was proud of her pretty, sulky daughter and mechanically-inclined son, and for years now she had managed to keep her family and her social interests in watertight compartments, so that the one never encroached upon the other. These were not, however, the only departmentalised aspects of her life. Just as she could retain an almost photographic image of articles read in Digests, so she was able to file her interests and obligations in the tidy, tier-like galleries of her brain. On the ground floor, so to speak, was the Dramatic Society and its by-products and on successive storeys were her modest financial investments, including expectations from Dad. Then came her health and appearance, her gardening activities and, up near the roof, her family. Sebastian, her husband, had occupied a top tier for years and sometimes remained up there for days on end, for her feelings about him were neutral. She regarded him as she might have regarded a blameless gentleman lodger and the fact that her lodger shared her large double bed failed to increase the tempo of their association. She was a woman who needed a husband, not only as a bedmate but as a seal of respectability, for at heart she was a conventionally-minded woman and lived in a neighborhood where tongues wagged at the slightest opportunity. Apart from this, Sebastian was a nice, comfortable, unexacting, dutiful little man, who kept out of the way when necessary and was always on hand as a sort of adjutant when she needed help with correspondence and matters of administration. In return for his presence and his clerical services she was happy to sleep with him and even to spend an occasional holiday with him. For the rest he could remain on the top tier and keep from under her feet.

When she saw him enter the room and make a puzzling gesture in her direction she remembered the Headmaster's phone call and at once excused herself and crossed over to where he stood, just inside the garden-room door.

"You've been a long time getting back, Sebastian," she said, gently, "are you better now?" He looked a little breathless and distraught and at once her tidy mind began to conjure with aspirins and hot-water bottles and a quiet lie-down at the top of the house.

"Yes, yes, I'm quite all right, Sybil," he said, but with an urgency that was not usual and caused her a slight prick of irritation. She supposed that he could see she was heavily engaged and decided that it was tedious of him to come home unexpectedly early on the second day of term after she had deliberately postponed the conference until after the end of the holidays.

"That little Mr. Whatshisname, the Headmaster, rang. He told me you weren't very well."

Sebastian looked rather startled. "He did? What else did he say?"

"Nothing, or nothing of any consequence, he just said you left early."

"That's so," said Sebastian, slowly, "and I walked part way home. The fact is, Sybil, I . . . I've got to talk to you! Something happened today and we ought to discuss it. How long will these people be around?"

She looked at him disapprovingly. Miss Teake and Tim O'Neil were standing less than two yards away discussing the latest French film at the Carlton and he at once interpreted her glance.

"All right then, let's go somewhere," he suggested but still urgently, as though what he had to discuss was important.

"Don't be so stupid, Sebastian," she said, firmly. "Whatever happened at your school can't be that urgent! It can surely wait until everybody's gone!"

"But it can't . . ." he began, but she turned away, pointedly taking a plate of cucumber sandwiches from the dumb-waiter and floating across to the group near the window.

He stood for a moment indecisive, staring after her, a hard knot of rage in his throat. The chatter of twenty people filled the room and odd words and phrases fell on him like drops of cold rain . . . 'revolting!' 'undeveloped!' 'over-em-

phasised!' and then 'quite enchantingly weird!' He stood by
the door chafing his hands and feeling sullen and helpless. A
few hours ago he had seen the Reverend Victor Hawley
for the first time and now, he told himself, he was getting his
first real glimpse of his wife's coterie, a group of affected,
class-conscious nonentities, dissipating nervous energy they
could ill-afford in attempts to impress each other and perhaps
Sybil. Why did she bother with them at all? What need had
she to fill her life with so many trivial people when she had
a family, a husband and plenty of money of her own?

Natural good manners, however, prevented him from pur-
suing these thoughts at the moment or doing what he might
have done an hour or so ago, that is, to take Sybil by the
hand and march her upstairs to the bedroom, locking the
door on the silly chatter and announcing that they had
reached a crisis in their lives. Instead he turned and drifted
across the hall and into the kitchen where a hired waitress
from Gatley's in the High Street was pouring cider-cup into
little glasses. The girl returned his glance without interest
and went on with what she was doing. The sound of a tinny
hammering came from the workshop-shed across the as-
phalted yard opening on to the vegetable garden and he
recognised the sound at once. It was Keith, his sixteen-year-
old son, tinkering with one of his greasy machines. A sudden
glow warmed him. After all, Keith was almost a man now
and his own flesh and blood. Surely this was something that
a father might discuss with a sixteen-year-old boy and hope to
get some kind of comfort from him. He crossed the kitchen
and yard and went into the shed.

"Hullo Keith. Are you finding it too much for you as
well?"

The boy looked up from the motor-cycle that was engaging
the whole of his attention. Sebastian decided that he was
growing quite good-looking, with strong features, a mop of
brown hair and a long, straight back. Through the thickness
of the cherry-coloured sweater Keith was wearing, Sebastian
could see the play of muscles as the boy moved his arms.

"They gone yet?" said the boy, briefly.

"Unfortunately, no," said Sebastian, but he felt slightly
cheered for it was obvious that Keith shared no community
of interest with the Wyckham Rise Operatic and Dramatic
Society.

"I suppose you're busy right now," said Sebastian, tentatively.

"Damn' busy," replied the boy, "this was a bad buy. Good mind to take it back. Transmission's lousy!" and he went back to his tinkering. Sebastian waited a moment and then cleared his throat. "I . . . er . . . I'm in a bit of a spot, son," he began and the boy looked up with a flicker of interest.

"Then why don't you kick the silly sods out?" he demanded.

"Oh, it's nothing whatever to do with your mother's friends," said Sebastian, hastily, "it's just something that happened at school. I . . . er . . . I've given notice! I lost my temper with one of the boys and gave him a damned good hiding!"

Keith's interest seemed to be caught at last. "You did? Well, bully for you, Dad! What happened? Did he fight back?"

"No," said Sebastian, "he didn't get the chance," and he briefly outlined what had occurred in the Lower Fourth at 3.20 p.m. that afternoon. "The Head seems to think his father will take it to Court," he concluded. "You see, son, you can't do that sort of thing nowadays. Parents are outrageously soft about discipline and the fact is, Keith, I'm a little worried."

Keith grinned. "I wouldn't lose any sleep over that if I were you! So you clouted a boy and so his father takes it to Court. They can only sting you a quid or so, can't they? It happens all the time!" and then, to Mr. Sermon's mortified astonishment, Keith dismissed the subject altogether and returned to the motor-bike. "Damn thing won't pick up like she should. Stutters and burps. Shouldn't be surprised if they hadn't cooked the mileage. Twenty-two thousand or so Mike said at the garage but I'll bet it's nearer forty!" and he stood up, rubbing his hands on a filthy rag. "Look here, Dad, suppose you talk Mother into coughing up the extra sixty for my two-seater? She might bite, she's dead scared of me running a motor-cycle and I'm seventeen in two months and can take a driving test for a car!"

Sebastian looked at him glumly. It was obvious that Keith's brief display of interest in the disaster at Napier Hall had been pretence, designed to humour him into an alliance for

the purpose of getting something he wanted. Disappointment
in the boy curdled in the pit of his stomach.

"We'll discuss that later," he said, grumpily. "I'm certainly
not in the mood to consider your problems just now!"

"Okay!" said Keith, lightly, "no need to get the needle
about it!" and he went back to his work.

Sebastian turned his back on the shed and stood for a
moment in the yard, listening to the sustained twitter that
issued from the open windows of the garden-room. It
sounded, he thought, just like a monkey-house at feeding
time and on a small wave of disgust he coasted round the
shrubbery and down the border path to the stone wall that
overlooked the avenue. He was leaning here, elbows on a
stone block, when he saw his daughter drive up in the family
Singer. She eased the car into the kerb and got out. He was
relieved to see that she was alone and studied her as she
reached into the boot and emerged with a tennis racket held
in a press. She looked, he thought, very dainty and desirable
in her sleeveless white frock and a mauve cardigan tied by
its sleeves across her shoulders.

As she entered the side gate he moved along inside the wall
and joined her.

"Your Mother has a 'do' on so I came up for air!" he said,
flippantly, but there was no response and glancing at her
sideways he noted that she was troubled about something and
instantly he warmed towards her.

"You upset about something, Jonquil?"

The girl swung round, pouting. "Me? No! Should I be?"

"I thought you looked a bit down in the mouth."

"Don't ooze sympathy, Daddy! I can't stand being oozed
over. And I don't like prying either. Do I cross-examine you
about your private life?"

Mr. Sermon winced. It occurred to him that this was precisely what he wished somebody would start to do and then,
unreasonably, he felt angry and deflated.

"I wasn't prying," he shouted but instantly he regretted having raised his voice for, inexplicably, Jonquil burst into tears,
flung down the racket and dashed up the path to the back
door.

Mr. Sermon forgot his own troubles for a moment. All his
life women's tears had distressed him and he stumbled after
her and caught her up as they entered the kitchen. Mercifully

the hired waitress was just leaving with the cider-cup and had her back to them.

"What is it, Jonquil? You can tell me. Don't go out there, the hall is full of those idiots . . . !"

She looked at him through a veil of tears.

"You wouldn't care, you wouldn't understand!"

"I would, I would!" he declared stoutly.

She swallowed, forcibly. "It's Derek!" she said, as Juliet speaks her final line in the crypt.

Mr. Sermon floundered for a clue. He thought he knew the names of all her boy-friends. He remembered two Tonys, one John, three Bobs and a speedway driver they called 'Tex' but he did not recall a Derek.

"Derek?" he said, and again, treacherously, "Oh, *Derek!*"

"He's going to Canada," said Jonquil, "just like that! Without saying anything! Can you wonder I'm upset? Can you wonder I'm making a complete fool of myself?"

What Mr. Sermon might have replied to this is problematical. Whatever he said would have been wrong but at that moment the phone rang in the hall and Jonquil reacted to it like a nervous filly under whose belly someone has flung a Chinese cracker.

"It's him!" she shrieked, "he's thought better of it!" and she plunged out of the room and dived between two middle-aged women, both of whom were reaching politely for the receiver.

"Yes?" she piped, her eyes sparkling. "Who is it? Jonquil here! Is it you, Derek?" and then, watching her from the kitchen door, Mr. Sermon saw the misery flood back into her face and she slammed down the receiver and returned to him with dragging steps. "It's for you!" and she began to sniff again. "Someone called Lane-Perkins."

It was as though someone had rammed a white-hot blade into the small of Mr. Sermon's back. He gave a little yelp of fear and clutched at her, dragging her back into the kitchen and slamming the door on the chatter in the hall.

"You've got to do something for me," he cried. "You've got to say I'm not here. This is important, Jonquil! Go to that phone and say you can't find me, say I haven't come in yet, do you understand?"

The sheer urgency of his appeal enabled her to forget her

troubles for a moment and she looked at him curiously.
"What's the matter? Who is Lane-Perkins?"

He gave a gesture of impatience. "Never mind, I'll explain
later! Just do as I say. Do it, you hear?"

"All right, all *right!*" she replied, sulkily, disengaging herself and opening the door, and then, bitterly; "You *see?* I
knew you wouldn't understand. Nobody understands!" She
went out and picked up the phone saying, "Miss Sermon
speaking. My father isn't here. He hasn't come home yet!
Very well, I'll tell him. Yes, I got the number," and she
rang off.

A kind of frenzy seized Mr. Sermon after his daughter had
replaced the receiver and hurried upstairs to her room. He
wanted most desperately to pursue and question her, demanding to know exactly what the caller had said and what
tone of voice he had employed. The phone call had pricked
the bubble of indifference inside him, telling him that Lane-
Perkins' father had lost no time at all in contacting the school
and then tracing the man responsible for the damage to his
son's bullet head and as he realised this a flame of anger
seared him. There was no comradeship in the Headmaster,
no courage or loyalty to his profession! He had been hectored
by Lane-Perkins Senior and had washed his hands of the
incident, even to the extent of supplying the angry parent with
his deputy's private telephone number. Sermon felt his knees
trembling and acidity rising in his gorge, and with fear and
wretchedness came disgust at the brutal indifference of everybody round him; the sheer, animal selfishness of his wife, son
and daughter, slavishly obsessed with their own trivial problems, a group of chattering poseurs, a second-hand motor-bike
and a complete stranger called Derek who was going to
Canada! Mr. Sermon, however, was no weakling. Self-pity
gave him no release and a little of the glow of his access to
power in the classroom and Headmaster's study remained with
him, like the last rays of a sunset lighting up a scene of
chaos and desolation. He reached out towards this gleam,
battling with panic and resentment and said, between clenched
teeth; "Damn them! Damn them all! But they *shall* listen, they
shall help! I'll tackle Keith and Jonquil in the morning. It's
time that precious pair gave as well as grabbed. And Sybil
shall listen too, if I have to take her by the scruff of the neck
and drag her away from that yammering mob out there. I'll

give her another ten minutes and after that . . . !" but while he was saying this and stomping upstairs to his little dressing-room that adjoined the main bedroom, cars were already reversing in the driveway and Sybil's guests were retrieving coats and hats and moving out into the garden.

He sat down in the basket chair facing the large round shaving-mirror and listened to their goodbyes and exhaust stutters. Then, with relief, he remembered that Sybil had a ritual for evenings like this and invariably came straight up-stairs when the last guest had gone and took off her shoes and dress to lie on the bed and 'recap'. Sybil's 'recap' was a natural sequel to a casting conference or rehearsal. She liked to make her decisions there and then, while impressions were still fresh in her mind and such decisions as she made at this hour were almost invariably translated into edicts and tele-phoned to the Honorary Secretary the following morning.

Tonight was no exception. A moment or so after the last car had scrunched on the gravel he heard her footsteps as-cending the stairs and the light go on in the bedroom. The door of his dressing-room was a foot or so ajar but he resisted the temptation to call out. Instead he sat very still, watching her reflection in the mirror. He felt that he needed a moment or so to collect himself, to muster his overriding sense of frustration and irritation so that he could talk quietly and rationally to her, setting out the facts in calm, chronological order.

He saw her stoop and wrench off her shoes and heard her sigh with pleasure as her feet were freed from their airtight prison. Then, as he watched, she looked in her dressing-table mirror and passed both hands round the nape of her neck, as though she was suffering from a headache or tension.

He was almost enjoying himself now. It was years since he had sat still and watched her in the privacy of their bed-room and it struck him that this was an odd state of affairs for a man and wife who had been living together for nineteen years. Suddenly she yawned, tapped her mouth, stood up and unzipped her grey gown, emerging from it, he thought, like a straight white sword from its sheath. The light fell on her shoulders and its sudden radiance must have pleased her for she studied herself in the glass and half smiled, as though more than satisfied with the reflection.

He had almost forgotten his problems now. He was like a

lover standing in a dark street watching the shadow-play of
his beloved on a window-blind. The physical yearning he had
felt for her upon the hill returned with a warm, sweet rush
and he began to feel like a gambler who sees his horse
drawing ahead of the others and carrying his winnings past
the post. Then she did another curious thing. With a shrug
she wriggled out of her silk slip and moved back a pace,
standing relaxed in her sheath-like corset, bra and black
lace panties, admiring herself and turning this way and that,
a warm flush upon her cheeks and her lips parted. Sebastian
resisted an impulse to chuckle. All the years he had known
her he had never seen her behave like this, never suspected
that, when alone, her conduct varied in any way from that of
the composed, ultradignified woman who never raised her
voice and walked without seeming to use her feet. Yet it was
so obvious from her pose and expression that she was delighted with her reflection. She patted her flat stomach and
lifted her large breasts. Then she turned sideways and studied
her profile, her glance travelling down until she could see the
line of her hips and heavy buttocks in the side-flap of the
dressing-table mirror. She did not seem to find this part of
her anatomy so pleasing for she frowned and wriggled her
toes, as though protesting at so much flesh. She was still
frowning when he gave himself away, leaning forward to
improve his view and forgetting that wicker-work creaked.

She gave a little gasp of dismay and he jumped up, giving
an apologetic cough and calling, "It's all right, Sybil, it's only
me!"—an admission he instantly regretted because it implied
that he had been spying on her since she entered the room.
She almost ran round the bed and flung open his door.

"What on earth are you doing, Sebastian? How long have
you been sitting there in the dark?"

She seemed very embarrassed and angry and he hastened to
calm her.

"Only a moment or so, I came up just as they were going."

"But you must have heard me come in!"

"Yes, I did, naturally I did."

"Then why on earth didn't you say something?"

He wanted to explain that he had been so absorbed in her
as a woman that he did not want to deny himself the pleasure
of looking at her and something like this rose to his lips but
he realised that this would only increase her displeasure. It

was obvious from the bright pinkness of her cheeks and the light in her eyes that she resented his Peeping Tom tactics, so he said:

"I was thinking, I've got a great deal to think about, Sybil."

"Really? What especially?"

"I've had a big row with the Head and I don't think I'm going back to Napier Hall."

"You mean you've given notice?"

He could see she was not only surprised but piqued and this disconcerted him for suddenly he was utterly bored with Lane-Perkins and the Reverend Hawley and everything else in the immediate past. It was obviously a day for seeing people as they really were. For the first time in years, he was seeing his wife as a glowing, healthy and extremely desirable woman and he did not want to be side-tracked into a dismal recital of everything that had happened that day. They could discuss Napier Hall later. They had the whole of their lives to discuss it and cope with any repercussions that followed Lane-Perkins' painful acquaintance with the hot-water pipes. At the moment what he needed was solace, the physical solace of the strong, handsome woman standing before him with light gleaming on her pale shoulders revealing the petal-like texture of her skin. She must have read his mind for she turned aside and picked up a flowered robe that was lying on the end of the bed.

"Don't bother with that, Sybil!" he said, hoarsely and reaching out to relieve her of it. "I'll explain everything later, afterwards!"

To his extreme mortification she swung round and stepped backwards until she was standing against the wardrobe. There was tension and anxiety in the way she braced both hands against the smooth mahogany of the door and in her eyes was not fear exactly but a kind of astonished dismay. He paused, facing her.

"What's the matter, Sybil? Why are you looking at me like that?"

"What's the matter with *you*?"

"Nothing's the matter with me!" he retorted, irritably, "except that I'm fed to the back teeth and I need you right now, more than I've ever needed you before!"

The hunted look went out of her eyes and she relaxed.

"Very well, Sebastian, let's sit down calmly and talk about it."

He almost snorted with disgust. "I don't want to talk about it, not at this moment. I did, but I don't now! I . . . I . . . want to make love to you, Sybil! There's nothing very extraordinary about that is there?"

She blushed again but covered her momentary confusion with a dry little laugh.

"Really, Sebastian, there is something the matter with you! You're behaving quite ridiculously. Now listen to me . . . !" and she made an attempt to side-step him and regain freedom of movement about the room.

" 'Listen' !" he suddenly shouted, " 'listen' you say? I've been bloody well listening to people all my life and now want to do something for a change!", and he emphasised the declaration by making a wild grab at her as she slipped past him round the end of the bed.

He missed her but only just, his fingers hooking in the taut elastic of her brassiere fastenings so that her rapid movement expanded it and it slipped from his grasp, snapping against her flesh with a vicious little smack.

"Owwww!" she cried, wriggling and backing quickly against the bathroom door and then "Owww-ohhhh!", as the small of her back struck the brass door-handle. They were the most unladylike sounds she had ever uttered, and for a moment Mr. Sermon was so startled by them that he paused in his pursuit. She was quite angry now from the pain, loss of dignity or both and he checked his impatience, realising that his tactics were getting him nowhere. She looked so unlike the Sybil he knew as she bobbed up and down, both hands reaching behind her back to massage her hurts, that he laughed outright and the laugh helped to steady him.

"You look absolutely wonderful tonight, Sybil!" he announced and this was not routine flattery employed to further his cause for it genuinely delighted him that this big, handsome woman wriggling her behind against the door and staring at him with pained resentment was indeed his wife, the woman who had married him, she whom he held in reverence and awe because of her money and assurance and subtle dominance over almost everyone she met. He was seeing her at last as a mate and an equal, a woman who could receive as well as give and whose big breasts and the deep cleft that divided them excited him as he had never yet been excited by a woman. A distant echo of the Reverend Hawley's warning about the male change of life reached him but he shrugged it off, surrendering to an overwhelming desire to possess her, and with a boldness that surprised him he caught her by the waist and jerked her sideways on to the bed, ignoring her squeals of protest and laughing openly at her violent struggles.

"Sebastian!" she screamed and gave a vast heave that carried them across the width of the bed and deposited them on the floor under the splintered wreckage of a light-weight bedside table that supported bedside light, carriage clock and an anthology of 1914–18 verse he had been reading the previous night.

Unfortunately for him, Sybil fell uppermost and her weight seemed to grind him into the floor, pressing his face into the boards and coating his lips with fluff, so that he thought fleetingly of poor Bateman whose face had been rammed against the desk when Lane-Perkins fell on him. He heard, as from the distance, the crackle of splintered wood and the sharp crack of the clockface glass, then the derisive tinkle of the china lamp rolling across the room and smashing to pieces in the fireplace. For a moment he lay there dazed, with Sybil's plump thigh clamping him to the floor and then her weight was removed and he rose dizzily to his knees, groping for his spectacles and conscious of Sybil standing directly over him and calling 'Jonquil!' at the top of her voice.

"Don't, Sybil!" he said feebly, but Jonquil was already there and behind her Keith, both looking down at him with wonder while Sybil struggled into her flowered gown and seemed almost to be whimpering between breathless protests. He found his spectacles and put them on, glaring at the children who said nothing at all but just stood there looking down at him.

"Get out!" he roared, "get to hell out of here, both of you!" and to his relief they fled, ignoring Sybil's "No! No! Don't leave me alone with him!"

He got to his feet slowly, rubbing his ear where it had been creased against the carpet. Then he saw her cowering in the window alcove, holding her gown about her like a helpless woman facing a troop of licentious hussars. The sheer idiocy of the situation struck him like a blow from a swing-ing door.

"Don't behave like a damned child, Sybil!" he grunted. "Be your age, can't you? I'm not going to hurt you, it was all in fun!" She almost choked with indignation.

"*Me! Me* be my age! I don't know what's the matter with you but if you think you can treat me like a . . . a . . ."

She did not complete the protest. As he took a single step towards her she jumped for the bathroom door and this time she got there with a yard to spare, slamming it and shooting the bolt.

For a moment he contemplated hurling his weight against it, knowing that the bolt was flimsy and would give at the first rush but the urgency had ebbed from him and although he still felt aggressive and masterful it was not in the same sense. He lifted his hand to thump the panels of the door and then let it drop.

"Sybil!" he said, evenly, "come out of there at once!"

"I most certainly will not," she said, "not until you go and lock yourself in your dressing-room."

"I could break through that bathroom lock with one kick," he announced.

"If you do I shall open the window and scream!" she countered but he noticed an unfamiliar quaver in her voice. Could it be, he wondered, that she was secretly enjoying this romp? Did she want to be pursued and manhandled? The malevolent imp inside him, who had been dozing since his final gibe at the Head, suddenly woke up and urged him to increase his stake and damn the consequences.

"Sybil!" he said, heavily, "I'm warning you! Either you come out and get into that bed or I walk out of here tonight and I'm not fooling, you ask them up at Napier Hall. There are times when a man needs his wife and this is one of them, so stop being so damned coy and come out this instant. If you don't you'll regret it, I promise you!"

He waited. Ten, fifteen seconds passed. He fancied that he could almost hear her heartbeats and could certainly feel his own. All around them was complete silence. The clock had stopped ticking and still lay where it had fallen amid the wreckage of the bedside table. He took out his watch and polished the glass with his sleeve. It was nine-forty-two and outside darkness had fallen. Through a gap in the curtains he could see lights winking on the hillside and the night breeze came soughing through the open window, striking cold on his temples.

"Sebastian," said Sybil at last, and now her voice sounded eminently reasonable, "suppose you stay where you are and tell me exactly what's happened? Then, when you've calmed down a little, and if you promise not to be too silly, I'll come out and we can discuss this like sensible people!"

He looked at his watch again. "I'll give you ten seconds to open that door, Sybil!" he said, "and I'm not making conditions, you understand?"

There was silence again while another ten seconds ticked by. Inside the bathroom she laid her hand on the knob of the bolt but she did not draw it, remaining quite still, listening. Her mind was a turmoil of astonishment, indignation and alarm but buried deep under these there existed an intense and burning curiosity that urged her to risk a second encounter with the man on the other side of the door, even to the extent of provoking him to commit further outrages on her person if she could determine exactly how far he was likely to go in the improbable role of satyr. Intense curiosity warmed and excited her, so that she felt her limbs trembling and her heart pounding and it surprised her that the sensation was not entirely unfamiliar for now she recalled feeling like this once before, just once, a long, long time ago before she had married Sebastian. The memory, flickering across her mind like a distant shaft of lightning, pleased and stimulated her, so much so that desire rose in her belly like a slow, strong tide, banishing resentment and the ache in her back where she had cannoned against the door-jamb. Then his voice came to her, very flat and thin it seemed and certainly not the strident tone of a moment ago, so that suddenly she felt deflated and disappointed.

"I'm going, Sybil. I'm going away and I don't know when I shall come back. Perhaps never!" he ended dramatically.

It was a little boy threatening to hold his breath until he died. She heard him go into the dressing-room and rummage in his chest of drawers, then descend the step to the corridor and move along to the back of the house. Slowly she drew the bolt and re-entered the disordered room, moving round to the far side of the bed to gather up the clock, the broken pieces of lamp and the fragments of splintered wood and

toss them into the window recess. Then, with great deliberation, she peeled off her foundation garment, removed stockings and brassiere and stood regarding herself in the mirror,
patting herself here and there as she had done when Sebastian
was watching her from the dressing-room. She saw her robe
on the floor and picked it up, musing awhile, then threw it
over the back of the chair and went softly to the dressing-
room door. There was a light in the corridor and she remained on the threshold a moment, listening but hearing
nothing except a goods train clank along the branch line in
the valley.

"Sebastian!" she called at last but there was no answer and
she pouted, moving across the dressing-room and into the
corridor. "Sebastian, dear," she repeated, and wondered at
the invitation in her voice. Still no answer and she began to
feel vaguely frightened, hurrying back into the room, slipping
on her gown and making her way along the corridor to the
head of the stairs. She was standing there, one hand on the
newel post, when the front door banged and the sound came
to her like the first rumble of an avalanche so that she gave
a little cry of alarm and darted across the landing to the
window that looked over the lawn, pulling aside the curtain
and peering down on to the short, curved drive.

She was just in time to see him pass out of sight behind
the laurels that grew down to the gate, a slight, shadowy
figure, with what appeared to be a lump on his back and
a stick in his hand. She gasped with astonishment and dismay,
unable for a moment to believe that she was not caught up
in an extravagant film in which a sober, blameless husband
walked out into the night with a bundle on his shoulder and
hate in his heart.

•   •   •   •   •

When the Imp's time-limit had expired outside the locked
door Mr. Sermon surrendered wholly to his directions. The
Imp said: "Well, you've issued a challenge, now make it
good!" and Sebastian obediently turned on his heel and
walked through his dressing-room, into the corridor and up
the stairs to the attic. He could not have said why he went
to the attic until he reached there but then he knew. He went
over to a rack where Sybil stored her theatrical props and

took down the one possession of his own that rested there, a huge khaki knapsack, with innumerable straps and pockets and buckles. Even empty, it must have weighed about six pounds.

He took it under the naked electric bulb and dusted it with his hand. It had never been used. He had bought it years ago, intending to take it on a Whitsun walking-tour but somehow, when he came to pack it, it had seemed a ridiculously clumsy accoutrement for a three-day trip to Snowdonia and he had taken instead a small two-section knapsack that they used on picnics. Now, however, he regarded it carefully, for to-night it was a good deal more than a mere travelling bag. It was a kind of symbol or banner proclaiming his new self, the reckless man who banged insolent boys about the head, defied his Headmaster, threw up his job and then marched home to rape his wife. It had up a rakish, devil-may-care look and its pockets seemed to wink at him and promise years of rewarding sin. Forgetting Sybil for the moment he threw it across his shoulder and went out on to the top landing where stood an oak chest of drawers that had been banished to the top floor because it lacked a leg and had to be propped against the wall. In here he kept his holiday clothes, a pair of thick corduroys, two or three check shirts, his swimming trunks, walking socks, brogues and an old, stained mackintosh. He made a selection, returned to the box-room and changed. Then he stuffed spare shirts, an extra sweater, the mackintosh, socks and three handkerchiefs into the main section of the bag and fitted it on his shoulders. It was not nearly so heavy as it looked and settled snugly against the curve of his spine. The brogues were stiff and he decided that he must buy some thinner socks, which made him think of money. He emptied his pockets of a scholastic jumble, leaving keys, letters and other odds and ends in his discarded jacket and retaining only a notebook, his fountain-pen, cheque-book and wallet. The wallet contained eleven pounds ten in notes and his P.A.Y.E. and National Insurance cards. He looked at the cards sourly, deciding that both were unpleasant reminders of servitude and was tempted to tear them up but he thought better of it and stuffed them back in his wallet. Then, with long, springy strides, he ran downstairs to the drawing-room where his glass-fronted bookcase stood in the window alcove and ran his eye along the top shelf where he kept a dozen or more old favourites, bound in soft leather and tooled in gold.

Mr. Sermon's books were not like other people's books, dust-hoarding and unused. They showed evidence of considerable handling over the years and the pages of all of them turned noiselessly, like considerate friends stealing past a sleeping man. He estimated the size of the long pocket in the knapsack and decided that he had room for three. *Treasure Island, Kidnapped* and *Robinson Crusoe* he knew almost by heart and he was almost equally familiar with *David Copperfield, Silas Marner* and Carlyle's *French Revolution.* He would have taken Froude's *English Seamen of the Sixteenth Century* had it not reminded him unpleasantly of the afternoon's riot. In the end he chose verse and took two anthologies, one modern and one classical. As an afterthought he added a well-thumbed copy of Baron De Marbot's saga of the Napoleonic Wars. At most of the crises in his life he had turned for solace to one or other of these volumes and he remembered reading Marbot's account of the Russian retreat when he was waiting for Jonquil to be born.

He paused and looked around the room for the last time, noting its clinical cleanliness and Sunday afternoon decorum. He decided then that he had never liked this room, never in fact liked any part of the house. It was utterly impersonal and if you lived in it long enough it reduced you to a two-dimensional person, without a past or a future. As he was re-entering the hall he heard Sybil call from upstairs and for a moment, he paused, miserably indecisive. Then he decided that she was still in the bathroom and this stiffened his resolution. 'To hell with her!' he thought. 'She can't really believe I'll do it but I can and I will!' It was as well for the new Mr. Sermon, however, that he could not see her at that precise moment, standing naked at his dressing-room door and manifestly ready to capitulate. Even so, it needed a great deal of determination to make him turn away towards the front door and it is doubtful if he would have succeeded in doing so had not the phone begun to ring, loudly and persistently, so that it sounded like the tolling of Newgate bell and conjured up a horrid vision of a crowded court, a savage-looking magistrate, a wan and bandaged Lane-Perkins standing in the witness-box and himself, manacled, perhaps, in the dock opposite, with a policeman at his elbow. It was,

his reflexes told him, a very improbable vision but it was
stark enough to make him leap for the open, his initial impetus carrying him through the front door at a sprint and
down the drive into the avenue, now empty and silent under
a sickle moon. He looked back at the house as he went along
under the wall and saw the lights at the big landing window
and then the curtain fall into place as Sybil, now apparently
watching, went to answer the phone. At the thought of what
she might hear over it he broke into a shambling trot, his
knapsack jolting on his shoulders, his stiff brogues punishing
the corn on his little toe. Only when he reached the bus stop
and boarded a 108 heading towards London did he exchange
alarm for a mounting exhilaration. "By George, I've done it!"
he said, almost aloud, "I've done something I've been wanting
to do for years and years and years," and he sat back, easing
his feet and slipping his knapsack on to his knees as a yawning conductor reached out for his fare.

"Where to?" the man asked, clamping a hand over his
mouth.

Mr. Sermon had no idea but he remembered that the bus
had had the word 'Vauxhall' on the front so he said: "Do
you pass near Waterloo Station?"

"York Road," said the conductor and then, regarding his
solitary passenger with faint interest, "Going to the country,
mate?"

Mr. Sermon beamed. It was years, he reflected, since anyone had addressed him as 'mate' and he warmed towards the
man.

"As far as I can get on these two feet!" he said and realising that it must sound somewhat unusual to hear Waterloo
Station named as the starting-point of a walking tour, he
added: "First lap by train, of course, then due West, Somer-
set or Devon to begin with."

The man shivered slightly for the night air was chill and
a strong draught explored the bus.

"Sooner you than me, mate," he said, emphatically, "my
terminus is Vauxhall Bridge Road an' then kip till nex' duty!"
and he rolled the ticket and gave Mr. Sermon change.

Inside the bus it seemed extraordinarily remote and isolated,
so much so that Mr. Sermon, closing his eyes and letting his
fancy rove, had the impression that he was in transit between
two worlds like a soul on its way to rebirth and that the

lugubrious conductor was a substitute for Pluto's ferryman or the barman in the play *Outward Bound*. This impression was so strong that he shuddered and then it struck him that perhaps it was not so fanciful after all for, in a sense, he was indeed being reborn and that at this very moment he was stepping out of and clear away from the drab frame of his existence. In a matter of hours, he reflected, he had shed the accumulated responsibilities of a lifetime and as yet had no new ones to replace them but simply a rough set of clothes, eleven pounds ten shillings and two books of verse as his passport to the new world.

CHAPTER TWO

Mr. Sermon Learns to Tap
and Finds It
Unexpectedly Profitable

WHEN Mr. Sermon awoke it wanted but a few minutes to broad daylight.

For the better part of this brief interval his half-conscious self wandered around inside his aching head, trying to recognise his whereabouts and relate them to a curious stiffness in his legs and the parched state of his mouth. His reconnaissance was unsuccessful. For several minutes he had not the least idea where he was, or how he had arrived there, sprawled full-length on three cushions that felt and smelled as though they had been stuffed with wire and dipped in a solution of creosote and tobacco juice. The stale odour in the carriage half-stupefied him and presently, because of it, he swung his feet to the floor and groped for the leather strap to adjust the window. Then, peering timidly into the thinning mist and down the line as far as the signal box, he suddenly remembered how he came to be the sole occupant of a third-class compartment on a stationary train in a deserted siding. He remembered this particular carriage first of all and used it as a guide rope leading to other discoveries. There had been the walrus-moustached guard who had piloted him to this carriage about 2.30 a.m. and before that . . . ? Ah, the change at Templecombe and the short journey on to Westport-Revel! Further back along the line was the wait at Waterloo for the 11.35 to the West and before that the silent bus flight from home. At this point the fog in his brain cleared and events stormed down on him in a body, his ludicrous wrestle with Sybil, his unsuccessful overtures to son and daughter, the two phone-calls, one of them certainly from Lane-Perkins' father, the trouncing of Lane-Perkins himself, all the seemingly unrelated events that had brought him here to this stuffy, evil-smelling railway carriage in the middle of nowhere.

For a moment his brain reeled under the impact of this improbable avalanche and then, as the cool morning air began to enter the carriage, he sat up, put on his spectacles and stared at himself in the misted mirror slotted between fly-blown views of Ramsgate and Penzance on the opposite wall of the carriage.

"By George!" he exclaimed aloud, "it really happened. It happened exactly as I'm remembering it," and he pranced to his feet and pulled his huge rucksack from the luggage rack, fumbling in one of the pockets for a packet of Players' he had put there when he left the train at Templecombe four hours previously.

Mr. Sermon was not a smoker. He had given up cigarette-smoking more than three years ago, when he had developed a smog cough that threatened to revive his youthful asthma. He had never missed that habit until last night when they told him that he had more than an hour to wait for the 11.35. Then, unaccountably, he had succumbed to an irresistible longing to smoke and as a gesture of defiance he had bought a packet of twenty at the buffet. On the journey down he had smoked four and this, no doubt, accounted for the dryness in his mouth and the slight ache in his head, but neither worried him much so he lit another and inhaled deeply. In the old days he had tried not to inhale but now inhaling seemed to him a devil-may-care habit, thoroughly characteristic of a man who struck out at everyone who crossed him and then ran away from home in corduroys and a grubby sweater. He leaned far out of the window, alternately gulping down air and smoke and he thought what manly comfort there was in a cigarette and what a milksop he must have been to let a suburban chemist talk him into denying himself such pleasure. For Sebastian Sermon, adrift

in the world, discovered that he was no longer a prey to innumerable abstract fears, like the fear of infected lungs. In
the space of fifteen hours, a mere nine hundred minutes
since he had thumped Lane-Perkins on the head, he had
sloughed off layer after layer of inhibitions and was still
shedding them, a craven host of prejudices and fads and
whims and caprices that had been leeching him since he was
a boy and their flight gave him a buoyancy and self-confi-
dence that sent his spirit soaring over the bluish tract of
moorland beyond the silent siding. In the whole of his life he
could never recall an awakening such as this, or a time when
he had felt more like exchanging banter with the first stranger
he met and it piqued him to notice that the little train was
shunted and abandoned by all but himself and that the wayside
station, marked 'Westbury-Revel' in white stones sunk in the
embankment, looked like the station of a ghost-town in the
mist of what promised to be a sparkling April morning.

He slipped on his 'mac', slung his rucksack and went along
the corridor bawling "Guard!" and "Hi there!" but it was
just as he feared, there was no guard aboard and when he
let himself out of the guard's van and stamped the length of
the short platform no one appeared at the windows of the
station-house and no wisp of smoke curled from the squat
chimney.

"Curious!" he said to himself but then reflected that perhaps it was not so curious after all, for the genial guard who
had accepted a florin to let him sleep in the carriage had
warned him that no train would depart for Exeter until 8.23
a.m. and that he doubted whether Fred Mimms, the part-
time level-crossing keeper at Westbury-Revel, would put in
an appearance until just before 8 o'clock.

Mr. Sermon had been so tired and so emotionally exhausted at 2.30 a.m. that he had given no thought to the
prospect of breakfast and a wash-and-brush-up but now he
felt a serious need of both. There was no water in the train
closet so he roved the platform until he found a tap under
which he soused himself thoroughly, using a vest as a towel.
After that he felt less frowsty but hungrier than ever and
after prowling round the shuttered station and shouting "Hi!"
once or twice, he set off resolutely down the winding road in
the general direction of the West. It was easy to discover
which was the West for a pale, yellow sun, tinged with

crimson, was peeping over the horizon beyond the station
buildings and this was clearly the East, so Mr. Sermon began
his march with confidence.

The way led over a wide heathland that seemed to Mr.
Sermon to be entirely uninhabited. Folds of heather were
dotted here and there with patches of gorse and lonely, wind-
whipped firs but as he went along, climbing slowly, he passed
through several small copses of beech, oak and ash, where
wild flowers grew down to the roadside, a straggle of prim-
roses, violets, campion and viper's bugloss, with here and
there the promise of bluebells in a week or so and once,
where a stream ran under the road, a white cloud of wood
anemones. It was an idyllic place to be at that time of day.
Behind him the sun was now clear of the earth's curve and
looked exactly like a vast poached egg, pale pink in the
centre and washed-out yellow at the edges. The sky was
stippled with ribs of cloud and the air was sweet and
heady. After a mile or so his corn began to twinge but this
was a trifling matter when measured with the glory of the
morning and only the steady gnaw of hunger made him
wish to share his solitude with other human beings. He kept
a sharp lookout for a village or hamlet, or even an isolated
cottage where he could buy some breakfast, any kind of
breakfast, but for all he saw of human habitation he might
have been pushing up the Amazon. He thought with mild
sympathy of all the millions of people who lived in cities
and suburbs like the one he had quitted the previous evening and such was his mood that he could find it in him to
think tolerantly of Sybil and the children, and even of Lane-
Perkins and the Reverend Victor Hawley, all not yet awake
but doomed the moment they opened their eyes to tread the
dismal round of come-day-go-day routine, slaves to the
tyranny of bells and meals and striking clocks. Presently,
however, the void in his stomach began to master him. He
could not remember when he last ate. Was it a canteen lunch
at Napier Hall an hour or so before flashpoint? He remembered that he had had no tea or supper, and that he
had bought nothing but the cigarettes in the station buffet,
but it seemed to him now that weeks had gone by without
his having swallowed so much as a cup of tea or a ham
sandwich.

He was plodding up a long, winding incline and praying

that the summit would reveal a village, no matter how distant, when he heard the crazy rattle of the van behind him. Looking round he saw it starting to climb, a battered and heavily-laden station-wagon, proceeding at not much more than his own pace and making a great deal of fuss about it as it was slammed into low gear and coaxed forward by the man at the wheel.

Mr. Sermon moved into the hedge to let it pass. He would liked to have called out or signalled to the driver but suddenly he felt self-conscious of his presence there at that time of day. He had plenty of time, however, to notice the eccentric appearance of the vehicle. It was, he would have judged, the bastard of a goods van. The chassis did not seem to be part of the general structure which had been added, not very expertly, from the remains of some other vehicle or vehicles. Its bodywork was a bilious yellow and its flat roof, fitted with a rack, was almost invisible under an assortment of household goods, all kinds of household goods, including a marble-topped washstand, two cane-bottomed chairs, a tatty-looking sofa and several copper pans tied on by the handles that boomed at every dip in the road. The back of the van presented an almost indecent appearance, for a bunch of chamber-pots were hanging from the handle of the door and these, looking like huge white pomegranates, chinked and pirouetted in an extraordinary manner presenting so compelling a spectacle that Mr. Sermon obtained no more than a glimpse of the inside of the van.

It roared past him, shattering the peace of the morning like the passage of a juggernaut and then, breasting the slope, lurched to an uncertain standstill as the driver poked his head out of the window and called: "Going on to the main road? Want a lift, mate?" and Mr. Sermon waved his arms and began to run, uplifted not so much by the prospect of getting somewhere as by the chance this would offer for a closer inspection of the outfit.

He was not prepared, however, for the risks he had to face in boarding the wagon. As he crossed the road, making for the nearside door of the driving cabin, the vehicle began to move backwards down the hill and the driver, clashing his gears, shouted: "Make it snappy! Make it snappy! The 'and-brake don't hold!" and began to lunge at the gear-lever like a swordsman battling for his life, while Mr. Sermon, one leg

on the ground and one inside the cabin, had to hop for a
clear ten yards before the gears engaged and the van began
to grind forward again towards the crest of the hill.

"Should have got her on the flat before I stopped!" said
the driver, with a gap-toothed grin. "I c'n manage 'er empty
but I got a good load on today. Is them jerries okay behind?"

"Yes," said Mr. Sermon, breathlessly, "they seem to be
managing and thank you for stopping, it's very good of you,
I'm sure!"

The man looked at him with interest and Mr. Sermon
looked back, thinking that the driver of this remarkable
equipage exactly suited it for he was quite as outlandish as
his vehicle. He was below medium height and as thin as a
beanpole, with a largish head crowned by a pork-pie hat
green with age. His face was broad and his expression genial,
advertised as it was by the wide gap in his front teeth. His
eyes, brown, tolerant and humorous, were very restless and
he had the pallor of a city-dweller. His accent Mr. Sermon
placed as somewhere between Hammersmith and Barnes,
with Hounslow as its extreme limit. His hands were large
and capable and Mr. Sermon noted this with relief for he
had very little confidence in the van but decided that although
it might get up to all manner of tricks this little man was
more than a match for it, giving it plenty of rope but calling
it to order when necessary.

"Made an early start, didn't you?" said the man amiably.

"From the station back there, I couldn't get any further last
night," explained Mr. Sermon. "I was hoping to find somewhere for breakfast, I'm absolutely starving! You . . . you
wouldn't happen to have anything to eat on board, would
you? A bar of chocolate, or a sandwich or something? I'd
gladly pay for it!"

The man gave him another curious look so that Mr. Sermon instantly regretted having mentioned his hunger, but he
replied:

"You're dead lucky, mate! I'm bloody sharpset meself.
We'll pull in at a transport caff at the crossroads. It's only
a mile or so but first we gotter shake hands with the Hangman!"

"The Hangman?" queried Mr. Sermon, anxiously.

"Terrible 'ill. Worst round here. One in five an' bends all

the way! Usually go round the long way an' dodge it but I got a full day ahead so I thought I'd chance it."

Mr. Sermon found this information disconcerting but he tried not to show it and at once broadened the conversation.

"You've got to deliver all this furniture at various places?" he enquired.

"Neow!" said the man, "this is stuff I got at yesterday's sale an' a lot o' junk as you c'n see! Nothing in it reely tho'. Flash, he's my old man, always brought me up to believe the big money was in junk an' not in good pieces. Something in it o' course, if you reckon by profit percentages. Buy an armchair for five bob an' sell it fer fifteen that's two 'undred-per-cent, ain't it? Lay out forty quid on a commode an' The Trade gives you forty-two-ten an' moan all the way down the bleedin' street! You made fifty bob but look at the percentage? No," he went on, dismissing the depressing economies of his calling, "I'm not delivering, I'm tapping today."

"Tapping?" said Mr. Sermon curiously, "tapping what?"

The man threw back his large head and gave a short neighing laugh and then, as though a little ashamed of himself, he winked, smiled and patted Mr. Sermon's knee reassuringly.

"*Tapping! Knocking!* On the knock!" he explained. "I got a shop see, down on the coast, place called Kingsbay, you prob'ly heard of it!"

Mr. Sermon had heard of Kingsbay. It was, indeed, almost famous in a way for its exclusiveness was sometimes the subject of a music-hall joke and had even been used by Television comics. It was, he remembered, a kind of ultimate in West-country resorts, a citadel to which colonels and admirals and Indian civil servants had retired in the days when we had an Empire, a place said to be ruled over by a Kiplingesque junta who sternly resisted the introduction of caravans and campers and the sale of iced lollies on the promenade. It seemed a most unlikely place to enter in a van with a cluster of chamber-pots on the door.

"I always heard Kingsbay was a very starchy place," he said, "a kind of Cheltenham-cum-Harrogate by the sea."

"That's it," said the man, sagely, "and that's the point! Good buying area, good class o' people. They got stuff 'anded down see? And most o' the pore bleeders are livin' on fixed incomes and 'ave to part with a bit every now and again to pay their flippin' golf sub. I milked some nice stuff out o' Kingsbay in me time but it's drying up mindjew, drying up fast! Too many bleedin' amachures and too many dabblers! Proper trade don't get a look in, not like they used to before the war." And he shook his head, looking quite fierce for a moment.

"What exactly do you mean by 'tapping' and 'on the knock'?" asked Mr. Sermon, who was enjoying himself when he could forget his frantic hunger.

"Oh it's just a term," said the man, "we tap see, tap on doors, any doors if they look like they got a bit o' French or Regency behind them. Never know what you might find, brace o' pistols, bit o' Georgian silver, chunk o' Spode or Rockingham maybe. Garden ornaments too, they fetch a good profit but there again, it ain't what it was, nothing like what it was, and if you ask me why I can tell you! You ask me and see!"

"Very well," said Mr. Sermon, dutifully, "I'm asking you. Why?"

The man looked at him gratefully as though Mr. Sermon had done him an unexpected favour.

"Magizines," he said, bitterly, "magizines an' T.V. talks and them bleeders who dabble a bit an' then glue their behinds to a chair an' write a book about it! Time was when you could get a silver rose bowl for a quid. Now everyone knows the flippin' marks and c'n date 'em to the year. Everyone's writing about antiques, see, everyone who c'n sit down to a flippin' typewriter. Ought to be stopped be law it did. Takes the flippin' bread out of your mouth it do!"

At this juncture they moved off level ground and began to descend a long, winding hill that Mr. Sermon assumed was the dreaded Hangman and soon he knew that this must be so for the gradient became alarming and the dealer's attention was fully occupied in keeping the van from running away and plunging off the road into the woods that grew on either side of the long curves.

Mr. Sermon clutched the side of the seat and set his teeth, trying not to imagine what would happen if the van was unable to negotiate one of the bends and shot off into the precipitous woods. Then, with a gasp of relief, he saw that the hill was flattening out and that houses were showing through the thinning timber on the right of the road and the van coasted down the last hundred yards of the hill to swing into a clearing before a seedy-looking bungalow flaunting a huge, crudely-painted sign that read: THE SAFE ARRIVAL— GOOD PULL-IN FOR TRANSPORT with the name of the proprietor underneath. Mr. Sermon thought that he had never seen a café more aptly named.

"You'll get a good fry-up here," said the man. "Ada, who runs it, is an old pal o' mine. I alwus look in when I'm over this way," and he led the way up wooden steps and into a long, smoke-filled room set with deal tables and chairs and hung around with what seemed to Mr. Sermon a whole gallery of calendars, all of them depicting young women in various stages of undress.

They sat down at a table near the window and Ada appeared, a forthright, blowsy woman of about fifty-five with a beaky face and hands coated with flour.

"The usual, Ada, but twice over," said the van driver, "and make it quick, my pal's got a big hole to fill!"

Ada, however, was disposed to chat and passed the order to a pallid girl behind the counter, after which she sat down between them, wiping her hands on her apron and lighting the cigarette Mr. Sermon's friend stuck in her mouth.

"Do any good over at Yardley Manor?" she asked. "I heard there was some good prices paid or so Hooker's boy said."

"No good at all, Ada," said the dealer, "London trade scooped all the best of it and the set o' chairs fetched four hundred in the knock-out."

"Was you in on it, Tapper?"

"No," said the dealer, gravely, "not on the chairs and top stuff I wasn't, I was on'y in the Rabbits' Ring but I come off with twelve-pounds-ten and a Persian rug. Mighter bin worse I suppose, tho' Flash, my old pot an' pan, created something awful when I got home. He said the foreigners should stick to their own areas, Kent and suchlike. They did in his day, o'course but times have changed, as I was just telling the perfesser here!"

Mr. Sermon, to whom the smell of frying eggs was refined torture, was only half-listening to the discussion but he caught the word 'perfesser' and it pleased him for somehow it gave him standing-room in this exciting world of tappers

and knockers. He had been extremely interested in his
friend's diatribe and already half-considered himself part of
The Trade, a beginner perhaps entering upon the very first
stage of initiation into what was obviously a very esoteric
community.

"Is he from Smoke?" Ada wanted to know.

"Search me," said Tapper and turning to Mr. Sermon
added, "are you mate?"

Mr. Sermon was not absolutely certain that 'Smoke' meant
London, but he took a chance on it and admitted that he
was a Londoner.

"What's in that there bag you got?" asked Tapper and
this time there was no amiability in his voice but professional curiosity, "it wouldn't be bits'n pieces you wanter flog,
would it?"

"It's kit," Mr. Sermon told him, "just some stuff I threw
in at the last minute." He drew a deep breath and looked
frankly at his companions, "I'm on a sort of holiday, you
see."

Neither Ada nor Tapper missed the hint of mystery and
Ada looked at him very sharply indeed.

"What do you mean—'sort of holiday'? Either you're on a
bloody holiday or you aren't! You can't have it both ways,
can he, Tapper?"

Mr. Sermon hesitated and then plunged. "Well, as a matter
of fact, I was teaching in school until yesterday afternoon,"
he said, "but suddenly, very suddenly indeed, I . . . I got
fed up with it all and . . . and walked out! Just like that! I
turned my back on it all!"

They were impressed, he could see that, and it would have
needed very little prompting on their part to have encouraged
him to elaborate but at this moment a vast plate of eggs,
bacon, tomatoes and fried bread was thrust under his nose
and Mr. Sermon forgot everything in an immediate attempt
to satisfy his hunger. He was halfway through his meal
before Tapper had picked up his knife and fork.

"Lumme!" said the dealer, "you were 'ungry, weren't you,
perfesser! Proper treat, idn't it Ada, to see a man go fer
his grub like that? Here mate, don't choke yourself, wash
it down with a drink o' tea!" and he poured from the large
enamel pot that the girl had set before them.

Mr. Sermon said nothing for the next five minutes and by

that time his plate was empty and wiped clean with bread.
He sat back with a sigh of contentment and watched Tapper
consume a leisurely breakfast. Ada got up and slouched
about the bungalow, serving one or two lorry drivers who
came in for tea and cigarettes.

"How far is this place, Kingsbay?" asked Mr. Sermon,
suddenly.

"About fifteen miles," Tapper told him, "was you thinking o' going on there?"

"I can go anywhere I like," said Mr. Sermon, more to
himself than to his companion, "anywhere at all, so why not?
Are you going on now?"

"No," said Tapper, "not until after the auction. That starts
at eleven but I don't need to get there till the lunch interval,
I got a dealer covering for me."

"You're on your way to an auction? But I thought you
said you were tapping?"

"So I am, on me way to the auction. Two birds with one
wallet, you might say," said Tapper and as he spoke he
extracted a leather case from his hip pocket and opened it,
fishing among the notes inside for an address card. Mr.
Sermon goggled. Only over the counter of a bank had he
seen so much money in one roll. The wad of five-pound
notes in Tapper's case was at least two inches thick and
must have contained all of three hundred pounds.

"Good heavens!" Mr. Sermon could not help exclaiming,
"do you carry all that money about with you everywhere
you go?"

"That ain't much!" said Tapper, disparagingly, "I usually
have twice that amount but I'm short this week. They keep
paying me cheques and the shop float is run down. Bloody
nuisance it is when you get nothing but cheques. What the
'ell's the good of a cheque? You gotter pay it in the bank
'aven't you and then where are you? Every flippin' nosey-
parker has a dekko at 'ow you're doin' and before you
know where you are the flippin' Bloodsuckers is on to you!
Cash is all that matters in my line, mate, you gimme cash
every time and stick the cheques where the monkey sticks
his nuts!"

He found what he was looking for, a neat, printed card
and replaced his wallet in his pocket. "Here we are, the
Hon. Mrs. Gliddon-Foster, Cedar Walk, Bletchley Wood. She's

the targit fer tonight! Wants to sell some picshures I'm told
but they couldn't be all that good or they'd have gone to
Sotheby's years ago. Point is, you never know what else
she's got that she don't know about. Got a feeling about her,
I have, down here, in me old barometer!" and he tapped
his stomach and sucked his teeth or such of them as remained.

Mr. Sermon was vastly intrigued, so much so that he over-
came his natural diffidence and blurted out: "Look here, Mr.
Tapper—that is your trade name, isn't it? Couldn't I . . .
wouldn't you take me with you today and drop me off in
Kingsbay tonight? I'd give you a hand lifting and carrying.
I'd offer to take turns driving but I don't think I could
manage your van very well. I'm interested in antiques, I
always have been and I . . . I'd enjoy it immensely, particularly the auction. Suppose I pay half for the petrol we use?"

Tapper looked at him kindly. "I'm easy," he said, "if you
don't mind messing around most o' the day. I like company
in the van, get sick o' me own in no time. Right!" He took
the matter as settled. "Let's pay Ada and get started. Bletchley
Wood? It's about six miles from here I reckon," and he
slapped a note and a florin on the table and called to the
proprietress.

"Look here, I can't have that, let me pay for the breakfast!" said Mr. Sermon eagerly.

"Don't be silly," said Tapper casually, "proper treat to see
you eat it! Ten bob and two for the girl, Ada. See she gets
it!", and winking and hitching his belt he led the way out
to the yellow van and swung himself aboard.

Mr. Sermon climbed in beside him feeling replete and very
much at peace with the world. He had taken an immense
liking to this odd little man and the trend of his adventures
so far both pleased and excited him. He would never have
believed that he could have embarked upon them so swiftly
and smoothly and the sense of entering a new world that he
had experienced in the bus the previous night returned to
him. He no longer felt any apprehension about the van, for
clearly Tapper was a man who could look after himself and
anyone along with him.

"By the way, don't call me Mr. Tapper," said his friend,
"just 'Tapper' will do. Me real name is Sugg, Algernon
Sugg, if you ever 'eard anything so daft but my old mum

thought 'Algernon' was classy and when it come to naming
people my missus run her pretty close. She called our boy
'Ewart Stuart' and then dropped it fer 'Blessing'. She was a
Plymouth Sister see, and regarded him as such, tho' I
reckon she'd change her opinion if she could see him now.
Proper young basket he is but keen mindjew, keen as mustard!
No one don't get past Blessing when Flash leaves him in
charge o' the shop, not the silver boys who want to give you
less'n you paid for sticks-an'-flat, or the bloke up the road
whose gran's just hopped it an' shows up with a laundry
basket full o' Goss china an' lustres with half the drops
missing. Equal to all of 'em Blessing is and him only four-
teen!"

As they went along Tapper talked easily of his family and
background but seemed not in the least curious about his
companion's antecedents. Mr. Sermon learned, for instance,
that 'sticks' meant candlesticks and 'flat' meant cutlery. He
also learned that Tapper's business establishment in the High
Street, Kingsbay, was called TABLESNCHAIRS, spelled just like
that, all in one word, and that he and his boy and his father
Flash ran it together, Tapper and Flash taking turns to
attend sales or go on the knock in search of stock which
was then resold to The Trade or to holiday-makers visiting
Kingsbay. The business sounded to be a very prosperous
one and Tapper explained that its title, 'Tablesnchairs', had
been selected after considerable thought. "You could have
called it something fancy, like 'The Copper Kettle' or 'The
Spinning Wheel'," he explained, "but after all, what do people
need most in life, what bits o' furnitchure—beds aside—is it
they can't do without? Tables to eat off an' chairs to sit on!
That's the beginning and end of the junk trade and everything else is a luxury. So Flash had a sign made out and it
pongs with people so they don't forget it easy, you get me?"

He went on to tell Mr. Sermon that the womenfolk of
the Sugg family were short-lived but the men came from
much tougher stock for Flash, his father, was now well
into his seventies but still active, alert and ready to retire
to bed on a quart of beer, a whole rice pudding and half a
jar of pickled onions. Tapper's mother had died in her
forties and was soon followed by Tapper's wife, the Plymouth Sister, and then by Tapper's sister, Beet. Bereft of their
womenfolk the men had not bothered to find replacements

but had moved into the rooms behind the shop. "Bit of a tip it is," Tapper admitted, "because we don't none of us eat regular but on'y when we feel like it and we don't do much in the way o' cleaning-up neither because it don't give you no heart when dirty stuff keeps going in an' coming out, day after day! We have a go at it Sundays sometimes and make the dust fly but it's as bad as ever by Monday midday, so we let it go for another week. We eat off stock see and have a big wash-up Saturdays and then carry it all down into the shop again!"

To Mr. Sermon this seemed a glorious way to live and he said so, thinking of the spotless kitchen and unfriendly drawing-room at home where Sybil's two dailies followed everybody about complaining of litter and marks on the furniture left by Keith's grease-stained jeans.

Talking this way they reached the village of Bletchley Wood, set in a verdant little valley on each side of a swift-flowing stream and after an enquiry in the main square Tapper drove the van beyond the last houses and into a steep drive that led between high clumps of evergreen to Cedar Walk, the home of the Hon. Mrs. Gliddon-Foster. It was a neatly-kept manor house in pseudo-Georgian style, with a mosaic terrace above the well-cropped lawn and tall windows hung with brocaded curtains. Tapper stopped the van and gave it a keen, professional glance.

"Gonner be tough, this is," he said, gloomily. "She obviously ain't 'ard up for a bob or two. I used to feel sorry for some of 'em in the old days but not now. Bloody sight tougher'n the trade they are, most of 'em, and that slick with their adding up it fair takes your breath away! Now we got to box clever here. You sit down and 'ave a fag like you was weighing things up and I'll go in an' do a rekky."

He got out of the car and marched boldly up to the front door, leaving Mr. Sermon with the impression that he was now almost a partner in the enterprise. A woman answered his ring and they exchanged conversation after which Tapper went in with a backward thumbs-up sign as the door closed behind him.

Ten minutes passed and Mr. Sermon sat back and relaxed, watching the rooks soar over the elms and an indolent gardener weed a bed near the drive. He was on the edge of

a luxurious doze when the van door opened so suddenly that
he almost toppled out onto an excited Tapper, who now
looked eager and conspiratorial and laid a warning finger
on his lips.

"You know anything about picshures?" he demanded.
"Oils, like they have in the National Gallery?"

"I used to go to the Gallery and the Tate quite often,"
said Mr. Sermon, "and I've read quite a bit about the lives
of painters."

"Just what the kewrater ordered!" said Tapper. "Now
listen, you want to do me a good turn? A real good turn?"

"If I can help I certainly will," said Mr. Sermon, "but I'm
not an expert on paintings."

"You don't have to be," said Tapper, "because she ain't
either. I twigged that right away and the picshures is wors'n
I thought. A flippin' landscape in there looks like a storm at
sea and God knows 'ow many of her flippin' ancestors are
looking down at yer like you was pinching the spoons from
out under 'em! No, I don't want the picshures, but I'm in a
bit of a spot, because I got to *pretend* I like 'em and you're
gonner be a Godsend mate because you look right an' talk
right, get me?"

"No," protested Mr. Sermon, "not altogether; you mean
you aren't going to buy the pictures after all?"

"Not if I can help it!" declared Mr. Tapper, fervently.
"But I am gonner buy that French bit if I have to camp on
the flippin' lawn for a week! Proper plum it is, bin in the
fam'ly fer a century or more. She knows it's good o' course
but she ain't up-to-date with prices because she's already sold
me a jardiniere for twenty and I c'n get twice that for it
from the trade be just making a 'phone call! Now listen,
mate, you take your cue from me, come in an' praise them
picshures an' make out you'd like to buy 'em all but can't
afford more'n two, an' want to get a partner down from
London to pick out which two, get me? You don't have to
say much, just let slip a few names an' types o' painting as
a smoke-screen!" and, presumably considering that this was
an adequate brief, Tapper returned to the front door followed
by a dubious Mr. Sermon who was already asking himself if
what he was called upon to do could be considered honest
trading.

He decided that it was the moment he met the Hon. Mrs.

Glfddon-Foster, who was precisely the type of woman Mr. Sermon had been at pains to avoid when he met one at Sybil's social gatherings. She was distant, patronising and utterly without humour. She spoke in a county voice, and kept her face stiff and expressionless but she could not hide the greed in her eyes. She tried very hard to give the impression that haggling over money distressed her but Mr. Sermon had no doubt whatever that in all matters pertaining to money she was as shrewd as a Petticoat Lane huckster and twice as pitiless. She was aged about sixty and well-dressed in country tweeds but the thing that attracted Mr. Sermon's attention were her hands which were like powerful little claws, with blue veins showing through taut, transparent skin. They were the hands of a selfish, acquisitive woman and seeing them Mr. Sermon put his conscience in his pocket and followed her across the wide hall and into a room on the left of the stairs.

"That's two of 'em," said Tapper, meekly, "the others are in the 'all Perfesser."

The title caused the woman to glance sharply and distastefully at Mr. Sermon but he ignored the look and concentrated on the two pictures adorning the wall that faced the big window. They were as Tapper had suggested, mediocre oil-paintings, the work of a Victorian artist obsessed with the cult of castle ruins and cloud-draped mountains. Both pictures vaguely suggested the Highlands and one had a bilious-looking stag in the foreground. They were the kind of landscapes that Mr. Sermon had seen hanging in provincial hotels and between them they covered the entire wall.

"Hum!" he said deliberately as Tapper and the woman hung back, and then, even more deliberately, "I see! Ah yes! Hum!"

He had never wanted to be an actor. Never once had he sought a part in one of Sybil's plays or operas but deep down he had always known that he could act a part as well as the next man and a good deal better than some of Sybil's amateurs. He was acting now and was very conscious of the fact. He could sense his audience hanging on his words and the feeling of power this gave him was very gratifying. He paused for an interval in order to build suspense and then said; "Interesting brushwork! Remarkable cloud movement! Remi-

niscent of Cot·nan at his best but leaning, I feel, towards the
younger Bonnington."

He heard Tapper hiss with pleasure and bowing slightly
in the direction of the Hon. Mrs. Gliddon-Foster, he added:
"Perhaps I could view the portraits, Madam?"

They moved out into the hall where a group of three-
quarter-length portraits were hanging under the staircase and
in semi-darkness along the wall leading to the kitchen. They
were not very good portraits.

"Remarkable!" exclaimed Mr. Sermon, at length. "Eight of
them and five in the Kneller tradition! Family portraits no
doubt?"

The woman made a strangled sound that was not exactly
non-committal but could have had several interpretations.
Tapper twinkled and slowly rubbed his hands together, his
eye roving along the hall and into the drawing-room where
stood the French commode he had marked down. Already
his mind was juggling with the telephone numbers of dealers
as far apart as Kensington, Richmond and Brighton and his
appreciation of the odd little man he had picked up on the
road grew in proportion to his estimated net profit. Mr.
Sermon was now completely immersed in his role of art-
dealer and turned to Mrs. Gliddon-Foster with a splendid
show of heartiness.

"The point is, Madam," he said, "I could make you an
offer for all of them, both landscape and portraits, but I
don't think I could do you the justice you and your canvases
deserve. I could offer to buy the landscapes, or two of the
portraits, and leave the remainder on reserve. How does that
strike you? Please be frank!"

"I had rather hoped to sell them all," grumbled Mrs.
Gliddon-Foster but it was clear from her tone that she now
accepted Mr. Sermon, placing him on an altogether different
level from his companion. "However, if you only want
two . . . by the way, which two?"

"Ah," said Mr. Sermon, gravely, "that's the difficulty! That
will be a matter for my partner to decide," and he looked
hopefully at Tapper who started and rubbed his nose.

"The Perfesser means his partner in London, M'm," said
Tapper, hastily.

Mrs. Gliddon-Foster had narrow arched brows and when

she drew them together she looked rather like a thwarted
Donald Duck.

"You mean you can't decide about them now?"

"We could pay a deposit," said Tapper, "and I'm willing
to pay cash down for the commode and the jardiniere. Sixty-
five and twenty was your rock-bottom, wasn't it, Madam?"

Mrs. Gliddon-Foster winced but said: "That's so, eighty-
five in all, plus the deposit on the pictures of course!"

"Then suppose we make it a round hundred?" ventured
Tapper, already groping for his wallet and somehow suggesting to Mr. Sermon that he was pulling a gun.

"Very well," said Mrs. Gliddon-Foster crisply, "one hundred pounds. Cash I presume?"

"By all means, by all means," said Tapper, counting out
twenty five-pound notes and winking at Mr. Sermon so
brazenly that the latter looked away in embarrassment.

"I must say it's bin a pleasure doin' business, M'm," said
Tapper, as they returned to the front door and paused on the
steps. "I'll send a carrier over for the furniture tomorrow and
the Perfesser here, he'll be in touch with you about the
picshures later in the week, won't you Perfesser?"

"Er . . . yes, certainly," mumbled Mr. Sermon, whose mind
had been occupied with an attempt to reconcile Tapper's
casual sacrifice of fifteen pounds for pictures that he had no
intention of collecting. The acting phase had passed and Mr.
Sermon realised that he was sweating slightly, so excusing
himself quickly, he ran down the steps and climbed into the
van. He raised his hat to Mrs. Gliddon-Foster who made an
extremely painful attempt to smile. They drove off down the
drive exchanging no word but once they were back on the
road and coasting along into the village, Tapper relaxed and
thumped Mr. Sermon's knee so hard that he cried out in pain.

"Marvellous," he said, "absolutely bang-on, mate! You
know what you are Perfesser? You're a ruddy natchrule! I
on'y wish old Flash could have been in on that. It's
like I said, she fell for the old Oxford talk right away,
just like I thought she would."

"I'm glad it was successful," said Mr. Sermon modestly,
"but I would have felt a good deal more confident if I hadn't
been dressed like I am."

"You got a point there, Perfesser," said Tapper, urging
the van up the hill and pulling into a space bordering a birch

wood. "You sound right but you don't look right. Now at this here auction we might come orf with a bob or two, so let's take a bit o' trouble an' dress yer for the part. What exactly you got in that there rucksack in the way o' duds?"

"Nothing very impressive, I'm afraid," said Mr. Sermon, "but at least I could put on a collar and tie."

"You do that," said Tapper, seriously, "you do that right now but before I forget let's settle up!" He took out his wallet and peeled four fivers from the depleted roll, pressing them into Mr. Sermon's hand and closing his fingers on them.

"I say, look here," began Mr. Sermon, "I can't possibly take that amount for a mere piece of nonsense. You've already forfeited fifteen pounds by paying the deposit."

Tapper looked at him in astonishment. "Lost fifteen pounds? Lost it? How do you mean, lost it?"

"Well, you aren't going back for the pictures, are you?"

"Well, o' course I'm not," said Tapper, "but that on'y means I paid eighty instead o' sixty-five for the French bit don't it? And what's eighty for a piece like that? Lumme, I ain't greedy like some of 'em! I'm satisfied with two hundred per cent. If I give you twenty pounds the commode stands me in at a straight hundred, don't it? And if I don't get three for it I ought to put the flippin' shutters up soon as I get 'ome!"

"Three hundred?" gasped Mr. Sermon, "you'll re-sell the commode for three hundred?"

"An' fifty fer the jardiniere," Tapper reminded him. "Ain't a bad start to the day, is it? Now go on mate, get changed an' we'll push on to the sale."

As they were pottering along at about twenty-eight miles per hour they heard an imperious hooting immediately behind them and Tapper glanced into his mirror and gave a snort of indignation.

" 'Ullo, 'ullo!" he growled, "if it ain't Old Chipper Trowbridge, blast his eyes! 'Ere, we'll 'ave a bit of fun with him!" and to Mr. Sermon's alarm he began to put on speed and hold to the very middle of the road while the man behind, driving a smart, unladen station-wagon, made several ineffectual attempts to pass.

"Is he a friend of yours?" demanded Sebastian, presently, as the man's hooting trumpeted the motorist's furious impatience.

"Friend? Christ, no!" said Tapper. "He used to be, a kind o' friend, tho' I never reely liked him. Too flippin' dicey and too smooth be' arf! Besides, I don't reckon he's honest!"

Mr. Sermon found this hard to digest. Coming from a man who had just purchased goods for a hundred pounds and hoped, within a matter of days, to dispose of them for three hundred, the remark seemed rather sanctimonious but Tapper must have divined his thoughts, for he said:

"We got standards! You mightn't think so but we 'ave and it's all a matter of how you approach a buy I reckon. Now when it comes to sellin', particularly to the public, the sky's the limit, perviding mindjew that you points out any restoration, fer that way you don't get no comebacks! But buying's diff'rent. Take that Mrs. Starch-an'-Vinegar we met back there, I didn't fault her stuff, did I? You didn't hear me tell her that French bit was late an' dolled up to look period? No, I told her the flippin' truth! I said it was a good, saleable piece, an' I give her gettin' on for what she asked for it. It wasn't up to me to tell her French was in the fashion was it? Or that the price o' that kind o' stuff was rocketing month be month? That's for 'er to find out on her own in them bloody magazine articles I was tellin' you about. But this bloke be'ind, Chipper Trowbridge, he gets all his buys be faulting. He comes into my place and tries to tell me that the Gillow couch I got ain't right because it's got two sabre legs an' two turned ones. Yet he knows as well as I do that they was turning legs long before Vicky days but still he comes the old Irish every time he looks in. An' that ain't all neither!" he added; weaving hard right just in time to prevent the infuriated Chipper from overtaking. "He double-crosses the Trade, not on'y me but others. I left him to bid for me at a sale one time because I had an important appointment and I asked him to get me one thing—*one thing* mindjew, a Persian rug it was that the missus wanted fer the flat. I didn't get that rug, mate, it went in the ring and Chipper held it when they dished out the kitty and when I offered him a profit on it you know what he said? He said he had a customer who was mad keen to buy it an' so I tracked that customer down an' found out what he paid for it. Twenty-eight pun-ten it was, an' Chipper bought it for seven and stuck on another fifty bob in the knockout. Now is that right? Is that fair? I ain't forgotten and I'm gonner fix him sooner or later!"

Having got this grudge off his chest, Tapper relented and pulled in to allow Chipper to pass. The station-wagon whizzed by in a flurry of blue exhaust and a triumphant blare on the horn, as though the driver was doing something extremely skilful in overtaking the ancient van. Mr. Sermon caught a glimpse of the driver, a plump, florid man about fifty, chunky and rather arrogant-looking, with a fair-haired woman sitting beside him.

"Is that Chipper's wife?" he asked, when they had settled down to their easy pace once more.

"Not 'er!" said Tapper. "His wife ran off with a Scoutmaster who was camping in Chipper's orchard a year or two back! Don't blame her, neither! Sexy bit she was, dark an' cha-cha-looking. No, that's Chipper's bit o' consolation, an' she's more upstage than wot he is! She sits in the car all the time he's buying, looking like the flippin' Queen o' Sheba when King Solomon's out on the knock!"

They were drawing near a large village now and Mr. Sermon saw signs of considerable activity on the outskirts, cars parked all along the road and a policeman directing traffic into a farm-gate on the right. There were saleboards announcing "Sale This Day" and knots of people sitting about on the grass verges of a lane that led to a largish house in the dip. He was amazed at the number of vehicles and the apparent prosperity of their owners. Some of the women were fashionably dressed and all the men wore heavy, country tweeds and looked as though they had just come from a point-to-point or an Agricultural Show.

"Are all local sales as popular as this?" he asked Tapper.

"This kind is, good-class property out in the country. You get a diff'rent clientele at town-houses, dozens of housewives taking the day orf an' a swarm of fringe dealers, dabblers mostly, but they don't show up at places like this. Nothing in it for 'em so they keep more to the kind o' stuff I got aboard, you know, bread an' butter lines. But this is a day for The Boys, for Chipper an' suchlike! I expect Steve Vinnicombe's here, in fact I know he is somewhere. Steve's the King-o'-the-Ring and a nice chap when you get to know him. Regular customer o' mine and fair mindjew, fair as they come!"

They nosed down the lane and found a place to park in the rear of the house. Tapper said: "Now you sit tight,

Perfesser, an' let me scout around a bit, I got a notion we might do a bit o' good here but first I'll have to see Steve an' the boys, an' find out what they're after an' 'ow much they're going up to. Yerse, it's a dealer's day orl right, the flippin' public won't get a look in! Wait here an' I'll be back in ten minutes or so!" and he writhed from the driving seat and disappeared into the house, shouldering his way through the crowd like a man with a definite purpose in mind.

He was back in ten minutes and Mr. Sermon noted that he was pleased and excited. His face glowed and there was mischief in his brown, restless eyes.

"It's our lucky day!" he said. "We're gonner pull a fast one on Chipper! I had a word with Stevie and Abey Steiner, and some of the others is comin' in, chaps like George Dickon an' Bill Cooksley. Bella McCoy an' her boy-friend, they're game as well, it's like I said, they all got it in fer Chippy! Now you c'n help work this Perfesser, in fact, I don't reck'n we could work it without you. Hurry up, mate, they're just about to restart. All the bedroom stuff has gone and they're half-way through the dining-room, up to Lot 201," and he almost dragged Mr. Sermon from the cab and steered him through the mob that was converging on the dining-room.

Tapper pointed out Steve Vinnicombe and several other dealers, who had congregated in a group near the fireplace and Mr. Sermon at once recognised them as an élite for they were calm and poised, chatting easily with one another and sometimes laughing quietly. They looked, he thought, like a knot of professional performers at an air-display, men and women to whom this was all in a day's work and very far from being an entertainment. There was a kind of aloof strength in the way they stood and gestured, holding their folded catalogues like batons and eyeing the auctioneer as jockeys eye the starter. Mr. Sermon, however, had little opportunity to enquire about any of them for Tapper whisked him into the little study that lay between the dining-room and drawing-room and pointed to a small, marquetry chest of drawers with a label announcing it to be Lot 311.

"That's the piece!" he announced, "that's what we're going to drop on Chipper when he don't expect it!"

"Good Lord!" exclaimed Mr. Sermon, involuntarily,

and then smiled at himself, for he realised that Tapper was speaking metaphorically and devoted all his attention to the dealer's instructions which were, however, almost incomprehensible to him.

"You're an up-country dealer, see? From York, where the family's gone. You come down special to get this one piece for the owners. A special bit, see? Got a history to it an' they want it real bad!"

"Then why would it be included in the sale?" asked Mr. Sermon, bluntly, but Tapper gave a gesture of impatience. "Executors have to put everything in the sale to stop argy-bargy from the bennerfisheries!" he grunted, "but don't side-track me, mate, we ain't got time. Chipper will be in here any minnit, they almost finished the dining-room before lunch."

"What exactly do you want me to do?" asked Mr. Sermon, plaintively, for he remembered the tough look of the dealers in the fireplace and was nervous of crossing the least of them.

"Look at it!" said Tapper. "No, not now, chum, when Chipper an' the others are here. Get down on yer flippin' grovellers an' sniff it! Worry it! Poke it! Keep looking at this here catalogue as if you was consultin' it, but make sure *he's* around. I know Chipper and the minute he sees you he'll start pumpin' you because Steve will have already told him who you are an' what you're 'ere for, got me?"

"Well, partly," said the harassed Mr. Sermon. "As I understand it, you want me to pretend to an interest in this one piece? Then, you hope to get this Chipper to bid against me?"

"You got it, you got it!" said Tapper, happily, "but there's a bit more to it than that! He'll try an' find out why the family's so keen on it and you'll tell him it's because of its 'istory, see?"

"But what is its history?" asked Sebastian.

Tapper clicked his teeth and glanced towards the door.

" 'Ow the hell do I know? You're the perfesser of 'istry aren't you? Someone well-known in 'istry give it to one of the fam'ly in the year dot—think of someone, someone who was alive when that piece was knocked up!"

Mr. Sermon looked hard at the chest but his brain was befogged.

"When would that be? About eighteen-ten?"

Tapper looked puzzled for a moment and then smiled,

revealing his half-inch gap. "Well, if you think so, why shouldn't he?" he said, jubilantly. "In fer a penny in fer a quid and as ter price, watch me, see? I'll give you the come-on or drop dead sign!"

"I say that's all very well," protested Mr. Sermon, "but suppose this man Chipper doesn't . . ." but he trailed off, realising that he was now talking to himself, for almost as though he had bounced, Tapper shot away and began to study some ivories on the far side of the room. At that precise moment, Chipper drifted into the room, looking about him with the air of a patriarchal squire who has been asked to put in an appearance at a village fête but is wishing that rain would relieve him of the obligation.

Mr. Sermon, his ears burning, knelt beside the chest as though it had been a prie-dieu and from the crowded dining-room he could hear the half-jocular, half-protesting mono-logue of the auctioneer . . . "Any advance on thirty-three-ten? I'm not going to dwell, it's going at thirty-three-ten . . . !" followed the almost inaudible tap of his gavel and the softly-spoken words "Sold to Mr. Vinnicombe."

As the auctioneer opened bidding on the next lot, Mr. Sermon was conscious of Chipper's bulk standing over him and a rather reedy voice saying, "Nice little piece, should fetch a good price, shouldn't it?" At the same time Tapper left the room without a glance in their direction and Mr. Sermon, feeling on his mettle, replied firmly, "I hope not too much, I came a long way to get it!"

This remark was interpreted by Chipper as an invitation to join Mr. Sermon in prayer, so that they knelt side by side, their noses almost touching the brass handles of the drawers. For a moment or so they communed in silence, then Chipper said: "You're trade, of course? Some distance away, I as-sume?"

"York!" said Mr. Sermon, sitting back on his heels, "but not in the trade, not exactly that is. I was asked to come and bid on behalf of the family."

No one, not even the cha-cha Mrs. Trowbridge who had lived with Chipper many years before running away with the Scoutmaster, could have divined from Chipper's reaction to this piece of information that it had already been passed to him in the crowded dining-room. He raised a pair of sandy eyebrows, showing just the right amount of interest and said:

"Really? They must be very keen to get it! I wonder why? It's pleasant but not exceptional, is it?"

"Sentimental value," said Mr. Sermon, feeling that he had got the measure of the man and reflecting how easy it was to lie to a total stranger. "Every family gets attached to one thing or another about the house, I suppose, and my clients—I'm a solicitor—have a special reason to want the piece."

Chipper pursed his lips, eyeing the back of Mr. Sermon's head speculatively.

"Would it be inquisitive on my part to ask that reason or . . . er . . . unprofessional on yours to tell me?" he asked but he was smiling now, a wide, tolerant smile that might have enlivened the face of an uncle teasing a favourite niece about boy-friends. Mr. Sermon's fears were exorcised by the smile and by the man's patently false urbanity which vanquished the last of his scruples. For a moment he groped about for plausible data and then, with a deep breath, he surfaced holding a name between his teeth.

"Princess Charlotte!" he said and was rewarded by Chipper's interrogative eyebrow lift.

"Charlotte? George IV's daughter? Was it . . . hers?"

"I . . . er . . . I can't swear to that," said Mr. Sermon, spellbound by his own recklessness, "but I'm given to understand that one of the family had a royal household post, that of tutor probably, in the early eighteen-hundreds and doubtless certain items of furniture . . ." His voice trailed away as Chipper went down on his knees again and seemed now to be crawling round and round the chest and looking, thought Mr. Sermon, rather like a St. Bernard scenting a tree. From behind them, through the open door, the monotonous voice of the auctioneer reached them, ". . . . not going to dwell . . . everything here is to be sold . . . seventeen once, seventeen twice . . ." and then another soft rap, followed by the words "Mr. Vinnicombe", respectfully uttered. Tapper was obviously right, reflected Mr. Sermon, it was a day for The Boys and the public were not getting much of a show, but then a confused sound told him the dining-room was emptying and Mr. Sermon found himself washed into the far corner of the room as what seemed to be hundreds of people trampled on him, filling the room to suffocation point. Twice he fended himself off the window seat and tried to struggle back towards the chest but bodies blocked him on every side and he almost

despaired of making himself heard or catching the auctioneer's eye. Fortunately, however, there were several lots to
be sold before the chest and in the brief interval Mr. Sermon
managed, by dint of much wriggling and knee-butting, to
work his way on to the ledge of the window alcove. Here, to
his great relief, he found he could look down on both Tapper and Chipper who were positioned each side of the auctioneer's stool.

"Lot three hundred and eleven," croaked the auctioneer,
"a marquetry chest of drawers in first-class condition. No
reserve on this, ladies and gentlemen, so give me a start; fifteen pounds shall I say?"

There was silence, a long, heavy silence it seemed to Sebas-
tian, and then, as the auctioneer opened his mouth to protest,
Tapper lifted his hand and the auctioneer said: "Thank you,
Mr. Sugg. Fifteen pounds bid!"

"Sixteen!" bawled Mr. Sermon, so loudly that everybody
looked at him and he blushed but remained defiantly where
he was perched, well clear of the crowd with his eye fixed
on Chipper Trowbridge. He noted that there was no smile
on the man's face now but a blankness relieved by a hard,
brightness of the eye. Suddenly Chipper lifted his catalogue,
whereupon Tapper lifted his and then Chipper lifted his a
second time and the auctioneer said "Nineteen? Come now
gentlemen, let's be serious, don't let's waste each other's time!"
and looked hopefully at Mr. Sermon.

Without knowing why, Mr. Sermon was sure that his bidding had excited more than an ordinary interest and that the
crowd, jaded after several hours in airless rooms, sensed real
competition and settled down to enjoy a blow by blow contest.

"Twenty-five!" he said clearly, and the auctioneer smiled
his thanks and turned back to the two men behind him,
watching not them but the rolled-up sale catalogues they
used to announce their bids. Mr. Sermon had a feeling of
being left far behind in the race, like a track-runner lapped
by two champions and in less than thirty seconds the chest
stood at sixty-five pounds and chatter ceased in all corners of
the room.

"Sixty-five once, sixty-five twice—it's against you, sir!"
said the auctioneer, looking at the impassive Chipper.

Mr. Sermon hesitated, unable to catch Tapper's eye and then, taking his courage in both hands he stood on tiptoe and waved his catalogue, feeling as he did so a sense of initiation that lifted him clear of the mass of people in the room and alongside the élite gathered in a patient knot round Steve Vinnicombe, King-o'-the-Ring.

"Seventy!" said the auctioneer. "I had an idea you weren't going to leave it at that, sir!" and then Mr. Sermon wilted, for he read tragedy in Tapper's brown eyes and suddenly felt chastened and helpless, a feeling reinforced by the recollection that seventy pounds was more than twice the amount he had about him and that the tough-looking auctioneer was almost certain to refuse a cheque from a stranger.

He need not have worried. Even dealers are not inoculated against auction fever and Chipper's blood was up. He said, crisply and disdainfully: "Eighty, sir!" and Mr. Sermon subsided with relief as the misery drained from Tapper's face and the auctioneer paused, gavel aloft.

"Have you done, sir?" he enquired politely of Mr. Sermon and Mr. Sermon cried out that he had, emphasising the fact by stepping down from the ledge and recoiling from the pneumatic behind of a plump woman standing immediately below.

"Sold to Mr. Trowbridge!" said the auctioneer loudly and Tapper passed his hand across his brow and eased his way back into the hall, whither Mr. Sermon was able to follow him as soon as the crowd had surged towards lots in a far corner of the room.

"Lumme!" muttered Tapper, leading the way out into the open, "you had me scared bloody stiff, mate! I thought we were gonner be stuck with it. Still, I ought to have had more confidence I reckon, seein' 'ow you did over the picshures!" and he rubbed his hands gleefully. "What did you tell the perisher to push him up that far? Did you say 'Enry Eight used the flippin' thing fer his trousseau?"

"I mentioned that it was once the property of Princess Charlotte," said Mr. Sermon, nervous reaction making his voice squeaky, "and I must say, he seemed to believe it. He semed very much taken with the piece."

"Who the 'ell is Princess Charlotte?" demanded Tapper, and when Mr. Sermon told him something of the unfortunate girl's history he gave a low whistle and placed both hands on his hips, regarding Mr. Sermon with unqualified approval. "I reckon you ought to get into the swim, perfesser! It's like I said, you got something, a kind of . . . kind of *or-then-tisserty* if you know what I mean? Old Chipper in there, he's a skate all right but he's nobody's fool an' never was! Yet his dander was up, I could spot that right orf. He'd have gone on and on and on sooner'n let either of us 'ave it. Funny that! You never can't tell at an auction, not even with the craftiest of 'em. Bloody-minded they get, and to think that flippin' piece 'as been standing in my back store all them months, with everyone faulting it right, left and centre! Almost makes you believe Princess Wotsit did pass it on when she kicked the bucket!"

"In your store!" exclaimed Mr. Sermon, "*your* store, you said?"

Tapper looked at him curiously. "Well, o' course," he said, "didn't I tell you?"

"No, you certainly did not!" said Mr. Sermon stiffly.

"That's right, I didn't," said Tapper, "because I didn't get the chance, did I? That piece was put in the sale a week or two back. Old Archie Coombes, the auctioneer, is a pal o' mine see, and as soon as this sale come up he give me a ring and sent the van round for it. And now Chipper's stuck with it at eighty, an' me thinking I was stuck with it at thirty-five, plus carriage! But we ain't finished yet! I daresay he'll stick a bit more on it at the knockout, tho' that might be risky and I'll have to have a word with Steve about it!" and he suddenly forgot about Mr. Sermon and dived back into the house, remaining incommunicado until the crowd had surged out into the courtyard to hear the garden implements sold. Then he re-appeared and led the way past the van and into a shrubbery beyond which was a rustic summer-house standing in a clearing.

Mr. Sermon was surprised to find most of the dealers already assembled there, sitting or standing round Steve Vinnicombe who was seated at a table, a sheaf of papers confronting him.

"What exactly is going on now?" demanded Sebastian, almost running alongside the fast-striding Tapper.

"Knockout!" said Tapper. "This is the real auction and don't say nothing see, you don't so much as open your mouth, got me?"

They took up their position on the steps and from what Mr. Sermon could make out from the grunts and gestures of the two dozen men and women enclosing Mr. Vinnicombe, it appeared that at least half the lots were being put up for auction all over again. He was not near enough to see or hear what happened when Lot No. 311 came up, but Tapper, who had abandoned him again, returned soon afterwards thumbing through a pile of notes that looked to Mr. Sermon to be as thick as the wad he had flashed in the café.

"Lumme, this is what I call a good day!" he said, drawing Mr. Sermon away from the summer-house. "Chipper put another fifteen on that flippin' bit o' markitry and now it stands him in ninety-five! He'll be buried in it I reckon because it won't take him long to find out that the family never heard of it, and then he'll come looking fer you with a chopper! Still, that's what comes o' chiselling in, don't it? He should've thought o' that when he was pumping you an' trying to get his claws in it so as he could ring up the family and say he held it and if they wanted it they'd have to cough up! Neat bit o' work that was, Steve himself said so. May teach him to leave a few crumbs around fer the rest of us now an' again!" and he dismissed the subject and devoted the whole of his attention to counting his money, finally peeling off another ten pounds and stuffing them nonchalantly into Mr. Sermon's pocket.

"I come off with fifty-seven!" he said, "and reckon ten o' that is yours be right, because the Trade wouldn't have looked at that markitry bit if you hadn't pulled the longbow. Thirty-seven, an' me a flippin' Rabbit! 'Streuth, I wonder what Steve an' the others'll get orf with today? Over the hundred apiece, I wouldn't wonder!" and he climbed into the van and started the engine, leaving Mr. Sermon to make what he could of his summary of the day's business.

It crossed Mr. Sermon's mind that he had no right at all to the two five-pound notes in his jacket pocket and scarcely more to the twenty pounds given him for his part in the private buy but he was reluctant to reopen the subject with Tapper, sensing that the little man would be offended if he challenged the amount. He was aware that he had contributed to the wad of money now nestling in Tapper's bulging wallet but his curiosity was suspended by an overpowering drowsiness that advertised itself in vast yawns.

"Will we be moving on to Kingsbay now?" he asked, as they turned into the main road and headed into the sunset. "I don't think I'd better leave it too late, I've got to find somewhere to stay for the night."

"You c'n kip at our place if it comes to that," said Tapper, "and then find somewhere a bit cosier in the morning. I'm peckish tho'," he added, "so we'll stop off on the way for high tea and after that I could do with a pint and after that grommet if I'm lucky. No sense in working like we have today an' grudging yourself a quid or two, is it?" Then, smiling reminiscently. "Who was it you kidded Chipper about? Princess Whowasit?"

"Charlotte!" said Mr. Sermon sleepily, and was on the point of asking his friend the meaning of 'grommet' when he dozed off in the very middle of a yawn, slumping down on the leather cushions heedless of the clank and roar and rattle of the grossly overloaded vehicle.

·   ·   ·   ·   ·

The sharp rattle of loose gravel awoke Mr. Sermon from a deeply satisfying doze. He noticed that it was dusk and that the wagon was slowing down to turn into a narrow arch that led to a cobbled yard, half surrounded by lighted windows.

"Is this Kingsbay?" he asked, rubbing his eyes.

"No, mate, it's two mile short of it," said Tapper, "but this'll do for a start. Nothing in the town to beat this for grub and home brew. Good service too, so long as Bella ain't swamped with visitors and she won't be, seeing it's on'y April and the season ain't started."

He parked the van and piloted Mr. Sermon through a swing door into the most cheerful-looking pub lounge Mr. Sermon had ever entered. Everything in it was clean and twinkling and dancing firelight played on half a hundred horse brasses and gleaming warming pans and copper measures fastened to the panelled walls and oak beams. There was a semicircular bar near the vast chimney piece and behind it, lit with green and ruby lights and electrically wired fisherman's floats, were scores of bottles and pewter tankards, an appropriate setting for the comfortable-looking woman behind the bar. The room appeared to be empty of customers and Tapper breezed in as one sure of a welcome, accosting the barmaid with a cheerful shout.

"How's me Home-Comfort? How's me Luvely?" he demanded and when Mr. Sermon hung back, still hazed with sleep, he pushed him forward and introduced him as "a-real-live-perfesser-who's-come-all-the-way-from-Smoke-just-to-drink-the-wallop-and-view-the-upholstery-at-the-bar-of-the-Cat-and-Carthorse!"

Bella, the barmaid, did not seem to resent this boisterous introduction and Mr. Sermon was surprised and elated at the impression she made upon him.

She was not exactly plump but very solid-looking so that Mr. Sermon recalled the phrase crime-reporters always used about barmaids found murdered in ditches—what was it?— 'The Body was partly-clothed and well-nourished!' That was it exactly! Bella was exceptionally well-nourished but her proportions were very pleasing indeed, fulfilling the description 'hour-glass' applied to her type of figure. Her bust was large and her hips rounded and heavy but Mr. Sermon thought it would be very pleasant indeed to encircle her waist with both hands in order to discover exactly how far round it his fingers would stretch. As he stood there, prospecting her as it were, she reached out to retrieve their tankards and as she bent forward her low-necked frock dipped to reveal a shameless expanse of bosom. It crossed Mr. Sermon's mind that Bella's action in stooping over the sink must have brought thousands of customers into the bar and been responsible, more or less directly, for selling oceans of beer. Then he gave himself a kick in the moral shins and told himself that if he didn't watch out he would soon develop into a dirty old man and in this briefly exalted frame of mind he followed Tapper to a table near the fire and when the girl arrived with the plates of cold meats and pickled onions he piously averted his eyes and stared into the fire. The penitent mood, however, did not survive the meal or even the next draught. A kind of pink cosiness stole over him, ironing away such quirks and creases of his old self as had survived the last thirty hours, and in the glow of the luxurious present he threw off the last of his inhibitions and began to revel in the banter Tapper and the girl were exchanging, laughing aloud when Tapper, who seemed never to have possessed any inhibitions at all, pinched her behind when she was slow at replenishing their glasses.

Towards nine o'clock customers arrived but no longer departed and the bar began to fill, the buzz of talk reaching Mr. Sermon as from a distance. Then several of Tapper's personal acquaintances came in and each was introduced to Mr. Sermon but by this time he had consumed too much liquor to differentiate between them and the only one who really registered was a round-faced woman with blonde, lifeless hair whose laugh was as arresting as the blast of a factory siren and who seemed to dissolve during a paroxysm and then coalesce again the moment it passed. At one stage of the evening they were all exchanging jokes and Mr. Sermon remembered feeling slightly sad because he did not know any, and later on they played darts and he scored a winning double-nineteen which almost shocked him into sobriety, but after that the mists of draught beer and the roar of conversation isolated him so that it was as if he was watching the party through an uncurtained window and somebody kept switching the light on and off, destroying continuity.

It must have been about then, and getting on for closing time, when he was conscious of Tapper dragging him by the arm and leading him towards an upright piano and then he found himself sitting at the instrument and letting his hands run over the yellowing keys while all the others stood around him shouting encouragement and waving their mugs in his face.

In a moment of comparative clarity he heard Tapper say: "He can play, o' course he can play, he's a perfesser from Oxford and Cambridge!" and, even in his totally uncritical mood, Mr. Sermon thought it rather foolish of him to name both Universities when either would have sufficed but nevertheless he began to strum, playing from ear, the way he had often played for the boys at school. For some reason his instinct led him to play songs of youth, of his own youth and the youth of most of those people around him, hits of the twenties like 'Ain't She Sweet' and 'Yes We Have No Bananas' and lively numbers like 'Valencia' and 'Bye Bye Blackbird.'

The success of his repertoire delighted everybody and a kind of mad and rapturous exuberance bubbled up from within him, demanding wilder and wilder expression so that he found himself bawling the lyrics at the top of his voice. In between each number somebody pushed a mug of beer to his lips and he sucked down a mouthful or two and then ducked under the mug to continue the concert, pounding his way into the thirties and down the years of popular sheet music as far as 'Roll Out The Barrel', the song that everyone was singing when war broke out more than twenty years before. And there Mr. Sermon stopped playing, right in the middle of what his friend Tapper would have called 'a twiddly bit', for the piano seemed to open up and engulf him and his fingers shot off the keyboard and clutched madly but unavailingly at the polished panel of the upright and Mr. Sebastian Sermon, until that moment the life and soul of the party, took off into outer space studded with constellations of flashing, soaring star-shells that hummed and whizzed and wailed as they rushed past leaving him floating in a blue, velvet emptiness bounded by the distant roar of the sea.

．　　　．　　　．　　　．　　　．

When Mr. Sermon opened one eye the first thing he saw was a woman's dress. It was empty and suspended on a hanger that was hooked to the picture-rail a yard from the narrow bed in which he lay. He studied it objectively, noting the cellophane sheath in which it reposed and the broad lace collar with exaggerated points that reminded him of the shirt stained with Charles I blood that he had seen in the United Services Museum, in Whitehall.

He studied the dress for more than a minute, deciding that it was too loud and flouncy for his taste but it was not until his single eye roved along the wall towards the window and observed other items of female clothing piled on a chair, that he related the garment to his present whereabouts and wondered what on earth he could be doing in a bed within reach of such things. Then, like a douche of ice-cold water, the two streams of thought mingled and poured over him and he jerked himself upright, gazing round the little room with amazement and alarm.

He did not recognise it or anything in it. It was neatly and simply furnished with a small wardrobe, a bedside table, a small rug laid on patterned linoleum and cretonne curtains that were half-drawn, but apart from the items of clothing there was nothing whatever to give it an identity. Sebastian at last opened the other eye, which seemed to have been gummed up during the night and was reluctant to view the daylight. He then saw his own rucksack, which brought him a little comfort for it was the only familiar object in the room and then, with both eyes open, he recognised his clothes, neatly folded and placed on a stool near the wardrobe. Like a swimmer far out to sea who has sighted a distant vessel, he projected himself upward and outward from the bed, giving a kind of yelp and springing on to the cold linoleum to dive for his trousers. It was only when he had fished out his wallet and found his money intact that he realised he was wearing nothing but his short cotton underpants and as though escaping from a burning building he plunged into his trousers, fastened them with trembling fingers and began a minute inspection of the room, half his attention on what he found and half engaged in a desperate grapple to reconstruct his last conscious period.

He remembered arriving at a pub with a ridiculous name, 'The Dove and Donkey' or 'The Dog and Dove'—no, that wasn't its proper name, it was something much more staid, the Something Arms, an old coaching hostelry approached by a narrow arch that led to the cobbled yard. He ran across to the little window and looked out. There was the identical yard and he was now looking down on it from a great height. He then remembered the party and rivers of beer, and himself roaring out choruses at the piano and a game of darts and then . . . ? He darted across and looked at himself in the mirror and saw that he needed a shave but apart from this his face looked familiar, a little drawn and bug-eyed perhaps, but not noticeably different from the narrow, thoughtful face he inspected every morning whilst shaving. It then occurred to him that he should have a hangover, surely a terrible hangover after all that draught beer consumed in that smoke-laden atmosphere, but he had no hangover, not a trace of one and the certainty that he had not helped to restore his confidence so that he said, aloud: "This is a rum do! Where the devil am I? A hotel, certainly, and the hotel Tapper took me to last evening but in whose room? Obviously not my own but somebody else's, a perfect stranger's!"

Then his eyes moved from the suspended pink dress to the pile of clothing on the chair and he reached out and picked up one of the garments, dropping it as though it was a live snake when he realised what it was, a pair of white, silk panties, with blue lover's knots embroidered on the hem. After that he began to panic. His mouth felt dry and his heart pounded so mercilessly that it hurt his ribs and he felt sick with apprehension. He looked carefully at the bed, relieved to discover that it had but one pillow upon which was the imprint of his head and nobody else's. The discovery steadied him somewhat so he was able to cross over to the marble-topped washstand and pour water into the china bowl and slop it round his face and over his neck and ears. Then he found his toilet bag in the rucksack and gave himself a proper wash. He put on his vest and shirt and was in the act of pulling on his socks when he heard the pleasant rattle of china outside the door and then a gentle double-knock that sounded to Mr. Sermon like an impersonal summons to the guillotine.

"Co . . . come in!" he squeaked, and the door opened to reveal a smiling Bella, with a small tea-tray skillfully balanced in the crook of her elbow.

"Hullo, Professor!" she said cheerily, "I thought you might like some tea. No extra charge. No charge at all in fact. Sleep well?" She indulged herself in a little giggle. "I'll bet you did! You was out cold when I laid you there, never moved a muscle you didn't." She glanced at the bed. "Tidy sleeper, too! There now, shall I pour you a cup?"

"Er . . . do . . . please!" stuttered Mr. Sermon, over-whelmed by her breezy warmth, and then, "I say, Bella—it *is* Bella, isn't it? Exactly where am I? I mean, whose room is this?"

"It's mine," she said, apparently surprised by the question, "whose should it be?"

"Yours!" He jumped up, stuffing his shirt into his trousers with frantic haste. "But Good Lord—I mean—how, why?"

She laughed and pushed him down on the bed.

"Here, drink it down. I bet you're parched but I'll also lay odds you haven't got a hangover, have you now?"

"No, I haven't," admitted Mr. Sermon, "but I . . . I should have, never in my life have I drunk as much as I did last night!"

"Well, you got me to thank for *that!*" she said triumphantly. "Tapper said don't bother but I came back when he'd gone, lifted you up and made you drink it. You did too, like a lamb. It's my special, Worcester Sauce base, dash of milk and egg yolk, with two Codeine dissolved separit and added."

"It was very good of you, I'm sure," said Sebastian, "but why . . . er . . . why didn't you book me in to an ordinary room as a guest?"

"In your condition? Don't be silly! We couldn't have got you up the front stairs without a scene and the boss would have heard all about it from the residents. On'y too pleased to bleat, they would have been, I mean to say, a bit of a sing-song in the Public's one thing but putting the drunks to bed on the premises is another, isn't it?"

"Yes," said Mr. Sermon dismally, "I suppose it is, but was I . . . was I quite as helpless as all that?"

"Helpless? Well I don't know how you coulder been more so. I mean to say, when a chap's legs trail behind him like empty bicycle toobs, and his head hangs down like a snapped-off crysant in a vase, you got to do something with him, haven't you?"

"I—I'm most fearfully sorry," said Mr. Sermon earnestly, "it came on very suddenly, I imagine, I don't even recall . . ."

"Oh, you don't want to apologise for it, Professor," said Bella gaily. "I mean to say, it comes over all of us now'n again, don't it? It's not as tho' you were a nuisance when we was hauling you up an' getting you undressed like some of 'em. Limp you was, right up to the time I come back with the head-lifter and propped you up to swallow it."

"What . . . er . . . what happened then?" asked Sebastian, nervously.

She threw back her head and laughed so that Mr. Sermon noticed her powerful throat muscles and the strength of her shoulders.

"Oh, I had to put up a bit of a fight for me honour you might say. Nothing reely but you kept catching me round the waist and trying to hoist me on to the bed. I couldn't help laughing, with you in that state! I dunno what you thought you could do if you got me there. We'd have both dropped off disappointed, I reckon."

She told him this without a blush but he blushed for the two of them. He was deeply ashamed, not so much because he had been guilty of such ungentlemanly behaviour but because it had been practised on someone who was taking considerable risks to help him.

"Where . . . where did you sleep, Bella?" he said humbly.

"Me? Oh, I was all right, I popped into Number 42 on the second floor and made up the bed again first light, so no one'll know, and in any case, the boss is away until after lunch. I'd have taken a chance on it mind you even if he'd been around. I know a gentleman when I see one!"

"I don't think I behaved very much like a gentleman," said Mr. Sermon sadly and felt extraordinarily deflated, vastly different, he reflected, from how he had felt when he began his wanderings the previous day at the abandoned siding in the country. What *was* the matter with him, and why was he behaving in this extraordinary fashion? Was this throwing off of fetters, this curiously powerful urge to begin again nothing more than sexual hunger, the final erotic flailings of a man approaching his second childhood? He shivered slightly and she noticed it at once.

"What's up? You cold?"

"No, no, Bella, I'm not cold—just, well, just a little afraid, I suppose!"

"What of? No one don't know and you'll be out of here before anyone comes."

"Oh, it's not that, it's not getting drunk and spending the night here. I dare say I'll laugh at myself over that in due course, but . . ." He stopped. He could hardly express his real fears to a barmaid whom he had attempted to assault a few hours ago.

"It doesn't matter, Bella," and he began to sip his tea.

"Oh, but it does! You're upset about something. Any fool could see that. Me especially because I know men. Now listen to me. You don't need to be! You didn't worry me a bit, I wouldn't even have mentioned it if you hadn't pressed me. Besides, it wasn't you reely, it was the liquor. After all, that's what we drink it for, isn't it? I mean, it lifts the lid off and lets your fancy roam around a bit. I'll tell you something else, too, it's a compliment to me in a way."

"Compliment?" he echoed, faintly.

"Yes!" She was slightly defiant now and her earnestness brought a pink flush to her slightly pendulous cheeks.

"You see, Professor, in the ordinary way, an educated bloke like you wouldn't look at a girl like me! I mean, if you wanted that you'd go looking for a real tart wouldn't you? But you didn't think that way, not even when you were full of beer. You just wanted . . . well, a bit of a cuddle, I reckon, someone to fall asleep on and feel safe, if you follow me, and if I hadn't been sure you'd have taken it the wrong way soon as you come round, I'd never have gone up to Number 42, I'd have stayed here all night. Matter o' fact I near as dammit did, so there! Here, what have I said now to make you worse?" and she took his half-empty cup from his hand, plumped herself down on the bed beside him and threw a vast arm along his shoulders.

He was weeping, not very obviously so for he fought against the flow of tears with all his strength and mastered it within seconds. He was weeping with a kind of humility and relief, humility at hearing this kind of admission from a plump, half-ignorant barmaid in a country pub where he supposed she had already spent most of her adult life. He was weeping because his entire conception of what constituted knowledge and civilisation, and the kind of teaching in which he had been engaged for twenty-five years, looked bloodless and sterile in the glare of her honesty and simplicity. He supposed Sybil and her suburban set would hardly deign to notice a girl like this, someone who prefaced everything she said with the phrase "Well I mean ter say . . . " and found it almost impossible to express the generosity and tolerance of her heart, yet somehow still managed to do it and reduce him to tears in the process. But as well as shame at his own watered-down philosophy he felt relief that he had stumbled through and beyond it to a place where he could at least begin re-learning about people, about what made them tick and about a world where people came out into the sun to laugh and enjoy themselves. Sitting there, with Bella's arm across his shoulder, he felt he had learned more in ten seconds than in all the years he had taught in school and crammed for examinations. He whipped out his handkerchief and blew his nose, letting the corner of the linen brush the moisture under his eye. Then he said:

"I think you're wonderful, Bella, quite wonderful! You don't know it and I'm at a loss how to tell you, but you've done me no end of good, no end, d'you hear me?" And then, briskly: "Do you think you could find me some hot water for a shave? And after that could I buy some breakfast before I push on into Kingsbay?"

"Why, that's better," she said, smiling, "now you're talking!

Put your jacket and tie on and come downstairs. You can shave in the Gents, there's hot water in there, and I'll fix breakfast in the dining-room because everyone'll think you're a late booker-in and early starter. You're not all stirred up with guilt no more, are you? No you aren't, you're all right again, I can see that!" and suddenly she took his face between her hands and kissed him on the lips and before Mr. Sermon could return the kiss she jumped up and skipped out of the room, shouting "Bring the tray!" over her shoulder.

Mr. Sermon put up his hand and touched his mouth almost as if the kiss had been a benediction and he wanted to trap it before it escaped. Then, slowly, he completed his dressing, picked up his knapsack and went out of the little room and down the backstairs where the smell of cooking was already circulating in the stairwell. At the very foot of the stairs he noticed a dog-eared calendar hanging on a disused gas-bracket and turning slowly in the draught. It was a Religious Tract publication, with the name of the month wreathed in scrolls of gold and surmounted by a text in cobalt blue. The text was the 31st verse of the 10th chapter of St. Mark and read: "But many that are first shall be last; and the last first." 'And very appropriate, too,' thought Mr. Sermon, 'if the Kingdom of God is a reality then I'd offer ten to one that Bella isn't even asked to produce credentials!'

CHAPTER THREE

Mr. Sermon
Crosses into Arcady

CONCERNING most things, Mr. Sermon was an exceptionally
modest man but in at least one respect he was very vain. He
was extremely proud of the general neatness of his mind
which, ever since his youth, had operated like a filing cabinet
maintained by an exceptionally diligent clerk. He could always find what he sought in it and that with the minimum of
delay. He did not, like most of us, have to forage about in
search of facts and figures, names, dates and arguments extracted from leading articles and statistics that were aimed at
reducing blustering opponents to stuttering impotence but so
seldom did. Everything he had read and learned was there
in its proper place and most people gave him credit for a
remarkable memory but this habit of ready-reference had
very little to do with memory as memory is generally understood; it was more the result of a careful sorting process,
deliberate and discretional. Mr. Sermon had once been impressed by a lecture delivered by a brain surgeon and had
learned, in the course of the evening, that no one ever forgot
anything but stored it away and lost the key. Mr. Sermon
rarely lost the smallest key. Even his dreams were tabulated
and filed away, and whenever he was free from emotional

stress each fantasy could be taken out, contemplated and, if necessary, re-classified before being returned to its locker. But there was a single flaw in his system. One dream could never be pinned down, labelled and tucked away. Always it had eluded classification for the reason that it never took on solid shape like the others, never stayed with him long enough to be saddled and bitted but hovered just out of reach, a tantalisingly beautiful dream utterly unlike all its brothers and sisters and cousins, a dream in which time and location and atmosphere, particularly atmosphere, were inexplicably interwoven and therefore defied analysis. And because it was so ethereal and diaphanous, because he could never decide what it was or where it was, he thought of it as his Arcadian or Avalon dream and had long since abandoned attempts to bring it to heel.

It had about it an air of eternal summer. He knew that because its sounds were those of bees humming and the sough of the south wind in spruce and larch and silver birch. Its scent was that of wildflowers carried on the breeze, coming to him out of deep, cool woods and across leagues of still, sunlit water. There was absolutely nothing positive about it, like his sex fantasies or his heroic feats that excited the envy of the handsome and successful, for all these lesser fantasies were enacted within the web of the Arcadian dream. Thus, in a sense, it was not a fantasy at all, having no separate existence except as a kind of frame for all his other fantasies. Yet it was the frame that fascinated him, the setting where all these other triumphs were achieved, and deeply rooted in his imagination was the certainty that triumphs would evade him unless he found the right field of operations. It was towards this Arcady that he was consciously directing himself when he walked out into the night but only now was he on the edge of discovering this important fact because, under the spur of his adventures, all his creative impulses were beginning to flower. He could feel the sap rising in him with every breath he drew and as he walked up the bare coast road towards the town of Kingsbay after breakfasting at the Cat and Carthorse that morning, he was suddenly aware of an absolute certainty that he was now on the very threshold of Arcady, not merely a physical conception of the setting that had eluded him so long but a realisation of himself as the man he had always yearned to be, a human being

with a purpose that was recognised by those about him. The
certainty of ultimate fulfilment enlarged and revivified him
to such an extent that his step seemed to lengthen with every
stride and the scent of Spring rushed into his lungs with such
force that it almost lifted him and ballooned him up the
gentle slope to the dark brown horizon that sat on the crest
of the moor.

He almost ran the last two hundred yards up the incline
and when he topped it, and stood gasping at the crest where
the road wound down between two plantations into Kingsbay
and the sea, he uttered an involuntary shout for he knew then
that his instincts had not betrayed him and that spread out
below him, like a relief map of Europe they used in Geography classes at Napier Hall, was his personal Shangri-la,
his Arcady, his Avalon, the place to which, like Arthur, he
had come to be healed of his grievous wounds.

. . . . . .

The white road plunged down from the wooded slopes and
ran almost straight between two sandstone bluffs, one impres-
sively high and bare of everything but gorse, the other, to the
west, a more modest promontory shaped like a fat paw and
clothed with pinewoods. In between, occupying a valley about
a mile broad, was the wedge-shaped town set on the gentle
slope, a town that did not seem to belong to Britain at all,
but had drifted there from the Caribbean Sea, for its houses,
or most of them, were a dazzling white and advanced on an
ever-broadening front to meet and touch the sea. The houses
were dotted about the valley with what struck Sebastian as
a careless but pleasing symmetry, here huddled together, there
interspersed with green patches of lawn and shrubs and sometimes a tall sycamore or a few Scots firs. The bay itself was
a sheet of silver but further out to sea, two miles or more he
would judge, were yellow sandbanks and here, where shallow
water caught the light, it was a deep greenish blue, flecked
with the white ruffles of wavelets breaking on the banks. There
were boats about, a dozen or so, seemingly stationary between
the breakwaters and at the extremity of the bay he could see
one or two cars gliding along the promenade. Apart from this
there seemed to be no movement in the town which lay
dreaming and waiting as it soaked up the April sun.

He stood there a long time drinking in the beauty of the scene and feeling like a man who, after incredible hazards, has crossed a continent and a formidable range of peaks, to view the sea. There was no doubt about it, this was it! This was Avalon, and hitching his rucksack he went on down the hill to the top of the wide High Street, glancing about him with a satisfaction that he could not have expressed in words but settled somewhere between throat and navel with a kind of pulsing glow.

One of the first shops he reached was Tapper's. He recognised it instantly by its clutter of furniture piled under the boulevard-like awning of striped canvas and its heart-shaped sign with the single omnibus word TABLESNCHAIRS painted in crude Gothic characters.

It was a much larger shop than he had imagined and from the outside it looked neat and clean. All the goods displayed in the open were priced in chalked figures and some of them he recognised as stock that had travelled there yesterday on the van. He looked through the window, shading his eyes against the reflection and saw a boy of about fifteen sitting at a davenport at the back, absorbed in a folded newspaper and presumably transferring memoranda into a notebook. The street was empty so, after a moment's hesitation, he opened the door and went inside, his action touching off a bell that brought the boy to his feet as if he had been prodded in the back with a bayonet.

"Good morning!" said Mr. Sermon, breezily, "I suppose you must be Blessing?"

The boy's expression underwent a sudden change. As he had advanced towards Mr. Sermon it had been obvious that he anticipated a sale. His rather pudgy features had assumed a painfully unctuous expression and Mr. Sermon would not have been surprised if he had bowed like a stage Chinaman and then 'washed his hands' as earnest of his desire to serve. Immediately Mr. Sermon spoke his name, however, his face straightened out, becoming almost sullen and resentful and he said, carelessly: "S'right! An' you're a bloke me Dad give a lift to yesterday. Said you might look in. He's out the back wi' Gramp!" and having reached and perhaps exceeded the limits he had set himself as host, he at once returned to his copying and left Mr. Sermon to find his own way through a pair of threadbare baize curtains and into a long, low-ceilinged room that had once been a bakery, for the ovens were still in position and sawn-off ventilators projected from the ceiling like a row of broken teeth.

The room was crammed with furniture: at the far end sat an old man shaped like a cider barrel with a grizzled poll and steel-rimmed spectacles perched half-way down a pomegranate nose. Mr. Sermon concluded that this must be Grandfather Sugg, or "Flash" as Tapper had referred to him, and it occurred to Sebastian that the old fellow was not disposed to be any more friendly than his grandson. The suspicion was confirmed at once. Flash rolled one poached-egg eye at the intruder and emitted a fruity grunt but he did not attempt to get up or remove his enormous calves from the backless chair on which they reposed. Looking down at him, Mr. Sermon was reminded of the porter in *Tom Brown's Schooldays*, whom the Rugby boys used to torment by whipping his calves. He seemed an extremely truculent old man and, like the boy outside, resentful of having been disturbed but Mr. Sermon was in such a cheerful mood that he pressed forward, extended his hand and said: "I'm a friend of your son, Tapper, Mr. Sugg. We . . . er . . . we did a little buying together yesterday."

"Arr, he told me!" growled Flash. "You're the one who dropped a bit o' marketry on that bleeder Trowbridge! Glad to hear about *that* I was," he went on, as though this could be offset against nameless other shortcomings on the part of the visitor, "taken all the profit out o' the game *that* type has. Easy enough to make a bob or two in the old days but not now, not now by thunder! Licked the plate clean they 'ave, what wi' their lah-di-dah talk an' their dashing about here, there an' everywhere in their stinking moters. Siddown! Tapper's making the elevenses in the scullery. *Tapper!*" and he roared the summons in a voice that would not have shamed a Company Sergeant Major quelling a mutiny.

The scullery door flew open and his son appeared, his mouth splitting in the familiar gap-toothed grin the moment he saw Mr. Sermon standing beside the foaming Flash.

"Well if it ain't the Perfesser!" said Tapper, cordially, putting down a tin tray on which stood three handleless and saucerless cups, seizing Mr. Sermon by the shoulders and rocking him gently to and fro, "I didn't reckon you'd show up for a day or so. I figured you'd be building up your strength for a bash at our Bella, mate. Proper struck on you she was! You're okay there boy, if you play your cards right. Likes a gent, Bella does! Never one to go for my type, 'cept in fun o' course. Here," he gave Mr. Sermon a painful jab under the ribs and closed one brown eye in a wink that could have had but one interpretation anywhere in the world, "how'd you make out when you come round, eh? Breakfast and usual in bed was it? Or was she too scared o' the boss coming in an' catching her at it? He has before you know, but he'd never sack her, not 'im! Brings too much trade into the place, and no wonder either! 'Streuth, where would you find a girl with a chassis like hers who can cook as well?"

He did not wait for Mr. Sermon to answer any of these somewhat intimate questions, but thrust a cup of cocoa into his hand and motioned to him to sit on a forlorn chaise-longue from which the stuffing oozed in several places. Mr. Sermon sipped the cocoa and told him briefly what had happened at the inn, not forgetting to mention the excellent effects of Bella's hangover cure.

"Gonner stay long, or just passing through, Perfesser?" asked Tapper, when Flash had returned to his newspaper.

"I'm going to stay," said Mr. Sermon, "I think this is a very attractive little town and I've decided to find lodgings and look around a bit. After all, if I'm going to walk I might as well have a base and it's wonderful country round here whichever way you go. Do you think you could recommend me a place? Somewhere quiet and near the sea?"

"Olga Boxall!" said Flash, without looking up from his newspaper, and Tapper exclaimed and thumped Mr. Sermon's knee.

"Just the job, Flash! I'd never have thought o' that but wait, she's going a trip somewhere, ain't she?"

"Not till June," muttered Flash, "the times I've heard about it!"

"That's right," said Tapper, "she ain't taking visitors this season and you—" and here he broke off and subjected Mr. Sermon to a steady, critical survey, "Yerse," he continued, "Olga'll take to the Perfesser! She's his type, educated an' likes a bit of a chat between times." He took out his note-book and a stub of a pencil and wrote, 'The Chalet, The Coombe' and handed the page to Sebastian. "Down the High

Street to the Front, turn right and second lane right opposite
the jetty. Can't miss it and I'll ring her an' tell her you're
coming! And lissen, Perfesser, I'll be in touch with you, 'cos
there's several sales coming up and I reckon you an' me
could pull something at one or two of 'em!" He turned to
the absorbed Flash, whose paper, Mr. Sermon noticed, was
a week old but nevertheless seemed to claim his entire attention. "You ought to hear the Perfesser when he gets goin',
Flash! Do you good, it would! Line o' sales talk drips from
him like a leaky tap—paintings, furnichure, everything! Cor
'streuth, wot money I coulder made if I had your brains an'
memry," he went on, turning to Sebastian again, "there ain't
a thing in this shop that wouldn't have a little bit of history
stuck to it and me with it all orf pat! Now I got to go over
to Podsmeade this morning but there's no sense in taking
you along there, it's on'y terrace-house stuff an' dead modern,
so I'll put you on the road to Olga's and tip her off on the
blower. I'll ring when something in your line comes up!"
and he steered Mr. Sermon back into the shop, past a
Blessing still doggedly transferring columns of figures from
newspaper to notebook, and out into the sunny street. Mr.
Sermon's curiosity had been aroused by the Sugg family's apparent absorption in old newspapers so as soon as the door
was closed, he said:

"Your father was reading a week-old newspaper and there's
today's sticking in the letter-box. Doesn't he know it's
arrived?"

"You bet he does," said Tapper, casually, "but he won't
give it a look until next Friday. Never does. Makes a pile
of 'em and then begins reading from the bottom. That's the
way he likes it, always a week behind!"

"But in Heaven's name, why?" enquired Mr. Sermon.

"I dunno, really," said Tapper, who had obviously never
thought about it, "I suppose because that way he can't get
worked up over what's happening to the world. Everything
he reads about is past, you see, and it's no good upsetting
yerself over it, is it? It's all over an' done with, like reading
a book. Come to think of it, that must be why he hates the
radio an' TV, I reckon. They're up-to-date and too bloody
worrying!"

"What about your boy, Blessing? That was Saturday's
Financial Times he was reading, wasn't it?"

"Oh, him, he's different again," said Tapper. "Never surprise me if he didn't turn into one o' them take-over tycoons. Marvellous at it, he is, marvellous!"

"Marvellous at what exactly?"

"Shares!" said Tapper and there was pride in his voice. "Do you know, that there boy can tell you what's going up an' what's goin' down any time o' the day or night!"

.   .   .   .   .   .

The town had one of everything, a rubbery-faced fishmonger in a straw hat, a grocer's with a bow window full of cheeses, a bookshop called 'The Two Nieces' (late Ada Brockett) and a Wesleyan chapel that was not the usual eyesore but a pretty little Regency building, displaying a text proclaiming 'To Live Is To Know God' on its notice board. The High Street, steep and ever broadening until it funnelled into a square, was just like the street in the song 'Old Fashioned Town' that Mr. Sermon's father had sung at half-forgotten soirées before World War One. It was bizarre and yet friendly, a Peggoty town that seemed to have stopped its town clock about the time Frith was painting his first Victorian seaside scenes. It was as different from Mr. Sermon's suburb or the modern industrial city as was Kandahar or Damascus, and when he passed the square and reached the promenade this impression was increased, for the pebble beach was dotted with boats turned upside down and sported a handcapstan draped with nets. Lean, yellow-eyed gulls strutted about, their plaintive wails muted as though they too had come under the Rip Van Winkle spell of Kingsbay. The scent of heather and pine, to be sniffed half-way down the High Street, did not reach this far, but in its place was the tang of the sea and dried weed and tar that carried Mr. Sermon back to the annual holidays of his childhood, so that he was not at all surprised when a caricature of a retired Colonel passed by in a Bath chair pushed by a human ramrod who had almost certainly served the veteran as batman in the days of Buller and Roberts. The old man in the chair lifted his stick (why a stick? thought Mr. Sermon) and said, gruffly but amiably: "Mornin' to you, mornin'!" and Sebastian respectfully returned the greeting and thought that if Kingsbay

ever issued a publicity poster, which seemed to him extremely
unlikely, it could hardly do better than to display colonel
and batman on their mid-morning jaunt. Such a poster, he
thought, would surely qualify as a gimmick to outgimmick
all gimmicks.

He ambled past the jetty and found The Coombe, a string
of cottages roofed with red pantiles that climbed an unsur-
faced lane as far as a pinewood that flanked the golf course,
the greens of which occupied the slope of the large headland,
but before turning off the promenade he lingered a few moments, leaning on the wrought-iron rail and looking out to
sea.

The beach was deserted, except for a long-legged young
woman reading a book and two young children in her charge.
The trio was grouped about twenty yards from where he
stood and from his elevated observation post he could study
the girl's profile, a little sharp-featured and serious-looking,
with dark hair and knitted brows. Then one of the children
threw a stone at a gull and she looked up and called, "Don't,
Geraldine! Don't do that, dear!" and he was struck by her
voice which reminded him of Sybil's but had more laughter
in it. Watching her, and hearing her call to the child, he had
a curious conviction that both voice and profile were familiar,
that he had heard her call out and seen her throw up her
head in that way somewhere before, a long, long time ago,
but he dismissed this as pure fancy.

Then, as Geraldine threw another stone, the young woman
got up with a gesture of impatience and moved down the
beach a few strides to collect and scold her and Sebastian
noticed that she scurried rather than walked, as though she
was not only impatient with Geraldine but with time itself.
As she took the child by the hand and turned to face him,
he again sensed recognition and smiled. She smiled back and
half lifted her hand in what might have been a tentative
greeting or an invitation to sympathise with her in the performance of thankless chores. He turned away, musing, and
climbed The Coombe, walking up the steep path until he
came to a house that might almost have been classified as a
miniature folly. Unlike all its neighbours, it was modern, half-
timbered and gabled but not quite large enough to dwarf
the cottages immediately below. Its pseudo-Tudor aspect
should have made it the odd man out in that setting, but

somehow it looked as if it belonged and even its banal name, 'The Chalet' seemed to suit it. He entered the gate and walked up the path flanked by daffodils and narcissi and was raising his hand to lift the lion's head knocker when the door opened and a woman stood in the doorway, smiling rather shyly and saying, with a slight stutter of nervousness: "Are you the gentleman Mr. Sugg phoned about? I'm sorry, he didn't mention a name."

"Sermon," said Sebastian, "Mr. Sugg said I might get a room here. I can't say for how long, I'm afraid, I'm supposed to be on a walking tour but there's so much to see round here that I want to use Kingsbay as a base and go out every day. Would it be all right if I guaranteed a fortnight?"

"Oh yes, a fortnight's quite all right. Ordinarily it wouldn't matter, but I wasn't really taking visitors this season. I'm going on a trip in June, something I've been meaning to do for quite some time. But do come in, Mr. Sermon . . . I . . . I really don't know why we're talking on the doorstep," and she led the way across the hall and into a pretty little sitting-room on the right.

Mr. Sermon found himself wondering at her agitation. She must, he thought, be accustomed to lodgers calling on her and in this case she had been warned of his impending arrival by telephone. Yet it was obvious that she was surprised and in some ways disconcerted and there could be no doubting her nervousness for she bustled about seating him and pulling aside the curtains to let in the sun. In the improved light he could see her more clearly and put her age at a little over thirty. She had fair, almost gingery hair, piled in what used to be called 'earphones'. She was tall, and her height was emphasised by her figure which was very slim and virginal, a boyish figure offset by some degree by very attractive hands with long tapering fingers that now fidgeted with a necklace of imitation pearls. He noticed that she wore very little make-up and that her small, almost prim mouth was scarcely touched with lipstick. Her complexion was very clear and she had a long, graceful neck, like the neck of a woman in a mediaeval painting. There was, indeed, something vaguely mediaeval about her as a whole and Mr. Sermon, who now had leisure to think about such things, pictured her in a conical hat with a draped veil attached to it, leaning over a balcony and offering a glove to a man on horseback

below. Her name, 'Olga,' wasn't it, did not suit her. It ought
to have been Elaine, or Petronelle, or Rosamund.

Yet the room, which was not at all mediaeval, suited her.
It was full of small pieces of furniture and silver-framed
photographs of young people in theatrical-looking costumes.
Over the painted mantelshelf, between two ostrich-feather
fans and two pieces of Coalport china, was a large glass frame
containing a spread of theatrical programmes and seeing that
he had noticed them her grey eyes smiled and her little
mouth twitched so that she looked neither mediaeval nor
young-old-maidish, but rather pretty.

"Yes, they are mine, Mr. Sermon, all I've got to show for
it I'm afraid."

Mr. Sermon had the laymen's veneration for the stage. He
had met thousands of amateur actors but never a single
professional, not even a retired professional.

"May I look?"

"Certainly," and she inclined her head gravely.

He studied the programmes and some of the photographs
beside the frame. One programme was that of a famous hit
of the thirties, *Autumn Crocus,* and others, lesser known
plays, were all of the same period. He could see nobody in
the cast list called Olga Boxall but several of the photographs
included a recognisable likeness of the slim woman standing
beside him. The face and figure seemed to have changed
very little but in all the pictures there was laughter behind
the eyes.

"Were you ever on the West End stage?"

"No, I'm afraid not, they're all repertory. We toured the
second-class dates and seaside resorts. It was before TV became popular and there was a demand in those days. I wasn't
very good I'm afraid. I gave it up when my father died and
couldn't help out with a sub. It was as good an excuse as
any!"

She said this without bitterness and without mock-modesty,
and then, rather pointedly, returned to the business of the
moment.

"A fortnight, you said? I could manage that or even a little
longer, I won't be shutting up the house until about June 1st."

"I shall have probably moved on by then," he said. "Could
I see my room?"

"Of course, this way," and she rustled out, mediaeval

again in spite of slacks and sweater and led the way up polished wooden stairs to what looked like a mock minstrel gallery built over the dining-room and having a door in the rear partition that opened on to a narrow corridor. As they went along the passage, he said:

"Have you many visitors in?"

She stopped, rather abruptly, he thought, her hand on the latch of the door and her nervousness, which seemed to have left her in the parlour, returned and brought a flush to her cheeks.

"I haven't any! I wasn't going to take any at all this year. I live here alone. Do you mind"—she was blushing furiously now—"you see, Mr. Sugg said 'a professor' and I . . . I imagined someone quite different, an elderly man," and she turned, forcing herself to meet his eye.

Even in his most defeated moments prior to his flight Mr. Sermon had never thought of himself as elderly so that her statement, and to some extent her confusion, could be received as an oblique compliment. He smiled and after a moment's uncertainty, she smiled back at him.

"I'm old enough," he said jocularly, "I'm forty-nine. I . . . I don't mind in the least if you don't, but if you'd rather we called it off, I'm sure I could find . . ."

"No!" she said suddenly, "why shouldn't you stay if you'd like to? We aren't living in 1900, are we?"

"No, unfortunately not," he said, with a schoolboy grin and the tension between them broke and they passed into a spotlessly-clean room furnished in oak, with a big latticed window looking on to the pinewood and links.

"This is wonderful," said Mr. Sermon, "I'll stake a claim right away if I may," and he tossed his rucksack on to a coffin-stool under the window.

"There's a much bigger room at the front, if you prefer it."

"No, no, this is fine and I'd like to pay a week in advance. How much?"

"It's out of season," she said, "and I suppose you'll be out for a midday meal. Would four pounds be fair? That would include cooked breakfast and a cold supper!"

"Very fair indeed I should think," said Mr. Sermon, "almost pre-war!" and he took out his wallet and handed her one of Tapper's five-pound notes.

"I'll get your change, and I dare say you'd like a wash."

"As a matter of fact I'd like a swim," said Mr. Sermon. "This is the first glimpse I've had of the sea since last August and it looked marvellous as I came along."

"A swim? You'll find it cold, surely?"

"I don't stay in more than a few minutes," he said, "I'll change here and take my togs down to the beach. Then I'll get some lunch in the town and go up to the Headland. What time do you have supper?"

"Any time," she said, "I've only myself to please for eight months of the year. Between June and September I have a sort of staff but the rest of the time I make do with a daily. Shall we say about 7.30?"

"Certainly. Until 7.30 then?"

"Do you like TV?"

"Some programmes."

"I've got a TV. You might care to watch it. There's very little to do in the evenings in Kingsbay, I'm afraid."

"That's why I came here," said Mr. Sermon, "there was far too much doing in the evenings where I come from."

"London?"

He nodded, "I loathe it, I always think the best sight in London is Waterloo Station."

"It can be a terribly lonely place," she said quietly and then, as though to herself, "even worse than this, I imagine. I'll get your change," and she left him with the feeling that she had told him the most important thing about her.

* * * * *

Olga Boxall was right, the water was so cold that it made him gasp and swim with frantic speed along the distance between the breakwaters, back again and then out to towel himself with terrific gusto. The dark young woman with the children was still there engrossed in her book but he noted with satisfaction that she had put it down and watched him as soon as she was sure he was going to swim.

As he went up the beach, glowing from exercise and thoroughly toned up by the dip, the young woman smiled again and said, "Excuse me, but haven't we met? You're Mr. Sermon, aren't you?" and he stopped, dumb with surprise, realising that his fancy earlier in the day was fact and that the girl was not a stranger.

"I . . . I'm quite sure we have," he said, eagerly, "but upon my word I can't recall where or when! People say I've got a good memory and I suppose I have for things I read, but I'm dreadful at remembering names and faces. I suppose it's because I'm rather short-sighted."

The young woman laughed, showing beautiful teeth. "Perhaps you'd better put your glasses on," she said and he did so but his frown told her this did not help in the least.

"It's no good," he said, "I used to put on an act and fish about for identity clues but I'm too old for that nonsense. I know we've met but it was a long time ago and I can't say more than that!"

"It was ten years ago," she said, "at that dreadful little school with that awful humbug of a headmaster, and I only hope you left long ago and had more luck than me!"

"School? Napier Hall? Ten years . . . ?" And then, although he was still unable to recall her name or anything of importance about her, he placed her, an aloof eighteen-year-old who had spent a single term at the school as Assistant Matron to the redoubtable Mrs. Fishwick but had left without giving notice and been swallowed up in the swarm of fugitives who used schools like Napier Hall as transit camps and got out of them at the first opportunity.

"I do remember now," he said, "but I'm extremely surprised that you should remember me. You weren't there very long and there must have been a dozen on the staff at that time!"

"Oh, I don't remember any of the others," she said gaily. "You stuck because . . . well, because I remember thinking of you as a fellow-sufferer. Apart from that you were kinder to me than anyone else and didn't nag or try and get me on my own on the pretence of dishing out avuncular advice!"

"Good Lord," he exclaimed, shocked by this information, "did some of the others do that?"

"Well, the Head did, the seedy old scoundrel! Several times in the study and once in the laundry room. He used to give me encouraging little pats in all the wrong places and he always smelled of mothballs. I remember he once offered me a bag of caramels. I've heard of all kinds of currency but caramels are a bit much, don't you think? Is he still bumbling around or have you lost touch?"

"I've lost touch," he said, "but only recently. As a matter

of fact I've only just left and I did it even more off-handedly than you did! I walloped a boy and caused quite a scene, then I gave notice on the spot and hopped it! I'm on the run from Napier Hall you might say, for I expect the boy's father will bring a summons against the place. I say, did you really hate it so much? I didn't you know, not then, or at all events, I didn't know that I hated it. It came on me suddenly like a brainstorm and I had to get out that instant and not only run from Napier Hall but from everything. Nobody knows where I am, not even my wife and family!"

She looked at him with amused surprise.

"Well, I'm damned!" she said at length, "you can never tell about people, can you? I mean, you can drive them so far and then—ping! The elastic snaps! Weren't you happy at home either?"

Her frankness disconcerted him. She had a trick of asking intimate questions in the ingenuous way of a half-grown child who embarrasses adults without the slightest intention of doing so. He said:

"I imagined I was, as happy as most people, but my wife and family seemed to be growing away from me all the time. We didn't wrangle or fight, not until the last moment, that is!"

"When did all this happen?"

"The day before yesterday!" he said and as he stated this the time factor staggered him, for it seemed a part of his life as distant as his schooldays or the time when this girl was drifting about Napier Hall dodging the lash of Matron's tongue and the furtive pawings of the Reverend Victor Hawley.

"Well I'm damned!" she exclaimed for the second time, "the day before yesterday. Forty-eight hours ago. You walked out, just like that! Do you know how long it took me to screw up courage to do the same thing?"

"Oh, come now, not that long, you were only at Napier Hall one term, weren't you?"

"I'm not talking about Napier Hall," she said, impatiently, "I've had a dozen jobs since then and at least four other schools. I'm talking about walking out on a husband and then nerving myself to face the divorce court!"

"You're divorced?"

"I'm afraid so, but isn't almost everybody these days?"

He was going to make some kind of conventional response

when they were interrupted by a shout from the promenade. Mr. Sermon looked up and saw the head and shoulders of an elderly woman thrust between the railings and staring down at them with an expression of extreme irritation. The woman's face was purple and she shook an umbrella in a very threatening manner.

"Benson has been hooting and hooting!" she screeched, "and you haven't taken the slightest notice! I said midday and I meant midday! It's ten after twelve now and past the children's lunch hour! Bring them up at once! At once, do you hear?"

"Oh my God!" groaned the girl, "I'd completely forgotten the old bitch. She's the grannie and an absolute horror!" She chuckled and waved her hand. "I'm supposed to be a Nanny, but I'm a dead loss at it, I keep forgetting and then meeting you like this . . ." and she raised her voice and called: "Coming right away, Lady Wilkinson! Ralph! Geraldine!" and she summoned the children and scuttled towards the steps leading to the promenade.

"Hi, just a minute!" protested Sebastian, "you've forgotten your book," and he picked it up and glanced at it. It was a dull-looking text-book devoted to veterinary surgery but he barely had time to note the title before she grabbed it.

"When shall I see you again?" he began, "there's so much I . . ."

But the purple face over the wall had frightened her and she said, breathlessly, "Any time, I'm usually here with the children, I must go . . . !" And disappeared, leaving him to relate her panic with his original impression of sturdy independence.

After a café meal he retraced his steps along the promenade to climb the towering bluff, skirting the slope of the links and mounting through winding paths to the summit where there was a coastguard's hut with a plank seat.

From here the view was magnificent, even more striking than that looking south from the crest of the moor. The cliffs ran down in a series of small peaks and the afternoon sun had turned the bay to molten bronze, with bars of gold where sand-banks were exposed by the tide. He had purchased a picture postcard in the snack-bar, intending to send it to Sybil telling her where he was but when he came to unscrew his

fountain pen, he found himself unable to progress beyond
'My Dear Sybil'. He would have found it possible to write a
casual message saying that he planned an extended holiday
had it not been for the shadow cast by Lane-Perkins. If the
wretched boy's father did prosecute then the summons would
find him in the end. In the meantime there was nothing to be
gained by making its delivery any easier. As it was, the
Reverend Hawley would almost certainly get in touch with
Sybil by telephone and if she had no knowledge of his whereabouts, Hawley would be unable to track him down and this
might even delay the issue of a summons until Lane-Perkins'
bruises had faded and everyone concerned had cooled off. On
the whole, he concluded, it was better not to write for a day
or so, and he rescrewed his fountain pen and tucked the card
into his jacket pocket, promising himself that he would make
a trunk call tomorrow or the day after and tell Sybil that he
was moving from place to place and perhaps give her a post
restante address at some other town in the West.

The incident, however, led him to contemplation of his
immediate future and the consideration of personal finance.
How long could one continue to lead this pleasant, vagabond
life on his present capital? He took out his wallet and counted
his money. Of his original eleven pounds ten, only about three
had been used for the journey west and the remaining eight-
ten had since been supplemented by Tapper's thirty pounds,
of which nearly seven had been spent on food and drink at
the pub and another four pounds paid out in rent. He now
had something over twenty-five pounds, surely enough to
support him for a month without drawing on his account.
Tucked away in Martin's Bank he had over three hundred on
deposit and another hundred, he estimated, in current account.
If he was careful, he could lead a simple life in a place like
Kingsbay for more than a year on such a sum and after
that . . . ? But here he deliberately checked himself from
looking more than a year ahead. Who in the entire world
could look twelve months ahead these days? All the same
fear of the future lay deep in his consciousness, the feeling
that there was not much time left to get about, to meet interesting people and root about for what remained of his lost
youth. It was the certainty that he had squandered his youth
that was the driving force behind him now and as he sat on

the hard plank and looked westward across the bay he did a kind of sum with his life, dividing it into periods and looking for profit in the total. He found none, or none worth having, until the moment of his awakening in the abandoned siding. He had been a lonely child, and a neglected weed at school, shouldered on one side by the strident and the mischievous. He had wasted his entire youth in study when other young men were dancing the Charleston and roaring about in Austin Sevens and playing ukeleles and kissing pretty girls in doorways. His marriage, despite Sybil's physical complaisance, had been arid. He could not recall a single occasion when, having embraced her, he had been rewarded by a flattering response, a thrill of gratitude or a sign of satisfaction in her having been mastered by a man. Their moments of intimacy had been achieved without recourse to words or even exchanges of tenderness expressed through the lips or hands and had become, year by year, a domestic ritual. Behind this mockery of a marriage lay his quarter-century trek as a schoolmaster and this had the same quality of sterility, the same absence of a single gleam of gold dust in the pan. As far as he was aware, not a single boy had been influenced by him, or had learned from him anything worth learning, not one pupil led through the golden gates of history or into the garden of English literature. A few, too few, might have imbibed his lessons parrot-fashion, sufficiently well perhaps to scrape through school-leaving certificate with a 61 per cent pass, but even this was by no means a certainty for he had always lost track of his boys at thirteen plus when they sat for Common Entrance and moved into the orbit of strangers.

Yet all this had changed, suddenly and very dramatically. He had been a complete success with Tapper, had fooled an astute man like Chipper Trowbridge, had been the centrepiece of a rip-roaring party in a public house and had so won the heart of a buxom girl like Bella, the barmaid, that she had put him to bed in her own room and brought him tea and kisses in the morning. Furthermore, almost by chance, he had located Avalon and pinned down his most elusive dream, and after that, for good measure, he had struck up a friendship in a matter of minutes with a woman like Olga Boxall, and as if that wasn't enough he had discovered the girl on the beach and learned from her that he had remained in her memory for years, he—a middle-aged nonentity, and she an extraordinarily pretty woman who was sufficiently sophisticated to have been through the divorce courts.

Taken all round it was an encouraging record and a very heartening one indeed, so with a certain jauntiness he lit a cigarette and set out along the cliff path, having made up his mind to walk eastward for an hour, strike inland and pick up the road he had travelled that morning, thus having encircled all the high land north of the town.

.   .   .   .   .

He arrived back at The Chalet as it was getting dusk. The circuit had taken it out of him for he had reckoned without the stiffness of his brogues and his lack of training. Three or four miles inland he had raised a blister on his great toe and the last mile or so was covered in great discomfort, so that he was very relieved when he descended the High Street and climbed The Coombe to see cheerful lights in the house under the pines.

Olga Boxall greeted him rather anxiously. "I was beginning to wonder if you'd got lost," she said, as he limped into the hall, "you did say seven-thirty and it's nearly nine. Here,"—observing his limp—"take off your shoes and I'll give them a brush in the morning. You must be famished and you can bathe your feet after you've eaten!"

He was too exhausted to protest at this unexpected fussing and gave her his shoes, climbing the stairs and having a quick wash before descending to the long dining-room where a table was set under the so-called minstrel gallery. It was a very inviting-looking table, laid with a gleaming cloth, dishes from which issued an appetising smell and a pretty pink epergne full of narcissi, daffodils and a few late crocuses. He sat down gratefully while she served him with thick vegetable soup. He was extremely hungry and could hardly wait for her to lay down the ladle.

"My word, this is splendid, splendid!" he exclaimed. "I'm famished after that hike and I'll do your cooking full justice, Miss Boxall." Then, pausing with his spoon half-way to his mouth: "It is Miss, I take it? You're not married, are you?"

"No," said Olga, smiling a little, "I'm not married, I'm Olga Boxall, Spinster, of The Chalet, Kingsbay, Devon; of uncertain age and semi-independent means."

He laughed and addressed himself to the soup, but after the first delicious mouthfuls he became conscious of her hovering attitude and said: "I say, how about you? Or have you had supper already?"

"No," she said, "but I'm not particularly hungry, I'll have mine in the kitchen when you've finished."

"Nonsense!" he protested, standing, "I hate eating alone!" and he lifted the lid from a dish and revealed a generous mixed grill. "I can't possibly eat all that," he added, "so lay a place for yourself, please!"

He could see that she was delighted by the invitation and she said, "Oh, very well Mr. Sermon, if you insist," and got herself a knife and fork from the sideboard drawer, returning to serve the grill which Mr. Sermon thought completed the most satisfying meal he had ever eaten, not excluding the one at the 'Cat and Carthorse' the previous evening.

Their conversation at the table was conventional, his walk, her garden and housekeeping problems, the state of the country's economics and the prospect of peace. After dessert, however, she seemed to shed her shyness and began to take the initiative, ordering him upstairs to soak his feet and apply salve to the blister while she cleared away and washed up. He was down again in time to help her dry and in the atmosphere of the little kitchen their relationship became guardedly cordial, rather like that of two passengers who find themselves unexpectedly stranded in a remote waiting-room and are there long enough to exchange information about themselves. He told her that he was a schoolmaster who had suddenly decided to take an extra holiday and was thinking of changing his profession, but for some reason, although he did not actually claim to be a bachelor, he did not mention Sybil and she did not ask him if he was married but talked about the impulse that had prompted her to close for the season and take the first extended holiday of her life.

At this stage she said she would bring the coffee into the sitting-room and when he entered there he found a bright coal fire burning and the most comfortable armchair set back from the smallest television screen he had ever seen.

"I'm not a TV fan, but it's company in the winter," she said, switching on and handing him his coffee. "I don't play golf and I'm a duffer at bridge and they say down here that if these two occupations are out you might as well be dead, but I seem to find plenty to do until this time of year. Time drags a bit after that and it isn't the slightest use my going to bed early. I only lie awake until the small hours and then feel hopelessly tired in the morning. You get used to living alone, of course, and in some ways it has a lot to recommend it, but I always find myself looking forward to late spring when the first of the visitors arrive. One is always surprised, I find, to hear oneself talking again after seven months' silence."

Before he could comment on this the TV set had warmed up and together they watched a travelogue about Brazil and half a Western about a gunman who wanted to reform but found his good resolutions baulked by a crooked saloon owner and a rather self-righteous heroine in a poke-bonnet.

"Do you want this on?" he asked at length, when the gun-man had reluctantly consented to fight a duel with two imported killers.

"Not in the least, if you don't," she said and switched it off, much to Mr. Sermon's relief, for Keith, his son, was a 'West-ern' addict and conversation at home had for years been punctuated by gunfire and the death-howls of Sioux. The ensuing silence was like a balm. Olga put more coal on the fire, and began to gather the coffee cups.

"Don't do that now," he said, "you've done enough for one day. Tell me about your trip. Is it a Scottish or Welsh tour?"

"Oh no!" she said, looking almost guilty, "it's a cruise to Istanbul!"

"Istanbul!" he exclaimed, as if she had said her route would take her across the Sahara to Central Africa. "Great Scott, I'd no idea, I thought . . ."

"Everyone reacts like that," she said mildly, "but really I don't know why they should. After all, I shall only be gone about ten weeks and although it sounds dreadfully expensive you can't live at home for nothing can you? It's something I've always wanted to do, see Greece and visit Gallipolli. I had an uncle killed at Gallipolli in 1915."

"You weren't born in 1915," he said gallantly. She smiled and he noticed that she smiled in a slightly mediaeval way so that at last he got an inkling of the reason why they called the Mona Lisa 'The Smiling Woman', something which had always mystified him for years, because she seemed not to be smiling at all.

"Come now, how old?" she asked.

"My dear Miss Boxall," he said, matching her mood, "I'm not such a fool as to go around guessing the ages of ladies!"

"As a matter of fact, you're right," she admitted. "He was killed before I was born but I can still claim him as an uncle surely? He was my father's only brother."

She told him that she was thirty-three and he reminded her cheerfully that he was forty-nine, and the exchange of information increased the feeling of comradeship that had been building ever since he came in from his tramp. He said:

"Look here, Miss Boxall, will you let me ask you a rather impertinent question? Is this trip of yours anything to do with your age?"

"Yes, it is," she said simply, "it's now or never!"

"Did that fact touch it off?"

"Yes, I think it did. Why?"

"Because it's really why I made up my mind to make a break, only with me it's a much more last-minute decision. In a way it makes us fellow travellers, don't you think?"

"Exactly what kind of a break are you making, Mr. Sermon?"

He considered. For a moment he was on the point of telling her everything, or very nearly everything, and certainly admitting to Sybil and the children if not to his fugitive status but then, as she waited, he succumbed to a clownish sense of pity for her, or perhaps it was not pity but an absurd idea that she would be disappointed to learn that he had a wife and grown-up children and might even reconsider her decision to share the house with him for the next fortnight. Whatever the reason, he compromised.

"I was very unhappy where I was working," he said, "I quarrelled with the Head and walked out. It was a silly thing to do at my age but I'm not in the least sorry that I did. Already it's given me a new kind of confidence in myself, almost like . . . like being young again, if you see what I mean!"

She gave him a long, thoughtful glance and as he met her eyes he noticed something that he should have noticed two hours ago, when he first sat down at the table. She had obviously dressed for him and gone to some pains to look her best for his return. When he had called on her that morning she had been wearing black slacks, sandals and an old sweater. He had noted her lack of make-up, her pale lips and old-fashioned hair-style. But he had not noted the changes she had made in his absence, the neat, biscuit-coloured two-piece, the matching suede shoes, the small pearl earrings, the touch of mascara, the heavy, reddish hair no longer coiled over the ears but parted in the middle and curled at the ends so that her face seemed less narrow and her forehead less high. She had been more generous with her lipstick and her mouth, which had seemed small and rather prim was appreciably riper. Even her finger nails had been touched up with a little polish and in place of her ugly string of imitation pearls was a Victorian locket enclosing a small Grecian profile. Suddenly he felt relieved that he had not mentioned Sybil.

"I see what you mean, Mr. Sermon, and if I don't who should? Forty-nine to a man approximates to about thirty-five in a woman and I think you were perfectly right to try again and I congratulate you. After all, you seem to have made a clean break, whereas mine is likely to be temporary."

"How can you be so sure of that? You haven't made it yet!"

"Oh, I know me, I'll come back with my tail between my legs, I always do."

"But you've never tried before."

"I've never been on a cruise before, but there are plenty of other ways of breaking a circle. After all, you managed it without Mr. Cook's help."

He leaned forward. Something told him that she had come very close to telling him a good deal more but had suddenly thought better of it.

"What happened? Was it the stage?"

"No," she said, smiling again, "it didn't take me long to find out that was a cul-de-sac as far as I was concerned."

"I don't want to sound inquisitive, but honestly, if you'd like to talk it does help sometimes. It's helped me a great deal since I broke the ice."

She got up and reached for the cups. Then, quite suddenly, she sat down again and stretched her legs to the fire.

"I don't know what it is about you, Mr. Sermon, but you'd make a wonderful sob-journalist. I believe you could coax people to tell you anything. Exactly what do you want to know about me?"

"All manner of things," he said cheerfully, "for instance, were you ever in love?"

"Twice."

"Was it reciprocated?"

"I think so, once."

"What happened?"

"That once? He was killed in Malaya eight years ago."

He noticed that she said this without emotion, as though she had long since come to terms with the loss but it did nothing to enlarge his theory that she was a person who was searching for a personal relationship that would release her from intolerable loneliness. She struck him as a woman who carried her sense of isolation through life as though it was a physical handicap, honourably imposed. She had not grown to accept it without resentment but in a perverse way she was almost proud of it. He said:

"In a place like this it should be easy to make friends. You must have several, some of them reasonably intimate."

"You don't make friends after your mid-twenties," she said, "just acquaintances, people you can take or leave and who can do the same with you!"

He realised that this was so for in all the years he had spent at Napier Hall he had not made a single friend, indeed, he was closer to chance acquaintances like Tapper Sugg and this woman than to anyone in the world he had shrugged off a day or so ago.

"How long have you been living here alone?" he asked.

"Since my father died. He was a doctor in the district and I bought this house with most of the money he left. I wasn't trained for anything, so I had to make a living somehow. I could run a house and it seemed to be the best thing to do in the circumstances. That was a few months after Bill died."

Eight years. She had been about twenty-five then and ever since time had submerged her as it had rolled over him, so that now, again like him, she was moving rapidly to a crisis, baffled and angry at futility and waste.

The reflection increased the sense of comradeship he felt for her and this to an almost physical degree, for he suddenly felt impelled to give it expression, to touch her, to stroke her hair, to kiss her perhaps but there was nothing sensual in the

impulse. It would have been simply a gesture from one lonely
soul to another, a faint-hearted desire to break the wall she
had erected around her and show her that contact could be
established if only shy people had the will to bypass the rituals
of introduction, the interminable exchange of small-talk, the
various stages of fusion that civilisation imposed upon people
of their age and social background.

Perhaps he might have found the courage to do just this,
to get up and put his arm around her slim waist and say,
without preamble: "Look here, Miss Boxall, I don't know why
you've shut yourself away all these years but it certainly isn't
to mourn a young man killed in Malaya! There's nothing on
a cruise to Istanbul that you can't find right here, so why
don't we settle for a few days or weeks of pleasant companionship in comfortable surroundings and have something to
look back on with pleasure, say, this time next year?" He
might have said this, but he did not for, as though sensing
danger, she fluttered and made a grab at the empty coffee
cups, saying:

"You must be very tired and I'm keeping you! Would you
like a hot water bottle? I can easily get one."

The remark was so obviously a parry that he almost
laughed, first at her, then at himself.

"No thank you, Miss Boxall, no bottle. What time do you
have breakfast?"

"About nine usually, but later if you like."

"I'll probably take a swim. The earlier I get used to it the
less I feel the cold. Good night, Miss Boxall, and thank you
for making me so comfortable."

"Good night, Mr. Sermon," she said and bent to put the
fireguard in the hearth.

Was he mistaken? Did she hesitate for a moment, as though
reluctant to bring their evening to an end? He stood up and
as he did so administered to himself one of his disciplinary
nudges. 'I really must try and stop myself hungering after
women in this rakish fashion!' he thought. 'There was Sybil,
the barmaid Bella, the girl on the beach and now this perfectly
respectable spinster who has gone out of her way to make me
feel at home but damn it, she did that out of politeness not
with an eye to the main chance!' and he nodded civilly and
marched straight upstairs to bed. He was just dropping off to

sleep when he heard her mount the stairs and softly close her door. Then a delicious ache of physical exhaustion settled over him like a soft blanket and he drifted away but somewhere beneath his drowsiness he was aware of a faint pinprick of disappointment at finding himself alone again.

CHAPTER FOUR

Mr. Sermon
Takes Over
in Two Spheres

THE passage of the next few days had a timelessness appropriate to Avalon. Each day spun a pattern and the patterns were very much the same but there was nothing featureless about them like days spent at Napier Hall or, indeed, at any other establishment where Mr. Sermon had lived or worked.

Each morning he rose about eight o'clock and took a swim, remaining in the water less than five minues but enjoying the virtuous glow the salt water kindled after he had towelled himself on the deserted beach and walked up to the promenade in lively anticipation of Olga Boxall's bacon, eggs and fried tomatoes, served to him the moment he returned home.

He learned to think of The Chalet as home in a way that the detached house in Wyckham Rise had never been. In some ways it was a ridiculously pretentious little building, with its brewer's Tudor appearance and its absurd minstrel gallery, but in other ways it was cosy and relaxing and cheerful with Olga's generous fires and comfortable chairs and excellent cooking. Their relationship improved day by day but although it was cordial and frank, so that they sometimes exchanged a little raillery and told each other a good deal about their respective backgrounds, it never approached the intimacy of that first evening, for it seemed to Mr. Sermon that each of them made a conscious effort to prevent this, almost as though they had made a pact not to meddle with the unpredictable but to accept the smaller mercy of easy, humdrum companionship.

One thing rather surprised him. The more he saw of Olga Boxall the younger and the more attractive she seemed to him. She never reappeared as the rather gaunt, slightly edgy woman in black slacks and jumper who had greeted him at the front door that first morning but seemed instead to develop, slowly but unmistakably, into a very feminine creature with a general air of cosiness that went along with her house and comfortable chairs. And often there was rather more to it than that, for her smile and voice had something in common with the lived-in quality of the little sitting-room where they watched television and chatted in the evenings. Her presence, he discovered, was as welcome to him as her shining grate and winking coal fire and this was not only because she was undemanding, and could sustain long silences without the slightest embarrassment, but also because she was his intellectual equal and had read what seemed to him an astonishing amount of biography and had even made a study of several periods of history, the fifteenth century for instance, and the French Revolution. She had very liberal views and an essential tolerance about people that even went so far as to make her champion traditional monsters, like Richard III, or crusty patricians, like the Duke of Wellington.

They were very pleasant evenings for Mr. Sermon when, replete after a good dinner, he could sit in the best armchair, watch a TV feature, drink his coffee and then silence the television in order to discuss the character of Edward IV or Danton, or argue the relative merits of Napoleon's marshals.

Sometimes, during the day, he went for a short hike, nursing his blister and hardening his feet and at least once a day he dropped in to see Tapper and his father and son, drinking cocoa in the littered bakery and listening to Flash Sugg inveigh against the modern trends of The Trade.

One day, when the boy Blessing was otherwise engaged, he took a turn at minding the shop and made his bow as a salesman, selling a copper warming-pan for four pounds ten and a Victorian scent bottle for two pounds seven and six, sales which Tapper described as 'not bad fer a start, mate, but you come down a bit too much fer the public!'

Tapper told him that it was their practice to open on Sundays in summer to cater for visitors but this year Blessing had refused to break the Sabbath because he considered Sunday was his day for a bit of fishing off the jetty.

"I'll gladly come in Sundays if I can be of any use?" volunteered Sebastian and Tapper eagerly accepted the offer, promising him a flat rate of two-and-sixpence an hour, plus five per cent commission on new stock and seven-and-a-half on back numbers, that is, stock that had been on show for more than a month.

The first Sunday, a bright and sunny day, Mr. Sermon sold very little, a fact which did not surprise Tapper for he explained that fine weather was the worst possible thing for the antique trade inasmuch as it kept people on the beach and away from the town. On the second Sunday, however, it clouded over about eleven o'clock and people were in and out of the shop all day. Sebastian sold about sixty pounds' worth of goods, including a battered corner cupboard that Tapper said had been gathering cobwebs for nearly two years.

"You're better at this lark than I am an' pretty near as good as young Blessing!" he declared delightedly, when Mr. Sermon handed over the cash and cheques and received four-pounds-fifteen in salary and commission. "You gonner be around all summer? I reckon you could pay your digs and fag money working one day a week here!"

"I really don't know how long I'll be staying," Sebastian told him and realised that he did not and that his future was as vague and unpredictable as on the first day he set foot in Kingsbay.

"How are you making out with Olga Boxall?" asked Tapper, shrewdly.

"I like her, I like her very much," admitted Mr. Sermon, but as he said this he felt a double prick of conscience, the first springing from his failure to inform Sybil of his continued existence and a second that could be traced to his failure to tell Olga he was a married man with two grown-up children. In the ten days or so since he had arrived at the coast he had made several half-hearted attempts to write to Sybil and on one occasion had even gone out to a call-box with the intention of 'phoning her but at the last moment he had relented, partly because he had an uncomfortable certainty that his idyll would cease the moment he heard Sybil's voice but more so because he could not determine upon the correct approach in advance. It all depended, he thought, upon Sybil's reaction. If she was shrill and shrewish he was confident that he could withstand her on the telephone, and, in the last extremity, hang up on her, but if she sounded unhappy and pleading he was not at all sure he could hold on to his new freedom and the fact was that this had become extremely important to him, so much so that he ultimately abandoned the idea of ringing up and reverted to his original idea of writing a postcard. About a week after his arrival in Kingsbay he did write a letter, but he did not post it for, as he stood beside the pillar-box, the terror of putting a term to his adventures and finding himself back inside Napier Hall rose up like a spectre and drove him to take shelter on the promenade where he promised himself another forty-eight hour respite.

His reluctance to admit the facts to Olga sprang from an altogether different source. He had convinced himself that it would shatter mutual trust and end in Olga putting him out of the house, to continue his truancy in some dreary little boarding-house or hotel. He did not want to get used to a new room and new people and he did not want to take a chance on hotel cooking when Olga's was so excellent and varied. He was very happy where he was and enjoyed Olga Boxall's company in the evenings. It was like being married with nearly all the advantages and without any of the disadvantages and on the few occasions when he was completely honest with himself he knew that a confession on his part would slam the door on the decorous flirtation that was beginning to bud at The Chalet.

Matters stood like this when they went on the charabanc trip and afterwards, whenever he thought of that dramatic occasion, Mr. Sermon blamed not himself or Olga but the driver of the vehicle for what happened. If the man had looked where he was treading, there would have been no crisis at Poppleford Steps and Mr. Sermon would never have been called upon to prove his manhood, either then, in front of eighteen strangers, or later with Olga Boxall, spinster, of Kingsbay, Devon, and semi-independent means.

It was while he was whistling his way along the front after his morning dip one Monday morning that Mr. Sermon noticed signs that Kingsbay was putting on its summer clothes. Modest strings of fairy-lights were being suspended from the esplanade lamp-posts and two or three longshoremen were erecting blackboards announcing the inevitable trips in the bay. There was slightly more traffic about and several early morning strollers from the three hotels on the front. Kingsbay, in short, was preparing its annual sacrifice to the urbanised tribes of the East and North, handing over its peace and selectivity in exchange for the money the invaders were prepared to pay for board, lodging and the strains of the stringed orchestra already tuning up in the bandstand near the jetty.

Near where The Coombe met the front stood a coach-tour centre and Mr. Sermon, whose blister was still giving trouble, suddenly made up his mind to take a day off and enjoy the country further afield from the cushioned seat of an excursion coach. Boards advertised day trips to Cornwall, Dartmouth, Exeter and almost everywhere else in the peninsula, and after studying the company's literature he selected the North Devon trip, taking in Lynmouth, Watersmeet, the Doone Valley, Ilfracombe and home via the uplands of Exmoor, with a stop for tea at Poppleford Steps. The ticket cost him fifteen shillings but as he was paying for it, it occurred to him that Olga too had earned a day off and that perhaps this would be a small way of repaying her hospitality. On the spur of the moment he bought two tickets and when he told her he was almost embarrassed by the pleasure it afforded her.

"Really, that's most charming of you, Mr. Sermon! It's years since I saw those places and years since anyone did anything like that for me without my having to suggest it! What time does it start? Ten o'clock? I'll have to change and there's the washing up. And the beds not made and . . . oh . . . no, you go alone, you'll enjoy it better."

"I shouldn't enjoy it half as much!" declared Mr. Sermon, stoutly, "so pop upstairs and change and I'll wash up while you're doing it. I shall go like this, in sweater and slacks. After all, it is an excursion."

He almost pushed her upstairs and carried the breakfast

things into the kitchen. He had almost finished drying when she reappeared and he gasped at the transformation. She was wearing a smart, navy blue costume with white piping and matching high-heeled shoes that looked both Italian and expensive. Her navy hat was a very daring affair for Kingsbay, a wide, down sweep over the left ear and a small white pompom over the peak. Her lips were scarlet and her eyes sparkled as he had not seen them sparkle before. She said, laughing at his expression, "Well, will I do?"

"Do? You look . . . quite wonderful, Miss Boxall!"

And he decided that she did indeed and displayed the kind of taste one seldom found in women who lived alone. He stood looking at her so long that she began to blush and as the colour flooded into her cheeks he dropped the dishcloth he was holding, bobbed forward and kissed her on the mouth.

It was an impulsive and rather clumsy kiss but all the safer for that, given as it was received entirely without embarrassment. A moment later they were sailing out of the house like a couple of children romping off to the beach.

The charabanc was almost full when they arrived at the park. There were several elderly women, of the kind that seemed almost to populate Kingsbay, matrons in heavy, serviceable tweeds, who talked in loud, hectoring voices, the product—or so Mr. Sermon imagined—of Spartan army homes, tough boarding-schools and hill-stations in pre-war India. There were one or two middle-aged tradesmen taking their wives on an excursion before the summer rush began and one very obvious honeymoon couple, who reminded Mr. Sermon that it was now the season of the year when young people rushed into marriage in order to save income-tax. This pair were Northerners and occupied a seat immediately in front of Sebastian and Olga. They engaged his attention almost at once because they were a kind of parody of a honeymoon joke, sitting so closely together that over their heads he had an uninterrupted view through the windscreen. The man was a thickset young fellow, moon-faced and pink-cheeked and the bride, almost as lumpish, had straight black hair, permanently parted lips that seemed to Mr. Sermon rather rubbery and a honeymoon glaze in her eyes. They communicated with each other by means of almost inaudible sighs and when the coach passed over a bump they merged together with a kind of sensual ecstasy. Sebastian winked at Olga who was also amused by them and after the lovers had occupied a straight stretch of road by gazing into one another's eyes and then resolved themselves into a mass once more as the big vehicle swung round a sharp bend, he leaned towards Olga and whispered the title of the currently popular Chevalier song, 'I'm glad I'm not young any more' and she giggled and had to take out a handkerchief and pretend to blow her nose.

They stopped at Lynmouth for coffee and Olga told him she had come here one autumn afternoon with the boy who was killed abroad and Mr. Sermon asked her outright if the recollection made her sad but she answered, brightly, "Not in the least because if one allows oneself to be nostalgic about every place associated with memories of youth one would end up quite static in a crowd of strangers!" and he thought this a sensible observation but could not help feeling grateful for a complete lack of nostalgic memories in his own background and a correspondingly heightened sense of living in the present.

The sun was warm but there was a pleasant breeze and he felt extraordinarily at peace with the world. Olga, sitting opposite him at the little table, looked prettier than ever, he thought, and glancing into an advertisement mirror behind him he noticed how tanned and healthy he looked and how little the streaks of grey showed at his temples.

"By George, I ought to have done this years ago!" he said, expressing his general satisfaction with life.

"You mean, come out on a coach excursion?" she said, but he laughed and added, "No, no, although this is very pleasant and relaxing I must say; no, Miss Boxall, I mean I should have set off looking for life instead of beetling round and round the inside of a glass hoping that someone would lift it up and let me out!"

They reassembled and went on up the wooded hill to Watersmeet, now in spate and a very impressive sight, and as they looked down at the tumbling brown flood Olga said; "I should never have lived by the sea, I much prefer rivers. Rivers are more personal and less moody, I think." He agreed but confessed to a lurking fondness for salt water, but she went on, "When I was a little girl I always wanted to live in the country with a river at the bottom of the garden. It probably came from reading *The Water Babies*. Were you impressed by *The Water Babies*, Mr. Sermon?"

"Very much," he told her, "particularly the bit where Mr. Grimes gets wedged in the chimney-pot and bullied by the policeman! After that I was always terrified of policemen and deeply suspicious of my father's repeated injunctions to approach them if I was in difficulty. I think I should have walked about London all night rather than approach a Bobby and chance being wedged into a chimney-pot and banged over the head with a truncheon!"

She laughed and it occurred to him that her laughter had a pleasant note and that this was the first time he had heard it, although she had smiled at several of his sallies in the kitchen and by the fire of an evening. Another thought struck him, the speed with which they had learned to communicate with one another, the simplicity of conveying an idea to her without an explanatory preamble. It was like talking to someone in shorthand and this was a new experience to him. He had known Sybil for more than two decades but it had never occurred to him to tell her of his fear of policemen. This, he reflected, was real companionship, the kind of association a man needed in his fifties, for by then one should have progressed beyond the stage when one sat thinking up things to say to a pretty woman one wanted to impress. He went on to develop this thought. Surely, at his age, one should be done with all that panting and sighing employed by the honeymooners in the coach. True he had kissed Olga that morning but 'kiss' wasn't the right word for it, there was another word, an old-English word, that conveyed the salute far more accurately—'*buss!*' that was it, and what was a buss between a man of forty-nine and a woman sixteen years younger?

"All in, sir, we got long ways to go!"

It was the coach-driver calling from above and Mr. Sermon started and found Olga waiting for him to emerge from his daydream.

"I say, we must be holding everybody up!" he exclaimed. "Here, it's too steep for those heels of yours, take my hand, Miss Boxall!"

She took it gratefully and he hauled her up the uneven steps but when they regained the level and were approaching the coach she said, breathlessly, "Look, Mr. Sermon, I don't think we can go on using each other's surnames, it makes us sound like a couple in a Brontë novel. What does your 'S' stand for? I've been peeking, I saw the initial on your knapsack! It isn't 'Sidney' I hope?"

"No," he said chuckling, "it isn't Sidney but to my mind it's worse! It's Sebastian!"

"Oh no, it couldn't be!" she protested.

"I'm afraid it is," he said, not in the least offended by her amused incredulity, "and I'd far sooner you went on calling me 'Mr. Sermon' than 'Sebastian'! I've got another name, thank God, but nobody's used it since I was a boy. It's 'Martin'. Is that any better?"

"Oh, much!" she said and, suddenly catching sight of the basilisk glare of one of the hill-station women, she added, "Come on, they're getting annoyed with us," and they ran the last twenty yards and regained their seats with a rush.

"Martin," she said half to herself, as the vehicle groaned up the hill, "that suits you far better than mine suits me. I think I hate 'Olga' as much as you hate 'Sebastian'. It's not simply the Russian spy implication, it's an ugly word and I wasn't even given another name."

"What would you have chosen if you'd been given the option?"

"Something French, I think, 'Madeleine', or 'Yvonne' or perhaps not, perhaps something very English like 'Mary' or 'Margaret'. There's a great deal in names, Martin, they have a way of typing people. All the 'Muriels' I've ever met have been saucy women attractive to men, and all the 'Gladyses' hearty and easy-going. Pick me one, pick one that suits your conception of a person like me!"

"Very well," he said and after a moment's thought, " 'Madge'!"

"Did you know a 'Madge' anything like me?"

"No," he admitted, "I don't think I ever met a 'Madge', but it's you somehow, down-to-earth and straightforward. One can't imagine a 'Madge' being artful or coy. A 'Madge' would speak her mind yet do so with due regard for other people's feelings, I think!"

She was silent for a moment and then, as the driver changed up and the hoarse roar of the engine changed to a persistent whine making conversation less effort, she said:

"Do you know, Martin, that's one of the most genuine compliments anyone has ever paid me," and she squeezed his hand and then looked quickly away across the dun-coloured moor.

*   *   *   *   *

About four-thirty the driver entered the steep, narrow lane that led to an off-the-map beauty spot known as Poppleford Steps, where giant boulders were spaced across a shallow river in the form of stepping stones. It was, thought Mr. Sermon, a foolish place to drive a 23-seater but the season was early and there was very little traffic about, so they made the descent without much difficulty and parked near the water's edge for tea. On the way down the Devon driver explained the origin of the name 'Poppleford'. "Yerabouts a 'popple' is a gurt pebble!" he announced, "and they moormen used popples to get across like, so it become known as the Poppleford!"

Most of the excursionists went into an isolated shack for tea but Mr. Sermon did not like the look of the place and having swallowed what seemed to him a quart of coffee at preceding stops he suggested they should walk along the bank to stretch their legs. Olga agreed but said she would leave her shoes in the coach, take off her stockings and go barefoot. There had been no rain for nearly a month and the turf of the water meadows was dry and springy. She kicked off her elegant but punishing shoes and peeled off her silk stockings without even indicating that he might glance the other way so that he noticed, with satisfaction, what unexpectedly shapely legs she possessed. He would have imagined that they would be thin like the rest of her but they were not, they were long and shapely, like the impersonal legs that advertise stockings in newspapers. They were also, he reflected, essentially young legs. She put her stockings in her handbag and they moved down the valley that ran between hanging woods, Olga dabbling her feet in the stream, Sebastian walking more soberly along the cattle path that followed the river.

The sun was going down over the western edge of the hill and the little valley was flooded with light ranging from yellow to white to mauvish pink, but a hard streak of blue-black showed where the woods met the sky. Wildflowers grew down to the water's edge, wild iris and small, wild daffodils, trefoil and periwinkle, and across the meadow under the heavier timber was a haze of bluebells looking, at that distance, like blue powder sprinkled on the grass.

"This is the most enchanting place I've ever seen," said Olga, wriggling her toes in the water. "Why have I never been here before? How far is it from Kingsbay, do you think? I'm hopeless at distances and measurements."

He said it was probably about twenty-five miles by road and perhaps fifteen as the crow flew, but he answered her absentmindedly because he was thinking how fresh and young and pretty she looked standing in the stream with her skirt clutched in one hand and her delightfully incongruous town hat in the other. Then, glancing at his watch, he suddenly made up his mind and called to her to paddle along round the sharp bend in the stream to a spot where the meadow narrowed and beeches grew down to the path, and the moment they were out of sight of the shack he took her by the hand, led her up the back and gently embraced her, kissing the nape of her neck and then her lips, not bothering to explain his conduct but leaving her in no doubt as to how much he appreciated the privilege.

She let him kiss her half a dozen times, conveying the impression that while she did not resent his attentions she found no particular excitement in them either but regarded a kiss or two as his due, like a girl seen home from a dance by a stranger. Ordinarily, he would have found this disappointing, but somehow he did not, for the act of kissing her reversed the age gap between them so that he felt, as his lips touched hers, no more than a youth to whom a mature woman was showing kindness and tolerance. Then, as he drew back from her, an owl hooted in a tree less than ten feet away and at the same moment there was an urgent rustle in the undergrowth behind them as a rabbit scrambled to safety and although he was visibly startled she only smiled, leaning against the grey bole of the beech and saying, very gently: "You see? Somebody was watching after all, Martin!" and they both laughed and turned towards the shack where passengers were beginning to straggle back to the coach.

As they walked along the valley the sky began to cloud over and all the warmth went out of the sun. The blue-black streak above the woods lengthened and deepened, so that it was obvious that one of the sudden storms characteristic of this area in early summer was about to break over the western edge of the moor. It was astonishing how rapidly the mood of the day changed. One moment it was early summer, the next spring and the next almost mid-winter, with a strong wind, great scudding clouds shutting out the sun and a rain-screen almost veiling the further bank.

They regained the coach without getting very wet, however, and the Kingsbay matrons exchanged a disapproving glance when they noticed that Olga had shed her shoes and stockings. Mr. Sermon loaned her a handkerchief to dry her feet and secretly hoped that she would put her stockings on in the confined space between the seats, but she did not, contenting herself with shoes and determinedly setting about the task of repairing her make-up.

Then it happened. The driver, reversing over a patch of stones near the river, misjudged his distance and ran the rear wheels on to a patch of soft ground where the big vehicle stuck, its wheels revolving madly as he wrestled and wrestled with the steering column.

Mr. Sermon could see that he was concerned and got up to offer help. Together, he and the driver descended and went round behind to study the situation, standing in the pelting rain and churned up mud. The driver said: "Christ Maister, we're in a praper ole fix! Us'll have to give they wheels something to bite on!"

"How about that old fencing over there?" suggested Mr. Sermon. "Unless you can get something better from the shack!"

"Us'll get no help from him," said the driver. "Crusty old customer he is and I don't stand well with him seeing as I give this place a miss all last season. Carrying on something dreadful about it he was but the truth is, Mister, I don't like bringing a coach down here. I don't know what made me do it today but there 'er be, us is stuck, ain't us? And no bliddy telephone neither!"

"Well at least we can try and move her!" said Olga, and Mr. Sermon saw with surprise that she had slipped off her shoes again and climbed out barefoot to offer assistance. She was the only passenger who had emerged, all the others were peering down at them through the misted windows.

"You'll catch a bad cold, Olga," said Mr. Sermon, "get back inside before you're soaked to the skin!"

"I'm soaked already!" said Olga, cheerfully, and he noticed then that she had left her hat in the coach and the rain was creating havoc with her hair.

They waded through mud to the edge of the river and tugged at a few yards of rotting fence near the stepping-stones. The crumbling posts yielded easily enough but the task of freeing the tangle of rusty wire was a difficult one. Still nobody joined them and the driver said, "Bliddy helpful they be in there! I'm obliged to you mister an' ma'am. Haul her back towards me—half a second, her's snagged up—there, her's free now—back this way and stuff her in the dent us've made in the bliddy ole marsh!"

They backed towards the coach, dragging the tangle of posts and wire with them and the driver made a neat job of packing the debris into the ruts gouged by the wheels.

"Dornee get in for a minute, I'll try her gently while you hold on to that post so as 'er don't skid away," he said and returned to the driving cabin, climbing in and starting up whilst Mr. Sermon and Olga held the posts level immediately under the wheels. The engine roared and the wheels revolved slowly, showering both of them with liquid mud. Glancing up Mr. Sermon saw the gleam of Olga's teeth through a black film and realised that she was laughing. "My word," he said to himself, "what a sport she is! Most women would be in a fearful temper if they got in a mess like that. I'll make this up to her somehow, I'll . . . I'll buy her a new outfit by God!" for he found himself thinking that somehow this was his fault.

Then he heard her shout with triumph as the tyres bit into the wire and timber and the coach came out like a tooth, with a final flurry of mud that covered them from head to foot. The driving door flew open and the driver tumbled out, beaming with relief and shouting through the pelting rain, "Us've made it, Mister!" as he ran back towards them. He should have moderated his pace for the wheels had dragged the wire well beyond the mud patch and strewn it between the loose stones of the valley. He caught his large feet in a trailing end and fell headlong and very heavily indeed, landing almost at Sebastian's feet and yelping with pain.

"I say, are you hurt?" exclaimed Mr. Sermon, stooping over him but it was clear from first glance that he was, for he sat up grasping his injured shoulder, rocking himself to and fro and gasping with shock.

"It's his collar-bone," said Olga, "look, a clean break!" and she pulled aside his dripping overall to reveal a splinter of bone showing through the flesh.

"Christ ha' mercy!" grunted the driver and then fainted into Mr. Sermon's arms, so that they remained for a moment in a huddle some ten yards behind the coach, open to the tumbling skies and dripping with black Exmoor mud.

"Look after him a moment, Olga," said Mr. Sermon. "I'm going inside to tell the others!" and he slopped towards the coach, climbing up the steps and addressing the passengers as though from a platform.

"The driver has just broken his collar-bone," he announced, "and we shall have to get him to a doctor at once! Is there anyone here who feels capable of driving as far as the nearest town?"

There was no immediate response. They regarded him sullenly so that he was reminded of a class of boys being ordered to perform something outside the usual curriculum. At length the honeymooner sat up and licked his lips and the two tradesmen nearer the back half-raised themselves but continued to stare at him almost accusingly. Suddenly he felt unreasonably irritated by their hostility and helplessness.

"There's no telephone at the tea-cabin and the man obviously isn't fit to drive," he snapped. Then, looking hard at the bridegroom, "You're a young chap, couldn't you drive the coach back to Kingsbay?"

The girl looked at her husband, who cleared his throat.

"It's against t'law," he mumbled, in a thick Yorkshire brogue, "tha c'n get pinched for driving a public transport vehicle without proper licence."

"I dare say you can," said Mr. Sermon, testily, "but what alternative have we? Surely the law would make allowances in a case like this?"

They were silent and Mr. Sermon now thought of them as a class of boys who had yet to become acclimatised to the tantrums of a new master. One of the tradesmen said, "Somebody should walk up to the main road and stop a car."

"Don't talk nonsense!" said Mr. Sermon, surprised himself at his own acidity. "By the time you got to the main road it would be dark and even if a car did come by, it's more than likely that it wouldn't stop!"

Olga spoke, appearing unexpectedly at the sliding door of the cabin. "Well at least somebody come out and lend a hand to get the poor man in the dry!" and Mr. Sermon noticed that she obviously shared his poor opinion of the passengers and also that she no longer regarded the incident as amusing.

The bride nudged the groom who got up unwillingly. Two of the tradesmen shuffled forward and the group followed Sebastian into the open. It was still pelting down and the wind had risen. The driver, propped against the sodden hedge, was conscious but when they lifted him he groaned with pain and they found it very difficult to negotiate the coach steps and squeeze down the gangway to the rear seats from which the Kingsbay women were ejected so that he could lie full-length.

"Sit beside him and put his head on your lap, Olga," said Sebastian, now assuming command of the situation and addressing her as though no one else was present. "I'm going to take the coach all the way back to Kingsbay unless we pass through anywhere that looks as if it had a resident doctor. In that case we'll stop off and get the poor chap attended to."

She looked at him with a half-smile: "Have you ever driven a heavy vehicle, Martin?"

"No," he admitted, "but I don't see that it can be all that different from driving a car. In any case, I can't see any alternative, so sit tight and hope for the best." He turned and addressed the coach as a whole: "Anyone who prefers can get out and wait here until I send transport back for them," he announced. "They could probably find shelter in the shack but they'd have to break in because the man has gone home and locked up."

There was a protesting murmur at this but nobody got out. Dusk was already creeping down the valley and there seemed little prospect of the storm abating.

Mr. Sermon was not an expert driver. He had held a licence for twenty years but Sybil drove herself and latterly young Keith, their mechanically-minded son, had taken to driving the family car, so that Sebastian was out of practice. In any case he had never driven anything larger than a private car and had never been in charge of a commercial vehicle of any kind. The prospect of handling so large a coach horrified him, but with a great effort he got his nerves in hand and made a minute inspection of the driving panel. The gears were the kind operated from the steering-column and he was not even sure which was forward and which was reverse. The risk of reversing unintentionally, and backing into the patch of swamp was therefore considerable, so Sebastian spent the next few minutes practising gear changes and finally satisfied himself about the positions of the four gears. Then he looked closely at the lights and switched them on and off three or four times, after which he adjusted the driving mirror to his satisfaction and then, very cautiously, turned the ignition switch and pressed the starter button.

The roar of the engine made his stomach turn over. He was awed by its deep note and by the sense of power it exerted, as though he had found himself in charge of an ocean liner during a violent storm or had been called upon, in the course of a nightmare, to drive the Royal Scot from Waverley Station to King's Cross. He sat rigid for a moment, gripping the big wheel so tensely that his knuckles gleamed and then, with a deep breath, he groped for bottom gear and gently eased the handbrake so that the coach slid slowly forward to the foot of the long winding hill, the beat of its engine keeping time with the thump of his heart and the speed alternating slightly as his right leg trembled under the thrust of the accelerator. Nobody offered a word of encouragement or advice but Mr. Sermon could sense the extreme tension among his passengers and deliberately put them out of mind, concentrating every scrap of nervous energy on the job in hand and inching up the steep hill at seven miles per hour.

After the first hundred yards or so the woods began to crowd in on either side so that he took one hand from the wheel and jabbed at the headlight switch, flooding the narrow road with light and probing with his left foot for the dip-switch which he failed to locate. The hill seemed endless, winding on and on round a series of atrocious bends and Mr. Sermon spared a fleeting thought of sympathy for professional drivers who did this kind of thing for a living. He was conscious too of an overpowering desire to smoke but he knew that this was out of the question. He needed all his fingers and thumbs for the steering-column which seemed so big and wide that it gave the illusion of expanding against his taut belly and crowding him into the back of the seat. Then, miraculously, the woods fell away and the light improved as they climbed towards the plateau of the moor, and Sebastian could see the march of violet dusk behind a curtain of rain and a whole ballet of raindrops dancing under the thresh of the windscreen wipers. Confidence began to return to him, enough at all events to encourage him to shift his grip and lean forward as though, by so doing, he could relieve the dragging weight of the vehicle. He was sitting thus, like a jockey coming into the straight, when the coach lumbered round the final bend and out on to the glistening tarmac of the main road and here he made a wild grab at the gear lever, slammed the engine into top and stalled, ramming his foot on the brake and grabbing madly at the handbrake. The coach gave a kind of shuddering leap and every passenger catapulted forward, hands clutching madly at seat structures, but from the very back of the coach came Olga's clear voice: "Well done, Martin! Jolly good show!"

He restarted the engine but forgot to disengage so that the coach gave another saurian leap. Putting them all out of mind again, he slammed into bottom gear and swung hard right, his left foot still probing for the elusive dipswitch in the hope of moderating the beam.

The moor was empty and utterly desolate. Patches of scrub and stunted trees made it look like a vast pantomime scene in the glare of the lights and although to Mr. Sermon it seemed quite terrifying there was a majesty in its emptiness and in the steady lash of rain and rush of wind. He jerked down the window and inhaled great mouthfuls of air and with each gulp courage and resolution flowed into him as though he was swallowing neat spirit. After a mile or so of straight road he changed up, successfully this time, and then up once more and finally into top gear, pushing her along at thirty miles an hour and sounding the horn, not because any other vehicle was in sight but because he wanted to prove to himself that it was indeed Sebastian Martin Sermon, late dogsbody of Napier Hall Preparatory School for Boys, who was propelling this vast, unwieldy monster into the gathering night and the teeth of hostile elements. He saw a signpost coming and glanced at it, making out the single word Porlock on one of the fingers. It was enough to enable him to get his bearings and he abandoned the idea of seeking help in a village en route and decided to push on all the way home, hills notwithstanding.

They passed two or three cars, snicking past at high speed and one of them blared at him because he failed to dip. Once or twice he looked in the mirror but the interior of the coach was dark, for no one had thought to switch on seat lights and all he could see was a blur of white faces on a blue-black ground. Then, as the road began to dip, he had to grope about for more courage for he recognised the descent to Porlock Hill and recalled the driver's remarks about it as they were ascending it earlier in the day. For a moment he had a horrifying vision of the coach going faster and faster as it slipped from his control and went screaming round the bends to shoot off the banks and turn over and over, a shapeless, shattered hulk rolling down the gradient with its load of dead and dying tumbling about inside. He grappled with the vision and had it by the throat in a matter of seconds, slamming into low gear, pumping the footbrake and feeling a wonderful sense of relief as the speedometer swung back to twenty, then ten and then almost to zero. Easing himself back he tackled each separate bend as though it was a straightforward, methodically-solved problem, so much pay out, so much pay in, a touch on the brake here, a split-second estimate of leeway there, until the road levelled off and the lights of Porlock showed on each side.

He knew that everyone, including Olga, expected him to stop here. He could sense their massed relaxation after the dreadful tension of the descent but now a kind of mad exhilaration took possession of him and he shot through the village and on towards Minehead, by-passing the town and emerging again on to the main coastal road to Kingsbay.

It was quite dark by now and he still had not located the dipswitch, but this did not worry him at all. He had full confidence in the new hand that Fate was dealing him, broad, straight roads, no bad hills and the slavish obedience of the monster under his hand, and he was prepared to stake life itself on playing these cards and calling the chips. He was like a hunting novice who, for the very first time in his life, finds himself out in front of the field and on the tail of the pack, the thrill of the chase conquering all sense of fear as the horse bounds forward, eating up miles as though they were furlongs and again like a horseman he was aware of a communicated sense of power quickening in his loins. He felt free and wild and reckless and triumphant, bold and eager and infinitely superior to the nameless ones behind. He charged through villages and past road junctions with his hand on the horn and when he was crossing the upland immediately above Kingsbay he began to whistle under his breath.

It was only when he was descending the steep High Street that he thought of the injured driver on the back seat and remembered to swing left and right into the courtyard of the Cottage Hospital and here at last he stopped, or rather he reined in, coming close to bringing his mount up on its haunches.

There was a kind of collective sigh from the passengers and Sebastian heard in it a great deal more than relief. They were admiring him, in a curious way they were showing that they were proud of him and realising this his contempt for them was transformed into a genial comradeship.

They began to disperse, muttering good nights but giving him respectful glances as they scrambled out. Only the bride-groom remained for a moment at his shoulder, like a sergeant awaiting the order to dismiss.

"I'll go in and tell them we've got a casualty aboard," he said, "maybe the porter will want a hand with him."

Then, with the terrible effort a Yorkshireman requires to pay a compliment, "You brought her along fine, chum! Nay, Ah doan't mind admitting, Ah were bloody scared the first few miles but it were a dam' sight better than spending night in t'open Dad!" and he reached out awkwardly and patted Sebastian's shoulder with a pudgy hand.

The driver was still in pain but not so much that he forgot to thank Mr. Sermon and ask him to explain the situation to the depot.

"Tell Mr. Symes I'll 'phone through the minute they fix me up," he said, but the honeymooner broke in with: "Nay, Dad's done enough for one night, I'll cope with t' depot."

"There's the coach," said the driver, "they'll have to send somebody up for it. I don't reckon it'd do for you to drive her in empty, Maister. Give Mr. Symes heart failure I reckon!"

"Never mind about the coach, get yourself attended to right away!" said Olga, adding, "I won't be a minute, Martin," as she helped him out and disappeared into the hospital.

Mr. Sermon took no part at all in the explanations. It was,

he suddenly decided, no longer his business, he had done his part getting them home but there was one thing that still bothered him and when Olga returned he was on hands and knees under the steering column.

"What have you dropped?" she wanted to know.

"Nothing," he said, "I'm locating that damned dipswitch. Imagine that! It's way out here on the left, tucked away out of sight. Wouldn't you think they'd make it more accessible while they were about it?"

She laughed. "Come on for Heaven's sake and let's get dry!"

He noticed then that her teeth were chattering and was immediately contrite. Under the tremendous stress of the drive he had forgotten the mudbath they had shared but now, as she waited for him in the circle of light shed by the porch lamp, he realised how disreputable they looked with half-dried mud coating their clothes and faces, mud in their hair and nostrils and shoes. He was not the slightest bit cold himself but it was clear that she was, so he took a rug from the coach and folded it across her shoulders.

"Would you like to wait while I get hold of a cab?"

"No," she said firmly, "let's get on home. The walk will warm us and the first thing I'm having, before a bath even, is a stiff tot and the same goes for you, Martin."

He took her hand and they cut through the back of the town to the golf-links gate that led to the head of The Coombe, walking swiftly and exchanging no word but when he saw her fumbling for the key he took her purse and opened the door and she said, simply: "You were wonderful, Martin! Quite wonderful!" and his triumph was complete.

She put a match to the fire and fetched a half-bottle of cognac, pouring two generous measures and holding the glass toastwise. "Here's to you, Martin! By God, it's good to stumble on a real old-fashioned male, someone who can make a decision and shoulder responsibility instead of spreading it all around, like those other weeds. What would any of us have done if you hadn't been there?"

"You came out of it pretty well yourself, Madge."

"Drop the 'Madge,'" she said grimly. "'Madge' was a game, wasn't it? You'll always be 'Martin' to me but you can revert to Olga now. We've grown up a little don't you think? You especially!"

She emptied her glass and pushed back her hair. "I'll tell you something, Martin, while I think of it and it's this. There isn't a damned thing you couldn't do if you wanted to or had to, so don't ever forget that and don't let anybody tell you differently!"

"Oh, go and get your bath!" he said, smiling. "We can build up each other's egos afterwards."

"How about you? You need one too, you know!"

"I'll boil some water on the stove and clean up in the kitchen."

"Nonsense, you're the paying-guest, I'm only the landlady!"

"Just do as I say, Olga, and then we'll eat."

She looked at him gratefully and went up stairs. He heard the water running and at once ceased to think of her as a cheerful companion but as the woman he had embraced a few hours ago and he remembered with pleasure the freshness of her lips and her lack of coyness. The glow of personal triumph continued to warm him so that he suddenly felt intensely virile but objectively so, telling himself that it was not simply her he needed to crown his achievements but any woman who could respect him as a man. He went into the kitchen musing and put the kettle on the stove, stripping himself and pouring water into the washing-up bowl. While it was cooling he took down the roller towel, wrapped it round his middle and padded upstairs to his room for some clean underclothes, another pair of slacks and a clean shirt. He stood for a moment in front of the mirror feeling more satisfied with his reflection than at any time in his life, as though his achievement had put muscle and bone into his limbs. Standing here he heard Olga splashing in the bathroom and the realisation that only a door separated them made him recall her pretty legs. Then, as his heart began to thump, his reserve of self-discipline launched a belated counter-attack and he said, half aloud: "This simply won't do! If things come to that she'll have to know the facts. She might be a good deal younger than you, my lad, but I'll wager every penny I have she hasn't had any real experience with men and it's time you stopped masquerading as a bachelor! We can't go on and on like this, being frank with one another about everything but the one thing that matters! Now if you had sense . . ."

But at this point she called to him through the bathroom door: "You'll need a big towel, Martin. There's a dry one here in the airing cupboard."

'My God!' he thought, 'the airing cupboard is inside the bathroom!' and securing his inadequate roller towel with finger and thumb he almost ran out of his room and along the corridor.

His arrival there was an anti-climax. She was standing on the threshold shrouded in steam and wrapped in a voluminous bath robe and when he scuttled up in his little towel she exploded with laughter.

"Oh, my dear!" she said, catching her breath, "is that the best you could do?" and at once withdrew, closing the door and leaving him to salvage what remained of his dignity with the large towel she had dropped at his feet.

He went downstairs rather sulkily, feeling like a victim of an elaborate hoax and scoured himself as best he could in the washing-up bowl and sink. Then he cleared away, refilled the kettle and dressed, making a pile of his mud-soaked clothes for the cleaner. She was up there, he thought, a very long time and in the interval he occupied himself going through his pockets. He found the letter, now limp and indecipherable, that he had written to Sybil and hesitated before tearing it into small pieces and putting them in the stove. It was, in a sense, a final renunciation, for he knew now that he was done with that life for good. If things turned out as he hoped he would set about tying up loose ends but not now, not at this moment, for his bones told him that the ordeal in the coach was exacting its toll and what he needed at this moment was plenty of hot coffee and relaxation in front of a blazing hearth.

He made the coffee, set the tray and carried it into the little sitting-room, pushing open the door with his foot and there, tending the fire, stood Olga. She must have descended and crossed the hall without making a sound.

She was wearing a blue housecoat over her nightdress and her hair, still very damp, was loose and pleasantly disordered. There seemed to be a great deal of it for it not only covered her shoulders but hung in curls and clusters about her temples where the light caught it and made it look more coppery than red. She had been attempting to restore some kind of order to it for she held a comb in her hand. Standing there, one hand on the mantelshelf, her head thrown back and a small slippered foot resting on the gleaming fender, she looked more mediaeval than ever, exactly like an illustration in a Book of Hours, or an idealised conception of the period from the brush of Burne-Jones or Rossetti. That was it—Rossetti!— one of those slightly gaunt, mysterious, ours-is-a-spiritual-re-lationship women whom Rossetti liked to paint against a back-ground of tombs and ruins, half buried in a tangle of improbable briars. She seemed to be pondering something and it must have been a serious matter for when he entered and said: "Hullo? I didn't hear you come down," she remained silent for a moment and then said, very quietly, "I'm not a bit hungry, Martin. I should be but I'm not! Are you hungry?"

"No," he answered, "I don't think I am any more, I was when I came in but somehow I'm not now!" and he placed the tray on a little table just inside the door and at once forgot about it.

He was aware then that this was the moment of crisis. Whatever was said, whatever movement was made by either of them, would, he was quite sure, have far-reaching con-sequences on their lives for there was an element of great suspense present in the room. The little carriage clock ticked on and on but somehow its ticks had ceased to mark the passage of seconds. He realised now why she was looking so preoccupied and a sudden panic seized him lest her ultimate decision should put her out of reach for all time. She had become a different kind of person and that in a very brief space of time, for when they had faced one another outside the bathroom less than half an hour ago she had been gay and relaxed but now she was tense and anxious, with colour in her cheeks that was not the result of confinement in a small, steam-filled bathroom. In the centre of each cheek was a bright, pink spot and as he watched her he could see her small breasts rise and fall under the pressure of an emotional stress. Then, quite suddenly, she faced round and began to say something but the words, whatever they were, did not emerge and all he heard was a harsh sound that might have been a sob. It broke the tension between them and time moved on, swiftly now, as though to make up for seconds lost and he crossed the room, taking her by the hand and turning her away from the fire, throwing his arms round her and holding her so fiercely that they swayed and his knee struck the armrest of the chair.

"Oh God, Olga, I want you so much, so dreadfully!" he cried and buried his face in her damp hair but she twisted her head, finding his lips before he could misjudge her unexpected movement as a frantic attempt to break from him. Her kiss had nothing in common with the light-hearted kiss of the morning, or the passive response in the beechwood that afternoon. It was greedy and demanding, so much so that it hurt his mouth and the pressure of her body against his was so sustained that he would have staggered had his leg not been braced by the chair. Then, with a swiftness that made him gasp, she was gone, tearing at the curtains and switching off the table light as she circled back to him, not seeking to renew the embrace but standing fully erect before the bright fire and shedding her housecoat and nightdress in what seemed to him a single, deliberate movement. It flashed across his mind then that perhaps he had been quite wrong about her after all, that perhaps the years since the death of her young man in Malaya had not been as empty and arid as he imagined, but this did not make her any less desirable, or the need to possess her less urgent, and he would have reached out and taken her there and then had he not sensed in the way she stood poised between him and the fire that, notwithstanding her nakedness, it was she and not he who was to make the decision.

He said, mastering himself momentarily: "You're very beautiful, Olga and I want you most terribly, more than I've ever wanted anyone in my life, but if it means you'll regret it, if later you'll feel . . ."

She cut him short, picking up his words where they faltered and using her own with a circumspection that was very odd in a timid woman standing naked before a man whom, only that morning, she had still addressed as 'Mr. Sermon'.

"I need you far more than you need me, Martin!" she said, speaking with astonishing determination. "I know very little about loving a man but I want more than anything in the world to know! I'm glad now that I waited because you're the right kind of man, gentle and decent, and that's something I don't have to learn! I sensed it from the beginning, you understand?"

Her frankness so humbled and amazed him that the moment he touched her physical desire succumbed to the discipline of his essential kindness, so that he was exceptionally gentle with her yet without abandoning male aggressiveness that is the basis of the sexual act.

And he was right after all. She was virgin and this fact alone helped to temper his ardour and when it was over and she lay very still in his arms, he was able to think of himself as a lover who had bestowed as well as demanded and taken.

They did not speak for the better part of an hour and the fire burned so low that the shadows subsided and seemed almost to have tired themselves out with their dance over walls and ceiling. He watched them absently, listening to her quiet breathing and stroking her back with short, measured strokes. She lay with her knees drawn up and her feet tucked into the cushion-well of the big armchair and the scent of her freshly-washed hair was as fragrant as the scent that had come from the woods in the little valley.

He felt no regrets, no pangs of conscience, and no sense of deflation that he remembered as the inevitable aftermath of his possession of Sybil, simply a great sense of peace and fulfilment that reached down from his heart into his belly and loins, a tide so strong and warm that it lifted him and carried him along like a piece of flotsam on the breast of a torrent. He was aware, subconsciously, of insignificant things, the lazy shadows and the tick-tock of the carriage clock but closer to full consciousness were the physical aspects of the woman he held in his arms, the smoothness of her shoulders, the firmness of the little breast half flattened by its pressure against his ribs, the tiny spirals of reddish-gold hair under his chin, the unusual length of her bare thigh half-thrown across his knee and glowing like a greave in the firelight. He thought: 'She's wonderful and I'm in love with her and this is surely what the Avalon dream held for me all those years. A man would be a fool to risk losing this kind of happiness to blurt out a piece of information that would send her scurrying into her clothes and upstairs behind a locked door!' And then, with a slight wistfulness, he remembered her virginity and thought of it with wonder, a woman of this day and age who cheerfully admitted to thirty-three years and was charged with so much positive energy, but had waited until she could find somebody on whom to bestow that energy, someone who would use her gently and match her loneliness with his own. And of all the men in the world he had been selected, carefully and with a deliberation that tempered physical desire. Surely this was the greatest compliment anyone had ever paid to him.

The coals slipped in the grate and a smoking fragment fell on to the hearth tiles. The rustle, and the pungency of smoke, must have awakened her for she stood up, smiling down on him and reached without haste for her housecoat. He waited for her to say something, trying to say all he felt with his glance and encouraged by her smile, the smile of a woman who, against all probability, is not subdued by shyness or reserve. She bent and retrieved the smoking coal with the tongs, popping it back into the fire with one of those neat, precise movements he had noticed as she moved about the house. Then, still smiling, she said: "Well, Martin?"

"You won't believe me, Olga, so maybe I won't tell you. You'll just shrug it off as an attempt on my part to be gallant—or gentle if you like."

"Tell me, nevertheless," she said.

"I should like you to know that never before was it so complete or real or rewarding."

Her expression changed and it seemed to him that now she looked at him with the eagerness of a child receiving praise from an adult it respects. Then, before he could speak again, her expression clouded again, almost as though her instincts told her he was making gentle fun of her and it was this shift of expression, this hint of disappointment, that finally decided him, for when she moved round the chair to pick up the coffee tray they had forgotten, he caught her by the wrist and said, "No, Olga, wait a little! I've got to tell you something before I find another excuse."

"I think I know what you want to tell me, Martin," she said, quietly, "and it can wait while I get fresh coffee."

He was disconcerted by the note of resignation in her voice and said, quickly, "I don't know why I've put off telling you until now, Olga. It was a very stupid way to begin. I've been married nearly twenty years!"

She smiled. "You surprise me after all: my guess would have been twelve to fifteen." Then, flatly, "Have you any children?"

"Two, a girl and a boy. The girl is eighteen and the boy nearly seventeen!"

For a moment they faced one another in silence.

"All right," she said at length, "now you've told me and perhaps we'll talk about it later. You've had nothing to eat, would you prefer ham on a plate with a salad or just sandwiches?" Her calmness was an affront.

"I've already told you, I'm not in the least hungry!" he growled.

"Well I am, I've suddenly developed quite an appetite!" she said, and picking up the tray went out into the kitchen, leaving him ruffled and uncertain. Presently, however, he heard her moving about and humming one of the Schubert songs they had played on her radiogram the previous evening and the sound of her voice above the rattle of china had a miraculously soothing effect upon him, so that his spurt of nervous irritation spent itself and he slipped back into the musing mood that had preceded it when she was asleep in his arms. He thought: 'Godammit, she's a most unusual person and quite maddeningly difficult to assess! Was she bluffing when she said she knew from the first I was married, or was it simply a defensive reaction that could pass as a sneer? What *does* she think about it? Does she look at me as a possible husband in spite of Sybil and the children? Or could it be that she just doesn't care one way or the other, so long as I go on living here? I wish to God I had more experience with women! Most men would know exactly what to do in this situation but I'm floundering like a seventeen-year-old boy at his first dance!' and he slumped back in the chair and tried to console himself with a cigarette while she went on getting supper and humming, of all things, 'The Merry Peasant Returning from Work'. Then, with the facility to turn his back on problems that he had acquired since his flight, he voluntarily surrendered to the cosiness of the room and when she walked in with fresh coffee and ham salad he was half-asleep.

"You'll have some coffee?" she asked.

"Yes," and he rose and joined her at the table, "I'll have supper too! What made you think of that tune, the one you were humming?"

"I didn't know I was humming. What tune?"

He chuckled, laughing because her serenity was so close to smugness that it went some way towards proving an equally smug theory, prevalent among the kind of men who boast of success with women. Perhaps, he reflected, there was something in the gibe after all, and perhaps women did change their personalities the instant they ceased to be virgins. He had found very little to criticise in her before and now, he decided, he liked her more than ever, but there was clearly a difference between the woman he had kissed in the beech-wood a few hours ago and this bustling, cheerful self-assured person helping him to salad and pouring coffee. It was a difference sensed rather than seen and he wondered briefly if a third party would have noticed it and then dismissed this as fanciful. It was there but surely only for him, and the thought drew her even closer so that he stopped himself saying 'This is excellent ham,' or something equally banal and instead reached across the table and squeezed her hand.

"It's for you to decide whether we talk about it, Olga. It was just that I suddenly felt cheap posing as a bachelor."

She said, lightly, "No woman alive would mistake you for a bachelor, Martin!"

"Are married men that easily identified?"

"Not all married men, just you."

He digested this, thinking that it explained a good deal, the indifference of pretty girls in railway carriages and 'buses, the amused tolerance with which middle-aged women had met his attempts to say something mildly gallant at social gatherings in and about the suburb. He *looked* married. Perhaps that was what was wrong with him.

"The curious thing is it seemed to me a happy marriage, at all events, a pleasantly humdrum one," he mused, thinking aloud. "We didn't quarrel or nag one another, it was all a bit flat I suppose but in some ways it seemed more satisfactory than most marriages nowadays. It isn't as if I ran away from Sybil or from home when I panicked at school, yet that must have been part of what I despaired of or I should have stopped running the moment I arrived home. I made straight for Sybil when the balloon went up, but there wasn't a thought in my head about carrying the mutiny past the front door. Things seemed to happen one after the other so that suddenly the entire life I was leading seemed futile and stupid, unbearably so! All of it! Sybil, the children, the suburb, the house, the furniture, the school, the lot!"

Most of what he said made no sense to her but she was attentive and some of her newly-acquired poise had treach-

erously abandoned her, so that she stopped eating and concentrated.

"Very well, Martin, tell me as much as you want to and
leave out any part you don't. Start where you like too, as
far back as you feel inclined or from the break onwards!"

He began to talk, easily yet carefully, sifting among his
memories for the relevant and isolating suppressed shames
and vanities so that he could assess their importance and
present them objectively, resisting the temptation to flaunt
them like a man enjoying psychoanalysis. He told her of his
childhood under the goad of his chapel-going father and
the soggy, protective mantle of his mother, who had always
regarded him as the intellectual swan of the family. He spoke
of his schooldays, the rather weedy boy who stood by the
railings with a Ransome's *History of England* in his pocket,
holding his hand over it lest some boisterous classmate
should turn aside from a game of Highcockalorum and de-
nounce him as a swot and arse-creeper. He told of his loneliness at University and how desperately he had sought to drug
it with study and of his meeting with Sybil at a Speech Day
to which she and her father had come to hear a boy-cousin
deliver a Latin Ode.

"I thought her very beautiful," he said, "and I suppose she
still is, for she hasn't changed very much except to put on
a bit of weight. I don't think I noticed that until the night
I ran off. The thing that staggered me after we met was
that she was interested in me, and I still can't explain that,
satisfactorily. In a few days I was calling there regularly,
you know, not as a suitor exactly but as a family friend. I
was ten years older than her and she had plenty of admirers,
younger, pushing men most of them, you know the type—
cars, golf-handicaps and a whole lot of slang, 'Chin-Chin',
'Down the hatch' and 'I say old bean', but I don't suppose
you remember that period do you?"

"I'm afraid I do," she said smiling, "just about, but why
should you be so surprised she chose you? I dare say you
were as good-looking as any of them and a lot less brash and
bossy!"

"You might have something there," he said, laughing a
little, "she was a strong-minded woman and I daresay in
the end she preferred a husband who was unsure of himself.
The main thing in my favour, however, was her father's ap-

proval. He rather fancied himself as an intellectual, which he wasn't, and I was sufficiently smitten to submit to being bored by him night after night! I daresay the others thought the price was a bit high, notwithstanding her money."

"She had money?"

"Oh yes, not a vast amount but more than a person in my position had any right to expect. After all, I hadn't a penny but I honestly didn't think of her money, not once, can you believe that?"

"I can with you!"

"Well, as I say, I didn't think I stood a chance. She was unofficially engaged to a noisy young chap called Norman who used to call for her in a sports car that could be heard a mile off. Then one week-end everything fell my way. This fellow dashed off abroad and Sybil and I were married almost at once. It was like . . ." But here he broke off, smiling down at her as she sat watching him, one knee clasped in her hands, "why am I boring you with this? It's a very ordinary story and it all happened twenty years ago!"

"I'm not bored, Martin. You could never bore me. What was it like?"

"I was going to say like Albert and Victoria," he went on, reassured by her obvious interest, "you see, it was Sybil who really proposed. She made a joke of it, of course, saying I should never get round to it and I don't suppose I should have done in the circumstances."

"And after? Did she go on taking the initiative?"

He thought a moment before answering.

"No, not really, although you might find that hard to believe. I don't think she ever gave other people the impression that I was a Queen's husband, or if they got that impression it wasn't her fault. Sometimes she made quite a point of pretending I was the boss, except as far as the children were concerned!"

"How about the children, Martin?"

"Jonquil and Keith?" He moved away from the fireplace, still thinking hard and choosing his words. "They meant a lot to me when they were little but not any more, not for some time now! I suppose that sounds heartless but it's a fact. They might be grown-up step-children or young people lodging in the house. Mind you, I don't think there's anything

very remarkable about that. I imagine it's the same with most
teenagers these days. Nothing's the same any more and the
different generations aren't within shouting distance of one
another."

"Isn't that true of every age?"

"No, no, it isn't, Olga, or not nearly to the same degree.
I wasn't particularly fond of my father but he stood for
something solid, permanent and worth having. I mean even
less to them than they mean to me and that's something else
I've realised since I came away."

She sighed and got up, drifting over to the fire and raking
among the coals. Presently she said: "Have you told your
wife where you are?"

"No! I wrote a letter but I tore it up!"

She seemed mildly surprised. "You haven't phoned or written since leaving?"

"No, and I know why I haven't. This last fortnight, particularly since I've been here with you, has been the happiest
period of my life and I daren't risk putting a term to it.
Sybil's comfortably off so it isn't as if she was likely to
need money and somehow I can't believe she'll be worried
about me or miss me much. Sooner or later of course I'll
have to get in touch, but it will have to wait until I've some
kind of proposition to put to her."

"Proposition? You mean, a divorce?"

She said the word without looking at him and he was surprised and a little alarmed to note that the mere utterance
of the word threw his situation, and perhaps hers also, into
a sinister focus for it was a word that he had never conjured
with, a newspaper and film word that had never entered his
personal life. Now, for the first time, it meant precisely the
same thing to him as it meant to the people one read about
in newspapers, for surely it was not improbable that both he
and she might figure in a divorce suit. This, he realised, was
an altogether new development, for whereas Sybil could not
divorce him on the grounds of a fortnight's desertion she
could certainly do so if she could prove adultery.

He knew that panic must be showing in his face and
turned away from her, looking gloomily into the fire. Then,
like the cheerful hail of a coastguard to a climber perched
half-way down a cliff face, her quiet voice reached him,
coaxing him down on to level ground. She was saying:

"You don't have to be scared of anything, Martin, and you don't have to make decisions, not about me, not now and not at any time, you understand? What happened here tonight was by my choice and I should be very ashamed if it encouraged you to think I had any sort of claim on you!"

He said, slowly: "All the things one feels about loving anyone have been cheapened by popular music, TV, plays and books, particularly the kind of books people seem to prefer nowadays. When you want to say what is in your heart you can't say it because, as the words take shape in your head, you find yourself despising them as clichés. I know very well what I feel for you, Olga, but I should need time to find words to express it, real words that is! Does that make sense to you?"

"Well, it's in character, Martin, but why should a single act of physical love between two people who are fond of one another become an issue at all? Does it have to? Do we need to let it?"

"You mean you can look at it like that, as something that doesn't necessarily make for a far closer development in a relationship between a man and a woman?"

"A man like you and a woman like me? Yes, I can, and I think I should! Would you think more of me if I tried to make a fetish out of my virginity? Is that what most women do? Exploit it for all they are worth once they've lost it?"

"Yes," he said soberly, "I think many women do in one way or another and maybe that's one reason why there are so many unhappy marriages."

She looked steadily at him for a moment and he had no inkling of what she was thinking save that somewhere at the back of her mind she was searching for words to comfort him. It struck him then that their roles had been reversed since the word 'divorce' had been spoken, for when she answered it was as if she was a brisk but tolerant mother reminding her little boy that it was past bedtime.

"Now listen to me, Martin, listen carefully! I don't regret what happened and I never will, so stop feeling that our relationship has changed so drastically. It hasn't, hardly at all. I enjoyed you and I hope you enjoyed me, so make up your mind to regard it as lightly as I intend to!"

"Ah, but do you?" he asked, wondering at the lengths to which she was prepared to go to reassure him.

"Yes, I do!" she said, with surprising emphasis, "I suppose you find that difficult to believe because it so happened that I reached the age of thirty-three without giving myself to any man but it's true for all that and I suppose the reason lies in what I said to you at the time. My lack of experience wasn't due to prudery and it wasn't really lack of opportunity either. I imagine fastidiousness played some part in it but tonight it seemed to me natural, right and almost inevitable! I'd always imagined that if and when it did happen I should be full of rue immediately afterwards but I can assure you I'm not, far from it! If I'm a hundred per cent honest I'll admit to being very pleasantly surprised and I don't imagine that's common to every woman!"

He smiled and shook his head, more puzzled than ever. "Men are supposed to regard sex more lightly than women, Olga," he said, "but I'm not such a man. It always seemed to me a very wonderful thing, not a casual thing. How do you set about reversing an old-fashioned attitude like that? You're a level-headed woman, what's your prescription?"

"I've got one," she said, smiling, "let's stop this gloomy post-mortem and go to bed and I don't mean together, because what you need right now is a good night's sleep and God knows, you've earned one, so off with you and leave me to clear away in here!" and she gave him a friendly push, picked up the fireguard, set it in place and began stacking the china on the tray.

He watched her for a moment or two and then, stifling a yawn, decided that she was probably right and that bed was very inviting indeed.

"The thing about you, Olga," he said, slowly, "is that you keep coming up with new surprises! Very well! We'll go over it all tomorrow!"

"Indeed we won't!" she said firmly, "hold this door open!" and she passed into the hall carrying the tray and kicked open the kitchen door with her foot and flicked the light switch with her elbow. He went up the stairs and along the narrow passage to his room and almost nodded off in the act of pulling off his clothes and flopping into bed but here, in the moment before sleep came to him, his serenity returned, seeping quietly into his mind and filling him with a delicious drowsiness. His adventures floated past him like galleons, Tapper's pictures, the auction sale, the mastery of the 'bus, and finally Olga asleep in his arms, and it seemed to him then that this last was not the least impressive of the fleet.

. . . . .

The little room was flooded with sunlight when he awoke and he knew without looking at his watch that it was late. He lay still for a few moments listening to finches squabbling in the gorse on the edge of the links and as he climbed from bed he heard St. Luke's church clock strike the hour and counted up to ten.

"Great Scott!" he said to himself, "that bus-trip must have exhausted me! I've overslept two and a half hours!" and as though this was important he hurried through his toilet and slipped into his slacks and sweater, determined to have breakfast and take his swim later in the morning. He expected to find Olga in the kitchen but she was not down, so he laid a tray and carried it upstairs, feeling rather like a newly-wed anxious to please.

"Tea up!" he called, thumping the panel with his foot, but there was no response and when he put down the tray and opened the door he was astonished to find the room empty, with the bed unmade and Olga's crumpled nightdress on the pillow. At that moment he heard the front door bang and hurried to the staircase, calling.

"Is that you, Olga? I brought tea!" and carried the tray down as she crossed the hall.

She had obviously been up to the town for she wore the hat and coat that had escaped the mudbath the previous day and he wondered if she had slipped out to make an early call on the gownshop. She said, quietly: "Hallo, Martin. I let you sleep on, I had to go up to Cook's place in the Square. I wanted to get everything fixed before you could talk me out of it and now it's done. Let's have breakfast!"

"Get what fixed? I thought your cruise was arranged weeks ago?"

"It was, but I managed to change it."

"You've cancelled it?"

"No, Martin, I've brought it forward. I was to have gone mid-June but I remembered there was an earlier one over the same route starting from Plymouth the day after tomorrow."

"The day after tomorrow! You mean, you'll be leaving then?"

"Tomorrow, Martin!"

He gaped at her, teacup half-way to his mouth. "You're pulling my leg aren't you?"

"No, Martin, it's all arranged."

"But in God's name—I mean—*why?* I wasn't sure you'd go at all and in any case there was another month. What made you panic like this?"

"It isn't panic, Martin, it's the reverse. Look, let's have breakfast and pour me a cup of tea. I went without any, because I was afraid you'd come down before I got out."

He poured her tea but his own seemed tasteless and flat. There was a drag in his stomach and his head began to ache about the brows. He sat down at the table with his appetite quite gone and watched her move about the room, cracking eggs into the pan and peeling rashers of bacon as though nothing had disturbed the easy camaraderie of the previous day, and he thought, savagely: 'Damn sex! It's always this way when a relationship between a man and a woman is pushed to its logical conclusion! The moment sex enters into it everything else takes to its heels! I wish to God I'd told her to put on her clothes and stop making a fool of herself and of me! Maybe we could have laughed it off, satisfied ourselves with a kiss or two and gone on in the same delightful way, chatting and laughing and behaving like dignified adults instead of a couple of panting adolescents!'

"Well?" he grunted, at length, "tell me what's made you so afraid of me all of a sudden?"

She looked at him calmly as she took her seat opposite. "Don't be silly, Martin, you know very well that I'm not in the least afraid of you!"

"What other reason could there be for this crazy decision?" he demanded and she gave a little chirrup of laughter that did nothing to improve his mood.

"You look more married than ever, Martin!" she said. "Now listen to me carefully and don't interrupt until I've finished. The decision isn't as crazy as I think you'll agree if you think it over as carefully as I have. Ordinarily, we should have spent the next four weeks alone here and by the time I was ready to go on the voyage neither of us would have known what we were doing or where we were going or what was to happen to either of us in the end. We should probably have ended up snarling at one another, just as you're spoiling for a quarrel right now; I didn't want that to happen and I'm not going to let it happen. I take full responsibility for what happened last night and when I thought it over it seemed to me that it was also my responsibility to take the initiative before we get out of our depth."

"Damn it, it was you who shrugged it off last night!" he protested, "I was the one who . . . !"

She raised her hand. "You promised me not to interrupt, Martin!"

"I didn't! You promised for me!"

"Well, go along with me for a few moments, please! I do mean that, it's very important to me!"

"Very well," he said, somewhat more gently, "you'd better say what's in your mind but I'm involved in this too, remember."

"Of course, I'll remember!" she said, sharply for her. "You were upset last night—any fool could see that. If you were the kind of person who took his fun where he found it and moved on it wouldn't have mattered in the least but you aren't. You're a very sensitive person and you couldn't subscribe to that kind of relationship, it would result in making you far more miserable than you were when you ran away to go looking for life."

He realised that she was right, that he was not and never could be a cheerful philanderer looking over his shoulder for the next encounter. Already this relationship, his very first essay in philandering, had surged far beyond the make-merry-and-be-damned stage, so much so that the thought of waking in the morning and finding himself alone in the house depressed him even more than the prospect of moving out and finding new lodgings. He said, "Suppose I hadn't admitted to being married, or suppose I had let it be understood that I was determined to get a divorce or some kind of separation? Would that have made any difference? Would you have been satisfied to wait for something permanent?"

"What profit is there in presupposing something that isn't true, Martin? The real point is that so far you haven't spared a thought for the domestic aspect of your truancy and until you do how can either of us know what the future might hold? You've been exceptionally honest and I appreciate that, but it seems to me damned unfair to penalise you for honesty! You haven't made up your mind to leave Sybil and if I stayed on here I should be a party to forcing a decision on you!"

"Is that altogether a bad idea, Olga?"

"It certainly would be if the decision was a wrong one."

He said, bitterly, "A month, two months, will it make that much difference? It depends on so many things, Sybil's view, what I propose to do with my life, and anyway I was never much good at making decisions."

"You were beginning to be and that's the crux of the matter! You need time to sort yourself out. You set out on the most important journey of your life less than a month ago and you're not half-way there yet, Martin. I've grown very fond of you and I don't want to be the person to stampede you in any one direction. Just think, Martin, what would happen if we stayed on here together until Sybil located you? You might find yourself in a position where other people made decisions on your behalf. I don't know, nowadays people seem to rush into marriages, second, third, or even fourth marriages without any thought at all but most of them are young and the young can afford to squander time. We can't, Martin, neither one of us, and if two people are set on breaking up a marriage at least they ought to be damned sure of each other."

The resentment was dying in him. He knew that she was talking and thinking good sense and also that she had measured to a decimal point the extent of his uncertainty. He understood, too, that she had been successful in isolating what had happened from their relationship as a whole. Perhaps all women were able to do this, perhaps the male assessment of the importance of physical possession in a woman was a fallacy and that women had the knack of weighing the true worth of an association on an accurate basis. He didn't know, he was beginning to realise that he knew almost nothing about women, not even the two women he had held in his arms. He could follow her reasoning so far but beyond that he lost the track in a labyrinth of possibilities and probabilities yet he was ready, grudgingly, to concede her commonsense. For a moment he was tempted to cloud the issue by telling her that he could never return to his old life and that this must inevitably sever him from his wife and family, for what wife with Sybil's notions of comfort would agree to uproot herself and drift about the country with a husband who had cut himself adrift from a settled, orderly existence? He resisted this temptation, however, and said: "Listen, Olga, I've been very happy here with you and I'm going to be desperately lonely when you're gone. If I show up when you come home, if . . . if I'm clear in my mind what's to become of me, if I've got some sort of plan that is, could we try again and perhaps stay together?"

It was a hollow and hedged-in kind of proposal and most women would have either resented it or laughed at it, but Olga Boxall knew exactly what he was trying to say, so much so that she had to get up quickly and turn her back on him, knowing that if he saw tears in her eyes they would find themselves in an emotional maze that would soon make nonsense of her decision.

"I don't think we can make any conditions about this, Martin," she said, when she had mastered her weakness and could stop pretending to refill the teapot. "I only know that every instinct I have about us told me to go out and switch boats because only that way do we stand a chance of making an intelligent decision."

Suddenly she stopped searching for words and addressed him directly, both hands gripping the guard-rail of the stove and holding her body rigid. "This has no bearing on me loving or needing you, Martin! Last night I wanted you and I took you, almost against your will, and in spite of the warning you were decent enough to give me. Well, as I said, I don't regret that one bit but now that I've had time to think I'm sorry for your sake because you have an instinctive chivalry about women and to use something as rare and fine as that for one's own ends would be contemptuous, don't you see? Now let's stop all this and enjoy what's left of the day. I'm going out of here early tomorrow and nothing you can say is going to make me go back on it. You can stay on—I'd be glad if you did, we'll go to Britton's, the estate agents and make you official tenant, but don't try and talk me out of it, I had quite enough trouble talking myself into it!"

A Verey light exploded in Sebastian's brain and suddenly he did understand and with a clarity that astonished him. He understood that this woman was in love with him but was deliberately removing herself from him because instinct told her that he was unable to return that love in a way that could bring either of them lasting happiness. He knew that she realised too many of his years had been spent within the orbit of another woman to whom he was bound by the chains of an attachment formed when he and all his world were young, and that although he might run from this he could never out-distance it. He understood that she was right when she said that his own journey was far from finished and that this involvement was a kind of half-way stage and a long way short of horizons that would have to be crossed if he was to learn anything worth learning from his odyssey.

"This house," he said presently, "I found peace and joy in it and I should like to stay here if it could be arranged but I must pay a proper rent, I don't see why you should lose by your decency, Olga. Let's go and arrange it and then I'll help you pack."

They got through the day with less difficulty than they had anticipated. He signed for the house at a rental of twenty-eight pounds a month and gave her a cheque in advance, the first he had cashed since leaving home, and when her trunk was locked and roped, and transport to the junction had been arranged, he gave her a gift he had bought while her back was turned, a lizard-skin bag that had caught his eye in the window of Gilroy's next door to the estate agents. He gave it to her after supper and when she kissed him and held him in a quick, nervous embrace her nearness disturbed him more than it had the previous evening, for it promised more than physical relief and the triumph of being the first man to possess her. They sat for an hour or so and talked in the manner of the days preceding the crisis and it gave him pleasure to realise that, beneath the restraints the new situation placed upon her, she was excited at the prospect of visiting towns and cities she had dreamed of since girlhood for this made her journey less of a flight and more of an adventure, sweetening the sour thought that he had been the means of causing her unhappiness. He said, summing up this conviction, "In a sense, you're doing the same thing as I did, Olga. We both waited overlong but I think you'll get the same kick out of it the moment the boat casts off. I haven't looked back, so don't you! For the next twelve weeks treat every day as a separate existence!"

He pictured her as he said this, going ashore in a chattering party to view Pompeii and Naples and the Piraeus, and part of him longed to be with her, drinking local drinks in little cafés and making tourists' observations, but he knew that this was not his road and if he was tempted by it he would only have to retrace his footsteps sooner or later and for him there was even less time to spare.

CHAPTER FIVE

Mr. Sermon
Enlarges His Audience

SEBASTIAN SERMON's physical, mental and spiritual enlargement moved on to its next stage within an hour of his waving goodbye to a rather tremulous Olga Boxall at the bottom of The Coombe, where she picked up her taxi. He had helped the taximan carry the trunk down the unmade roadway to the sea-front and when the car had passed out of sight among High Street traffic he felt so glum that he yearned to do something strenuous and grabbing costume and towel he turned his back on the empty house. He crossed the edge of the links and went on down the bluff to the eastern edge of the Bay where there was a section of shingle beach not much patronised by the paddlers and shrimpers.

The water was warm and he swam slowly westward, making for a moored launch that lay about a hundred yards offshore and being careful to skirt the most westerly groyne that projected eighty yards into the Bay. He had reached its point when he saw the child, a girl about four or five wearing a sunsuit and carrying a shrimping net with which she probed the concrete buttresses of the breakwater. He regarded her warily, thinking that the adults in charge of her were taking a chance to allow a child of that age to walk the slippery planking with deep water on either side and as he thought this he caught a glimpse of her mother, or whoever it was, standing on the concrete drum nearer the beach and gesticulating at the perched infant.

Perhaps the child's attention wavered between the swimmer and the mother, or perhaps a ninth wave submerged the groyne and caused her to lose her footing. At all events the child suddenly toppled backwards into deep water and the woman on the beach uttered one of the most piercing screams Mr. Sermon had ever heard, not excluding those practised by despairing actresses on the telly.

As he rose on the swell Mr. Sermon caught a glimpse of people converging on the woman as she stood knee-deep in the water and then he was over the groyne and diving deep at the point where the child had disappeared.

He was not much of a diver and without glasses his range of vision was limited but he had the sense to turn inland and ride the surge of the next breaker and as he surfaced he saw his quarry, a threshing, rolling bundle turning over and over in the swell and bobbing up just long enough to glare at him with a desperate ferocity, so that even in the tumult of the moment Mr. Sermon decided that she was likely to prove a difficult handful. He went after her however, with wild, chopping strokes and just as she disappeared for the second time he grabbed her by the shoulder-flounces of her sunsuit, tugging her backwards so that he could enlarge his grip before they went under together and he swallowed what seemed to him a gallon of water.

They seemed to struggle there a long time, Sebastian on his back, the child held by her shoulders against his belly, and all the time the breakers thundered over them and pitched them this way and that until Mr. Sermon felt that he too was on the point of drowning. Then, as he kicked out madly, they dropped into a trough and before the next wave broke over them he got his breath and his bearings and without relaxing his grip worked himself into a more horizontal position so that the next wave swept them inshore. It went over them nevertheless and the child gave a violent belch, striking out with her feet and hitting Sebastian in the groin, the blow causing him to yelp and swallow yet another mouthful. Then, with a sense of unspeakable relief, he felt bottom and somebody fully-clad reached out and relieved him of his burden and he

was able to struggle ashore. Reaching the tideline he fell
forward on hands and knees, gasping and retching as the
beach swam before his eyes. Kneeling there he was hardly
conscious of the fact that he was surrounded by excited
holiday-makers and that a fisherman was crouching over the
child and working her arms like pump-handles.

As soon as his vision cleared Mr. Sermon succumbed to
yet another wave, this time of indignation directed at the hys-
terical woman he had seen waving to the child before she
toppled into the water. 'Damn them!' he thought savagely,
'why the devil can't people look after their children properly?
Any fool should have seen the danger of letting a child that
age walk the length of a slippery breakwater with a shrimping
net! I hope she *was* scared! She damn well deserves to be
scared! Supposing I hadn't turned aside whilst making for
the launch, supposing . . .' but at that moment the little devil
he had rescued rolled over, sat up and began to shriek and
everybody round her cooed and exclaimed, and the fisherman
stood up beaming round on the ever-growing circle as though
he and not Mr. Sermon had been responsible for averting
tragedy. Sebastian was so disgusted by the man's bearing that
he got up, spat out more water and began to plod down the
beach towards the spot where he had left his clothes and
spectacles. Then everybody seemed to notice him at once and
a young woman shouted "Wait! Hi there! *Wait!*" and people
turned away from the fisherman and the screaming child and
began to thump him on the back and exchange first-hand
accounts of the rescue, as though they were talking about
someone they had read about in the newspaper. Scraps of
their conversation reached him as he stood there hemmed in
by spectators and some of whom prodded him as they might
have touched a curious exhibit taken from its museum case:
'Jolly Good Show!'—'Saw it all!'—'Came up with her four
times—wouldn't let go!'—'Ought to get one of those medals!',
and so on, until Mr. Sermon's bewilderment gave way to
acute embarrassment and he shuffled forward mumbling,
"Excuse me—my clothes—rather cold—get something on."

It was the most ill-advised remark he could have made for
at once he was half-buried under a rain of blazers and mackintoshes, and hands led him up the beach to a refreshment
hut and somebody thrust a cup of tea in his hands and urged
him to 'drink it up before he did another thing!' He sipped

the tea gratefully enough and then a very plump, rubicund man wearing office clothes that made him very conspicuous among so many bikinis and beachshirts, elbowed his way forward with an air of indisputable authority and said, "Excuse me, sir, but would you mind giving me your name? It's official, for the record! I'm the Town Clerk here—Bignall's the name —and I'm sure to get asked, bound to in the nature of things, huh?" He ended his request on a note of query, the 'huh' coming out sharply and authoritatively, so that Sebastian was browbeaten into mumbling, "Sermon's my name, but please, I . . . er . . . I really don't want any fuss about it! It was just lucky I happened to see her go in, I . . . er . . . I had a presentiment she would! Is she all right now?"

"Right as rain, right as rain, huh?" barked Mr. Bignall. "Coming up the beach now and none the worse, none the worse, huh?" and he pointed to a little group picking its way up the shingle with the child in the centre. She was still uttering dolorous cries and being ineffectually comforted by the woman, the fisherman and the few hangers-on who had not yet deserted her in favour of the hero.

"Well, I'm glad about that!" said Mr. Sermon, privately deciding that what the child needed in addition to more competent supervision was a good spanking, and then, as he was about to tell Mr. Bignall something of the circumstances, he checked himself for he recognised the nursemaid as the girl who had spoken to him that first morning on the beach, the one who had remembered him from her brief sojourn at Napier Hall Preparatory School and had been frightened away by the Reverend Victor Hawley.

"God bless my soul!" he exclaimed, "will you excuse me a moment, sir? I . . . I'd like to speak to the young lady and there's still my clothes and towel—" and draped in a stranger's raincoat, he pushed his way through the crowd and touched the girl on the arm.

"Hullo there! It is you, isn't it? I hadn't my glasses, I didn't realise."

The young woman turned a harassed gaze on him and then, with some difficulty, allowed her features to relax in a wry smile.

"Yes, it's me, up to my neck in trouble as usual! Geraldine, for goodness' sake—this gentleman saved your life! Won't you stop howling long enough to say 'Thank you'?" and Mr.

Sermon recognised the child as the little girl who had hurled
stones at seagulls, a memory that confirmed him in his opinion that she was not a child he would have elected to save
had he been given the choice.

"All right, then I'll say it for you! Thank you a thousand
times, Mr. Sermon! And if I hadn't been so horribly involved
I should have clapped and cheered like mad! Geraldine, for
pity's sake!" and she lifted her shoulders in a gesture of hope-
lessness as the child, her wails rising an octave, tore loose
and rushed into the embrace of the testy old woman Mr.
Sermon remembered as the owner of a car half as big as
Grosvenor Square.

"Oh, God, that's put the tin lid on it!" said the young
woman, her hand flying to her mouth.

"I say, are you likely to get into trouble about this?" asked
Mr. Sermon and suddenly found himself ashamed of contrib-
uting to the sensation. The girl looked very glum and seemed
reluctant to emerge from the thinning crowd.

"Trouble? I shall be fired like a gun! You'll hear the report
from the far side of the town. Well, here goes! Let's get it
over with and I suppose I ought to be glad in a way but I'd
much sooner have fired them!"

"Wait a minute!" said Sebastian, "perhaps I can do something."

He pulled the borrowed raincoat closely round him and
went up the stairs to where Geraldine was burrowing deeper
into the embrace of the old woman who glared at him as
though he was soliciting alms.

"Sermon's my name," he began, rather breathlessly, "I
pulled the little girl out but I think you ought to know that
the young lady looking after her did everything possible to
avoid the accident. I saw her walk into the water in an attempt to make the little girl come back to the beach."

The woman gave him a searching glance and then dismissed
him to devote her attention to the nursemaid.

"How did she get out there in the first place? That's what I
should like to know! What were you doing to let her risk her
life in search of a few shrimps? What do you think I send
you down here for? To sit and read about animal diseases?
To sunbathe? To let the child go where she likes without let
or hindrance? You ought to be thoroughly ashamed of yourself, Miss Grey, you hear me? When my son and daughter-

in-law hear about this they'll be devastated, devastated, you hear? Take her home at once! Take her home and give her a hot bath! Dawson! Where are you, Dawson?" as the poker-faced chauffeur stepped forward and touched his hat. "Take us all home at once, do you hear?"

"But I say, you must listen . . ." began Mr. Sermon, dismayed by her manner and annoyed by her cavalier dismissal of a man whose groin ached from the impact of the child's heel, but before he could utter another word, Mr. Bignall joined issue, sailing into the group like a man-o'-war bearing down on a huddle of rowing-boats.

"You are addressing the man who saved the child's life, Lady Wilkinson!"

The old lady blew out her lips and made the kind of face she might have made after tasting a sour plum. If gratitude stirred in her it was not noticeable and Mr. Sermon found his indignation jockeyed aside by amazement at such incredible arrogance.

"*Him? He* rescued her? Well, thank you, I'm sure, but what interests me is why she *had* to be rescued? This young woman is paid a good wage to look after the child, instead of which she reads and gossips! She was gossiping to that very man the last time I called for her!" and as though in response to an afterthought she opened a vast handbag, plunged a fat, freckled hand into its depths and came up with a purse about three inches square. Fascinated, Sebastian watched her tuck her bag under her arm and extract a pound note from the purse. With a small part of his mind he knew that she was on the point of offering him a tip but his brain as a whole rejected this as a monstrous improbability. Nobody, he thought, could be so purse-proud and arrogant as that, and as he watched her unfold the note and smooth it between her palms he wondered what on earth she would do with it when it had lost its wrinkles. Then, as the woman's hand completed the smoothing process, the girl acted. She bounded forward, pushing between Mr. Sermon and her employer and thrusting her body forward so vigorously that the old woman raised her hand as though she expected a blow in the face.

"How *dare* you! How *dare* you, you . . . you disgusting old woman!" shouted the girl. "Mr. Sermon is a gentleman! Mr. Sermon wouldn't touch your filthy money, so don't offer it, don't you dare offer it, or I'll . . . I'll stuff it down your horrible throat!"

Mr. Sermon gasped and even the stolid Mr. Bignall raised his eyebrows and murmured "Huh!" in an unexpectedly subdued voice. Some of the bystanders grinned and tittered but the majority succumbed to a sudden embarrassment and began to shuffle away in various directions. The old woman's face twitched, the child stopped snivelling and the chauffeur coughed gently, discreetly. Then, with great deliberation, Lady Wilkinson shifted her grip on the handbag, opened it, returned the note to its depths and gestured Geraldine towards the car, following her without a word. The chauffeur hesitated, glancing interrogatively towards the girl, who said: "Don't bother, Dawson, I'm not coming! Tell them I'll send for my things later!" and walked quickly away as a breathless boy tugged at Mr. Sermon's arm and handed him his clothes and towel.

Mr. Bignall pretended to ignore the little scene.

"Change in one of our tents. On the house, huh!" he said, and Sebastian, now feeling cold and bewildered, followed his directions to a row of council bathing tents near the refreshment hut and escaped into one gladly as the last of the crowd melted away.

When he emerged it was to find that Mr. Bignall had departed leaving a neatly-written message with the restaurant-hut attendant. The note ordered him to telephone the Council Offices at once and ask to be put through to the Town Clerk's office. Mr. Sermon pocketed the note promising himself that he would think twice before obeying the order for he had no desire at all to figure in a public acknowledgement of his action. For the moment all he was interested in was the girl and what was to become of her now that she had sacked herself and sacrificed all prospects of a reference. He climbed the steps slowly, still conscious of the ache in the groin and suddenly there she was standing beside a promenade shelter, beckoning and smiling.

He was surprised to see her looking so cheerful. He had had the impression that she was very much upset by the encounter with her employer but it was obvious that she had more buoyancy than most people, for she said, taking his arm in a friendly fashion; "I waited because I remembered that we haven't had a real chin-wag Mr. Sermon. I've got a sort of car in the park and I feel like a drink. Let me buy you one!"

She led the way across the promenade to the car-park and pointed to her 'sort of car', a bull-nosed Morris at least twenty years old. "She passed her roadworthy test but you have to hold on to the door, I never seem to get around to having it fixed."

Sebastian got in and they climbed the High Street to the moor. Conversation was impossible during the ascent, but when they reached the summit she pulled off the road and turned so that they could look down on the bay and enjoy the view that Sebastian had of the town the morning of his arrival. It was a familiar view now, so much so that he felt he had been living there years instead of less than a month, but he got the impression that she did not share his affection for Kingsbay and was glowering at the prospect, as he might look down on the Wyckham Rise estate as a place where dreams had no room to grow. He said: "Do you belong to this part of the country? Is Kingsbay your home town?"

"Good heavens, no!" she said, emphatically, "I'm from Canada. Can't you spot the accent?"

He could now that she spoke of it, a shortening of the 'a' and a barely noticeable slurring of consonants and it surprised him for she looked very English with her brown eyes, dark hair and fresh complexion, the kind of girl one might expect to find in a house with lawns, tumbledown stables and sporting dogs asleep on the terrace.

"I've been over here since I was a child," she went on, "but ever since I grew up I've been meaning to go home. It's like everything else, somehow I never got around to it! I hardly ever get around to anything, Mr. Sermon. Daddy's dug in here and more English than the English but then you'd expect that, seeing where he lives and works. I'll never get him to uproot himself now. If I do go home I'll have to do it on my own steam and I don't think I'll ever raise the fare!"

"What does your father do?"

"He's a Headmaster, you probably know the school, because it's quite near here, Barrowdene!"

"Barrowdene! *The* . . . Barrowdene? The Public School?"

"Why yes!" she laughed. "Am I such an improbable Headmaster's daughter?"

"Yes, you are," he admitted, "and come to think of it, you're an improbable person altogether!"

"I don't think I'm any more improbable than you, Mr. Sermon," she said, laughing.

"Ah, but the difference is I wasn't in the least improbable at your age," he said, "in fact, I've only been improbable for a matter of weeks. Until then I was probably the most predictable man in Europe!"

"How do you like it?" she asked, smiling, "being improbable I mean?"

"I like it fine," he said, "and I wish I'd taken the leap years ago!"

"Oh, don't wish that," she said, with unexpected seriousness, "I dare say you're enjoying it as a change but when it's part of your make-up it's a damned nuisance, take it from me! Sooner or later everybody you know loses patience with you and in the end you lose patience with yourself! If I'd had any say in it I should have made myself a very different person, I can tell you! I should have settled for a quiet, demure little thing ecstatically happy with a husband who came home at 6 p.m. every night and gave me a couple of kids who occupied me until bedtime. There's peace in that kind of existence, you can grow old with dignity."

"Indeed, you can't," he argued, thinking of himself, "that's the one thing you can't do! You begin to panic every birthday and each night, as you're going off to sleep, you feel that's one more day wasted!"

As he said this he was aware of a curious affinity with the girl, for here was someone rooting for tranquillity as he rooted for adventure and change, and somehow it made them partners and fellow-travellers so that they were able to arrive on common ground with the minimum of talk.

"Here we are discussing one another's compulsions," he said, "and I don't even remember your name! The one I'm using right now is 'Martin', I've changed it along with my background. What is your name?"

"Rachel," she said, "Rachel Grey. Grey is my maiden name and I've gone back to it. I didn't like my husband's name, it was Follet-Smith. Double-barrelled names always irritate me. I think most people invent them like famous ancestors and even the genuine ones seem pretentious. That was one of the things Steve and I quarrelled about, I would persist in signing myself 'Smith' and introducing myself as 'Smith' over the phone!"

She leaned back and tried to stretch her long legs in the cramped space under the steering-wheel. "That's enough about me, tell me more about your dramatic abdication from the Prep. School!"

"No," he said, firmly, for the factual recital of his flight was beginning to bore him. "You tell me more about yourself. How did a girl with a father head of a famous school like Barrowdene come to embark on a career of assistant matron, or nannie for that matter? And what happened in between, apart from your marriage to Mr. Follet-Smith? Oh, and why do you go about with a book on veterinary surgery?"

"Oh, it's all a frightful muddle," she said lightly, "and when I look back it seems a fearful waste of time, not the least bit like I planned when I was seventeen and starry-eyed at Montreux! One ought to settle for reality making nonsense of dreams, of course, but I think mine must have gone far wider of the mark than most girls', particularly the kind of girl I met over there. I think it was in Switzerland that they started going wrong. Oh I liked it at Montreux at first, but that was probably because I love mountains. We used to ski a good deal and I made lots of friends, but I didn't learn anything, not even conversational French. You see, I'm a very lazy person—intellectually that is—and I suppose I also acquired expensive tastes in Switzerland. Most of the girls had wealthy fathers and we've never had more than just enough to get by. I was a bit conscience-stricken about this when I came home, that's why I took the job at Napier Hall."

"How old were you then?"

"Nineteen when I left. I tried two more Prep. Schools but I absolutely hated the life. Men can be tiresome enough but thirteen-year-old boys! All those bleeding knees and gaping socks! Besides, I suppose I rather hoped I'd meet a real man on the staff, but I never did, they were either tired old failures or self-opinionated young boors. Mind you, I felt sorry for some of them, you for instance, but that only made the background more depressing. I went home for a spell and then took an art course in London. In some ways that was worse."

"In what way?"

"It was all so hopelessly phoney. Most of the people I met

had no more real love of art than I have for quantity sur-
veying! They used it as a kind of sloppy backcloth for acting
out their personalities, or the personalities they thought they
had! They used to spend hours and hours convincing themselves that they occupied advanced outposts in politics and
philosophy and artistic appreciation. They were so full of
fads that it was like . . . like living in a mental hospital,
where everyone is pretending to be a cherry tree or Savo-
narola or Snow White and the Seven Dwarfs! I soon found
out I couldn't paint, tho' I wasn't bad as a potter. I stuck it
out for almost two years and then I got a job as a stewardess
on a South American line. That was fun in parts but it got to
be very exhausting. I don't mean the work, I mean the all-in
wrestling with the crew and passengers. The only way to get
by was to learn ju-jitsu, so I did, but the only time I used
it was on a Bolivian who had a seat on the Board. That's
just me. I was paid-off while he was still in sick bay. It was
soon after that I met Steve."

"Steve Follet-Smith?"

"Yes, he was a Yale man doing research on the magazine
I worked on for a time. He was a terribly brainy person and
I admired him, particularly his powers of application and
concentration which was something I lacked so badly. I wasn't
all that attracted to him physically, tho' he wasn't bad-looking,
lean-faced, very intense, with high cheekbones and rather
husky for an intellectual. He was a bit Caius-Cassiusy, you
know, wiry but strong as a bull. His folks had money and he
was over here getting material for a thesis. I forget what it
was on, I fancy a French poet . . . 'Shen' or 'Chen'—some-
thing-or-other!"

"Chenier. André Chenier?"

"That was it! Aren't you brainy? I remember now, the poor
little toad wrote reams of verse to a girl who didn't give a
damn about him. Steve was crazy about him and we went
all over France tracing clues, at least, he did, I usually
stayed at a little place in Brittany and lazed around, waiting.
I liked that part of our marriage, it was a kind of stop-go
honeymoon and I was always thrilled to see him come loping
down the path to the farm where I'd been dumped."

"What went wrong?"

"Oh, all kinds of things. I suppose he got bored with my

laziness and general dimness. He should have married a girl
with something upstairs as well as down, someone a bit better
balanced, if you follow me. We got along fine in bed and
often out of it when we hadn't seen one another for a fortnight or so, but when we went to his home in New England
he began his drive to turn me into something he didn't have
to apologise for to all the other long-hairs. He just didn't
realise what he was up against. Dozens of well-meaning
teachers had already broken their teeth on me and he wasn't
any more successful than the best of them. We had some
dreadful rows but I don't think he realised that I did try.
If I'd been madly in love with him I might have succeeded,
but I wasn't, I just liked and admired him, and it wasn't
enough, you see? Then I blew my top—reaction to all the
intellectual pressure, I suppose—and had a rather dreary
affaire with a boy who hadn't got an idea in his head outside
horses and baseball, and then Steve's mother chipped in and
finally he divorced me. I couldn't quarrel with that and I
don't now, he was more generous than I had a right to expect
and even paid my expenses home and gave me a bit over. I
hope to God he found somebody who could give him a
better deal."

The thing that Sebastian found himself admiring most
about her was her breezy honesty. He was beginning to discover how rare this kind of honesty had been in the world he
had deserted but how often it cropped up now that he had
gained a little elbow-room and had time to consider people
objectively. It was one of the things that had attracted him
to Olga and, before that, to Tapper Sugg and the barmaid at
the Cat and Carthorse just over the hill. People had never
been anything like so frank about themselves in the suburb
and a conversation with any of Sybil's devotees, or member
of the staff at Napier Hall, always left him with a feeling
that they had drawn a tight circle round themselves and that
nothing but a violent shock would cause them to step outside
it and be themselves for a few moments. It had made all his
personal contacts stale and profitless, as though every sentence
he exchanged with the few people he did meet was the kind
one might exchange in a railway compartment and this
stricture, this hedged-in feeling, had extended even to Sybil
and certainly to his son and daughter. As he pondered this,

however, a new thought struck him. Were the kind of people he had met during the last few weeks different or did they merely seem different because his own personality had undergone a radical change, so that he was now able to meet them half-way or, in the case of the shy ones like Olga, more than half-way? He was so struck with this that Rachel Grey made the error of thinking his attention had wandered and said: "Look here, Martin, I'm boring you to tears! I didn't volunteer the story of my life, you asked for it, remember? Let's have a drink and something to eat!" and she pressed the starter button.

"I'm not in the least bored," he said, "I was comparing your story with my own. After the divorce what happened? Did you come home again?"

"I always come home! Father's a very tolerant person and one of the wisest people I know. He doesn't probe, he enjoys watching me get my breath back. I'm the youngest you see and all the others have turned out rather well. One brother is a physicist and another brother and a sister are both happily married with two kids apiece. He's been very lonely since Mother died and the one tidy thing about my life is my relationship with Fred. He's a poppet and we're buddies! There isn't much left to tell anyway; after a bit I took the job as companion-nannie to Lady Wilkinson."

"What I don't understand," he said slowly, as she reversed and moved back on to the road, "is how few bruises you've got to show for it. You aren't bitter about anything, not Steve or bad luck, or mistakes or even those awful Wilkinson people. You're like . . . like someone who has stood all day throwing rings at a hoop-la stall without winning a prize, but remains as optimistic as when you started out. You think of yourself as a muddler but you aren't really, you've got something quite rare and I can't think of the word for it. It isn't 'resilience' exactly and it isn't a thick hide. Can you name it? Do you know yourself that well?"

She gave him a shrewd glance as though she was not at all sure how she should take this, then she laughed and said: "It was smart of you to spot it that quickly. I feel things as much as anyone but I don't bruise, at least, if I do the bruises don't stay and I know why all right. It's because I had a happy childhood. I discovered that as soon as I left home and you can spot it in other people, all kinds of people. It's armour against fate and most things bounce off it, Martin. You'll understand when you meet Fred." Then, eagerly, "I say, would you like to? Now? This afternoon?"

"Go over to Barrowdene with you?"

"Yes, after we've had lunch at the pub."

"I would indeed, I've dropped schoolmastering but I'm still interested in schools, particularly schools like Barrowdene. Would your father mind?"

"He'd love it, you'd get on like a house on fire. I'll introduce you and then you can wander round. He's been there over twenty years and it oozes from the pores. He likes showing people around, particularly pros like you!"

"Then I'd like to very much, Rachel, and if he's busy I'll pose as a parent prospecting the ground."

She drove fast but extremely well and in a few moments they reached the pub where he had set out for Avalon. As they passed the crest of the hill he made a mental genuflexion and for the first time since Olga had announced her intention to leave he felt the spread of excitement and happiness in his belly, a sensation that he was beginning to recognise as the warning note of a new adventure.

"There's one thing you haven't told me," he said, as they drank their beer and waited for Bella's pastries to warm. "Where does the veterinary book come in? Is it a hobby?"

"It began as one," she told him, "but it's developed into a bit of a penance. I'm good with animals, dogs, cats, horses, anything that can't answer back, and I always had an idea I should enjoy working with them, particularly if they were sick and needed looking after. I couldn't nurse people but I think I could nurse animals and during the time I was at the Wilkinsons I took refuge in the dream of becoming a vet. For one thing there's sex equality in that field, people accept women vets and it's just a question of finding the staying power to pass the exams."

"You'll find it, Rachel!" he said, and regarding her comically through the glass bottom of his tankard he found himself wishing with all his heart that his own daughter, Jonquil, had the same zest for life, the same introspective modesty that concealed courage, warmth and a kind of impish gaiety. He remembered then what the girl had said about the legacy of a happy childhood. Perhaps Jonquil's had not been so happy and he wondered how much blame for this attached to Sybil's determination to dominate her background and how much to his placid acceptance of that domination.

. . . . .

A romantic in a variety of fields, Mr. Sermon was almost an addict when it came to the Public School, or what he thought of in his mind as the Public School and the name 'Barrowdene' conjured up a picture of all that was good and vital and permanent in the system, for while it was old and traditional it had not become the exclusive preserve of the privileged, as had Eton or Harrow. Instead it might be said to occupy a leading position in the second flight and was reputed to provide a good modern education as well as inculcating into boys what most people recognised as 'the Public School spirit', a combination of self-reliance, good manners and qualities of leadership. The fact that he had never taught in a school of this type did not make him in the least envious of those who did. He merely considered them fortunate, like people who won football pools or enjoyed perfect health. As regards schools, in fact, he was a little bit of a snob.

Thus it was that he approached Barrowdene that May afternoon in a state of suppressed excitement, finding it difficult to realise that he was being taken there by the youngest child of the man who had ruled over this establishment for twenty years, a man to whom she referred, somewhat disrespectfully he thought, as 'Fred, a Poppet!'

The buildings occupied a long ridge of moorland about ten miles inland from Kingsbay rising clear above the valley woods that grew on each side of the river. There were one or two white farms within view but no villages, not even a hamlet, and Mr. Sermon recalled then that Barrowdene was famous for cross-country events and that several old Barrovians had made reputations for themselves in Olympic Events in post-war years. Much as Shrewsbury was a rowing school Barrowdene was a steeplechasing school and a glance at the country surrounding it told him why it had so specialised. On all sides of the square-sided steeple, the brown hills rose in great, gorse-grown folds and every cleft was dark with pine and beech through which, here and there, ribbons of silver water moved along little valleys to feed the Dene that flanked the school to the west.

"By George!" he exclaimed, as the old Morris chugged clear of the woods and tackled the steep road to the east drive, "what a wonderful setting for a school! What a marvellous place to live and work in! It's the epitome of every Public School in literature!"

She glanced at him and smiled, finding his enthusiasm rewarding but because she was familiar with the scene and, as a girl, unresponsive to the mysticism of the cult, she did not feed his excitement with a running commentary on the various pitches and outbuildings as they passed between two rows of evenly-spaced beeches to the quadrangle. Only when they reached the war memorial on the edge of the playing field did she say, "Fred holds two services there every year, one on November Eleven and one for the R.A.F. in September. I used to think it was all pious bunk until one day I went in to see him after he had come in from a service. I found him alone and weeping and I didn't think of the services as mere ritual after that! We had twenty-nine boys killed in World War Two and Fred knew most of them by their nicknames! It makes a difference I suppose!"

Her comment helped to establish in his mind a picture of the man whom he already respected. He saw him as a calm, dignified figure of medium height, greying and also inclining to baldness, with a quasi-military erectness and a sternness that could change in an instant to gentleness and understanding. He would, thought Mr. Sermon, be neatly and quietly dressed in blue serge or dark grey, and there would be about him the repose of a village rector wedded to the purposeful air of a professional man of affairs, something between Doctor Arnold and an Edwardian Cabinet Minister, with just a dash of the kind of man glimpsed in launches that follow the eights at Varsity boat-races.

Rachel pulled into a semicircular court outside the chapel and hailed a good-looking seventeen-year-old in blazer and flannels who was carrying an armful of cricket pads.

"Hi, Buster! Is the Head around?"

"Talking to Mr. Raven on the library steps Miss Grey, shall I tell him you're here?"

"Please, and tell him I've brought a friend and we're going in to tea now!" and she led Mr. Sermon into the Headmaster's house, a suite of high-ceilinged rooms that cowered between two greystone blocks three storeys high.

The drawing-room was simply furnished with one or two pieces of mahogany and modern, handmade furniture in soft wood. There were one or two engravings of landscapes and along the length of a shelf a set of Coalport plates, rather late Coalport, thought Mr. Sermon in his character of dealer. The room as a whole was less expensively furnished than he would have imagined but it looked very much lived in, with piles of books and papers on the table and most of the chairs, and some silver on the sideboard that needed cleaning. There was a vase stuffed with foxgloves under one window and the smell of tobacco was so strong that Mr. Sermon sneezed.

"I'm sorry about the fug," said Rachel, opening a window that looked out on to tennis lawns. "Fred's absolutely immune to it. We all follow him round opening windows and sometimes the boys put on a choking act when he comes into a classroom. If smokers really do die of lung cancer he should have died long ago. He gets through about two ounces a day and he uses the same old pipe until it falls to pieces! Sit down and I'll tell Mrs. Brennan there's two for tea, I hope to God nobody shows up!" and she disappeared through a green door leaving Mr. Sermon to take a seat near a window and gulp moorland air while he had the chance.

He was sitting there watching the boys stream in from the nets when he heard a sharp rap and the door which opened to reveal a small, fat, bespectacled boy about thirteen years of age in regulation grey trousers and a grubby unbuttoned jacket. The boy inspected the room cautiously, obviously expecting to find the Headmaster there but when he saw Mr. Sermon he did not seem much surprised and piped, "I've come to say my rep sir! I've got it now I think. Is the Head having his tea?"

"He's about to, I believe," said Mr. Sermon, gravely, and then, curiosity getting the better of him, "To say your *what?*"

"Rep!" said the boy, "I had an extra four lines and I got it all word-perfect but that bit during the rep session! I got stuck on these but I've got 'em now!" and without further preamble he at once began to recite in a shrill, sing-song voice—

"And in the back false Sextus
Felt the good Roman steel
And wriggling in the dust he died
Like a worm beneath the wheel!"

"That's word-perfect, isn't it, sir?"

"I should say it was," said Mr. Sermon, trying not to smile, "but I'm new here, so you'll have to tell me what 'rep' means. Does it stand for 'repetition'?"

"I don't know, sir," said the boy, "I've never thought about it, it's just 'rep'! You learn it in detention, four lines for every ten minutes they've booked you, and it works out about a page an hour. Here . . . I got from there to the cross this week!" and he thrust a small green text-book into Mr. Sermon's hand and pointed to a page scored with heavy pencil marks.

"Do you learn this for punishment?" asked Mr. Sermon wonderingly, and the boy gave him an odd look as if making a casual assessment of his mental capacities.

"Well, you wouldn't learn it of your own accord, would you, sir?" he said, respectfully but still managing to imply that Mr. Sermon had asked a very stupid question indeed. Sebastian was so conscious of this that he was relieved when Rachel suddenly appeared with a loaded tea-tray and asked the fat boy what he wanted.

"He's come to repeat his rep!" said Mr. Sermon, helpfully, "he's got it by heart and presumably has an appointment with the Headmaster."

"Oh rep!" said Rachel, casually. "How many lines, Kirkwall?"

"Twenty-four this week, Miss Grey," said Kirkwall with a certain pride, "but I kept muffing the last four. The Head was pretty sporting, he gave me three chances and several prompts but I couldn't get 'em. I've got 'em now though, haven't I, sir?"

"You have indeed!" said Mr. Sermon and at that moment the Headmaster himself burst into the room, pounced on the impassive Kirkwall with a kind of jocular fury and bawled:

"I'll wager you those four plums on the dish over there against this week's copy of the *Eagle* that you muff them again, Kirkwall! Is it on? Quick now? Are you willing to back yourself?"

Kirkwall's hand shot to his jacket pocket and the astonished Mr. Sermon now noticed the crumpled edge of a magazine protruding above the flap. The boy glanced at a plate on a side-table whereon rested one apple and four plums, blinked, took one pace forward and piped:

> *"And in the back false Sextus*
> *Felt the good Roman steel*
> *And wriggling in the dust he died*
> *Like a worm beneath the wheel!"*

"Splendid!" roared the Headmaster. "Collect and depart! If you go on like this, Kirkwall, you'll be the only man in the world to know *Lake Regillus* right through!"

"Thank you, sir," said Kirkwall solemnly and scooped his winnings into bulging pockets, watched by an astonished Mr. Sermon and an amused Rachel.

"I do apologise for that but at least you've met Kirkwall," said Mr. Grey. "Quite someone is Kirkwall! A poor memory but the makings of a successful businessman. Did you notice how accurately he weighed his chances? Come my dear, introduce me!"

"Don't talk as if you were brilliant at introducing people yourself, Father," said Rachel, kissing him affectionately. "This is Mr. Sermon, also by way of being an usher. At least he was but he came to his senses and threw it up, didn't you, Martin? He was at that first place of mine, Napier Hall and we met again on the beach a fortnight ago. This morning he did me a great service but humanity an injury by saving that little wretch Geraldine from drowning off the breakwater. He's a lot tougher than he looks and can swim like a shark!"

They shook hands and Sebastian welcomed Rachel's raillery for it gave him a moment to recover from his bewilderment. Fred Grey was quite unlike any Headmaster he had met or read about and infinitely removed from the man he had imagined whilst on his way up the drive. To begin with he was gigantic, at least six feet three and as muscular as a navvy. He had hands like a navvy, huge, rough and broad-fingered, and every movement he made with them heightened an impression of enormous vitality. His hair was white and stood up in tufts, the centre tuft being larger than those on each side, suggesting snow-covered mountains with one peak dominating a range. He had a youthful complexion and eyes as mild and brown as his daughter's, his eyes softening an otherwise rugged face. His nose was long, sharp and inquisitive and his jaw square and jutting in a way that suggested bull-headed determination or extreme obstinacy. The impact of his personality was so powerful that Mr. Sermon thought with respect of fat little Kirkwall and the ease with which he had challenged it in the matter of the bet.

Mr. Sermon could see the man as a successful parson of a slum parish but not as a Headmaster who would impress doubtful parents. There was far too much force about him and the fact that it was a cheerful and tolerant force did not make it easy for a stranger to meet him on anything like level terms. Sebastian wondered why father and daughter got along so well, for surely a tornado like Frederick Grey could have little patience with a drifter like Rachel. He said: "Don't be taken in by her tale of heroics, Headmaster! I was swimming near by when the child slipped and I fished her out. It was only her struggles that attracted attention and anyway the whole incident had a disastrous sequel. Your daughter quarrelled with her employers on my account!"

"I've packed it in, Father, they were absolutely insufferable!" confirmed Rachel.

"Ha, ha, I had a notion you wouldn't stick that family long," said Mr. Grey jovially. "I hope this means that they'll withdraw their boy's name from Barrowdene. He was due here when he leaves Prep. School. Didn't like the father! No sense of humour and in a Civil Servant that's disastrous! Pass the sugar, Rachel!"

"I put in four lumps," said Rachel, "if you want to reduce . . ."

"Oh, to hell with reducing, I'm not that much overweight! I refereed the house games all last term, surely that entitles me to a little sugar in my tea, don't you think, Mr. Sermon?"

Sebastian said it did but the Headmaster did not require an answer, preferring to do most of the talking himself. He did this not so much in the manner of a man who resents an interruption, but as a genial company-director might enjoy putting a newcomer 'in the picture'. He talked almost exclusively about the school and Mr. Sermon was surprised to note that he never returned to the subject of his daughter's loss of employment. Perhaps, he thought, he is accustomed to her popping up again and was more than half expecting it. It was Rachel who checked him at last and Mr. Sermon had another insight into their easy relationship, for suddenly she said, "Oh, wait until you show him round, Father! Half the things you're saying don't make any kind of sense to him. He's never been here before and he's only taught in Prep. Schools."

"I should very much like to look round," said Mr. Sermon, "if you can spare the time, that is!"

"Delighted!" said the Head, and obviously meant it. "How long are you with us this time, Rachel?"

"Oh, until the hols, I expect," said Rachel, carelessly. "After that I shall try for a job at the riding stables over at Marley. I mean to have a shot at the vet idea in the autumn, I'll go and tell Mrs. Brennan I shall want my room again." She turned to Mr. Sermon: "Well, thanks for everything, Martin, and I'll get in touch later in the week. Where are your digs in town?"

He wrote down Olga's address and told her that he had taken the house for the season. Then the Headmaster took him by the arm and they began a tour of the school, passing across the quad and beginning with the handicraft section where Mr. Sermon recognised furniture similar to that in the Head's drawing-room.

"Do the boys make those chairs here?" he asked, surprised at the quality of the carpentry.

"They certainly do and we've come on very fast in that direction. We have a first-class man on the job, young feller called Pratt. The boys call him 'Chips' of course. To his face, I believe! What did they call you?"

"'Preacher'!" said Mr. Sermon glumly, and as he said it he felt a faint pang that nobody was likely to call him 'Preacher' again.

They passed through classrooms and corridors to the dining-hall and dormitories and after that the gymnasium and chapel, Grey pointing out the original sections of the great building which he said were mostly late Tudor and drawing attention to the various additions made at peak periods in the school's history. "Curious rhythm about places like this," he said, 'they go up and down rather like old-established business houses. There's been a school here since 1690 and during that time we've been down as low as twenty-five boys and up to over five hundred. We're not far off capacity now and I keep hammering at the Governors to call a halt. Nothing worse than a school that outgrows itself. Four hundred is about right, over that it loses something and becomes unwieldy. Since the war has been a good time for places like this, more money about and a strong prejudice in favour of the medium-priced boarding school. When I came here it was not so long after the slump and we were right down, there was even talk of the County taking us over. Hi—what's the forecast, Cooper?" This remark was thrown at a tall, thoughtful-looking eighteen-year-old, who walked past carrying towel and trunks. "School Captain, Mr. Sermon, but I daren't use his nickname in front of a visitor! He's sorting them out at the pool for Sunday's house-swimming trials, like to watch?"

"I would indeed," said Mr. Sermon, and the three of them fell into step and crossed the corner of the cricket-field towards a pavilion under the lee of the plantation.

"Stormside is the favourite so far, sir," said Cooper, gravely, "but Whitton's have one or two dark horses. That new boy from St. Kitt's is said to have a terrific crawl but I haven't seen him in action yet."

They entered an enclosure surrounded by corrugated iron and for the next half-hour watched the house-trials for free-style, backstroke and breaststroke. As he stood there surrounded by splashing, shouting boys, Mr. Sermon had a strong sensation of belonging, so strong indeed that it produced a curious shrinking sensation in the pit of his stomach. So, he imagined, must Paul Bultitude have felt when the Garuda stone changed him into a boy in *Vice Versa*. 'It's odd,' he said to himself, 'but nothing here is really strange or new to me, not this delightful chap, Grey, or the boys, or the buildings! I think I could find my way about without a guide. God help me, how different it might have been if I had started at a place like this instead of those ghastly private schools that all had the same cabbage-water smell. Damn it, it's not as if I'm bad at my job or hated teaching, real teaching! If only . . .' and then he realised that Grey was asking if he would like a drink before Choral Society practice which the Headmaster had arranged to take that evening. They re-crossed the fields as twilight stole down and in the Head's study he expressed his thanks over a stiff whisky and soda and said how thoroughly enjoyable the visit had proved. Rachel could not be found so the Head escorted him to her car and shook hands warmly, saying: "I know I'm a bit of Barrowdene bore, Sermon, but the truth is, this is the whole of my life and I wouldn't mind living it through again from the day I came here. I shall be sixty-five in December and due to retire but they've given me a five-year extension, thank God! I'm still very fit and I should die of boredom if they retired me now. Maybe at seventy I shall be glad to put my feet up!"

"I don't think you will, Headmaster," said Mr. Sermon, smiling, "and as for boring me, you've got rid of a whole cluster of cobwebs." He hesitated a moment and went on, rather recklessly: "I was fed up with teaching and I suppose I still am with the way it's done in most corners of the educational field, but the thing that strikes me so forcibly about this place and yourself is the optimism you generate! I think I was running from the nuclear bomb as much as anything and it doesn't seem to bother you a bit, Mr. Grey!"

Grey looked more serious than Mr. Sermon thought possible and when he replied the heartiness had left his voice. He said; "It bothers *me* all right, my dear chap, but don't fall into the common error of imagining it bothers youngsters! It doesn't, any more than the losses on the Western Front clouded your dreams at sixteen, Sermon! What one tends to forget after forty is that Mankind is an extremely adaptable animal. After all, he survived the Dark Ages, the Black Death, Passchendaele and Adolf Hitler, and I wouldn't mind wagering he'll find a way out of all this more or less intact. As I see it, one's job as a schoolmaster is to improve his chance in any way one can!"

"How *does* one contribute?"

"I only know one way," said Grey, slowly, "by distilling into every word of instruction a few grains of tolerance aimed at broadening minds and enlarging personal horizons. There's the bell, I must go but you'll come again? Get Rachel to run you over any time you wish and I mean that! Goodbye now!" and he scurried off and disappeared almost at a run, diving into the arch that gave on to the quad.

Mr. Sermon drove slowly down the drive and stalled the engine turning into the narrow lane that led to the main road. While he was groping for the unfamiliar starter a sound came to him from beyond the beeches. It was the Choral Society singing 'Greensleeves', a melody that Sebastian had always loved and one which, for a reason unknown to him, conjured up memories of all that was most pleasant and rewarding in the years he had spent in and about schools. He listened for a few moments, the car half in and half out of the drive and then, feeling almost drunk with nostalgia, he restarted the engine and drove on into the dusk.

CHAPTER SIX

Mr. Sermon Dons
a Uniform ... of Sorts

SEBASTIAN arrived back in Kingsbay about eleven o'clock and left Rachel's car where it would be handy to the garage people. He felt pleasantly tired as he walked up The Coombe to the house on the edge of the links, reflecting that one way and another it had been a very full day. As he entered the gate he promised himself a nightcap, half-hour with the daily paper and then bed. But routine was eluding Mr. Sermon these days.

He was in the act of putting his key into the door when a bulky figure stepped from the shadows and Sebastian saw, with a sharp in-take of breath, the gleam of mountings on a policeman's helmet. A deep voice said: "Mr. Sermon? Mr. S. M. Sermon?" and when the fact was acknowledged, "Do you mind if I step inside a moment, sir? I'd rather like to have a word with you."

Mr. Sermon had a law-abiding man's dread of policemen, any kind of policeman. He opened the door and groped for the hall light with trembling, fumbling fingers and together they went into the sitting-room where Sebastian glanced irrelevantly but guiltily at the armchair he had shared with Olga. The policeman seemed friendly, however, and beamed at him so that Mr. Sermon groped in his pockets and offered him a cigarette, feeling as he did so that he was passing a bribe. The policeman accepted the cigarette, took off his helmet and mopped his brow.

"Warmish night, thunder about," he said, pleasantly.

And what kind of thunder, thought Sebastian gloomily. Then, pulling himself together, "Is it about that business on the beach this morning?" although why he should half-apologise for saving a child's life he could not imagine.

"No, sir," said the policeman, pulling hard on his cigarette, and then, with the air of a man anxious to come to the point, "We . . . er . . . we've been asked to locate someone of your name. Had a call through this morning and just missed you when you left the beach!"

Sebastian's stomach turned over. This was it! This was where Lane-Perkins finally caught up with him! Somewhere in the pocket of this man's tunic was a folded summons to appear in answer to charges of assault and battery. Perhaps it was more serious than that, perhaps Lane-Perkins had sickened and died from the effects of brain lacerations and his attacker was on the point of being arrested for manslaughter. He said, weakly: "What is it? Who . . . who wants me?"

"Your wife!" said the policeman simply and now it was he who sounded apologetic.

Sebastian's heart gave a leap but when it settled again he felt in command of himself. His wife. Sybil. Tracking him down as if he was a common criminal! Great God, this was monstrous—unless of course she was acting as decoy for the father of the injured boy and he passed his hand over his face and found that he was sweating very freely.

"Look here, officer, what is all this? I'm here on a holiday and I'm not in any sort of trouble that I know of. My wife isn't ill, is she? I mean, was it she personally who was enquiring after me?"

The policeman did not seem much concerned with the subject of the enquiry. He relaxed as though glad to be sitting down smoking instead of alone in the dark on his beat.

"Oh, I wouldn't say there was anything to worry about, sir," he said kindly, "but we have these kind of enquiries every now and again. Routine you might say, not even strictly in the line of duty," and he took out his notebook, rubbed his nose thoughtfully and thumbed through one or two pages.

"Here it is, call from a London suburban station. Your home district, I imagine, Wyckham Rose—no, *Rise*."

"That's where I live, or rather where I did live," said Mr. Sermon. "Can't a man take a bit of a holiday without the police having to check his movements?"

"Well, I don't know about that," said the policeman defensively, "but I have to do what I'm told and the Sergeant gave me instructions to pop round here and see if you were the person concerned. I take it your wife was worried about you. Can't think of any other reason she would have asked us to check up, can you?"

"No, I certainly can *not!*" said Mr. Sermon sharply and suddenly his fright subsided and in its place came a fierce resentment that he should be harried in this fashion. "The fact is, officer," he said, "I left rather hurriedly . . . I . . . I needed a holiday and I needed to be by myself for a spell! Hang it, this is a free country, isn't it? I had no idea wives had the right to . . . to ask policemen to check on their husband's movements, unless maintenance comes into it, of course!"

"Well, in a way, I suppose you came into the category of missing persons," said the policeman gently. "Not that I don't blame you for being a bit upset over it. Must have given you a bit of a turn, I reckon. I told the Sergeant tomorrow would do but you know what sergeants are, he said 'tonight' so here I am. We can leave it at that if you like, sir. I can go back and say you're located, in good health and that's all there is to it. Shall I do that? Would you like it that way?"

Suddenly Mr. Sermon felt rather sorry for him.

"Look here, I'm sorry if I sounded rude," he said. "But I do realise you are only doing your duty and there's absolutely nothing personal about my resentment. I suppose it's my own fault in a way, I should have written or phoned and I certainly would have done if I'd realised this kind of thing could happen. As I say, I needed a change and took one. I told my wife I was going and I can't imagine what all the fuss is about or, for that matter, how on earth she located me!"

"I can tell you that," said the policeman with a grin, "but keep it to yourself for my sake. You cashed a cheque a day or two ago and your wife got the address from the bank at her end. Quickest way of locating anyone that is and the confidential lark you hear so much about don't seem to

operate in banks like it should. You'd be surprised how
many maintenance arrears the Justices collect that way but
I don't suppose maintenance comes into your case, does it?"

"No," said Mr. Sermon, emphatically, "it most certainly
does not! But thank you for the tip, I ought to have thought
of that myself!"

The man stood up but lingered. Obviously he would have
been glad to learn more, not as a policeman but as a married
man. Beneath his professional phlegm, Sebastian could see
his curiosity stirring but years of training prevented him from
putting a direct question and unwittingly Mr. Sermon rushed
to his rescue.

"Do you mind telling me what steps you'll take to pass
this information back to its source?" he asked politely.

"Why no, sir," replied the policeman gratefully and
promptly sat down again, stubbing his cigarette and nodding
his thanks for the replacement Sebastian offered. "All that'll
happen now is I shall tell the Sergeant you're in one piece
and any steps you take after that are your concern, not ours.
I suppose he'll have to ring through to Wyckham Rise and
tell them and they'll doubtless pass the information on to
your wife but by that time, you'll have moved on, won't you
sir?" and he winked or came very close to winking.

Mr. Sermon smiled as the pressure of humour cracked the
crust of his resentment.

"I don't know about that," he said, "I'm very comfortable
down here and I've enjoyed myself since I made the break. I
certainly shan't jump on a train and go home if that's what
you mean but I'll promise you one thing, I'll write straight
away and save you chaps any more bother on my behalf!"

The policeman nodded. "Yes," he said, "you'll have to do
that, I reckon!" but made it sound as if he thought it a great
pity.

Mr. Sermon saw him out and went back into the kitchen,
opening the back door and looking out into the night where
stars twinkled over the links plantation and the soft wash of
the sea came to him from the foot of the hill.

What an extraordinary thing for Sybil to do, he thought,
and then, more tolerantly, but was it? Did she think I might
have done away with myself? The possibility intrigued him.
Was she, he wondered, genuinely worried about what had
happened to him and if so what had become of her pride

that she should enlist the police to track him down? It then
occurred to him that she might have received a severe emotional jolt by his abdication, might in fact have changed as
much as he had changed himself over the last few weeks. He
wished Olga was here, feeling that she might know the answer
to this question and thinking of Olga he realised that he was
still far from clear in his mind about his feelings for Sybil.
There was one thing that he was clear about, however, and
the visit of the policeman had helped to get it into sharper
focus. He was not going to return to Wyckham Rise to live
or to Napier Hall to work! He was not, in fact, going to pick
up the fallen threads of his life and follow where they led,
to old age in an impersonal suburb. 'I ought', he told himself,
'to announce this at once and perhaps I should write and tell
Olga also, for surely this decision is vital to both of them!'
It was of Sybil, however, whom he thought most, for he was
still unable to come to terms with her bizarre method of
locating him, almost as though he was important to her after
all. This genuinely astonished him, for never had she given
the slightest indication that he meant very much to her, less
for instance than did the toothy bank clerk she hoped to cast
in her next play!

He stood there thinking a long time, looking up at the stars
and sniffing the salty air and then, as the church clock chimed
the half-hour, he went back into the sitting-room and opened
Olga's bureau, taking a sheet of her printed notepaper and
writing: "Dear Sybil, The police have just been here enquiring
after me. This is ridiculous! I told you I was going off on a
tramp in order to sort things out and I'm perfectly fit, fitter
than I've ever been in my life. I've done a great deal of thinking about everything but I haven't come to any hard and fast
conclusions except about two things. I won't live in London
any more and I won't waste what's left of my life in places
like Napier Hall. I may go into the antique trade or I may
find something else that suits me. I'm sorry if you were worried but it never occurred to me that you would be, perhaps
because you never gave the impression I meant very much to
you or the children. I hope you are all well and I'll let you
know what I intend doing as soon as I know myself."

He read it over and gave some thought as to how to con-
clude the letter. At first he was inclined to write "Sincerely",

but then he thought this sounded rather pettish and in the end he wrote, "Affectionately, Sebastian", sealed and stamped the envelope and put it in his pocket.

He sat thinking for a moment, trying to compose the opening sentences of a letter to Olga telling her all that had happened that day but the shock of the policeman's visit after such an eventful day made composition trying, so presently he gave it up and went to bed.

The telephone rang while he was frying his breakfast and thinking it must be Rachel with instructions about the car he hurried to the phone. It was not Rachel but Mr. Bignall, Town Clerk, who addressed him with mock severity.

"Hullo there! Sermon? You didn't ring, you rascal! Come now, you're too old to be coy. The *County Press* has been on to me about that rescue and they want a picture."

"They won't get one!" said Mr. Sermon, firmly, thinking of what might happen if his picture appeared in the paper. "I've no patience with all the fuss newspapers make over everything nowadays."

"Ah, I'm with you there, Sermon," agreed the Clerk, "and nobody has more right to that opinion than a man holding public office but these fellows are very persistent and they know where you're domiciled, so watch out on your way down!"

"On my way down where?" queried Sebastian.

"To the Council Offices," said Bignall with a trace of impatience, "you promised you'd call this morning."

"Did I? I don't remember. I'll come of course, but why don't we meet for coffee in the town somewhere?"

"Café coffee? Not on your life!" said the Clerk. "I've got the best coffee-maker in the West. She's a dreadful typist but I keep her on for elevenses. How about it then?"

Nobody could ever have mistaken Benjamin Bignall for anything but what he was, Town Clerk of an Urban District Council in the provinces. He was Kingsbay in person and Sebastian felt that over the past four decades not one among the few changes that had taken place in the Urban area had been instituted without his sanction, that no gardener would dare to convert a half-moon flower bed into a circular or rectangular bed without first having conveyed his intention to the Town Clerk through the proper channels, or that no local farmer could have secured by cajolery, bribery or any other means permission to allow a caravan to remain on one of the headlands overnight. Extending his hand across the vast desk, Mr. Sermon felt acutely conscious of the fact that he had called upon the Town Clerk wearing slacks and an open-necked shirt, but Bignall seemed far less patronising than on the previous day and motioned him into a comfortable chair, while a chinless girl crept in with coffee, laid the tray on the desk like an apprentice priestess tending an altar and crept out again. Bignall boomed: "You're not doing anything particular in our part of the world, are you, Sermon? By way of employment, huh? For the next two months or so?"

Sebastian was rather taken aback by the directness of these questions and had the impression that, for a reason unknown to him, the Town Clerk had had his eye upon him ever since he entered the town and took up his abode at Olga's.

"Well . . . er . . . no, not exactly," he stammered, "but I'm really on holiday. I'd heard about Kingsbay but I'd never visited it before, so I . . . I just came!" he concluded, apologetically.

Bignall's eyebrows shot up and he tapped his horsey front teeth with a pencil. Without quite knowing how it had come about, Sebastian realised that what had begun as a social visit had suddenly developed into an interview and at once hastened to make his position clear.

"I'm . . . er . . . I'm not looking for a job," he said, "I have a sort of an agreement with Mr. Sugg, the antique dealer and that keeps me busy on Sundays. Beyond that . . . well . . . I . . . er . . . I mooch about, swimming and . . . er . . . tramping you know!"

He said this as though no one with the faintest regard for propriety would dare to admit to Benjamin Bignall that he was altogether idle.

"Well, we won't beat about the bush," said the Town Clerk, briskly, leaning forward and handing Mr. Sermon his coffee. "Fact is, something unusual has come up and with the season opening I find myself in a difficulty as regards supervision. Now I flatter myself I'm a good judge of character, Sermon! Never had a real wrong 'un yet and I've been engaging men and women since 1908! You *look* like a supervisor. Yes, you look like one, Sermon!"

"A supervisor of what?" asked Sebastian, not unreasonably, he felt.

Mr. Bignall blew out his big red cheeks and the trick made his face look like an inflated pink balloon. "Why the beach, man, the beach," he barked, "what else? I'd hardly offer a man of your education an artisan's position. Up to now we've not needed a supervisor in the real sense of the word, but with the pressure they're putting on me to convert Kingsbay into a miniature Blackpool—and that's what it amounts to, Sermon, that's exactly what it amounts to, mark my words—some kind of official supervision is obligatory! I'm committed to engage a full-time man by early spring next year but a man like that takes finding and vetting and the so-called Progressives on the Council"—he almost sneered the word 'Progressives' so that Mr. Sermon was sharply reminded of Pooh-Ba inviting an insult—"with *that* kind of pressure I'm compelled to appoint a stop-gap and I intend to find a man of my own choice before some irresponsible ass is foisted on me, you understand?"

Mr. Sermon did not but he gathered that somewhere in Kingsbay there existed a faction opposed to Mr. Bignall's tyrannical determination to put the clock back to 1913 and that, for a reason that had very little to do with the rescue, Mr. Bignall not only trusted him but thoroughly approved of him.

"What would this . . . er . . . position entail exactly?" asked Sebastian doubtfully, "and how many hours a day would it require?"

"We have here a number of beach undertakings," said the Town Clerk, now fairly launched. "Some are quite harmless —refreshment huts, deck-chair hire, public conveniences etcetera, but others have been wished on me during a process of infiltration perpetrated by a gaggle of till-hungry trades-men! I don't care to imagine what will be the end of it all," he went on, darkly, as though he envisaged a Kingsbay in the year 2000 A.D. full of brothels and one-armed bandits, "the donkeys and yachting pool and this new-fangled Chil-dren's Zoo they've just opened may seem innocuous to the uninformed, Sermon, but to me they are the thin end of the wedge, sir, and a lethal wedge it will prove if I'm any judge!

"What I'm looking for to tide me over until September is a responsible man to help keep an eye on our various under-takings, to check money, catch litterbugs, restrain vulgarity, oversee the temporary staff in the car-parks and chair-ranks, and, above all, to watch out for hanky-panky in the bathing-huts and band enclosure. Now this isn't an exacting job but it's a job for a gentleman and I'm sufficient of a snob to have you marked down for a gentleman the moment I saw you side-step that yammering crowd yesterday. Moreover—" and he lifted his hand for silence as Mr. Sermon opened his mouth to reply, "moreover, I'll wager you're accustomed to exercising authority. Am I right, sir?"

"I was a schoolmaster for many years," said Sebastian, "but . . ."

"Ha! There! I knew it and it confirms me! You have an additional advantage. No one knows you, you have no local affiliations that might encourage you to turn a blind eye to, say, short-charging the Authority on a parking ticket. Further-more, something tells me you wouldn't condone hanky-panky. You wouldn't, would you?"

"No," said Mr. Sermon, doubtfully, "I don't think I would, but . . ."

"Now the salary I am authorised to pay is a modest one," continued the Clerk. "Suppose we say ten till four, five days a week, at two-pounds-ten per diem, a total take-home, less the insurance stamp, of eleven pounds a week."

"But I know absolutely nothing about supervising beach undertakings, Mr. Bignall," wailed Mr. Sermon, "I hardly know my way around town and I should imagine that quite considerable sums of money . . ."

"As to the topography," said Mr. Bignall ruthlessly, "I shall take you on a personally conducted tour and as to the money —all you have to do is to collect twice a day and pay in at the sea-front Information Bureau in exchange for vouchers. Perfectly straightforward system. Initiated it myself! That fool of a Finance Officer was getting into an unholy muddle, so come on, give it a try, man! If I'm willing to take a chance on you why should you question your abilities?"

"Well, really, I hardly know . . . it's very flattering of you, Mr. Bignall, but I can't help feeling I . . ."

"We'll tour the Foreshore at all events," said Mr. Bignall decisively, rising and pressing a bell that brought the chinless clerk into the office like a figure on a mediaeval clock. "Miss Vesey, I shall be gone precisely one hour. Hold all appoint-

ments! Come, Sermon, and see for yourself what a sinecure
it is!" and he gave Mr. Sermon a prod that projected him
past the priestess and half-way across the outer office where,
so subdued were the staff, that not one clerk looked up from
ledger or typewriter as they passed through the flap counter
and down the stairs to Mr. Bignall's car in the courtyard.

Touring the Foreshore in the wake of Mr. Bignall was
rather like inspecting a front line behind a four-star general.
Wherever they went, U.D.C. employees and tenants sprang to
attention and the Town Clerk treated them all as though, like
the Duke of Wellington, he regarded his troops as the scum
of the earth. They visited the three refreshment huts, leased,
Mr. Bignall explained, to the highest bidders at the annual
auction of beach rights, the yachting pond and paddling
pool, the deck-chair depot, the Sea Angling headquarters
on the jetty, the four public conveniences, the lifeboat station,
the two municipal parking lots, the cove where the donkeyman plied for hire and finally the two bathing-stations desig-
nated 'East End' and 'West End'. At almost every stop, Mr.
Bignall was given respectful attention, with the word 'sir'
interpolated between every other word, but there were three
among the Foreshore staff who were not impressed by the
majesty of the Clerk. The donkeyman seemed to Mr. Sermon
to be short of wits for he bobbed and grinned like a village
idiot when they approached and seemed bewildered when
neither of them ventured to hire one of his mounts. To everything Mr. Bignall said to him he replied: "Oo-ahh, us is in
business!"—a statement that appeared to Mr. Sermon to be
an affirmation of faith rather than of fact, for the dejected
donkeys remained tethered to a stake-rope and such children
as were in the vicinity were occupied in building sand-castles
along the strip of shore where the shingle petered out and
sand stretched as far as the western headland.

"I trust," said Mr. Bignall censoriously, "that you feed the
animals adequately. Some of them seem to me to be rather
undersized, even for children to ride."

"Oo-ahh!" the youth assured him, "us veeds 'em now us
is in bizness, mister!" and he bobbed up and down, whirling
his goad.

"Am I to understand from that," asked Mr. Bignall, "that
if business is poor you under-feed the poor beasts?"

The youth wrinkled his nose and looked to Mr. Sermon for enlightenment, but at this juncture Mr. Bignall, never a patient man, uttered a contemptuous growl and began plodding back to the promenade steps. "You see what I mean, Sermon," he complained, ploughing steadily through the soft sand, "they would have the donkeys and now they've got them the poor beasts stand around from morning until night waiting for hire."

"I expect they'll be in demand during the school holidays," said Mr. Sermon hopefully, but he realised that far from seeking reassurance as regards financial possibilities of donkeys, Mr. Bignall was condemning recent Foreshore policy as a whole. "The busier we are in August the more bitterly I shall oppose progressive policy," he snorted. "Don't imagine that I'm one of those misguided fools who regard beach income as a source of relief for the rates. No, sir! That isn't progress at all but a policy calculated to reduce Kingsbay to the level of every other coastal resort, spa and watering-place, places that have forfeited their birthright and are now caught up in a spiral of competitive tragedy."

Mr. Sermon tried hard to imagine what a spiral of competitive tragedy would look like, or whether or not it could be reduced to a graph on Bignall's office wall but the Town Clerk became more lucid when he reached the esplanade and continued: "What town councillors as a body have overlooked here and elsewhere," he explained, "is that the entire holiday pattern of the country has changed since the introduction of the Welfare State. In the old days the *hoi polloi* couldn't afford Kingsbay and now that they can they don't want it! Most of them would sooner spend a fortnight in gaol than in a place like this! They go abroad, Sermon, they gad about the Riviera and Spain and Switzerland, whereas the people who are looking for a place like Kingsbay, or like Kingsbay was, people on fixed incomes who are victims of the Welfare State, resent the new tempo the town is setting and prefer to do without a holiday altogether! Thus we lose our old visitors without attracting new ones, for today my friend, there is no middle course for coastal resorts. Either they run up their chromium stores, cinemas and dance halls or they stagnate. Yes, Sermon, they stagnate!"

"But I say," protested Mr. Sermon, feeling defensive about

Kingsbay, "this place hasn't stagnated. It's kept its character, it hasn't changed very much since Dickens' time I imagine."

Mr. Bignall stopped and seized his arm, looking into his eyes with an expression that came close to pathos.

"You think so? You really think so?" he said, piteously. "You're not saying that to flatter me? You *mean* it? You *feel* it?"

"Certainly I do," said Mr. Sermon, a little embarrassed by the Town Clerk's emotion. "It's what attracted me the moment I saw Kingsbay, it's got a . . . Peggoty look . . . you remember, those Cruikshank illustrations in early editions of *David Copperfield?*"

"Bless you, Sermon!" said Mr. Bignall fervently. "Bless you for those words of encouragement! Sometimes I despair, sometimes I say to myself, 'Benjamin Bignall, you're an ass! You're an ass to care, to go on kicking against the pricks!' and then I remember how Kingsbay looked to me as a child at the turn of a century, with round bathing-machines drawn up and down the beach by cart-horses, with no sea-front as you see it now, a mile of tarmac garnished with hideous kiosks and shelters, but a mile of sandhills, sir, and with quaint characters at every turn of the street, dead now, dead long ago, God rest them! And then, sir, when I remember that I rededicate myself to the local rapists, the Men of Mammon who have succeeded the gentlemen I served as a younger and more hopeful man!" and apparently braced by his reaffirmation he quickened his step and regained the car for the last two ports of call, the bathing-stations at either end of the half-moon bay.

The two men in charge of these blocks of huts were close relatives, either cousins or brothers-in-law, Mr. Sermon never discovered which, but it was plain that they were engaged in one of those feuds beloved of the writers of Western paperbacks. The intense rivalry between them had existed for as long as the bathing-stations had stood there but Mr. Bignall, who fostered the quarrel as something that fitted into his picture of the original Kingsbay, did not know its origin and did not seem to care.

Mr. Bridgeport, the custodian of the East End, was a savage-looking longshoreman with the appearance of a retired buccaneer, and his rival at the West End was a blubbery individual called Pearcey, with small red-rimmed eyes and a variety of near-pornographic tattoo marks on chest and fore-arms. Each man welcomed the Clerk's visit as an opportunity to complain bitterly of his rival.

"He's at it again, the bleeder!" growled Bridgeport, the moment Mr. Bignall asked to see his register, "lets 'em park anywhere he do! *Free!* Fer Sweet Fanny Adams! I mean, you carn't compete can yer? Down my end they 'ave to pay and wot would *you* do? Suppose you had a motor and wanted a dip, what would you do? You'd go to 'is end, wouldn't you? The end where you could park for Sweet F.A.! I ask you, is it fair now? Is it fair, Mr. Clerk?"

"No, it isn't," said Mr. Bignall pacifically, "and I'll speak to Pearcey about it. This is Mr. Sermon, our new supervisor I hope—Sermon, this is Bridgeport, one of the few local characters left to us."

Sebastian shook the horned palm but Bridgeport was so obsessed by his grievance that he barely noticed him, turning again to the Clerk. "He'll 'ave an excuse ready, you c'n be sure o' that," he snarled. "Biggest bloody liar in Kingsbay Pearcey is, an' not too partickular as to what goes on down there neither! Bathing in the rude they was, so I heard! Three of 'em! Maids too! Stark they was! I 'ad it from Mrs. Gavin at Number Three. She sore 'em! In the rude they was! In the altogether!"

"Oh, come now," said Mr. Bignall, with unexpected mildness, "we went into that last week and I don't see how Pearcey could be blamed. It happened after he'd gone home, by moonlight I understand."

"Ha-ha!" sneered Bridgeport. "If I know Ned Pearcey he was parked somewhere 'andy, Mr. Clerk. Take it from me, he knew about it. Left a key under a stone for 'em, I shouldn't wonder!"

"Well, I'll go along and warn him about the parking," said Mr. Bignall, "I don't suppose you're very busy yet, are you?"

"Busy?" said Bridgeport, and again, *"Busy?* 'Ow can I be, with 'im taking all the trade by lettin' 'em park free?" and apparently despairing of securing municipal justice he strode into his hut and slammed the door.

They had hardly descended from the car at the West End bathing station before Pearcey, noting the direction from which they had come, launched the counter-attack.

"Lettin' 'em get away with it, he is, Mr. Clerk. Seed one yesterday, bold as brass! Seed 'im through that!" and he flourished a squat brass telescope under Mr. Bignall's nose.

"Bridgeport says you're letting people park free at the top of the steps," said the Clerk gently. "Now you know that isn't allowed, Pearcey, you know we have police permission to keep this bit clear."

"All right," said Pearcey sullenly, "when you stop him letting 'em undress on the beach I'll send the free-parkers packing soon as they draws up!"

"Aren't people allowed to dress and undress on the beach?" asked Mr. Sermon mildly, remembering that he had been doing so for the last month and wondering if the brass telescope had ever been focussed upon him.

"Officially no, but strictly speaking we can't stop them providing their towels and wraps are adequate," said the Clerk. "However, come to that, we aren't legally entitled to charge for parking on the highway but we've been doing it for years, not for gain of course but in order to keep trippers at bay." He turned back to the sullen Pearcey. "Now look here, Pearcey, why can't you and Bridgeport make it up over a glass of beer? You've been squabbling like two old hens for twenty years and you must be thoroughly tired of it."

Mr. Sermon noticed that he said this as a sop to the cause of peace but entirely without conviction. It was obvious that he relished the feud and did everything he could to inflame it, for he went on, "It's odd you should complain of people undressing on the beach. Bridgeport told me you not only permitted young ladies to bathe in the nude but left a hut key for them under a stone!"

"That's libel!" roared Pearcey, "I can sue him for it!"

"It isn't libel, my dear chap, but it might be established as slander, providing of course that you could prove he said it, and I wouldn't give evidence against a Kingsbay man. Now listen here, if I undertake to urge Bridgeport to warn off the next beach-undresser, will you promise me to make motorists use the official car park?"

"Mr. Clerk," said Pearcey, soberly, "you always played fair wi' me and I'll do it for you, but you won't have no peace on this here Foreshore till you sack that old soak an' pay someone to wash out his dirty mouth wi' carbolic!"

"Wonderful!" said Mr. Bignall, beaming, "just like Sam-pick-up-tha'-musket, isn't it, Sermon? But don't take these two seriously, they'd be miserable without one another. Now let me introduce you to our new Supervisor, Pearcey. Come, shake hands, man!"

Mr. Sermon was on the point of protesting that he had not yet accepted the post but the Clerk was now looking anxiously at his watch, so Sebastian shook Pearcey's flabby hand and returned to the car after a final and apprehensive glance at Pearcey's telescope.

"What an extraordinary pair!" he said as they drove back along the esplanade and the Clerk swung dangerously into the High Street.

"In my young days," said Mr. Bignall sadly, "almost every-one in Kingsbay was an eccentric, yet the place ran like clockwork. Nowadays everyone here conforms and look at the mess we're in! Well, my dear fellow, I take it you're engaged? Could you start tomorrow?"

But here Mr. Sermon reasserted himself, clinging to the tatters of his independence and saying, "I'll think it over and I'll phone you my answer by five this afternoon."

"Just as you wish," said the Clerk stiffly, "but you have to admit it's a sinecure, man. Come now, you have to admit that!"

"I think I could do it but I'm not yet convinced that I want to," said Mr. Sermon, surprised at his defiance. "By the way, we didn't call at the Children's Zoo."

"It isn't open yet," said Mr. Bignall, "we await the appoint-ment of an attendant, the bunch we interviewed yesterday were useless."

"Suppose," said Mr. Sermon, "that I could put you on to someone, a girl with an impeccable background and a knowl-edge of veterinary work?"

The Clerk looked at him with astonishment.

"You know of such a person?"

"I might," said Sebastian, enjoying ascendancy for a mo-ment, "if I did, would you take my word for her?"

"I'd interview her on your recommendation," said Bignall, cautiously.

"Right," said Sebastian, getting out of the car, "I'll ring you regarding both matters at five sharp!" and he strolled away feeling that he had joined the minority of people who had succeeded in astonishing the Town Clerk of Kingsbay.

∙   ∙   ∙   ∙   ∙

It is doubtful if Sebastian Sermon would have accepted the post of temporary Beach Supervisor of Kingsbay's Foreshore Undertaking had it not occurred to him that here was a chance to share a prolonged joke with Rachel Grey. He was not interested in Rachel in the way he had been interested in Olga. If it is possible for a man of romantic temperament to cultivate a platonic friendship with a pretty woman twenty years his junior then Sebastian's interest in the Headmaster's daughter was platonic. He liked her and she interested him but he was far too modest a man to assume that she was interested in him, except perhaps as a fellow rebel against the twin cults of Respectability and Regular Routine. The idea of seeing her every day, and sharing Kingsbay Foreshore with someone who possessed a strong sense of humour made a great appeal to him and by lunch-time he had telephoned her and told her of Bignall's offer. He was surprised and delighted by her enthusiasm.

"You put in a word for me? You think I stand a chance? Well, you're a poppet, Martin, and I'm terribly grateful. Yes, of course I'd like the job and I don't care what they pay! I'd like it and I'd be damned good at it! I read about the zoo in the *County Press* but it never occurred to me to have a try. Don't you see, if I got a bit of practical experience down there, it might make all the difference when I came to apply for a County Grant to get a vet's training. I'll come over this afternoon—all right tomorrow afternoon then, but ring again tonight, ring and tell me if you're taking the job. Yes, I'll tell Father right away, and you don't have to thank me for introducing you. He loved having you here and he wants you to come over for Sports Day, Saturday week. Goodbye and thanks again, it was wonderful of you!"

Her excitement decided him and he made up his mind to gamble on her getting the job. He rang Bignall accepting the post and then made an appointment for him to see Rachel the following day.

"When are you prepared to start?" asked the Clerk and when Sebastian told him the following morning at ten, he said: "First-class! Good man! Can't stick a shilly-shallier, never could. Deep end and kick out, Sermon! Know where you are and a good example to everyone watching, huh?"

Mr. Sermon smiled as he rang off, reflecting that he was beginning to get the measure of the Town Clerk. 'Come to that,' he said to himself a little smugly, 'I think I'm beginning to get the measure of most people. And situations!'

Yet he was unprepared for the final incident of the day, which was the arrival, about six o'clock, of a pimply youth carrying a small, round parcel bearing the letters K.U.D.C. on its outer wrapping. Wonderingly he carried it into the kitchen and when the brown paper was removed he extracted a very smart, rakish cap with a broad, shining peak, starched canvas cover and the word 'Supervisor' lettered in gold on the band. A note accompanied the parcel and Bignall had written—

"Ordinarily an overseer of your grade would not wear uniform but I felt something must distinguish you from our better-class loafers! Faithfully, B. Bignall."

Mr. Sermon sat staring at the cap while his tea grew cold. At last he rose, put it on, looked in the hall mirror, tilted it slightly and then looked again. He stood quite still for almost a minute, studying the quasi-nautical reflection and then, with a loud hiccough, he began to laugh.

It was many years since Sebastian Sermon had laughed at his reflection in a mirror.

*   *   *   *   *

Mr. Sermon, his canvas cap-cover dazzling white in strong June sunshine, swung along the Promenade in the general direction of the Children's Zoo. He walked with the stride of an Alpine Guide and the uprightness of a man whose past is blameless, whose present is satisfying and whose future is secure from want, oppression and fear.

More than three weeks had passed since he had enlisted as Supervisor of the Kingsbay Foreshore Undertaking and stepped out in public wearing his rakish yachting cap embroidered with the letters K.U.D.C. in gold. He liked the job and he enjoyed wearing the cap. In the old days he would have been ashamed to wear a nautical cap in public, much less enjoy wearing it, but now he had come to terms with himself. He was like a drunkard who, on being told that alcohol will make him blind, replies: "Doctor, I've already seen most things!"

It had been strange at first to find himself in command of half a dozen parking attendants, a lady zoo-keeper, two bathing-station custodians, six deck-chairmen, a donkey-driver and two lavatory attendants, but he soon got used to it. They were far easier to handle than, say, twenty-eight twelve-year-old boys banded together to resist instruction and although each day brought its problems, internal jealousies and occasional cash discrepancies were smoothed out with the minimum of effort and he was aware that his standing was already high at Kingsbay's equivalent of City Hall.

It was a few minutes to eleven when he made his way to the long, one-storeyed building where the zoo was housed.

It was not much of a zoo judged by Regent's Park standards but Rachel Grey, in sole charge of it, much preferred this title to that of 'Pet's Corner', which had been the Foreshore Committee's choice. After all, she had argued, one can hardly call snakes pets and there were several snakes on exhibition. There were also eight monkeys, a fox, a badger, two stoats and several other exhibits, in addition to the Shetland pony, and a variety of dogs, cats, rabbits, hedge-hogs and hamsters. There was also a limited selection of birds, including a toucan and Mr. Sermon's favourite, a grave, bespectacled owl.

Mr. Sermon, in his capacity of sponsor-supervisor, called at eleven every morning and was given coffee brewed on Rachel's Primus-stove in the food store behind the zoo. Sebastian preferred it out here. He had ceased to be a fastidious man but he retained a sensitive nose and in June weather the smell inside the zoo was a little too much for him.

He sat down on a crate and watched her attend to the Primus and as she straightened up he gave her a friendly smack on the bottom, giving way to one of the little weaknesses he had agreed to tolerate in himself since donning the rakish yachting cap.

"That's enough!" she said, but without resentment. "I never can seem to convince men that my behind is not public property."

"It's pure symmetry," he said, lightly, "symmetry in relation to the narrowness of your waist. Breadth of beam such as yours and emphasised as it is by the kind of garments you wear, must surely constitute an eternal temptation to men. Fashions affect the impulse. I feel sure the late Victorians were tempted, whereas few men could have been disposed to wallop a Tudor wench wearing a what was it—farthingale or stomacher? It was right out again in my young days, when girls wore tube-like dresses designed to disguise their shape but now, with all these tight jeans on display—why I believe I could write an essay on it!"

"I believe you could, you dreadful old man!" she said, handing him his coffee and sitting down on a crate close by. "By the way, talking of your accomplishments, Father was impressed by your off-the-cuff lecture on the American Civil War last night. He gets a real kick from your visits and looks forward to Saturdays. I suppose schools go a bit stale after half-term, even for fanatics like him and you."

"I doubt it," he said, lighting two cigarettes and giving her one, "if ever there was a man who enjoyed his work that man is your father. And I doubt if he looks forward to Saturdays as much as I do. There's a wonderful atmosphere over at Barrowdene and Fred Grey is the source of it. I wonder if the men on the staff know how lucky they are?"

"Do you ever get a yen to be back on the treadmill, Martin?"

He thought for a moment. "Yes," he said finally, "when I'm up at your school I do, but if I ever returned to teaching it would have to be at a place like Barrowdene, with an intelligent man in charge, someone who has the knack of marrying tradition to a modern approach."

"Gilbert's coughing again," she said, changing the subject. "I gave him his medicine but he seems very depressed since he was recaptured."

"Let's take a look at him," said Sebastian and went into the zoo tilting his cap at the owl and scratching a leaping dog under its chin. The cages and glass cases were ranged along each wall with a narrow corridor in between. They were all, he noted, spotlessly clean and the animals looked more like the Robinson Crusoe family than captives. There was hardly one of them you did not want to stroke and spoil. 'She's wonderful with them,' he thought, 'and getting her down here was a brainwave on my part! She's happy too, a great improvement on the harassed kid I met looking after that awful

Geraldine on the beach!' and he called to her: "Rachel! I must go, I'll see you at the 'Wagon-Wheel' ten after one!"

They usually ate lunch together in a chintzy little café near the West End bathing-station. The holiday season was now in full swing and the café proprietress, a Miss Anson, reserved them a table each working day. He went out into the bright sunshine and turned eastward towards the larger of the head-lands. As he approached the parking ground he noticed a group of people congregating outside the nearer of the two public conveniences and seeing him, Travers, the attendant, detached himself and trotted across.

"I was looking out for 'ee, Mr. Supervisor, hoping you'd show up! Emmie Slater is in a rare ol' fix, 'er is! One o' the ladies is stuck!"

"Stuck? How do you mean, stuck?"

"Far side o' the turnstile. Locked in! Tiz they forrin coins again an' Em says customer's got 'erself to blame but it hain't no good arguing the toss till us gets her out is it? Us is busy too, proper queue there is. Us've had to shuttle 'em over to the other one further along the front."

Mrs. Emmie Slater, the female attendant, was standing at the entrance of the winding path leading from the esplanade to the sunken brick-built building marked 'Ladies' but at once Mr. Sermon found himself in a difficulty. Could he, even in his capacity as Beach Supervisor, walk boldly into a 'Ladies', or would the investigation have to be made by a female? His doubts were soon resolved for Mrs. Slater, a red-faced and rather aggressive woman, called out: "Jammed it is! No good rattling an' thumping! Serve her right! Been waiting a long time to catch one of 'em, I have. Go on in an' see for your-self, Mr. Inspector. A good mind to send for the police, I am!"

Sebastian had very little confidence in Mrs. Slater and decided to silence her before she succeeded in attracting an even larger audience.

"Do stop making a scene, Mrs. Slater," he said severely, "and leave this to me! Is there a key to the coin box inside? If so, give it to me at once! Travers!"

"Yessir?"

"Go across to the boatshed and chalk on a board 'Tem-porarily out of order' and come back here with it straight away!"

"Yessir! Right away, sir!" said Travers and shot off as Mrs.
Slater sulkily surrendered her key. Bracing himself and trying
to look as if he did this kind of thing every day of the week,
Sebastian marched down the winding path and approached
the turnstile that did duty for a door. He was surprised to
find the lavatory in semi-darkness. The light was switched off
and the small frosted window was screened by overgrown
laurels. Peering through the grille, however, he observed a
well-dressed woman standing well back against the further
wall. He hesitated to say 'Good morning!' so he compromised
with—"I'm the Supervisor, madam! I'll have you out of here
in a moment!"

He heard her give a stifled exclamation, a protest to his
sex no doubt, but turned aside and unlocked the coinbox, slipping the money into his pocket. Travers was right, a coin
roughly the size of a penny had failed to clear the slot and
it was stuck fast, a fraction of its edge protruding. The woman
edged forward and Mr. Sermon, regarding her out of the corner of his eye, noticed that she was middle-aged and pretty
in a fluffy kind of way. She said:

"I . . . I didn't realise it was a foreign coin, it must have
been passed to me as change. That dreadful woman out there
declares I did it deliberately! As if one would—I mean—as if
one would?" and her voice indicated that she was on the edge
of tears.

"Now, just keep calm, madam, and don't worry about the
wretched penny," said Mr. Sermon. "I may be able to do this
myself and save everyone a lot of fuss, but I can't do anything unless you stand away from the bars and give me the
benefit of what light there is."

She stood back against the cubicles and watched him
tensely as he wrestled with the coin.

"Excuse me, I'll have to take my coat off," he said, but
at that moment a plump, 'teenage girl rushed down the steps
at the head of a tumbling group of girls and cannoned into
him, leaping back with a shriek and shouting: "Stop! Stop!
It's a Gents!" a cry that produced a chorus of squeals and
sent the intruders tumbling out again with Mr. Sermon at
their heels.

"For goodness' sake, Mrs. Slater," he protested, "I told you
to keep everybody . . . !"

But suddenly he stopped dead, dumbfounded at the sight of

a girl in the forefront of the group standing on the pavement. He was looking into the startled face of his own daughter, Jonquil, and as his brain registered this fact he had an even greater shock, one that sent him diving below like a sub-mariner spotting attacking aircraft. "Great God!" he said aloud, "Jonquil! And two yards behind her, Sybil!"

With a tremendous effort he collected himself.

"Er . . . you er . . . wouldn't happen to have a torch in your bag, madam?" he asked and it seemed to him as though he was listening to a playback of his voice on a tape-recorder.

"No, but I've got a lighter," said the woman, "will that do?"

"A lighter?" He had a lighter himself and took it out, hold-ing it inside the coin-box and flicking the wheel half a dozen times before the small flame lit up the interior of the box.

"I . . . I really need a screw-driver," he said, less than half his concentration directed to the mechanism and that only held there by an effort that made him sweat.

"I've got a nail file," said the woman helpfully and pushed a strong, bonehandled file between the bars. He thanked her and held the lighter in his left hand while with his right he jabbed the point of the file between the lower edge of the coin and the small spigot against which it had jammed. To his relief, the spigot gave a little leap and the coin dropped into the box.

"You've done it!" said the woman excitedly. "Oh, you are a nice man, you really are!" and she swung back the grille and ran at him with such enthusiasm that he would not have been surprised if she had clasped him in her arms and show-ered him with kisses.

As a matter of fact he would not have been surprised by anything at that particular moment. An earthquake or tidal wave would have found him submissive and resigned, inca-pable of further shock, so that when, still gibbering her thanks, the fluffy little woman pulled open her bag, whipped out a ten shilling note and stuffed it into his hand he could do nothing but stand there in his shirtsleeves and gape after her as she tripped up the steps to be greeted by an ironic cheer. He thought: 'This is terrible! This is absolutely farcical. What are they doing in Kingsbay? And what evil fate directed them here at this precise moment when I was coatless in a ladies' lavatory?'

Mrs. Slater restored a sense of reality to his nightmare by appearing round the bend in the steps and saying: "Are you all right Mr. Inspector? You aren't stuck are you? There's someone here asking for you."

He lifted his hand in a hopeless gesture and then, dragging on his jacket, turned towards her and began to climb. He still held the woman's nail file in one hand and the lighter in the other and when he emerged on to the promenade the little woman was there, asking for the file and saying over and over again, "It was awful! I thought I was there for the night and I would have been but for him. It was dreadful! I've always hated those things and somebody ought to abolish them by law!" but when he looked left and right there was no sign of Jonquil or Sybil and for a moment he thought he must have been the victim of an hallucination. Then Travers appeared with his chalked board and Mr. Sermon noted with detachment that he had spelled 'Temporarily' TEMPRY. He said, "It's all right now, tell Mrs. Slater I've emptied the box and I'll pay it in later." And at that moment he saw them again, sitting side by side on a Corporation seat about twenty yards nearer the Bowling Green.

They were both looking directly at him and in the eyes of mother and daughter was agonised despair, as though they were witnessing his hanging. For a good ten seconds he returned their stare and then, as upon rubber legs, he tottered towards them, more than three shillings-worth of pennies jingling in his pocket.

CHAPTER SEVEN

Mr. Sermon Journeys On,
Wifeless
But in Good Company

JONQUIL made a sudden decision.

"I'm going to the hotel, Mother," she announced. "I'm sorry but I don't want any part of this, it's too awful for words!" and she clacked off in her high-heeled shoes, ignoring her mother's cry of protest. Then Sebastian approached slowly and looking after his daughter's receding figure said, quietly, "Let her go, we can talk better without her, Sybil. Would you . . . could you do with a drink? Or a coffee, perhaps? There's a place over there."

"For goodness' sake, take that . . . that dreadful cap off!" she burst out and he obediently removed it, tucking it into his pocket and sitting beside her.

"I'm just as surprised to see you, Sybil," he said. "You got my letter I imagine? I must say you've been very quick getting here."

"I didn't get any letter," said Sybil stonily and he seemed mildly surprised.

"You didn't? I posted one the day before yesterday, when did you leave?"

"Yesterday morning."

"Then it must have arrived by midday post," he said, adding rather ruefully, "I would have written before Sybil and I mean that but I was very angry about the police calling. You shouldn't have done that, you should have known me better than that!"

"Why should I?" she was angry now and had recovered her composure. "Why should I know you any better? You stalk out of the house leaving me without an inkling of whether you're alive or dead! You wrote, you say, but even if you did it was after many weeks without a letter and now that I have found you, what are you doing? Superintending public lavatories—*you*—who were supposed to be so shy that you could hardly exchange a sentence with anyone I asked into the house. I can't pretend to understand what's happened to you or what's driven you to . . . to humiliate me in this dreadful way. I can only think you must be ill . . . or . . . demented or having a breakdown of some kind." She looked at him closely, noting his strained expression and relented. "Of course, if you are ill it's quite a different matter . . ."

"I'm not ill, Sybil, and I told you so in my letter. As a matter of fact I've never felt better in my life and I've never been happier either!"

He saw from her expression that this angered her and added, "However, that doesn't mean I'd willingly cause you any distress but it's the truth. Whatever's happened to me since I left home has been good and in a way a great deal has happened, though I can't expect any of it to impress you very much."

"I'm quite sure it wouldn't," she said. "And you can hardly expect me to congratulate you on your choice of profession!"

"Well, that isn't quite what it appears," he said, smiling a little. "I was only using my initiative to help someone and after all, that's what I'm paid for, that and to keep an eye on the staff."

"What staff? For whom do you work?"

"For the Urban District Council," he said simply.

"But why—why? You aren't penniless, are you?"

"Not me!" he rejoined, with some satisfaction. "I left home with eleven pounds ten in my pocket and now I've got over two hundred, not counting the forty odd I paid out to Olga of course."

"Olga?"

"Olga Boxall, whose house I rented but you must know about that if the bank told you of the cheque."

"I was on my way there just now."

"You wouldn't have found anyone there, Olga is away."

The information relieved her slightly but she thought it strange that he referred to his landlady by her Christian name.

"Who is this Olga?"

He looked at her calmly, hiding a smile. He was over his moment of panic now and surprised to discover that he still held the initiative. Not only had she come searching for him but she was concerned about the company he kept and this was something new in their relationship.

"I've just told you, she's my landlady but she went off on a Mediterranean cruise soon after I got here. You see, Sybil, I've made lots of friends and that's something I was never able to do before. I run an antique shop on Sundays and the Town Clerk is delighted with me. I've become friendly with the Headmaster of a famous school near here and I go there on Saturdays. Yes, one way and another I suppose I've changed quite a bit."

It made her feel absolutely helpless sitting there listening to his boasts as though she was his mother and he was assuring her that he had settled to a new routine, and that she was not to worry because he was a big boy now well able to look after himself. It was as though she wasn't talking to him at all but reading a long, egotistical letter, a wish-you-were-here from a bustling holiday centre and posted to a dull home town where nothing ever happened.

She passed a hand across her brow and he regarded her anxiously. "You're feeling all right now, aren't you, Sybil? I mean, you've been keeping well, you and the children? You look wonderful, I don't think I've ever seen you looking so young and attractive!"

He spoke sincerely for she did look attractive and certainly nothing like her true age in a trim biscuit-coloured suit and spotted silk blouse, although privately he doubted whether the kind of hat she was wearing had ever been seen on Kingsbay's promenade.

Her shoes, gloves and handbag were obviously very expensive accessories and he reflected that she had always been a woman of excellent taste, with an unerring instinct as to what suited her age and figure. The latter, he thought, had improved since he last saw her, for she seemed much slimmer and he wondered if she could have lost weight through worry. He felt a little ashamed of the satisfaction her presence here caused him, for there remained in him no trace of the rancour that had driven him from the house. Instead he was able to look at her with a steady, half-amused affection that would have needed very little encouragement to develop into something more demonstrative. He thought: 'It's very strange, but she's not in the least like the high priestess of the Wyckham Rise Operatic and Dramatic Society that I remember! Who would have dreamed she would come posting down here before she even received my letter? And who would have imagined that she would go to such pains to find me when she had every excuse for waiting for me to make it up?' Then it crossed his mind that perhaps there was a more sinister reason for the sacrifice of her pride, perhaps she had sought him out for the purpose of putting an end to their marriage, and he made the rather surprising discovery that this would upset him very much—that the possibility of losing her depressed him more than he had any right to be depressed, particularly if Olga was taken into consideration. Yet even in her presence he felt no conscience prick regarding Olga, or for walking out on her that night, for it seemed to him that their future as man and wife now lay with Sybil rather than with him. He had initiated the change of direction and was resolved that such change must at all costs be maintained, yet, if she was prepared to adapt herself, their marriage might not only be saved but infinitely strengthened and with this possibility in mind he said, bluntly:

"Look here, Sybil, let's go across to the café and have lunch together. It's quiet there and I can get the alcove seat. It's high time we had a talk about our future and I imagine that's what brought you here!" She made a gesture of refusal but he went on, "Dammit, we can't plan the rest of our lives on a Council seat and when you've had a meal we'll go back to my place and spend the rest of the day getting things straight if you wish. Where are you staying?"

"At that big hotel over there, the Royal Albert, I think it's called. It's quite dreadful!"

"Well, I know one thing, I don't want Jonquil in on this,"

he said, decisively. "She can kick her heels for a bit and we'll call her up later."

Then she knew that despite the shock of meeting him again in these shameful circumstances she still wanted most desperately to come to terms with him but that this was not nearly so easy as she had imagined it would be, for whereas she was by no means sure of herself, he was maddeningly self-possessed and had in fact acquired an entirely new personality during his brief absence, so that it was like two people walking the same path in the dark, one possessing first-class vision, the other near-sighted and conscious of faltering steps. As they moved off along the sea-front a ravaged old man in a blue jersey saluted Sebastian and growled: "Marnin' Mr. Supervisor!" and Sebastian returned his salute with a careless lift of the hand, like an officer crossing a parade ground. It was not, she reflected, the kind of salute ordinarily given by a man in charge of public conveniences.

They entered the 'Wagon Wheel' café where a woman in blue overalls greeted him with restrained enthusiasm.

"Oh, you're early, Mr. Sermon, but I've saved your corner," and she piloted them to an alcove made by a bow window at the far end of the room. As they ate Sebastian talked about the town and seemed to display enthusiasm for it.

"You mustn't judge it on that barn of a 'Royal Albert'," he said earnestly. "That place is badly managed but Kingsbay as a whole has a very definite policy. It sets out to provide something quite different from the usual resort, to preserve what was calm and cosy about these kind of communities in the last century but attract a select type of visitor. You can call it stuffy if you like but it has a wonderful effect upon the nerves. Down here nothing seems urgent. People still give value for money and there's a dignity about life. It isn't a scurrying from point to point with an air of let's-get-all-we-can-out-of-'em-and-be-damned-to-'em, like most seaside towns in summer."

"Do you intend making a career of this . . . this beach inspecting?" asked Sybil presently and he laughed.

"Good Lord, no!" he said, "this is only a stop-gap! I was talked into it by Ben Bignall, the Town Clerk and promised to tide him over until September. They're getting a professional on the job next year but I haven't found the job difficult or worrying. Come to that I don't find anything very difficult nowadays. Six weeks ago, if anyone had asked me, I should have told them that the only way I could earn a living was as a schoolteacher but now I could earn enough to keep me any number of ways. I suppose I've developed confidence in myself and, anyway, you remember how I always hated cities and suburbs."

"You mean you intend to stay here? For good? In this town?"

"Not necessarily here, but somewhere like it. Listen Sybil," he began to speak rapidly now as though he might lack the resolution to say what was in his mind if he paused to choose his words, "why don't you make a break too? What future is there in the kind of life we were leading in that suburb? All those people who lived near us, who shared our kind of life, what do they amount to, any of them? They're all trying to be someone they've dreamed up and it isn't until you get away from them that you realise there's a whole world outside where most people accept life as it is and themselves for what they are. I became so absorbed in the microscopic life of a prep. school that I came to accept the spurious for the real and we lost contact with one another in the process. We never even talked like this, frankly and without regard as to what one ought or ought not to say. We could have been happy enough if we'd broken the circle but it never occurred to us to break it because none of the people around us did. I think I've reached a cross-roads, Sybil, and at last I know where I'm going, the kind of things I want to do, and what kind of person I want to be in the time left to me. You can call it drift if you like but at least it's drift on a free range and not down a groove about two inches wide!"

"How was I to know that you hated it all?" she asked, suddenly. "You didn't say so, you seemed happy enough at home. I didn't nag you into sharing my kind of life. I always let you follow your own inclination."

"But don't you see, Sybil, that's no way at all for a married couple to live. We didn't mean anything to one another and all the time, without even knowing it, I was shrivelling into a husk of a man. You must see a difference in me now! I'm a different kind of person altogether!"

"Yes, you are," she said, slowly, "so different that I can't even begin to understand you, Sebastian. All this talk about a change of air and scene and occupation doesn't sweep me off my feet however, I know very well that I couldn't go rural to please you or anyone else! And anyway, you're obviously content to lead a kind of vagabond life, devoid of all social contacts. You can't expect me to share that at my time of life!"

"Damn it, I'm not asking you to . . . to cut yourself off from everything you like, Sybil. All I want is that you should break free of that bloody suburban set. Look, I could get a steady job down here, a job I enjoyed and could do well, a business perhaps, anything, but that isn't important because you don't have to live on what I bring home on pay days. And where we live isn't important either, so long as it isn't in a city or a suburb, like Wyckham Rise. I wouldn't ask you to move into an insanitary country cottage or anything like that! There are some first-class properties about here that people like us have spent a lifetime saving to buy. But this is beside the point too, the vital thing is we'd be starting fresh and free from clutter and if we built the kind of marriage I want to build we shouldn't need to rely on outside interests and acquaintances! I'd be very happy indeed to give it a go!"

"Well, I wouldn't," said Sybil, "and I don't think that's unreasonable of me! Think what you're asking me to do. You're asking me to sell up, to leave a house and district I like, to turn my back on every friend I've got and lead an altogether different life in a place that may be nice enough for a week's holiday but wouldn't suit me at all as a permanent home. It's too big a change and too big a revolution. I like nearness to London, to decent shops and a decent hairdresser. I like my amateur work and the people it brings into my life. If you hate where we live as much as you say you do, I'd . . . I'd be willing to compromise, I'd sell the house and look for another further out, somewhere like Thresham or Bickley or even Sevenoaks but certainly not here among the chaw-bacons! I'm not that kind of person and it would be silly to pretend that I am or could be. I value our marriage as much or more than you pretend to, Sebastian. After all, it was you who put such a strain on it by storming out of the house in the middle of the night and leaving me to trace you via a bank and a police station!"

She was speaking off the cuff and not one statement was

the result of reflection over the lonely days and nights that
had preceded this reunion, yet, in so far as she was aware
of what she wanted, it was an honest response and therefore,
to his mind, a final one. He realised then that they really
had grown away from one another and that the longer they
lived the more widely their paths would diverge until, any
moment now, they would pass out of hailing distance and
push on alone, or with somebody who happened to be going
their way. Perhaps this was the best thing that could happen
but it seemed a sad enough ending when a little pliability on
her part would have given them a chance to start out afresh.
She was her old self again now, the Queen of the Amateurs,
cool, detached, and mistress of her emotions. He had been
touched by her when she looked bewildered and helpless on
the sea front and had even thought how exciting it might
be to win her all over again but now the impression of girlish
uncertainty had gone and she was the woman she had been
on the night he left home, the woman who had married
him on the impulse because she did not seem to be able to
make up her mind which of the over-confident young men
she wanted as a husband.

She stood up and he followed her to the door. Her abruptness irritated him and when she said, stiffly, "I should like
to pay my share, Sebastian!" his temper flared up and he
snapped, "Don't be so damned silly, Sybil!" and flung down
a pound note, walking into the street without waiting for the
change.

"Look here," he said, turning back for a final try, "let's
go home to my place and talk. We can't leave things like
this. Or, if you prefer it, let's get the car and drive out
somewhere?"

"I think we've said everything we have to say for the
time being," she said quietly. "If you are as happy as you
seem to be down here working as a beach inspector then good
luck to you, Sebastian! I mean that, I'm not sneering at you
—but it surely proves we no longer have a thing in common
and talking won't bring us together. We might as well shake
hands and part like civilised human beings!"

He winced at the word 'civilised', recognising it as a suburban cliché almost invariably applied to the man and
woman whose marriage had worn threadbare and who had
agreed to separate without acrimony. It was a much misused

word. The final parting of a man and woman who had lived together for twenty years was not 'civilised', no matter how much people like Sybil persuaded themselves that it was.

"What do you intend doing, then?" he asked sourly.

"I suppose that depends very much on you, Sebastian."

"How on me?"

"Well, I shan't take any steps to divorce you until I think you've had long enough to arrive at a final decision. That doesn't mean, however, that I'm prepared to wait indefinitely! If you decide to act sensibly and come home with me now I dare say we could pretend that it had never happened at all."

It staggered him that his plea had made so little impression upon her and he said, wonderingly, "You . . . you don't even begin to understand what's happened to me, do you? I believe you still think your money is important to me and that I can be collected like a . . . like a stray dog and taken home to be scolded and forgiven for running away!"

"I think you're making it far more complicated than it is," she said coolly. "The point is you would be welcome now but in the end I might have to take certain advice."

"You might be very surprised at the 'certain advice' given you!" he retorted, battling with a temper flayed by her polite arrogance. "After all, I've offered you a home down here and within limits a wife is legally obliged to live where her husband works!"

"Not this wife," she said grimly, her glance sweeping up the busy High Street, "and within limits can mean different things to different people!"

He made one last effort, taking her by the arm and turning her towards him. He had forgotten that holiday-makers were passing up and down the street and that some had to move round them as they stood in the middle of the pavement immediately outside the café.

"Sybil, I can't let you go like this! If you took all that trouble to find me and come down here on the off-chance, then it must mean you . . . !"

"Hullo there! I missed you! They told me all about the spectacular deliverance from the Bastille . . . !"

It was Rachel Grey, shouting to him from the kerb where she had succeeded in parking the Morris in a tiny space between a van and a private car. It was obvious that she did not connect him with Sybil for she bounded out of the car and bustled across, radiating high spirits.

Her sudden appearance confused Mr. Sermon. He had forgotten their luncheon appointment and he saw Sybil give the girl one of her quick, appraising glances, noticing also that Rachel recoiled from the inspection, as though contrasting Sybil's smart clothes with her own jeans and sweater.

"I'm sorry," she said, stepping back, "I didn't realise you were with somebody," and she looked so awkward that Sebastian spared something of his own embarrassment to feel sorry for her.

"This is my wife, Rachel," he said gravely, "Sybil, this is Miss Grey who runs our Children's Zoo. Her father is the Headmaster of the school I was telling you about."

"How do you do?" said Sybil, striking a neat balance between disinterested acidity and common politeness. So she might have responded to the arrival of a breathless and untidy schoolgirl introduced into the house by her daughter Jonquil.

Rachel reacted like a schoolgirl. She did not exactly say 'Ooo-er!' but a passer-by could have been forgiven for thinking she had. The exclamation, however, was not without its use for it revived Sebastian's sense of humour and he said: "If you're jumping to the conclusion that it was my wife I rescued from the ladies', Rachel, you're wrong. That would be stretching coincidence too far! Sybil arrived when the actual victim was tipping me a ten shilling note for services rendered!"

"You don't mean to say she coughed up ten shillings!" said Rachel, forgetting Sybil for a moment. "My God, that must be a record in Kingsbay. They're notoriously mean with small change around here," she said, turning back to Sybil but then Sybil's expression froze her exuberance and she said, awkwardly, "Have . . . er . . . have you had lunch?" and when Sebastian nodded, "Fine! Well . . . er . . . if you'll excuse me, I'll pop in and get mine, I'm famished!" and she disappeared into the café without saying goodbye.

"What an extraordinary young woman!" said Sybil. "The daughter of a headmaster, you say?"

"Yes," said Sebastian, crisply, "but a very eccentric headmaster I'm afraid, not in the least like the Reverend Hawley!" They walked silently down the High Street and along the promenade towards the Royal Albert. He felt more deflated

than at any time since he had left home and this was not
only because their reunion had been such a failure but
because he sensed he had once again lost the initiative and
had been driven to defend himself like a child called to
account by a disapproving parent. It was odd, he thought,
how a single hour with Sybil could puncture a man's self-
esteem and reduce his stature sufficiently to pop him back
in a place like Napier Hall. He was sure that she did not
intend to have this effect upon him, but she had and was
obviously prepared to take advantage of it for when they
reached the hotel she stopped and offered her hand.

"I don't think there is much point in you seeing Jonquil.
She's not the easiest of children and she was very upset
when you came out of that place wearing that cap!"

"I don't see why you all want to make such a bloody fuss
over my cap!" he burst out. "It's only a badge of office
and most people wouldn't find anything ridiculous in it! The
fact is Sybil, you and Jonquil are a couple of snobs and I
suppose that's one of the snags we foundered on!"

"Yes," she admitted, quietly enough to make his outburst
seem childish. "I am a snob! I was born one and it's far too
late to do anything about it. One would imagine," she went
on, looking round in a general way and lifting the conversation from its personal groove, "that in a remote provincial
town like this old-fashioned prejudices would have survived
the Welfare State but I see that this isn't so. If anything, the
general levelling process has made more progress here than
it has at home. Well now, I expect you've got to get back to
your duties so I won't detain you any longer!" and somehow
made it sound as if she was keeping a conscientious workman
from his sewage pipes. "You'll write again I suppose and
perhaps you had better give me your full address. I'll write
it down before I forget," and she extracted a tiny address
book and propelling pencil from her handbag and waited,
pencil poised over the page marked 'S'.

Sullenly Sebastian repeated his address and she wrote it
down in her small, careful script reserved for addresses and
telephone numbers. A kind of smouldering rage took possession of him and he longed to shatter her studied detachment but realised that there was absolutely nothing to be
gained by a public quarrel on the steps of Kingsbay's largest
and stuffiest hotel.

"You won't change your mind and stay a day or two, Sybil?"

"No, Sebastian, I won't, I realise now that it was rather unfair of me to descend on you like this. We shall start back in an hour or so but there is one more thing, I talked on the telephone to that man Hawley before I left and he told me he had managed to straighten things out at school. If you want to take a term's holiday you can, without vacating the post. He told me to tell you that."

"I'm damned if I'll return there!" growled Sebastian, "and you can tell him so if you like!"

"It's for you to tell him," said Sybil. "I shan't have any reason to contact him will I?" and she smiled, as though enjoying her pitiful little triumph and walked briskly up the steps to the swing doors.

●   ●   ●   ●   ●

It was a week before he could put Sybil out of mind and begin to enjoy life again. For several days following her visit his new friends found him taciturn and listless and during this period he was grateful for the company of Rachel, the only one among his Kingsbay associates who had actually met his wife and been able to form an independent estimate of her character. Rachel's estimate was not a flattering one and she announced it with characteristic outspokenness.

"I don't know why the hell you're mooning over the woman, Martin," she said bluntly, as they faced one another across the identical café table where he and Sybil had lunched. "Physically I thought her attractive and she has a dress-sense I envy but she just isn't *you* any longer. She may have been once but she isn't now, and sooner or later you'll have to face the fact. Damn it, I had to once and now I'm better for it, at least, I hope I am! I dare say you've got old-fashioned ideas on divorce, so if I was in your shoes I wouldn't do anything at all, I'd just wait for her to make the first move. Surely even people of your generation don't find anything sordid in divorce on grounds of desertion, or do they?"

"But I haven't deserted her, not in the legal sense," argued Sebastian. "I've changed my job and my place of residence, and I've invited her to join me. Legally I'm in the clear, particularly as she enjoys two thousand a year in her own right!"

He had never mentioned Sybil's income to her before and Rachel was staggered by the figure.

"You ran out on two thousand a year?" She looked at him admiringly. "Then, that surely proves my point, you and she are incompatible. *She* wouldn't run out on five hundred! Come to that, I don't think I would! You're absolutely unique, Martin, the only middle-aged man I've ever met who doesn't show evidence of Shelley's 'world's slow stain'!"

He reflected that she had her father's childlike ability to select certain aspects of life, enjoy them to the full and neatly side-step everything that threatened more than sixty seconds' depression. Suddenly he had the urge to confide in her, to explain not only the nature of his quarrel with Sybil, and the flashpoint of the explosion that had blown him westward, but also his indeterminate *affaire* with Olga Boxall. She listened carefully and he was surprised that he could tell her so much without embarrassment.

"What the devil gets into these women I wonder?" she mused after he had tried to explain Olga's motives for insisting on a prolonged separation. "One would suppose that life was five hundred years long and they had all the time in the world to enjoy it! How old is she? Thirty-three you say? Well, she wants her head examined and in a way she's as bad as Sybil, she just doesn't deserve luck with men. Imagine that! A virgin until thirty-three, then finding a sweetie like you, then running out on him! But maybe I'm wrong, maybe she's a natural spinster!"

"She isn't anything of the kind!" protested Sebastian stoutly. "She's a very affectionate woman, so much so that I sometimes think it was damned unfair of me to take advantage of her."

Rachel's shout of laughter was so loud that he had to hiss at her and cast a warning look at neighbouring tables.

"Oh, you're absolutely priceless!" said Rachel merrily. "What makes you think you took advantage of her? You really aren't fit to be out alone!"

He supposed that some men might have resented this but he did not although he said, guardedly; "I'm not going to discuss this kind of thing in a crowded café."

"All right," she said cheerfully, "let's continue it this after-

noon. It's Saturday isn't it and you'll be coming over to
school, won't you?"

"There's not much point in my coming, your father's got
a Governors' meeting and won't be free until after seven."

"Well, that's fine," she said, "you and I will go up the
Dene and have tea at the 'White Rabbit', under Barrow Tor.
I could do with stretching my legs a bit, so long as you don't
expect me to scramble over rocks and through gorse thickets. Then we can take it easy on the way back and Father
can put you up in the Old Boys' dorm for the night."

He was tempted but remembered his arrangement with
Tapper Sugg.

"I have to open the shop on Sunday. Would you lend
me the car to drive back early in the morning?"

"Sure, providing you run over and pick me up for Monday."

He accepted the invitation gratefully. Not only did he
enjoy her company but the prospect of forty-eight hours at
Barrowdene lightened his spirits. There was a serenity about
the place that soothed him and it even occurred to him that
he might discuss certain of his problems with her father,
whose judgement he respected.

They finished their lunch and walked back to the zoo,
where Rachel issued instructions to her deputy and collected
the old Morris from the garage where it seemed to spend
most of its time.

She seemed thoughtful during the journey, concentrating
on driving but looking at him from time to time with a side-
long smile and he thought what a relaxing person she was,
for all her shiftlessness and sudden spurts of enthusiasm that
spent themselves without achieving anything in particular.
What she lacked, he felt, was her father's steadiness of vision
but at least she was aware of this and in this respect differed
from all the women he had known, Sybil and all Sybil's
friends for instance, who were unable at any time to say to
themselves: 'This is worth having and that is not, this is
genuine and that is phoney.'

As they turned in at the east drive she suddenly gave expression to a thought that showed him some of her father's
love of the place had rubbed off on her over the years. She
said: "I believe I understand what you and my father find
here, Martin. It's a kind of refuge, like a faith in a world

stampeding towards nothingness. I wish I could believe in something like that, something that had a chance of surviving the sputniks and the bomb, but to have such a faith one would have to be born before the First World War and remember the little that was left of the old world after nineteen-eighteen!"

She stopped the car near the chapel and turned off the ignition. "Listen, Martin. It's a kind of litany, isn't it?" and they sat there for a moment listening to the snick-snack of balls at the nets across the field and the muted shouts of boys in the quad behind the chapel. Then, as always, the pensive mood left her and she bounced out of the car and pulled him by the hand. "Come on, let's get started! I know what! I'll take you to a place I used to go to when I was a kid growing up here. I'd go out there and read on summer afternoons when I wanted to escape from the spots and blushes of all these half-grown males. I remember I took *Wuthering Heights* up there and *Westward Ho,* and even dear old *East Lynne* or *Dead-Dead-And-Never-Called-Me Mother!*"

They went across the rugby pitch and through a gap in the hedge that led to the birchwood bordering the shallow river. The sun was high overhead but it was cooler down here, with blackbirds rustling in the undergrowth and a persistent kingfisher flashing and dipping along the curves of the stream. There was an overgrown footpath where the trees thinned out and she led him to where it wound over the lower slope of the bracken-crowned tor and in and out of vast stretches of briar and wild rose and foxglove clumps, so that he thought of Tennyson's 'brambly wildernesses' and wondered at her obvious familiarity with the ground. He had never thought of her as a person with his kind of appreciation of the countryside although she had lived hereabouts since she was a child. Presently they left the woods and began to climb towards an outcrop of granite on the steepest side of the tor and it was here, scrambling after her up the pebble-strewn path, that he noticed a breathless eagerness in the way she pressed on as though she had an overdue appointment with her youth and had forgotten that he was stumbling in pursuit. Then the path levelled out at an almost rectangular slab of stone as big as a cromlech and behind the stone was a dell that was half a cave, roofed by an overhang of boulders but affording a view of the countryside for miles around. It had a floor of soft turf and she threw herself down, out of breath, leaving him to look out beyond the low entrance rocks to the ribbon of the Dene moving in and out of the plum-coloured woods to the gorge where the 'White Rabbit' lay like a toy farm two hundred feet below. To the left, beyond the shoulder of the hill, he could just see the school and playing fields and the dark green lines of beeches marking the drives but the heat haze in the valley shut out all but a general outline of green field and grey stone, with the top of the chapel steeple silhouetted against the sky.

"This is a wonderful place," he said, "and I don't wonder you've kept it in your heart all these years!" and then, with a touch of pride, "Have you ever brought anyone here before, Rachel?"

"Never a soul," she said, "not even the man I married!" and there was a harshness in her voice that he had never previously noticed. He thought little of it, however, turning back to the view and noting that up here, high above the valley, they were beyond the range of the hum and rustle in the thickets or the murmur of the river, and the loneliness of the place was almost tangible. He said, half to himself, "It's beautiful but sad somehow, as though it was cut off from the familiar and the remembered," but she made no answer and when he turned round he experienced a sharp, physical shock.

She was lying flat on her back with her eyes closed, her hands outstretched and her fingers gripping the short, tough grass. One long leg was fully stretched but the other was bent at the knee so that her stained grey skirt had slipped back revealing the top of her stocking and a generous expanse of thigh. He realised at once that the gesture was deliberately provocative, a plain invitation to him to make love to her, here in this secret hideout of hers that she had never shared with anyone. She looked, he thought, almost unbearably desirable and this surprised him for he had never thought of her as anything more than a big, healthy adolescent, impulsively affectionate perhaps but with a child's impatience for everything not directly concerned with the present.

He thought, with a mixture of wonder and distress, 'Why

should she do this? What on earth prompts her to make such a primitive gesture? It isn't me she wants! If it was I should have known long before this, during the times we have been alone during the last weeks.' And then it occurred to him that she might be testing him in some way but he rejected this as improbable. She was not that kind of girl, the kind young men had had an abusive term for when he was young. 'Well,' he decided, 'I'm not going to oblige! If my guess is right, I should be rebuffed and be made to look damned ridiculous, and if it wasn't things would never be quite the same again, not between us or between me and her father!' and he sat down, looking across the valley, very troubled and uncertain.

But it was impossible to ignore her and soon he found that he was sweating and trembling and, turning his head once more, noted that she had not moved a muscle but that her eyes were now wide open and looking directly at him. Her glance did not match her posture for her eyes were troubled and she looked more adolescent than ever, almost as though someone had demanded this performance of her and that she was aware that he was finding it both ridiculous and embarrassing. Yet even then she did not sit up or withdraw the invitation in any way but lay quite still, looking at him and waiting.

He made a feeble attempt to speak but his mouth and throat were dry. She was so shamelessly exposed that the temptation to exploit the situation was almost irresistible, yet he continued to resist it and at that precise moment he could not have said why except that in some remote way his decision was bound up with the future, his and her future, and the future of all the other people in their lives. It needed a great deal of will-power on his part to remain there pressed against the rock, and resentment burned in him so fiercely that for a moment or so he almost hated her for her clumsy challenge.

At last he forced himself to speak, his voice shrill with exasperation.

"Don't do that, Rachel, don't!"

She made a little grimace, turning her head to one side and a minute passed before she said, "You don't have to talk like a schoolmaster. You haven't caught me cribbing or throw-

ing a paper dart!" but she flung out her arched leg with a
kind of defiance and her skirt fell back across her knees.

She had replied to him, he realised, without a trace of
her characteristic humour but the rebuke snapped the tension
inside him and he flung himself down beside her, reaching
out his hand tentatively and letting it pass over her hair and
down her cheek. It was a simple, tender caress, expressive
and renunciatory and it must have touched her for she
shuddered and then, twisting round violently she threw her
arms around his neck and crushed her cheek to his, holding
him awkwardly and convulsively, less like a woman demanding a lover than a child frightened of the dark.

"Is it Sybil or Olga or both?" she said, when something of
the urgency had gone from her first embrace.

"It's nothing to do with Sybil or Olga," he said gently. "I
want you to believe that, Rachel."

"Then, why? Why don't you want to touch me even?"

"I do want to touch you! I want to most dreadfully but
I don't know how I could make you understand. You're so
different from me, so much more free and less complicated.
Dear God, I'm flesh and blood, do you think it's easy for
me?"

She seemed strangely comforted by his vehemence and
some of the tension left her.

"All right, Martin, you don't have to explain. Keep your
privacy! I wish to God I could share it with you!"

She detached herself, turned her head slightly and kissed
him softly on the cheek as the moment passed. "All right,
you don't owe me an explanation, it's I who owe you one!"
and she smiled ruefully so that he recognised the Rachel
Grey of their earlier association and welcomed her return.

"You don't owe me a thing," he said, "whereas I owe you
a great deal. And don't go away from here with the idea that
I don't find your need of me a source of pride. I know very
well that I shall look back on this moment with the kind of
regret most men have about lost opportunities but that doesn't
make it right, right for us, that is."

"That bloody fool Sybil doesn't know you at all!" she
burst out.

"I didn't know myself for almost half a century," he said
simply.

"It's time you did!" she said, leaning back against the

smooth upright of the granite wall. "You have a kind of strength that makes muscularity look insignificant. You'll win out in the end, Martin, because of that strength and balance. I wanted you just now, more than I ever wanted any man, but it wasn't good old-fashioned lust or even a whim of the moment, it was something bigger than that. Close contact with you has helped me a great deal and I suppose I wanted the very closest contact, a kind of . . . of blessing. Does that sound so silly?"

It did not sound in the least silly, for her words brought him far more pride than he would have derived from possession of her. They did as much or more for him as had the incident with Olga, the driving of the 'bus, the rescue of the child, all the steps that had advanced his emancipation up to the moment that Sybil had halted and reversed it. Now it was moving forward again and once more he felt himself growing, sensing the growth in an almost physical way, for here was one more human being who found in him the succour that the lonely sought in the strong. All the resentment he had felt for her when she was lying on her back with her thighs exposed in that childishly provocative manner left him and he felt for her nothing but affection and gratitude. He said: "If I took advantage of you, Rachel, it wouldn't be a matter of bestowing a benediction. I'm certainly no wiser than you and I find it a matter for pride that someone as young and as pretty as you should even want me as a potential lover. When I made up my mind to start afresh, however, it wasn't with the idea of satisfying the sexual panic men get at my age, but rather to find whatever purpose there was in life and fulfil myself in some way. I haven't found the whole answer yet, only part of it and an involvement of this sort would only complicate things, particularly as I've grown so fond of you and your father." He paused a moment, then went on, "There is one thing, however, I'd like very much to kiss you, to . . . to hold you for a moment." She seemed surprised by this request. "Why, Martin? If you won't have all of me why should you want to kiss me?"

He said, slowly: "There are things a man likes to remember. I should like to remember this afternoon, the day a woman who could attract any young man had an impulsively generous notion to give herself to a man like me and that isn't humility, Rachel, it's simply facing facts and I'm not nearly so reluctant to do that as I was in the days before I met you."

She scrambled to her knees, smiling.

"I've got to inject more confidence into you, Martin. Sometimes I think you're coming along all right on your own and then, quite suddenly, all the air hisses out of the tube. You've been more than half-deflated ever since that wife of yours swept down on you and perhaps . . ." She broke off, shaking her head, "No, I won't try and bamboozle myself! I was going to say that this was one of the reasons I wanted you just now but it wasn't, mostly it was just honest man-hunger I guess, so why dress it up in fancy language?"

She leaned forward and took his face in her hands. "Stop feeling grateful for every woman who takes a fancy to you, Martin—Sebastian—I'm-a-bit-of-a-droop-Sermon! Women like your type! Intelligent, dependable and virile, too, I wouldn't wonder given the right sort of encouragement!" and still smiling she kissed him on the mouth and held him there, enlarging the kiss in a manner that was half-sensual, half-humorous.

Then she got up, caught him by the hand and led him into the blazing sunshine that was beating over the shoulder of the hill and down the steep path to the 'White Rabbit' and as he followed her striding figure, marking the grace of her long, swinging strides, he reflected; 'I'm an even bigger fool than I thought I was! Why can't I adopt her code? One day is like another so why not eat all the fruit you find beside the road? The time will come when you'll never be able to explain to yourself why you held back just now. A woman's lips freely given are one thing but that would have been really something to remember in your old age, you idiot!' Yet, notwithstanding his ruefulness, he was able to smile at himself a little as well as at her and he doubted if he would have been able to do this had the encounter been carried to its logical conclusion. 'I know one thing though,' he added to himself, as they emerged from the wood and crossed the paddock to the tea house, 'I shall feel a damned sight more easy in my mind when I meet her father tonight and at my time of life I'm all for possessing the tranquil mind that poor old Othello set so much store upon!'

.   .   .   .   .

Looking back on that blazing afternoon Sebastian came to regard it as a kind of half-way house in his odyssey, a place where he got his second wind after the distressing days that followed Sybil's descent upon Kingsbay.

For one thing it was the beginning of a run of luck and the run began as they entered the farm. At the end of the paddock they passed close to an open shed and Sebastian's Tapper-trained eye caught a glimpse of lumber among which were three wickerwork perambulators, high built, strap-slung vehicles of early Victorian design. He pointed them out and asked if she thought they might be for sale.

"What do you want with a pram?" Rachel asked, her humour now thoroughly restored. "I could make a really nasty crack about that but I won't, providing you'll tell me what use you would put them to."

"I think they'd sell," said Sebastian, "I think they might start a fashion. People have been using old wheelbarrows and carts for flower-stands for some time, so why not period prams?"

"I dare say the new people here would pay you to take them away," she said. "Come on, let's see what they've made of the place, I've heard it's gone contemporary since old man Thorn died and his family sold up."

She told him that when they first came to Barrowdene the 'White Rabbit' had been a cider-house kept by an explosive old character called 'Dido' Thorn.

"He was a bit of a hermit," she added, "and people would come from miles around to be insulted by him and then go home treasuring his abuse like famous last words. He had the place so stuffed with junk you could hardly see out of the windows!"

A severe-looking woman served them with china tea and open Danish sandwiches and he pressed Rachel for more information regarding the late Dido Thorn's junk.

"Oh, I can't remember what he had here," she said, "pistols and blunderbusses and stacks of pewter plates and tankards. There was a horrid tankard with a frog in the bottom I remember and I'm thankful it's all gone. I like smooth surfaces and fresh air!"

"I wonder what happened to it all," mused Sebastian, "it sounds like a very good buy for someone," and when he paid the bill he asked if the Victorian prams were for sale and was referred to a young man tending fowls who was identified as the new proprietor. The man agreed to sell the perambulators for a pound apiece and looked at Mr. Sermon as though he was doing business with an escaped lunatic. When Sebastian enquired if there was any more lumber for sale the man suddenly became very businesslike and said that some of the effects of the late owner were still in the loft and that he had plans for converting the outbuildings into a battery-house for his hens and was prepared to dispose of the litter en bloc, providing Mr. Sermon would undertake to take it away himself. A brief inspection of the loft and stables encouraged Sebastian to make a spot decision. He could see a variety of saleable goods under cobwebs and mouldering sacks, an oak dresser base, a set of copper measures, several battered oak coffers containing pewter ware, firedogs, ponderous kitchen utensils, a hanging bookshelf of Regency design, chairs with broken backs and missing legs, and a dozen or so pictures in heavy Victorian frames.

"It's quite hopeless to sort all this out now but it looks to me as if at least half of it is valueless," he said cautiously. "I'll give you two hundred pounds for the lot and undertake to remove it all by next Wednesday."

The young man was unable to conceal his satisfaction and Mr. Sermon reflected that had Tapper Sugg been negotiating the deal he would have probably closed at a hundred less. He was certain, however, that he had driven a good bargain and when they were returning along the track to the woods Rachel said; "You're a deep one, Martin! How much do you stand to make on that rubbish?"

"That's the glorious thing about The Trade," said Mr. Sermon jubilantly, "one never knows but I can tell you this, we're in on it already. I can sell the prams, the dresser base and the pewter for the outlay and whatever else is there, is profit less transport costs! There's no such word as rubbish in The Trade."

"Martin," she said solemnly, "I don't think we've heard the last of you! Why on earth didn't you branch out years ago? Why did you waste so much time bogged down at places like Napier Hall? Was it Sybil?"

He thought for a moment before answering, then he said, deliberately: "No, Rachel, it wasn't Sybil or Sybil's money. It was something more fundamental. I'm a teacher at heart not a businessman. This kind of thing is all right as a hobby, a kind of private joke with myself like the post of Beach Supervisor but it isn't basic. I'd sooner be your father than the most successful tycoon in Threadneedle Street. I don't think I could spend my life dealing in things, I'm too interested in people."

"Two hundred pounds seems to me an expensive joke," she said, "I hope it doesn't end in hollow laughter."

"It won't," he said simply, "I feel lucky today. Maybe it's because of you!"

He said this lightly, supposing her to have put the incident in the cave out of mind but he misjudged her for she gave him a searching look and thereafter became thoughtful again, answering him with monosyllables and sometimes not at all as they walked into the sunset towards Barrowdene. Then, as they were emerging from the coppice to take the track across the water meadow to the rugger field, she called to him, sharply: "Martin!"

He stopped and turned back, thinking for a moment she had stumbled and wrenched her ankle.

"What is it?"

"I won't have a chance of a word alone with you when we get in, Father will monopolise you as he always does."

He was struck by the earnestness in her voice. "There's Monday Rachel, and you're not thinking of resigning from the zoo because I didn't come up to scratch, are you?"

"I might even do that!"

"Look here," he said, sharply, "this isn't fair! I've already said it doesn't make any difference and you agreed. I thought . . ."

"It isn't what happened back there, Martin, we aren't talking about the same thing."

"Then what the devil are we talking about?"

She said, slowly and distinctly, "I believe I'm in love with you, Martin, and I'm not in the least sure what I can do about it! I know one thing, two in fact, I won't become a damned nuisance to you and if you ever do break with Sybil, Olga Boxall won't be the only one in the queue. Something else too, the next time I'd go about it with more finesse!"

He had not the least idea how to reply to this or what face to put upon such a declaration. He stood there with his

mouth slightly open, finding her words more bewildering
than her behaviour on the tor but she gave him no chance
to comment, walking swiftly past and almost running across
to the gap in the hedge that marked the Barrowdene
boundary.

He went after her but she could move faster than him and
had jumped down on to the rugger pitch before he had
reached the gap. Then, seeing a group of boys practising at
the long-jump pit, he abandoned the pursuit, annoyed with
her for once more destroying the balance in their relationship.
"Oh, to the devil with women," he said grumpily, "from now
on I'll concentrate on making money!" and he waved vaguely
to a boy who greeted him and crossed the field to the quad,
applying his mind, but not altogether successfully, to the less
erratic vagaries of The Trade.

CHAPTER EIGHT

Mr. Sermon
Is Faced with a Choice
of Professions

SEBASTIAN'S life in Kingsbay now fell into a pleasant rhythm. He was a success at his job on the Esplanade which occupied him five days a week and on weekday evenings he usually took a walk, or drove out with Rachel, or drank a pint with Tapper Sugg in one or other of the local taverns. On Saturdays he usually went over to Barrowdene and spent the day with Fred Grey, occasionally helping out with school routine, as when he took the Sixth for a double-period history and amused the staff, most of whom he had come to know well, by tempting the science section to join the class and learn some spicy details regarding the character of the Bourbon court. All day Sunday he presided over Tapper Sugg's antique shop at the top of the High Street hill. Tapper liked to have him there and would have preferred to engage 'The Perfesser' as he continued to refer to him, as a full-time scout and salesman.

He was elated by news of Sebastian's overall purchase at the 'White Rabbit' and made three trips out there within twenty-four hours of receiving Sebastian's telephone call. Privately, Sebastian wondered whether Tapper would decide that he had been too generous with the vendor but during the lunch break that same Monday, Tapper appeared on the parking ground in a state of considerable excitement.

"Lumme Perfesser, you struck oil! You reely struck it this time. Two 'undred you give 'em? Streuth, you peeled the pants orf 'im! You'd have been flippin' lucky to get it for five!"

"Oh, come now," protested Sebastian, "there were one or two nice pieces there but a great deal of it was junk."

"Junk!" exclaimed Tapper, extracting a small but carefully wrapped object from his pocket and peeling away the tissue and newspaper, "you call this junk? It's a fammy-rose plate and it ain't got a chip nowhere. If there's more o' that stowed away we're home an' dry, not countin' the pewter an' copper and all them witch-doctor's masks!"

"Well, I'm delighted to hear it," said Sebastian, "so, suppose I come up tonight and help you sort and price?"

"It's a date," said Tapper. "I'll nip over for me third load this afternoon. Lumme, it's like fallin' A over B into the treasure o' the perishin' Incas this is!" He stopped and looked at Sebastian keenly.

"How you off fer crinkly? You want a bit to go on with?"

'Crinkly' was Tapper's term for paper currency but in his mind it excluded everything but the five-pound note. Mr. Sermon told him that he had paid for the goods by cheque.

"That's bad, that's real bad!" said Tapper. "We'll have to break you of that habit. Worse'n bitin' your nails that is!" and he lumbered off towards his estate van, leaving his promising pupil to equate two hundred and thirty-two parking tickets with a leather bag full of loose silver.

When Sebastian entered the shop that evening he had great difficulty in making his way as far as the green baize door for Tapper had unloaded the furniture and dumped it higgledy-piggledy into every available corner. He was in high spirits and beamed up at Sebastian from a recumbent position he occupied beneath a converted spinet.

"Looker this fer a start, mate," he chuckled. "Right as royalty this is an' the conversion job already done for us! We oughter get twenty-five for this when I've got Blessing to give her a rub with Mansion polish. The dresser base is seventeenth century, an' as fer that there 'anging bookcase wi' the fretted shelves, you wait till we got leather books in it. Look as if it had come out o' Blenheim Palace it will!

There's money in the bits an' pieces too. No more fammy-rose worse luck, but the pistols is all flintlocks an' there's a Wild West Colt there, that oughter fetch a tenner now all them bang-bang programmes on the telly is startin' a fashion in six-shooters! I tell you, Perfesser, you on'y made one slip up with this load. Chap said you give him an extra three quid fer them prams! I told him you muster made a mistake but he said no an' loaded 'em on me roof!"

"There wasn't any mistake!" said Sebastian, indignantly. "It was the prams that put me on to all the other stuff."

"But why? Who the 'ell wants prams? Young married couples wouldn't be seen dead pushing one o' them!"

"Good heavens!" exclaimed Mr. Sermon, "they aren't for babies, they're for flowers!"

"*Flowers?*"

"Yes—freesias, flowering geraniums, hydrangeas standing outside shops and as centre-pieces in cafés. You've seen wheelbarrows used for that purpose, so I thought we'd have a go at prams. It's a gimmick and a very fashionable one too. The Royal Family are using nineteenth century perambulators and as soon as that gets in the magazines everyone will want one!"

Tapper regarded Sebastian like a father whose favourite son has arrived home with news of a scholarship to University.

"Perfesser!" he said solemnly, "I said it before an' I'll say it again. You're a natchrule! I knew it the minute I picked you up on the road top of the Hangman's! Flowers! Royalty! Outside shops—here—," and he rushed through the baize door and reappeared a moment later staggering under the weight of an orange box containing nine pots of lilies.

"Stick 'em in an' wheel 'em out!" he urged. "Start wi' one an' keep the others in reserve. It never does to show two of anything unless they started life together!"

Mr. Sermon arranged the pots and negotiated the perambulator through the piles of stock to the door where he wedged the handles against the angle of the porch.

They listed the stock, entered up and priced. Tapper put 'a starter' as he called it, on the witch-doctor's masks, explaining that African curios had been a drug on the market in his earlier days, but, like most things, their turn had come round and collectors were now scrambling for voodoo items.

"Pistols is the same," he explained, "time was you could buy a sackful for a fiver but now, lumme, I see duelling pistols fetch sixty and seventy a pair, perviding they match and got all the twiddly bits to go with 'em. It's like I said, you can't never tell in this lark, one day's dustbin is tommorer's safe-deposit box! You seen the prints?"

Mr. Sermon examined the prints, a bunch of five tied up with string and spotted with mildew. He spread them out on the floor and went down on his hands and knees, removing some of the dirt with a duster. Then he sat back on his heels with an exclamation.

"I believe they're Rowlandsons!" he shouted.

"Rowlandsons! The poor man's 'Ogarth? Get on with you, let's have a look!" and he joined Mr. Sermon on the floor where they carefully examined the five prints, setting three aside as doubtful and taking the remaining two to a desk where they could inspect them under electric light. One print was of a naval shipyard in the Medway area and the other was a barrack-room scene, reminiscent of Rowlandson's 'Hussar Barracks.' All the characters had the happily debauched look of the eighteenth-century poor and the firmness of line and general vigour of the scenes indicated the work of a first-class artist.

"We'd never know for certain," said Mr. Sermon, "I can make nothing of the signatures, if they are signatures, but we could try them out at Christie's, couldn't we?"

The profit-look had perched on Tapper's lean face. "We don't 'try 'em out' as you say, mate, we enter 'em as Rowlandsons and 'ope for the best. You got any idea what a Rowlandson print fetches?"

Mr. Sermon had not neglected to read sales catalogues since his entry into The Trade and he remembered exactly. "They're not terribly valuable," he said, "but one fetched a hundred and fifty at Sotheby's a month or so ago, I remember thinking it wasn't enough!"

"Well, it ain't bad in the circumstances, is it?" said Tapper, tolerantly, "we stand to get three-quarters of our outlay back on one item!" and he placed a fatherly hand on Sebastian's shoulder. "I'll tell you what we do," he went on, "I was gonner pay you the usual commission on this lot an' refund the two hundred now but seein' it's come out so well I don't reckon that's square. We'll go halves on the outlay and

fifty-fifty on the profits!" and before Mr. Sermon could object
he pulled out his customary roll of bank notes and peeled
off exactly one hundred and one pounds, ten shillings. 'He
may be sharp,' reflected Mr. Sermon, pocketing the money,
'but he's got his standards. How many dealers would have
remembered the odd three pounds laid out on the prams?'

The next moment they had confirmation of success for a
big car stopped outside and a prosperous-looking couple got
out and rattled the door on which the 'Closed' sign was
displayed.

"Open up, Perfesser," said Tapper, casually, "there's no
such thing as overtime in this lark. I daresay we shall have
to lissen to a description of her Aunt Matilda's log-box in
Alabama but you never know, do you?"

The woman wasted no time on preliminaries. "That pram,"
she said briskly, "how much is it?"

"With or without the plants?" said Tapper, before Mr.
Sermon could reply.

"Without them," said the customer, "I've got plants. That's
what I want the pram for."

"Well, it's not reely for sale," said Tapper slowly, "it's part
o' my shop window."

"I'm sorry, but I must have it!" said the woman and turned
to her so-far-silent husband. "We must have it, mustn't we,
Barry? I mean, it's a ducky! It's just what we need for the
conservatory!"

Barry neither confirmed nor denied this claim but smiled
a little fatuously and Mr. Sermon, who was learning fast,
knew that he was a man sadly resigned to sudden stops in
High Streets all over the country.

"Come now, I know you people," said the woman, "you'll
take a profit if I offer you one."

Tapper rubbed his blue chin and Sebastian heard the
stubble rasp under his palm.

"You don't see many of 'em, do you?" he asked, almost
piteously, and the woman said no you didn't and that was
the reason she wanted to buy.

"I ferget what it cost us," said Tapper, guardedly, "it was
so long ago. Sling over the stockbook, Perfesser, an' let's
see if we can oblige the lady. I know one thing, my missus
isn't gonner like it, she sets a big store be that there pram!"

Mr. Sermon gave him the book, his face betraying nothing

of the blatancy of Tapper's sales-talk. 'I wonder if she would
still buy if someone told her that the pram had been there
five minutes, that it wasn't even entered in the stockbook,
and that Tapper's wife had been dead for years?' he mused.
Tapper thumbed slowly through the pages of the ledger and
Sebastian wondered whether he should begin lifting the plants
from the pram, for there could be but one end to the
incident.

"Ah, here we are," said Tapper, presently, "one early Victorian per-am-bew-later! Eighteen-ten, ten bob on the carriage!" He snapped the book shut. "Stands us in at nineteen,
m'm. It'll cost you twenty-four!"

"Twenty-two ten!" said the woman unexpectedly and Tapper shivered as though someone had doused him with cold
water.

"Can't do it, m'm, worth more'n that to me as a 'bringer
in'. It brought you in, didn't it now?"

The woman relaxed and smiled. She was, thought Mr. Sermon, accustomed to this kind of thing but was not nearly so
good at it as she imagined herself to be.

"You look like a sport," she said, "I'll toss you twenty-two-
ten or twenty-four!"

Tapper cheered up a little. "I never could resist a gamble,"
he said, "but either way I got some explaining to do to the
missus!" and he took a half-crown from his trouser pocket
and without attempting to spin it whacked it down on the
back of his hand. "You call, m'm!"

"Heads!" she said.

It was tails and Tapper showed her the coin. "Will you
take a cheque?" asked the woman.

"From a sport like you? 'Course I will!" said Tapper, "so
long as you write your name and address on the back!"

The husband wrote the cheque and they helped him stow
the pram into the boot, wedging it with wads of newspaper.
While they were occupied with this the woman found a
Staffordshire poodle and paid for it with cash. The profit on
the poodle was ten shillings.

"Well, there you are, mate," said Tapper, rubbing his hands
as the car roared off up the hill, "you bin proved right an'
I bin proved wrong but who cares so long as we shift the
stuff!"

They spent a pleasant evening sorting the stock and when it was dusk Sebastian said good night and strolled down the High Street and along the front to The Coombe. His mind was chiefly occupied with Tapper's offer of a permanent partnership which had, he was bound to admit, considerable financial advantages. If the stock sold well and the prints did turn out to be Rowlandsons, he stood to make something like three hundred pounds on this deal alone and obviously he had a flair for this profession. On the other hand, did he really want to drift to that extent? Was it a full life for a man who still had something creative to give in a profession for which he had been trained and for which he still felt he had a calling? He would have very much liked to have discussed the matter with Olga and when he arrived home he was pleased to find a fat letter from her, posted in Athens a few days before.

He took the letter into the kitchen and read it over supper but his pleasure soon changed to disappointment. As he unfolded the sheets a sheaf of snapshots fell out, coloured pictures taken in brilliant sunshine and he looked at them incuriously until he came upon one of Olga standing against the rail of the ship beside a lean, saturnine man about his own age. The man, who wore a yachting cap not unlike Sebastian's official headgear, had his arm about Olga's neat waist and there was in Olga's expression an archness that Sebastian associated with wedding pictures in a local paper. He studied the snap with disapproval. Somehow it seemed almost indecent that Olga Boxall, shy and virginal all these years, had progressed as far and as fast as the snap seemed to indicate. Who was the man in the yachting cap? How came she to let herself be taken in a quasi-honeymoon pose and have the nerve to send him evidence of her emancipation? He read the letter sulkily, skimming through two or three pages of descriptive matter until he arrived, with a nasty jolt, at the operative paragraph. *"I think one of the reasons I kept putting off this trip,"* she wrote, gaily, *"was the feeling that I should find travel of this kind lonely. I had the idea that I might be shut up on board with a crowd of people who weren't 'me' and from whom there was no escape but quite the reverse is true. I've rather surprised myself with the ease with which I've made friends among the passengers and in the pictures you'll see one or two of them, particularly An-*

drew, taken on board as we got into Naples. He is a very charming man and reminds me very much of you in some ways, a publisher from Boston making his first trip to Europe which I thought odd because he's very comfortably off and the kind of man one would imagine was often over here on business. His wife died a year or so ago and he has a daughter about nineteen. I think they were a very happy family and after his wife's death he forced himself to make the trip because he couldn't readjust himself. He's like you inasmuch as he's a very interesting talker and you know what a good listener I am! We had a wonderful time ashore in Naples and went to Pompeii, where I always wanted to see those naughty pictures on the walls but they wouldn't let the women in! We've all been teasing him ever since to tell us what they were like but he . . ." and suddenly Mr. Sermon found that he was unable to read on for irritation choked him as he pictured Andrew, the rich, widowed publisher, surrounded by a giggling group of English spinsters giving their inhibitions an airing at the expense of a few 2,000-year-old paintings on the wall of a brothel. It was all too silly and schoolgirlish, he thought, and he was surprised and disappointed that a woman possessing her kind of commonsense and dignity should subscribe to such a scene. It was very clear that a few weeks on board ship in the Mediterranean were having a distressing effect upon her.

Moodily he finished the letter and then drifted into the little sitting-room where he stood leaning on the mantelshelf a moment, studying the theatrical photographs of Olga Boxall during her brief and improbable stage career. He found nothing to confirm the idea that a kittenish spinster had lain dormant in the shy-looking girl who had looked back at him from the frames. He could relate this girl to the woman who lay in his arms in this very room barely a month ago but not with the author of the letter, the coy voyager who let herself be photographed in the cuddly embrace of a middle-aged American publisher 'very comfortably off'!

Musing alone in the twilight it occurred to him that one way and another he might soon find himself in an extremely complicated situation. Women, he decided, were becoming something of a nuisance! There was Olga whom he had seduced, and Rachel who had tried to seduce him, and had now openly declared that she was setting her cap at him!

And, in the background, far away in the half-forgotten world of Wyckham Rise, was Sybil, who had also presented an ultimatum—come home or wipe the slate clean! If he ignored this ultimatum then Sybil would drop out of the running and so, it would appear, would Olga if she continued to write him letters like this. There remained Rachel, but Rachel was in a class apart, an attractive young woman whom it would be perfectly delightful to spoil, but was he seeking this kind of companionship? Could Rachel Grey offer anybody a lasting relationship?

He was preoccupied with these thoughts when the telephone rang and he jumped up startled, wondering if the insistent bell (a sound he had never heard without a degree of apprehension) was about to introduce further complications into his life and when he heard the fruity voice of Fred Grey, Rachel's father, he was quite certain of the fact.

"Sermon? I didn't think you'd be in but I took a chance! I'm in Kingsbay right now, up at the station. Look here, old chap, there's something I'd rather like to discuss with you, is it too late if I run over, or shall I leave it until the morning?"

Mr. Sermon's apprehension increased. Something Grey wanted to discuss! Something that couldn't wait until they met next Saturday! It could only be Rachel, he thought and said, hesitatingly, "Er . . . no, it's . . . er . . . not too late. Come over for a drink but don't drive up The Coombe, leave your car at the bottom and I'll look out for you."

"I'll be with you in ten minutes," said Grey and rang off, leaving Sebastian gnawing his lip and wondering if Rachel had been fool enough to tell her father what had occurred on the Tor on Saturday afternoon. 'Yet he didn't sound annoyed or disturbed,' he thought, striving to reassure himself. 'I really must get out of this habit of presupposing that every human contact I make poses a new problem. I must learn to take things as they come!' and he helped himself to a stiff whisky, turned on the porch lights and went down to the gate to watch for Fred Grey's headlights.

They showed up almost at once and soon he discerned the tall, slightly stooping figure striding up the path, walking like an eager crane with beak out-thrust and wings gently flapping. They went straight into the house and the Headmaster flopped

down in Olga's armchair, his face glowing with the climb
and his white tufts of hair more like an Alpine range than
ever as he thrust his fingers into the tangle. His first words
set Mr. Sermon's mind at rest.

"Have you ever thought of going back to teaching,
Sermon?"

Sebastian was so surprised by the question that he left
his finger on the syphon and made a pool on Olga's sideboard.

"Teaching? You mean, at a school like yours?"

Grey nodded, reaching out for his whisky.

"It suddenly occurred to me as I was seeing Bradley off
just now. You remember Bradley? He's been with us four
years now. He taught History as far as the middle school and
French to some of the juniors, a nice lad but his heart was
never really in teaching! He's very much the outdoor type
and now he's going off on a climbing expedition in the
Caucasus. He can well afford it, the lucky young devil, and
he's gone with my blessing although where it'll get him I
don't know beyond having something exciting to look back
on when he finds his joints getting stiff. Apparently he has
the same pessimistic leanings as you, Sermon, thinks everybody's time is running out and the world is going to go bang
one of these mornings! Wants to do everything he dreamed of
doing before it's too late!"

"You mean . . . you would consider me as a replacement?"

"Why not? You aren't likely to go gadding off to the
Caucasus are you? And you always seem so happy over at
school I imagine we should get on well enough."

"I'm quite sure we should!" said Sebastian, enthusiastically,
but his mind was in a whirl for this was something he had
never imagined could happen. On the staff of a school like
Barrowdene! And with a man like this jovial giant as one's
Headmaster! Already he felt he had belonged to the school
and the prospect of really belonging, of being able to play
an active, useful part in the establishment was enough to
make him whoop with delight. Then he remembered Sybil
and after Sybil, Rachel and finally Olga, due back in a month,
and as a double postscript his half-promises to Tapper Sugg
and the Town Clerk. 'God damn it!' he said, almost aloud,
'I'm no more free than I was before I left home! I've escaped
one trap to run headlong into half a dozen others and if

they aren't as saw-toothed as the old one their jaws are sharp enough to remind me that I can only please myself about trivialities!'

"Do you want an answer now? This moment, Mr. Grey?" he quavered and the Headmaster, surprised by his tone, jumped up and exclaimed: "Good Lord, no! What kind of man do you think I am? I've rather knocked you off balance, haven't I? I didn't mean to do that, my dear fellow, I only rang up because I happened to be in Kingsbay and I had a call from the Chairman of the Governors before I left school today."

"A call concerning this vacancy?"

"Well, yes, and I put your name forward as a possibility on Saturday and they agreed to consider it. Naturally I didn't mention it when I saw you on Saturday night because I didn't know how they'd feel about it. A vacancy should be advertised of course, but well, you know me—if I can cut a few inches of red tape I'll do it, and I think you'd be an admirable choice."

"Why?" pressed Mr. Sermon, conscious of a dry mouth and an uncomfortable stirring in the pit of his stomach. "Would you mind telling me *why* you think I'd fit into Barrowdene? I've never taught at a school like that, I'm forty-nine and perhaps it's a bit late to start in an entirely new field."

"Yes, I'll tell you why," said Grey, readily, "you're a man with a great respect for tradition but you're content to let it ride lightly on your shoulders. Some of the men they send me haven't a moment's patience with any idea preceding the jet age, while others use tradition like plaster on a wall, stuffing it into every available crack in the system. This distinction might not seem an important one to many educationalists but it's damned important to me! I've steered a middle course through all the years of controversy as to what or what not Public Schools ought to offer and I like to surround myself with men after my own heart. It's as simple as that, d'you see?"

"Where did Bradley live?" asked Sebastian. "Was it on the premises or did he have one of the cottages?"

"He lived in school," Grey told him, "but a cottage becomes vacant in September. Old Henshaw is retiring and has bought a bungalow here in Kingsbay. Those cottages are stone built and very comfortable I'm told, you look around one next time you're over."

He hasn't asked about Sybil, Sebastian thought, and surely that underscores the fundamental decency of the man. Almost any person in his situation would want to probe a little into my domestic background but he doesn't, he's prepared to take me on trust! I could be wonderfully happy with a man like that in a school like Barrowdene! I know that but what I don't know is could Sybil and I make a fresh start in these new circumstances?

He stood up and turned frankly to Grey: "I know I should love it there and I think I could make a success of it," he said, "but it does rather depend on other factors, my wife chiefly, who is very attached to London and hasn't had any experience at all of life in the country. I should naturally have to discuss it with her . . . as a matter of fact Headmaster, it is this very thing that threatens our marriage but I haven't given up hope of persuading her to change her mind! The pity of it is she's financially independent and that does put a man at a grave disadvantage. Suppose she flatly refused to leave London? Would it make a difference? I mean, is there particular preference for a married man?"

Grey looked thoughtful and reached for his second whisky absentmindedly.

"I suppose I could say 'no' to that, Sermon," he said, at length, "but I wouldn't be telling the strict truth. The Governors much prefer married men because there is always the question of taking over a house in the future. Let's put it this way, your prospects at Barrowdene would be infinitely brighter if you could persuade your wife to join you down here."

"Thank you," said Sebastian, "I rather imagined that would be the case. How long can you give me to think it over?"

Mr. Grey stood up. "It's July now and we break up for the holidays in three weeks. Could you give me your final answer by the middle of August? That shouldn't be too late to find someone if you turn us down!"

"It's very generous of you," said Sebastian, "and I hope I can give you my answer before then," and he walked Grey to the door and down the path to The Coombe.

Back in the sitting-room, knowing that it would be a long time before he could retire with any prospect of sleep, he re-read Olga's letter and found to his surprise that it no longer irritated him, that he could contemplate the comfortably-off publisher with a tolerance that had eluded him earlier in the evening and he thought, as Rachel might have said, 'Jolly good luck to her! I hope she lands him,' and then he dismissed Olga altogether, his thoughts turning to Sybil and what approach he should make to her. As he took a sheet of notepaper from Olga's bureau and wrote 'My dear Sybil' he chuckled, reflecting that he had not even asked Grey what salary he could expect and this would astonish the daughter of a man who had founded a chain of grocery stores.

He sat there for a long time, toying with his pen and wondering whether to adopt storming tactics or a softening-up process in the opening paragraph. Then, looking up, he saw the telephone and tossed the letter aside, nerving himself to pluck at the receiver and ask for trunks.

The operator put him through very quickly and he told himself that he would give the phone twenty double-burrs before concluding that Sybil had retired to bed. At the fifteenth summons the receiver was lifted and a startled voice said: "Yes? Who is it?" and Sebastian, smiling a little, said: "It's me, Sebastian! Long distance! Are you alone, Sybil?"

He heard her catch her breath and then, in a somewhat indignant tone, she replied: "Of course I'm alone, it's gone midnight! Where are you? Are you still in that Kingsbay place?"

"Yes," he said, "I'm still here but something interesting has developed. I was going to write and then I thought I'd sooner phone. How are you, Sybil?"

"I'm very well!" she said evenly, and then, "Are you ringing to tell me you're coming home?"

"Not exactly," he said, "but I might have to come to London very shortly. There's something I should very much like to discuss with you. It concerns the future of all of us and I'm hoping it might prove the ultimate solution."

"Oh," said Sybil, guardedly, "the solution to what exactly?"

"Look, Sybil, for God's sake drop that tone!" he exclaimed almost involuntarily. "This is vital to both of us! I've been offered a splendid job with a real future!"

"Oh?" she said, incuriously. "What as? A *County* lavatory attendant?"

He fought his temper, reflecting that after all it might have been wiser to write. Then, biting his lip so savagely that it hurt, he said: "That big school I told you about, Barrowdene, the Headmaster has just been here. He offered me a permanent post with living accommodation outside the school. I could start in September and in time it might lead to a house if things work out satisfactorily. The point is, I'd like to accept and I should have accepted right away if we hadn't been separated in this ridiculous way. Suppose we both agree to let bygones be bygones? Or if you need time to think, I'll come up and see you next week-end. How does it strike you?"

There was a long pause and he pictured her standing by the little table in the hall with the sitting-room door ajar and light streaming across the plain fitted carpet. It was like looking back on a scene of his childhood, where domestic objects had fixed themselves in his mind as part of a particular setting. Then her voice reached him again and now it seemed to be coming over a trans-Atlantic cable.

"This is nonsense, Sebastian, how can we possibly decide a thing like that on the telephone in the middle of the night? Do what you intended doing, set it down on paper, but if it means burying myself alive in a damp village on the moor I warn you that it will be a waste of your time. That doesn't necessarily put the idea out of court of course, we might easily come to some alternative arrangement, providing you really are serious about returning to a respectable profession. There are other schools . . ."

"Damn it woman, I'm not interested in other schools!" he almost screamed. "I've been offered a post at Barrowdene! Not Eton, or Harrow or anywhere on the doorstep of that jungle you live in! It's Barrowdene or nothing and I've got to know!"

She replied in the same calm tone. "Very well then, get on the train and come home tomorrow. It's ridiculous to expect me to make a decision, or even to express a considered opinion under these circumstances. What time can you get a train?"

He said, between his teeth; "I can't come up just like that! If I come at all it would have to be on a Saturday and I should have to return again at latest Sunday night but if you feel this way about it why should I waste five pounds on a fare? I've got a better idea. *You* get in the car and drive down and see me! You've done it before and you can do it again, but don't bring Jonquil, d'you hear? I'll expect you by tea-time on Saturday!" and with a flourish that helped him to regain control of his temper he slammed down the receiver and stumped off to bed.

. . . . .

Sybil heard the sharp click signifying disconnection but for more than a minute she remained standing by the telephone, holding the receiver to her ear and repeating, over and over again, "Hullo? Are you there, Sebastian? Hullo? Sebastian, are you there?" for never in her life had anybody hung up on her and even now she could scarcely believe it had happened. Then, as she remained with her back to the garden-room door jiggling and jiggling at the hook, an arm encircled her waist and she felt the sly tickle of a moustache on the back of her neck, and although her instinct was to shrug herself away she resisted the impulse and yielded slightly to the pressure. She said, replacing the receiver, "It was only Sebastian, he's been offered a teaching post down there, Kelvin!"

Kelvin Scott-James had never been this close to Sybil Sermon and her nearness seemed to affect his breathing, so that he was unable to reply at once and his silence gave her the chance to extricate herself without offending him. She returned to the living-room and he followed looking like a disconsolate collie.

Here, however, noting Sybil's distress, he suddenly found his voice. "He's a bounder!" he said and then, firmly, "This rather buttons it up, doesn't it my dear?"

The phrase 'buttons it up' was very typical of Kelvin Scott-James, who was plump, pink-cheeked, dramatically moustached and still a bachelor at forty-three. He had been christened Eustace Kelvin James, the 'Scott' having been added on July 23rd, 1942, the date he had been commissioned in the Royal Air Force. Almost everything about Kelvin Scott-James dated from that day in 1942, so that one might have said that for him the march of time stopped dead the moment he received his first grudging salute. From that moment, for instance, he had ceased to call a match a match and it became 'a metch', just as an unwelcome obligation became not a worry or a nuisance but 'a bind'. If his car-fender became entangled with anyone else's car fender it was not a collision

but a 'prang', and when he worsted someone in argument, he
invariably described his victory as having 'shot so-and-so down
in flames'. It was from this red-letter day in his life that he
started to sprout his thick ginger moustache and now, in
1961, he was as much an anachronism as, say, the K-nut, the
Masher or the crossbow.

When he left the R.A.F. in 1945 he returned to his father's
photographer's business in Kipley and when his father died
he inherited the business and a certain amount of money, but
the money was so securely tied up in trusts that he could
never get at it and was always short of ready cash. He lived
fairly well, however, for he was a reasonably efficient photographer and it was a professional engagement that brought him
into contact with Sybil and the Amateurs. Later he joined
the Society and played one or two heavy character roles in
her productions, but until a few weeks ago he had occupied
a place on the outer edge of the circle surrounding Sybil.
Only latterly, to his amazed delight, had he suddenly moved
in and was now firmly established as her adjutant and confidant, for, following her abortive raid into the West Sybil had
sought his counsel rather than carry out her threat about
consulting a solicitor.

On the evening that Sebastian rang through with his news,
Kelvin had been sitting on the sofa listening patiently to
another recital of woes and wishing she would stop talking
if only for a moment. Then the telephone rang and he
listened, slightly shamefacedly, to her conversation with
Sebastian. When she seemed to be growing annoyed with her
caller he had taken heart and tiptoed to the door, standing on
the threshold and studying her back view with a degree of
satisfaction that increased the rate of his pulse. The click of
Sebastian's withdrawal from the conversation had been a
signal to advance or 'to press on regardless' as he himself
would have put it, and he moved forward and placed his arm
round her waist, drawing her gently towards him and inhaling
her expensive perfume with the kind of sigh attributed to
lovers in Restoration poems. At last, it seemed, he was
making progress and one aspect of this rather gentle embrace
that encouraged him to make his subsequent leap in the dark
was the sensation of her plump buttocks resting for a matter
of seconds against his almost equally plump loins.

"Look here, my dear. I'm going to speak plainly!" he

announced, when he had closed the door and followed her back to the fire. "If you really want my advice you ought to go right ahead and . . . call it a day. Damn it, how long can he go on dodging the column like this? You could divorce him for what he's done already!"

Sybil continued to look irritable and undecided. There was an emphasis in his voice that suggested he needed very little encouragement to advance from courtier to usurper but the conversation with Sebastian, and the abruptness with which he had brought it to an end, had left Sybil in a mood where she was inclined to be led rather than to lead so she forced herself to smile a warm smile and to say, softly:

"I don't think I *can* divorce him, Kelvin. He's offered me a home down there and if that came out in court, as it most certainly would, the judge would throw the whole thing out in a moment! As a matter of fact he's just practically ordered me to go down there on Saturday!"

Kelvin had met Sebastian on several occasions and had great difficulty in reconciling his memory of the man with someone who issued orders to a woman like Sybil over the telephone.

"Ordered you! But you're not going, of course?"

"Well, no, of course I'm not, but . . . doesn't that leave me in an even more difficult situation? I mean, he could probably prove he asked me a second time. There might even have been someone listening in at that end—a lawyer or somebody!"

She said this without any conviction for she had, in fact, already half-decided to obey the summons as being the one action on her part likely to set a term to this intolerable situation but Kelvin pounced upon her suggestion like a seal after a herring.

"You can depend upon it, my dear, somebody *was* listening but I'll lay odds it wasn't a solicitor! It was that scruffy girl you told me about, the one who messes about in a zoo. It wouldn't surprise me in the least to learn that she was having an affair with him, probably living in the house if the truth's known. If you could shoot him down while he was putting up that kind of black, then everything would be in the bag. From your point of view and from . . . er . . . from *ours!*"

He had not meant to commit himself but it had slipped out and he was a little astonished by his own recklessness but instead of turning a cold and disapproving gaze upon him or challenging his presumption in any way, Sybil coloured and looked away with what he could only think of as a charming display of nervous pleasure. Scenting triumph, he blundered on, a R.A.F. Regiment tank running amok, "I . . . I *mean* that, Sybil! . . . I . . . I'm very much in love with you! I can't stand seeing that bounder treat you this way. I'm not a rich man but I'm not poor either and I'd like you to . . . to *think* about us in that way, even if we could make no real decision until things had sorted themselves out. I'd wait years, you understand me? *Years!*" and swept towards her by the impetus of his declaration he almost bounced across the hearthrug, gathered her in his arms and began raining random kisses on her neck, brow, cheeks and chin.

Sybil was bowled over by the fury of the assault and they collapsed on to the sofa which, fortunately for her, was so positioned as to break their fall. She let the first wave of the attack pass over her and then, with a few dexterous wriggles, held it sufficiently to gasp: "Really, Kelvin! Stop it, Kelvin! Wait, you mustn't! You mustn't, really!" with just sufficient conviction to give him pause although his heart was bursting with triumph.

"I'm not divorced yet!" she stated firmly, "and I'm certainly not going to put myself in the wrong, particularly not if what you say turns out to be true, do you understand?"

Excited as he was, he yet recollected the necessity of consolidating a newly-won position and withdrew an inch or so, continuing to hold her firmly by the hand: "Very well, Sybil," he said briskly, "our next move is to get the gen! You mustn't go to Kingsbay, but I will!"

"*You* will?"

"As soon as I think he's had time to feel secure. In the meantime don't answer the telephone and don't answer any letters he sends. Leave everything to me and if what I feel certain of is true—namely that there's method in his madness and he's giving you cast-iron grounds for divorce—then I'll get the evidence and you—we—can go right ahead!"

A gleam of Sybil's common sense lit up the turmoil of her thoughts and she said: "Why should he invite me down there if he's having an affair with that zoo woman? Surely Kingsbay is the last place he would want me to appear?"

"Bluff!" replied Kelvin, patting her knee with the air of an all-wise male instructing the helpless little woman. "It's a manoeuvre any man might employ if he was determined to get what he wanted without involving himself or his mistress in a public scandal!"

"But what does he want?" cried Sybil, piteously. "I don't know and I don't think I ever shall know!"

Kelvin considered a moment, hesitating to say something that might wound her pride yet realising that the correct strategy now was to push on while she was confused and indecisive.

"I'm afraid that is becoming all too clear, my dear. He intends to end your marriage but he wants to do it in a way that allows him to emerge as the injured party! That's very important to a schoolmaster, remember! If he really is in a position to get a job at a good school then it is essential that he puts you in the wrong. In my opinion he's quite cold-blooded about it and all this flannel about wanting to live in the country is pure camouflage. Nothing more, nothing less! Now are you going to let him get away with it, or are you going to give me permission to call his bluff and shoot him down in flames? It's up to you, Sybil. I'm at your disposal and you must know that by now!" and he gave her two more little pats, one on each thigh.

Sybil hesitated. Her intellect told her that Kelvin was talking sheer nonsense, that Sebastian was not having an affair, that he did not want a divorce and wished with all his heart for a reconciliation on his terms, but latterly her intellect had been on holiday and most of her decisions had been dictated by her emotions. If this bull-calf of a man who was clearly enslaved by her wanted to do a little investigating on her behalf then she might as well let him while Sebastian had another week or so to come to his senses. She said, taking him by the hand: "You're very good to me, Kelvin. I don't know why you should be but you are. You're the only real friend I've found in all this trouble and if you really want to go down there and find out what Sebastian is up to I don't think I should stop you, providing of course you promise to be very discreet and don't get involved in a scene!"

"Ha, ha!" said Kelvin, "I don't think you need to worry on that score! If I find what I think I shall find it will be a matter for a solicitor! By the way, you don't think he'll recognise me? We've met, you know, at one or two of your parties."

"I'm quite sure he won't recognise you," she said bitterly. "He's never done me the honour of recalling the name of any single member of the Society whom I introduced."

"Very well!" said Kelvin, enthusiastically, "we'll let Saturday go by and I'll pop down mid-week. By that time he'll be convinced that you aren't running to his whistle, confound him! Give me his address and where he works, that ought to be sufficient."

She gave him Sebastian's letter and he put it carefully away.

When he was gone she went back into the living-room to turn out lights and empty the ashtrays. An irritating thought nagged at her that perhaps, after all, Kelvin Scott-James was not the man to trust with a mission that required tact and discretion, but the memory of Sebastian's hectoring tone returned to her and she shrugged off her misgivings.

"I don't give a damn either way!" she told herself, "by the time he gets there, Sebastian will probably be here and I'll cure him of this madness one way or another. He can't have changed that much in three months!"

She rummaged in a drawer until she found what she sought, a box of tiny, heart-shaped sleeping pills and as she swallowed two with a glass of soda-water it occurred to her that they were Sebastian's pills dating from over a year ago and that never had she used this means to get a night's rest on account of anyone so utterly predictable as Sebastian Sermon.

CHAPTER NINE

Mr. Sermon
in Damp Clothes

THE long spell of fine weather broke towards the end of July and for the first time since he strode down the hill into Kingsbay Mr. Sermon saw Avalon under seeping skies and ragged hedges of low cloud, the harbour a sombre shadow behind a veil of mist and the twin headlands blotted out by thin, slanting rain. Day after day passed without a gleam of sunshine and visitors, hunched under mackintoshes, slouched along the esplanade looking as though they were victims of a monstrous confidence trick on the part of fate and their landladies.

He spent a good deal of his duty periods in the deserted zoo, brewing endless pots of coffee with Rachel and sloshing out to the sheds in the yard under the cliff where the food for the animals was stored. He was foraging here one morning when he noticed a broad crack in the stone buttress that had been built into the cliff face beneath which the zoo premises were situated. Flood water from a network of culverts immediately above was already cascading over the twenty-foot retaining wall and the fissure between the blocks of stone seemed to him menacing.

He went back into the zoo kitchen and told Rachel, afterwards putting through a call to the Town Clerk and asking for a squad of workmen to be diverted to the spot before the wall collapsed. Ben Bignall sounded snappish and out of sorts. "I can't send anyone down there until next week," he told Sebastian gruffly, "the Mill Brook is blocked at Crowley Bridge and water is a foot deep in Moorend Road. People have been ringing us day and night and if we don't take immediate action we shall have a rent strike on our hands! I'll ask Hesketh to come over and see what can be done in the way of sandbagging."

Hesketh, the Town Surveyor, looked in during the lunch break and dismissed the wall fissure as a trivial matter. He was tired and short-tempered after a day and a night out at the Moorend Road flood and all he did was to send over a vanload of sandbags which Sebastian, Rachel and the two parking attendants filled and placed in position between store sheds and holding wall. It was back-breaking work and when it was done, and the parking attendants had left, he and Rachel sat for a long time over the stove listening to the monotonous drip of water in the yard.

"I don't know what I'm expected to do if that wall collapses and the water comes down on us," Rachel complained. "What does one do with seventy to eighty birds and animals caught up in a flood?"

"Turn them loose, I imagine," said Sebastian, "all but the snakes, that is! Most of the cages are too heavy to load on to lorries unless we were lucky enough to find a dozen volunteers!" and he stood up, stretching himself and yawning. "Damn the wall! I'm for getting warm and dry, Rachel. How about you?"

"I'm staying here tonight," she said briefly. "I'm not going to lock up and turn my back on the poor things with the wall in that condition!"

He noticed then that she had erected a camp bed and put blankets beside the stove and wondered whether he should try and talk her out of remaining at the zoo overnight. She had the telephone of course, but if she needed help urgently it would take at least twenty minutes to reach her at this end of the promenade.

"Are you sure you'll be all right here alone?" he asked, and she shrugged her shoulders, a gesture that reminded him she had been far from her cheerful self during the last few days.

"Has the weather got you down to that extent?" he asked, smiling, and she said, or snapped, "It isn't the weather, it's you!"

"Me?"

"I know about the job Daddy offered you and I know you haven't accepted yet."

"No," he said, unhappily, "I haven't, and your father knows why I haven't. But leave me to sort it out in good time. It's a job for a married man."

"You aren't married," she flashed out, "not really married! If Sybil won't live with you why should you regulate your life by her? You could land that job without Sybil and it's a job you've set your heart on! Fred wants you to have it but he can't keep it open indefinitely. If you don't make up your mind in a day or so you'll lose it, you can take that from me!"

He said, slowly, "Are you sure of that, Rachel? Your father gave me until mid-August!"

"He doesn't tell you everything," she said, sulkily. "He's under pressure from the Governors, I heard him on the phone to them last night."

"You want me to accept very much, don't you?"

"Yes, but it isn't personal!" she said emphatically. "I want it for your sake far more than mine. I stand by what I said when we were coming back from that walk a fortnight ago. I'd grab you if I thought I could but I don't, not really! No one will ever really get you away from that woman and that makes me mad! I want to see you stand on your own two feet and you've got a real chance to do it now but you won't, you're still hoping for a miracle! You are, aren't you, Martin?"

"Yes," he admitted, "I suppose I am. When your father came up with the offer of that job I saw a chance of Sybil and I making a fresh start but I dare say you're right, she'll never bury herself down here, two hundred miles from the West End and her damned Amateur Circus!"

"So you'll let this slip and eventually drift back?"

He gave her a wry smile. "You don't know me as well as you think you do, Rachel." He studied her a minute wondering how much of her acrimony for Sybil stemmed from genuine affection for him, and how much from bruised pride

dating from the afternoon on the Tor. He felt nothing for
her now but comradeship and speculated on the possibility
that she might ultimately arrive at maturity if she became
his mistress but rejected the fancy almost at once. She would
live and die an adolescent, despite her marriage, her series of
jobs, her gallivanting about the world in search of stability.
It was not in her to mature and perhaps herein lay her
appeal. He reached out and ruffled her hair but she did not
respond to the gesture, remaining with head cupped in hands
and elbows on knees staring into the stove. He left her for a
moment to take a final look at the sandbag wall and on his
way back stopped by the door.

"I'll tell you what, Rachel. I'll give Sybil until Friday
night. If she hasn't written, phoned or shown up by then
I'll go over to school and tell your father to put me up for
the interview!"

She looked up, surprised: "What will you tell them?"

"The facts; that I'm separated from my wife and likely to
remain so. It may work if I impress them in other respects.
People are pretty broadminded about that kind of thing
nowadays. They have to be, don't they?"

"If they turn you down I'll write to every Governor telling
him what I think of him!" she said. "Will you ring me before
you turn in tonight?"

"I was going to in any case. Good night, Ray."

Sebastian fought his way home and let himself into the
empty house, turning on the electric fire and peeling off his
wet clothes to drape them round the stove. He drank a
whisky while he was waiting for the kettle to boil and went
out to the wire letter-box to see if there was any mail. There
was nothing from Sybil but Olga had written another fat
letter describing her descent upon Rhodes. Mercifully there
were no more snaps of Andrew the publisher.

He read her letter over supper and found it rather twittery.
Somehow this globe-trotting Olga did not seem the woman
with whom he had shared this house for three carefree weeks
and the realisation saddened him, for at the back of his mind
Olga had always stood four-square as insurance against loneliness. He knew that he could never find the permanence
and tranquillity he needed with Rachel and that her almost
glowering passion for him would soon go grey and cold,

like every other enthusiasm of her zigzag journey through life. Sybil, it seemed, was determined to hold fast to her way of life, a way that could never be his now that he had seen the other side of the hill and Olga—? As in a series of rapidly revolving pictures he saw his life as Olga's husband, a source upon which she fed, intellectually and sexually, with demands made upon him no less exhausting for being amiable and conciliatory. 'I don't know,' he thought, 'I seem to have come full circle. When I left home I broke up the jig-saw pattern of my life meaning to remake it but now none of the pieces seem to fit! I'm stuck with antique selling and beach supervising when I really want to be a teacher, and I'm vacillating between Olga and Rachel when I know in my heart that I want Sybil, providing Sybil would let me lead. I've enjoyed myself these last few months but have I really learned anything that has a direct bearing upon the future? Only that I won't return to the old life, so it all ends in deadlock!'

He did what he usually did on these occasions, deliberately shelved the problem until something should happen to compel re-assessment. He took up a book he had borrowed from the Barrowdene Library, a history of the Dukes of Burgundy, and settled down to read, but he was very tired after all that sandbag filling and was soon fast asleep in the famous arm-chair, the heavy book open on his knees, his reading glasses balanced on the end of his nose. The little clock chimed ten, then ten-thirty but he did not hear it.

It was the telephone bell which brought him stumbling to his feet. It had settled down to a steady burr-burr and some-how he knew that it had been ringing for some time. Bemused, and shedding book and glasses en route, he blundered into the hall and grabbed the receiver. Rachel's voice reached him and he recognised desperate urgency.

"Martin? Oh, thank God! Are you dressed? Can you come right away? The wall is down and water is coming into the yard like Niagara!"

"Have you phoned the Surveyor's office?"

"There's no one there, everyone is up at Moorend Road, if . . .", and then the telephone went dead and he stood a moment staring at it and saying, "Listen . . . listen, Ray!" before he realised that there would be no reply.

He thought, savagely, 'Damn it, I must get help from

somewhere! What about the police?' and then, as he jogged
the receiver, the picture of Rachel waist-deep in flood water
and surrounded by terrified animals projected him out of the
front door and into the teeth of a raging south-westerly gale,
without cap or coat and wearing a pair of loose-fitting carpet
slippers. The one thing he did grab as he rushed past the
hallstand was the torch that Olga kept there for lighting
strangers down the porch steps to The Coombe.

It was the wildest night he ever remembered, tumultuous
with threshing rain and a wind that came bellowing over the
western headland like a maddened giant determined to flatten
everything in his path. Gusts screamed through the elms on
the edge of the links and slates crashed from the steep roofs
of The Coombe cottages, a fragment striking him on the
shoulder as he ran down the hill, holding his torch outstretched like a rapier and losing both slippers in the loose
pebbles at the foot of the gradient. He did not stop to retrieve
them but hurried on barefoot along the glistening pavement
of the Esplanade, thankful that down here there was a glim-
mer of light from the widely-spaced street lamps. To his right
the sea crashed to the foot of the wall and twenty-foot showers
of spray soared over with every other wave, drenching him
before he had gone fifty yards. Where the seafront curved he
remembered to take a short-cut across the parking ground but
he forgot the presence of Symes' motor-coaches, parked in
line near the eastern exit. The feeble gleam of his torch on
the bodywork brought him up short but not in time to avoid
a collision and he bumped knee and chin on the vehicle,
recoiling and shouting a curse into the storm. Then it
occurred to him that the accident might have been providential
for transport would be a Godsend over at the zoo and he
scrambled into the driving seat and groped in the glove
pocket for the ignition key that Symes' men usually left
there for relief drivers in the morning. It was there and he
started the engine but failed to locate the panel light, so that
he had to try every knob and switch before he found headlights and windscreen wiper.

A moment later he was off, sweeping round in a half-circle
and shooting between the exit posts at full throttle. He
handled the bus as if it was a small saloon, driving it full-tilt
along the esplanade to the patch of yellow light that showed
inland from the last lamp-post, and when he arrived in the

gravel yard of the zoo he remembered to swing round in the wide arc and ram the gear into reverse so that the rear faced the building. Then he jumped out and sloshed through a foot of swirling water to the main door but it was locked so he returned and ran round to the side entrance.

The scene here was chaotic. There was a light burning in the kitchen and in its glow he saw what had occurred in the yard. The holding wall was now less than three feet high and there was a twenty-foot subsidence on the bank immediately above. A torrent was rushing through the rent with such force that it was obvious the timber structure below would be overwhelmed in a matter of minutes. Even now the store sheds were disintegrating and a mass of flotsam was swirling about in the yard. He plunged through to the back door, the water reaching his thighs and banged despairingly on the panels, calling Rachel's name at the top of his voice.

"I daren't open the door, get in through the window!" she shouted, appearing suddenly in the door connecting kitchen and zoo. He grabbed a barrel-lid that was floating past and used it to smash the glass, hoisting himself sideways through the frame and falling headlong at her feet, breathless, battered and bleeding about the hands. Water was already more than a foot deep in the room and she was standing in the pool of light with the zoo lamb, Bambi, under one arm and a rope-handled crate under the other.

"The bloody fools!" she shouted at him, "I could see it was going to happen. I phoned two hours ago and they said they'd send somebody with a lorry . . ."

"I've got transport. It's out at the front," he yelled. "Go through and open up before the water reaches the engine," and he splashed through into the zoo, pushing her before him.

There was more light here for the bus headlights were on and she waded between the cages to the main door unlocking it and pushing it outward with her feet. The flood water caught her off-balance as it sought a lower level and she stumbled but he caught and steadied her and together they staggered down the steps to the coach where he flung open the rear emergency door. Bambi and the box were hoisted inside and they battled their way back to the zoo. She shouted; "Open the bird-cages, they aren't locked, only the toucan's! I've got the monkey cage key here," and she turned her back on him while he groped his way along the upper tier opening the cages of the canaries and budgerigars but not waiting to see if the birds flew out. At the far end of the hut was the railed-off enclosure for the dogs, two spaniels, a labrador and a fox-terrier, none of them chained and all barking furiously. He tore at the flimsy gate and it came away in his hands. The dogs splashed past him and he heard them yapping around Rachel near the door. Then he remembered Teena the Siamese cat, who occupied a run built against the east wall. He climbed on to the rail of the dog-run and opened the wire door, expecting the cat to emerge but she did not and when he flashed his torch into the cage he saw her crouched behind her basket, glaring at him with eyes full of fear and hate.

"Come on, Teena, run for it!" he called, hoping the cat would pick her way along the top of the bird cages, but Teena remained motionless so he lunged forward, grabbing her by the scruff of the neck and jumping down into water that reached his waist. The cat bitterly resented his rescue attempt, writhing and spitting in his grasp and attempting to claw his face but he managed to hold on and wade along to the monkey cage where Rachel was coaxing the last monkey from the topmost trapeze. He was so concerned with getting the cat to the coach that he spared her no more than a glance. It was enough, however, to impress him for she stood thigh-deep in water with both arms raised, detached from the chaos around her, and calling softly to the terrified Charlie, encouraging him to join his mate on her shoulder. Sebastian thought, 'That's her vocation all right! Nobody in the world could improve on Rachel Grey in a situation of that kind!' and he felt a kind of reverence for the degree of trust she was able to instil into birds and animals.

By the time he had deposited Teena in the coach, Rachel had rejoined him, carrying out another crate but he had to tell her there was no time to save the remaining animals for flood water, cascading down the zoo steps, was now knee-deep in the yard.

"Drive on the cottage foundations near the gate!" she said. "It's higher ground over there. I'm going back for the hamsters and rabbits," and before he could protest she was gone.

He jumped in and drove the coach across the yard to a spot where the foundations of a demolished coastguard cottage made a little island in the flood. Somewhere behind him was Bambi, the Siamese cat, and whatever pets Rachel had managed to save in the rope-handled crates. Rain was still falling in torrents and as he jumped down into the flood and sloshed his way back to the zoo he heard a warning crack and saw the south wall bulge and the swirling water shift its course to sweep away the topmost planks of the entrance steps. He pulled himself up by the handrail, calling, "Hurry, Ray! The building's coming down on us!" and suddenly she was there, silhouetted against the light of the kitchen lantern, with a small wicker basket under her arm and a terrified hamster on each shoulder.

"Take the basket," she said calmly, "I'm afraid Dinah will lose her nerve and jump!" and she passed over her burden and put up both hands to steady the terrified animals. 'Great God!' he thought, 'she went back to save a couple of rats!' but he grabbed the basket, lowered himself and waded over to the coach. He was in the act of closing the emergency door when he heard a second and louder crack and swung round in time to see the entire front of the building subside and slither outward. Debris spewed across the yard into the wash created by the collapse and then Rachel materialised from the wreckage.

"I'm afraid the snakes have had it," she muttered and then, almost casually, "Open the boot, the monkeys are inside but they'll travel together—not wide!" as he gripped the handle, "just a crack in case one of them pops out."

He did as she asked, feeling curiously humble. She was not so immature after all, not in her own private world but only in the world of people like Sybil and himself and Ben Bignall the Town Clerk. Out here, in a tempest of storm and flood, she was a goddess, exercising a mystical influence over all creatures that flew and crawled and swung from hoops and each of them acknowledged her power as the sick place themselves in the hands of a surgeon. He recognised something else too, another legacy of her father who possessed the same unexpected strength in the world of the young. It was this that he had transmitted to her but it had taken a freakish turn, converting itself into power over animals.

She said, closing the boot: "All right, let's go! And thank

you for coming, Martin. We've done what we can I suppose, I don't see how we could have done more."

The coach engine was still running and he hesitated a moment before choosing a route to lower ground.

"Pull over left and then hard right!" she said decisively, "there's a patch of rubble alongside the putting green, the lorries come in that way when it's wet."

He followed her directions carefully, inching down from the foundation block and groping under the flood water for the half-made path that ran beside the greens. The water had spread out here and was not more than a few inches deep so he was able to follow the line of the palings until he reached the esplanade. The animals seemed quiet, all save Teena who was snarling and swearing on the luggage rack.

"Well, what now?" he demanded, when they had turned east on to the sea-front. "Where the hell can we take the wretched things?"

"I've thought of that," she told him, "drive up to the main Council Stores in Coastguard Road. Someone is on duty and I can find a place for them in the bins and sheds. I'll sort them all out in the morning."

She was right again, the depot was showing lights and two or three of the Surveyor's staff were there to help them unload and house the animals in various corners of the store sheds. There was plenty of packing straw and shavings and between them they made a rough check of the survivors. None of the birds had been brought away but Sebastian told her he had opened the cages and she said it was likely they had flown off when the front of the building fell out. The snakes were drowned and so were most of the rabbits but Rachel had saved two Chinchillas in the first crate. Only the fox-terrier had had the sense to jump aboard when he had released the dogs but Rachel had no fears for the spaniels and the retriever. "They'll show up in the morning," she said, "and I dare say we can track down some of the birds. You didn't manage to free the toucan, did you?"

"No," he said, "the cage was locked and I didn't have the key."

"That was my fault," she said, glumly. "It was on the monkey house ring and I should have thought of it when I was opening up." Then, bitterly, "Someone is going to get the rough edge of my tongue for this! I warned them by phone two hours before I rang you and they promised to send some-one with a lorry!"

One of the Surveyor's men overheard her and growled: "We got enough on our hands up at Moorend. Twenty to thirty houses flooded and some people lost half their furni-ture!" Rachel said shortly: "Damn their bloody furniture! Furniture can't drown!"

He noticed then that she was shivering, perhaps more from shock than cold for the rain was warm and only his feet were cold. "You'd better come home with me and have something hot. You'll get short shrift at those digs of yours at this time of night," he told her. "You can have a bath and I dare say I can find some of Olga's clothes to tide you over until you can drive over to school. We'll borrow a Council van, old Bignall won't mind, after all we've saved the ratepayers!" and he piloted her to a van used by the head gardener and they drove back to The Coombe. She said very little on the way and seemed very cast down by the disaster.

"Don't blame yourself, Ray," he said, "you were wonder-ful and I shall see to it that everyone knows what you did!"

"It's a curious thing," she said as though she had not heard him, "everything I take up develops into a washout one way or another and I didn't intend to make a pun! It's just that I seem to be bad luck for everyone, including animals! I keep thinking of that toucan drowned in its cage!"

"Everything there would have been drowned if you hadn't kept your nerve!" he said. "From here on I take over," and he opened the door and flung her his raincoat that had been drying before the stove. "Wrap yourself in that while I light the fire and run the water. You can soak first and have your soup afterwards. I'm not giving you alcohol, you're suffering from shock!"

She submitted meekly to his fussing and sat warming herself by the stove while he bustled about lighting the sitting-room fire and filling the bath. He found a skirt and a high-necked sweater in Olga's chest of drawers and took two bath towels from the airing cupboard, leaving one in the bathroom and throwing the other across his shoulder. When the bath was ready he called to her and went into his own room, stripping off his wet clothes and towelling himself until he was breathless. As he rubbed it struck him that there was a curiously repetitive pattern about the evening for here he was, once again peeling off wet clothes while the woman who had shared his adventure took a hot bath, exactly the way it had been with Olga when they came home after the incredible coach journey.

When he was dry he went down to the kitchen and opened two tins of soup, helping himself to a large tot of whisky while he watched the saucepan bubble on the stove. A year ago, he reflected, he would have been very alarmed over the prospect of catching a severe cold but now he hardly gave the matter a thought. He supposed he was getting thoroughly used to wettings, and rough living and adventures, they were just part of his new way of life and new personality. He looked at his hands and found them criss-crossed with Teena's scratches and when he rolled up his sleeve there was blood on both arms from a dozen small cuts inflicted by the broken glass of the kitchen window. Casually he wiped his arms with a dishcloth, thinking that if something like this had happened to him in Wyckham Rise he would have scampered all over the house shouting for disinfectant and sticking plaster.

When she came down wearing Olga's skirt and jumper he was relieved to note that she was her cheerful self again.

"That hot bath was heavenly, Martin," she said, "what a thoroughly domesticated creature you are! Soup? Whacko! Give me a quart of it and, in passing, why doesn't Olga throw away garments like these? Does she hoard everything, like those girlish bath cubes I found? I used to give that brand to people for presents when I was a little girl!"

"Drink your soup and shut up!" he said. "We've had enough excursions and alarms for one night. And the moment you've finished you're going to bed!"

"In Olga's bed? Why can't we keep one another warm?"

"You'll find this just as effective," he said, carrying a hot-water bottle from the pantry and filling it from the kettle.

She watched him, grinning broadly and he realised that the sense of failure that had oppressed her an hour ago had now bounced away like every other mood she had revealed to him. He envied her resilience, thinking it must be wonderful to possess that kind of nature, almost like being reborn every hour. Then he went up to Olga's room and stripped the blankets from the bed, carrying them down and making them up on the sofa in the living-room. The arm-chair and a stool would have been comfortable but somehow he could not bring himself to put Rachel to bed in that arm-chair. The fire had burned up brightly and the room was cosy now so that when she came in from the kitchen, having accounted for two plates of soup and three cups of coffee, she cooed delight.

"Martin, you're a dream husband!" she said. "No one ever made this kind of fuss of me! Are you really such a stuffy old puritan as to want to retire modestly to your cold little room upstairs?"

He said, half-seriously, "Yes, I am and it isn't because I'm a puritan but because I don't care to get involved with you when I'm relying on your father to do me the biggest favour anyone has ever done me in my entire life."

"Ah, so that's it," she said, thoughtfully, "I rather thought it was and it takes some of the sting out of it but that doesn't account for your not wanting to marry me, does it?"

He looked exasperated for a moment and then laughed. He was finding it increasingly easy to laugh at her. "I know exactly what would happen if I was fool enough to do that," he told her.

"What?" she said. "Tell me, Martin!"

"In less than a year you'd be wondering how the hell it all happened. I'd be high and dry again, your father would be made miserable and you'd mope around for twenty-four hours telling yourself what a Jonah you were! Then I should be replaced by some other fad and that's about the middle and both ends of it!"

She wriggled herself into the blankets and sat up hugging her knees like a child. "You're probably quite right, Martin," she said, "but what a wonderful year it would be for us both. Are you going to kiss me good night?"

"It's nearly four in the morning," he reminded her, "it will be daylight in an hour. However, I'm not that pedantic I hope!" and he kissed her lightly on the mouth, evading the grab she made at his shoulders.

"You'll never stop treating me like a child, will you, Martin?"

"No," he said from the door, "because you'll never stop being one! Don't put anything more on that fire, I should hate Olga to come home to a charred ruin and learn that a wanton I'd brought in from the streets had started the blaze!" and he turned out the light and went cheerfully up-stairs to bed.

．　　　．　　　．　　　．　　　．

He did not hear the knocking at the front door but opened his eyes when he heard Rachel call from the foot of the stairs. He struggled up and looked at his watch. It was a few minutes past eight o'clock and for the first time in days the sun was shining through his window.

He had left home without a dressing-gown and had not yet bought one but had made do with a threadbare bathrobe of Olga's. He threw this over his pyjamas, hurried along the passage and half-way down the stairs but there he stopped for Rachel, barefooted and wearing his old mackintosh, was standing in the hall talking to a heavily moustached stranger. Or was it a stranger? At second glance Sebastian had an impression that he had seen the man before and linked his pink plumpishness with some kind of official business, insurance or income tax or licensing of some sort, he could not remember what.

"Who is it, Ray? What does he want?" he demanded, embarrassment making him sound irritable.

She shrugged her shoulders. "Better ask him!" she said, yawning, "I didn't even hear him knock, he came round and rapped on the window."

The man addressed him in the kind of voice novelists some-times describe as 'fruity' and Mr. Sermon at once decided that he did not care for his manner. It was too confident for an insurance man but not confident enough for someone sure of his ground. He said, with a note of query: "Mr. Sermon? Mr. Sebastian Sermon?"

"Yes, that's me," said Sebastian, "have you come about last night's affair?"

A flicker of amusement lit up the man's face and then died away as he recaptured his expression between blandness and shiftiness.

"And this will be Miss Grey?"

Rachel, who had been taking no more than a cursory interest in the exchanges, stifled a second yawn and stared at the visitor.

"What is all this?" she demanded. "We didn't get to bed

until four a.m., so if it's about the damage at the zoo and what happened to the animals, go over to the Council. We'll be over there after breakfast."

"It's not about the zoo," said the stranger, and suddenly it occurred to Sebastian that the visitor was enjoying their bewilderment.

"Then what the devil is it about?" asked Mr. Sermon, sharply.

"It's about you, I'm afraid," said the man, "you and this young lady! I need not have introduced myself at all since I have what I came for but I thought it wasn't fair dinkum to go away without telling you!"

Mr. Sermon recognised 'fair dinkum' as an Australian term but his knowledge of dialects told him that this man was not an Australian but a Londoner and a South Londoner at that. The certainty of this made him uneasy for in the back of his mind he caught at a wisp of memory that associated this evasive ass with Wyckham Rise. It had something to do with a group of people sitting in a row and smiling cheesy smiles, and a lot of people in fancy dress with this man and his idiotic moustache bobbing about in the foreground . . . and then the combination clicked, and out walked a drivelling photographer who attended Sybil's dress rehearsals in the Manor Hall.

"Good God!" he exclaimed, "you're Scott-Jones, or Jone-son Scott or Something. You're a photographer!"

The man looked startled for a moment and then made a brave show of relaxing.

"Bang on, Sermon! I didn't think you'd remember me. Sybil said you wouldn't but there, you have after all! It's 'Scott-James' as a matter o' fact, old man!"

"*Sybil?* My wife Sybil?"

"That's right, and I'm acting for her."

Sebastian rode out the impact of this statement with his calf braced against the seventh stair where he had remained during these exchanges. He now rubbed his eyes, wishing that he had remembered to pick up his glasses on leaving the bedroom and then, moving slowly and carefully, he descended to hall level, hunching his bath robe around him like a toga. He went right up to Scott-James and looked him in the face.

"*Acting* for her, you said?"

"That's it, unofficially I suppose you'd say but I'm no

longer certain about that, not in the . . . er . . . circumstances!" and he turned his gaze to Rachel who had remained over by the sitting-room door with both hands thrust into the pockets of Sebastian's brown mackintosh. Following the man's glance Mr. Sermon was shocked to note that the mackintosh appeared to be her sole garment. He took a deep, reassuring breath.

"Go and get something on, Ray and leave me to deal with our friend. Now, sir, *acting* for my wife you said! In . . . er . . . what capacity may I ask?"

Scott-James, who had been slightly intimidated by Sebastian's approach, now assumed a kind of waggish heartiness, a trick of expression acquired almost unconsciously in the anteroom when aircrew were ragging each other about popsies.

"Now look here, Sermon old man, let's be thoroughly adult about this! You know very well what I'm doing here and you'll have one hell of a job to bluff your way out of this! I'm a very close friend of your wife's, metter o' fect she came to me for advice and that's why I'm here."

Mr. Sermon studied him bleakly. "That's what I mean," he said quietly, "but I don't understand *why* you are here, I don't understand that at all! I intend to find out, however, even if it involves taking you to court, you understand?"

"I shouldn't rely too much on courts, if I was in your shoes!" said Scott-James, unpleasantly, adding, "I should imagine that it will pay you to keep clear of the courts, old man!"

"I want to be clear on one thing first," said Sebastian, continuing as though the other had remained silent. "I should like to know, for instance, if you have my wife's written authority for calling on me and forcing your way in here."

"I didn't force my way in," blustered Scott-James, "your . . . er . . . Miss Grey invited me inside when I indicated that I wanted to speak to you."

"Please answer my question," said Sebastian, stubbornly, "have you my wife's authority for this . . . this monstrous impertinence?"

"Yes, I have!"

"*Written* authority? You mean you are a solicitor as well as a photographer?"

"No, I'm not a solicitor!" shouted Scott-James. "It hasn't

got to a solicitor yet but it will, Sermon, and when it does you won't have a leg to stand on!"

Rachel joined in now and Sebastian noticed that she had ignored his order to get dressed but had remained standing by the door.

"Who the hell is he? A private detective or somebody?"

"No," said Mr. Sermon, grimly, "he's not a private detective, just a snooper and a very amateur one at that!" and without a flicker of warning he shot out his right hand, grabbed Scott-James by the jacket collar and planted a powerful, short-armed left in a region of the stomach that would have indubitably disqualified him from any boxing contest, amateur or professional.

The success of the blow amazed him. Scott-James uttered a loud grunt and folded like a half-severed bullrush, bending almost double and spreading his arms wide like a diver. The overcoat he had been carrying across his arm slithered across the polished floor and landed at Rachel's feet and Mr. Sermon, unable to resist the tempting target of Scott-James' head, moved in with a right and a left swing, the right landing a heavy blow on his victim's ear, the left—by far the most powerful of the two—striking home on the side of Scott-James' thickish nose.

"Good God!" exclaimed Rachel, putting a hand to her mouth and stepping back across the threshold of the sitting-room door as Scott-James, dazed under the impact of the three blows swayed left, then right and finally plunged forward to sprawl across a hall chair in an attitude of prayer. His nose began to spurt blood and he groped wildly for his polka-dot scarf while Sebastian, now as white as a sheet, watched him incuriously, not even holding himself in readiness for a counter-attack but breathing hard as though at the end of a strenuous round.

"Now, sir," he said, breathlessly, "you hinted something about evidence you had. I assume you mean photographic evidence. Where is your camera?" and he bore down on the helpless man as though he meant to conduct a search.

"It's in here!" said Rachel suddenly and picked up the overcoat. "But . . . how did you . . . I mean, why did you . . . ?" and she surrendered the coat with a gesture signifying wordless amazement. Mr. Sermon turned his back on

Scott-James and delved into the pockets, his hand emerging with a camera in a canvas case.

"Ha, I thought as much!" he said, triumphantly. "Peeping Tom at the window, eh? Well, it won't avail him very much!" and he extracted the camera, threw the case on the floor, took out the roll of film and put it carefully in his bathrobe pocket.

"Right! Now open the door, Rachel," he said briskly, "and then do as I say. Get dressed at once, do you hear?"

Rachel slipped across the hall and opened the door and when she turned Sebastian had replaced the camera in its case and was holding it suspended by its strap. Scott-James, who seemed to be losing an alarming amount of blood, had now struggled into a sitting position and seemed to be trying to say something but his words were muffled by the scarf clamped to his face.

"You can add this to your account of what happened down here!" said Sebastian and whirling the camera round his head in the fashion of a mediaeval slinger he flailed it against the door with such force that the strap fastenings broke and it rolled down the steps and bounced into a clump of herbaceous border plants.

The deliberate destruction of his camera roused Scott-James as the assault upon his person had failed to do. He rose to his feet and rushed through the open door with a bellow of rage.

"By God, I'll have satisfaction for this!" he shouted. "I'll get the police up here you . . . you vicious little swine! You won't only be cited for divorce! I'll have you in court for assault and battery! My Leica! My God, my Leica!" and he plunged down the steps and began scrabbling among the beds where the camera had rolled. When he found it he raised it in both hands, gibbering half-articulate protests and suddenly the sight of him in this posture, with the ruined camera held up as evidence of his assailant's vandalism, must have struck Mr. Sermon as mildly comic, for he smiled a very tight-lipped smile and said:

"Take it to court, my dear fellow! Label it exhibit Number One! And perhaps your nose will be Exhibit Two, you unmitigated busybody!" and he slammed the door as though upon a spectacle that, whilst having diverting aspects, was nauseating to a man of good taste.

He marched into the sitting-room and found Rachel watching a retreating Mr. Scott-James from the window. Even now she had only partially obeyed his twice-repeated instructions to get dressed, for in place of the mackintosh she wore only a semi-transparent pair of briefs. The sight of her brought a blush to his cheek but she seemed not to notice this and said, dismally: "I warned you I was a Jonah! Now perhaps you'll believe me! I hadn't the faintest idea he was snooping. I thought he was someone from the Council Stores about the animals we dumped there. He didn't say anything, he just rapped on the window and pointed to the front-door, so I nipped out of bed and let him in without another thought. Did I do wrong? Have I let you in for something dreadful? Oh dear, I do hope not."

"Well, you might at least have pulled the damned curtains and slipped something on before you invited him into the house!" growled Sebastian. "However, it might have been worse I suppose, the idiot might have got away with his disgusting photographs and we shouldn't have heard another word about it until they were handed up to the Judge!"

"He . . . he took pictures? You're . . . you're sure he took pictures?"

"Of a sort through the windows no doubt, although I can't really see the purpose of them even now. It isn't as if we were both in the room but I suppose they'd be admissable as evidence that you spent a night in the house! Well, thank God I managed to floor him and get hold of them!" and he bunched a newspaper, put it in the grate and set a match to it, tossing the roll of film into the flames and watching it burn.

"You were absolutely marvellous, Martin!" she said admiringly. "It was just like a Western! One, two, three and he was out for the count. I didn't know you could box. I find out something new about you every day!" and as she rattled on she wriggled into her girdle and brassiere as though dressing in his presence was in the natural order of things.

So indeed it seemed for he was preoccupied with other matters. He sat thinking deeply, legs outstretched, hands deep in the pockets of Olga's robe and when she said, "Hi! I was asking where you learned to box?" he looked up with a smile and replied: "I never did, I watched the boys over the years and I suppose I acted instinctively. He was the kind of man it was a positive pleasure to strike. I wish I'd hit him half a dozen times more and knocked all his teeth out!" Then, as though to himself, "I just can't imagine Sybil doing a thing like that, it's not like her at all. It's something many women might do I suppose but not Sybil, it's too . . . too cheap and stupid!"

He stood up, suddenly, addressing her directly.

"I suppose you know what this might mean to you, Rachel?"

"That I could be cited? Yes, I realise that, I'm not really the 'teenager you make me out to be, Martin and frankly I don't care a damn! If Sybil does divorce you I think I'd be glad about it and not simply because you might ultimately come round to taking me seriously. I think it would be right for you and the only aspect of it that worries me at all is the effect it might have on Fred. He'd pretend to be broadminded of course but it would upset the old boy and that's what you're concerned about too, isn't it?"

"Yes," he said, "but there's rather more to it than that, Ray. If Sybil uses you to divorce me it's goodbye to a job at Barrowdene, I'm afraid!"

She looked shocked. "Oh no, Martin, that wouldn't be fair!"

"It's inevitable none the less. Can you imagine the Governing Board approving the appointment of a man whose wife divorced him on grounds of adultery, citing the Headmaster's daughter?"

She stopped tugging at her hair and sat down, looking very troubled indeed.

"Will that idiot really summons you for assault and battery?"

"Not him, we've seen the last of him," said Sebastian, "but what I have got to discover is how closely Sybil was involved in getting him here. I think that will decide the future more than any one thing and I might as well start on it now. The fact is, I'm getting tired of events overtaking me, I'm going to start shaping them again!"

"You'll go to Sybil? But suppose it's true? Suppose she did send him and won't even talk to you except through a solicitor?"

"Then she can do what the hell she likes about everything!" he snapped.

"Will you come back again?"

"Of course I'll come back! I shall go into partnership with Tapper Sugg if she goes ahead with the divorce."

"Then oughtn't you to ring Father?"

He hesitated. "No," he said at length, "I don't feel like talking to him. At the moment I only feel like talking to one person—my wife! You go to him and tell him the whole truth, exactly as it happened and say I'll be over to see him by mid-week. If he can hold that job open until then well and good."

"But if he can't, Martin?"

"If he can't, it's just too bad," and he turned to go upstairs but she ran forward and caught his arm.

"I'm sorry, Martin, really sorry! You believe that, don't you? I didn't want anything like this to happen . . . me letting him in, me being here; after what I said to you that day it's almost as though I deliberately . . ."

"You never did a thing deliberately in your entire life, Ray," he said, for he could see now that she was genuinely distressed and now considered herself wholly responsible for the situation. She followed him out to the stairs and at the foot he turned to her. "Look Ray, don't blame yourself and stop worrying! I believe I can cope with this and anyway I mean to try right now! You've got things to do about those animals and I've got to pack and get time off . . . !" and he turned his back on her and went upstairs, marching along to his room, pulling open the wardrobe and throwing his knapsack on the unmade bed.

He had intended stuffing a few things into the bag, hurrying into his clothes and going straight over to Bignall's office in order to tell the Clerk he would be away for a couple of days but the sight of the big, shapeless knapsack checked his rush and he stood beside the bed looking down on it, realising that it still had for him the significance of a banner. He recalled so vividly how he had plucked it from the shelf in the spare room a few months ago, or was it half a lifetime ago? It had all seemed so straightforward then, a mere stuffing of necessities into that bag and a slamming of doors on a life that he was shedding like a pair of worn shoes but now it wasn't anything like so simple as it had appeared on that mild April night. One could go through the motions of changing the course of one's life but was never able to shed old ties and old loyalties. No matter how far or fast one ran they were always there, tagging along in pursuit, sometimes below the horizon but sometimes, as now, breathing down one's neck. And with this knowledge the futility of all that had happened since he began his odyssey came down on him like a wet fog bringing a sensation of fear, frustration and helplessness. The blows he had struck upon the person of the egregious Scott-James had carried him through the immediate crisis but now that the man was no longer there to be used as a punchbag he felt like a castaway waving his arms and shouting at a vessel steaming past the island. The improbability of his situation maddened him. If Scott-James had appeared on any other morning but this he would have had to return to Sybil with his tail between his legs and it seemed to Sebastian quite monstrous to be called upon to account for wild oats that had not even been sown, notwithstanding strong and consistently applied temptation on the part of the girl downstairs. As he remembered this, his anger against Sybil rose in his throat and into the furnace of his rage he threw not only Scott-James and his camera, but all Sybil's prejudices and vanities that separated them like a prickly hedge preventing them from building a life worth living, and this at a time when the minutes of history were ticking away with terrifying speed!

He stood there looking down at his fallen standard, the folds of Olga's bathrobe hunched about him, the bluish stubble on his chin giving him the haggard look of the defeated, and then he was suddenly aware of Rachel standing in the doorway looking across at him with a kind of communicated comradeship, as though evaluating his sense of loss and yearning to share it without trespassing further on this privacy.

As their eyes met, she said, deliberately:

"There's an old story, Martin, the one about the innocent man who served twenty years for murdering someone who was still alive."

"What about him?" he growled and she said, quietly:

"When he came out of prison he took a gun and shot the man he was supposed to have killed in the first place!"

He said, gruffly: "Very well, shut the damned door and

make sure you lock it this time!" and when she had done this and crossed to him, lifting her face to be kissed, he took hold of her with a kind of savage frenzy, as though she represented all the people and forces who had prevented him from becoming the man he wanted to become and believed he had become up to the moment when he identified Scott-James in the hall below. His use of her was not only impatient but almost painfully demanding, and the words and expressions that issued from him were alien to all she knew of the man, but she did not resent this any more than his roughness because she was aware that he did not at that moment identify her as Rachel Grey, the woman who had been importuning him for weeks past but simply as a means of release from the almost intolerable oppression within him, a chance of hitting back at everything that had harried him down the years. It had been the certainty that such a release was vital to him that had impelled her to lock front and back doors and follow him up to his room, for she wanted now to offer herself not as a woman in search of physical gratification but as an instrument that would enable him to reassert himself to himself, as someone who was not wholly defeated. He had often surprised her and now he did so once again with his strength and brutality but when the climax passed and he had subsided physically and emotionally she sensed triumph at having been the means of such reassertion, at having restored to him by a few moments of turmoil a dignity that he could never have found in the body of a stranger without full knowledge of his inner conflict.

She held him to her while he became aware of what had occurred, while the sun beat into the room and the silence of the house settled about them like a presence. She thought, wonderingly: 'He's never really had a woman before, not really, not like this! Those other women, his wife and that experimental spinster of his, they only took from him, the one regularly, the other spontaneously. They didn't yield anything of themselves in the process because he was too gentle and considerate and had so much essential kindness. Now perhaps he's learned something about women, that it doesn't do always to be kind and gentle and after-you-madam! I'll never have him again but it isn't necessary that I should because he's moved on now and perhaps I have too, and

when he meets his wife again he'll be a different lover altogether and my guess is that she'll be grateful in the end.'
She said, aloud: "This is the one and only time, Martin, but
it wasn't so one-sided as you imagine, dear. At least it has
established something, two things!"

"What did it establish, Ray?"

"That you really are the man I thought of you as being
and that I've been of real use to someone at last. Remember
that, because I won't be around to remind you when you
come back. Knowing you has taught me so much I needed
to know and could never have learned from anyone else!
I'm not going to risk you going sour on me!" and she got up
and went out, closing the door.

He lay still for a few moments thinking but his thoughts
no longer seethed and tormented him as they had done
when he was standing by the bed looking down on his
knapsack.

CHAPTER TEN

Mr. Sermon Takes
Mother-in-Law's Advice

MR. SERMON caught the train for London that same afternoon.

He set off without any preconceived plan or notion of what
he would do on arrival home or, in fact, where he would
go when he reached the Paddington terminus.

It may seem odd that Mr. Sermon gained impetus to
project him towards his wife from an act of adultery but it
was so, for Rachel's almost compulsive act had opened his
mind to a conviction, perhaps an unconscious one, that if
one woman desired him then the other necessarily must. To
simplify it further, if Rachel Grey, young, unattached and
undeniably attractive, was prepared to go to such lengths to
demonstrate her affection for him, then Sybil, his wife, was
unlikely to set aside a man who had remained faithful to
her for twenty years and had fathered her children.

Sebastian arrived at the Junction soon after two o'clock
and having so much on his mind had forgotten to supply
himself with reading matter for the journey. He sat in his
empty compartment and studied the landscape until the express roared in and then, having no necessity to change trains
(for the coach was switched to the main line train by a local

engine) he watched passengers leave the express and pass
his window on their way to the branch line.

It was high season now and there were a good many of
them, mostly elderly couples, for despite the Kingsbay
U.D.C.'s donkeys and paddling pool the town had yet to
attract a family patronage. One of the first to pass Sebastian's
carriage was a lean, sun-burned traveller wearing a new
panama hat and suit that did not look as if it had been made
in Britain. He was carrying a heavy case and a large leather
grip, both bearing labels 'Marseilles'.

The man's face was familiar and Sebastian had a good
view of him as he passed. He marked the panama-hatted
man's arched brows and slightly aquiline features and
thought: 'He must be a Kingsbay worthy home after a
holiday and I probably met him during my first weeks in
town', and then a sharper memory focus brought him to his
feet with a rush as he realised that this man was exactly like
the American publisher who had been photographed in
Naples with his arm round Olga's waist.

"Good God!" he exclaimed to himself. "He can't be! Olga
is supposed to be in Casablanca and isn't due home for
another ten days!' But it was and Olga wasn't in Casablanca,
for here she was on the 'Up' platform of Haversham Junction, mincing along in four-inch heels some ten yards behind
the Boston publisher and his porter, and fumbling in her
handbag as though searching for a tip.

He was so surprised to see her that he shouted without a
second thought, projecting head and shoulders from the
window and yelling "Olga! Olga!" and at once she stopped
fumbling and looked right, executing a little jig of delight
and calling "Andrew! Wait Andrew!" at the man ascending
the footbridge that spanned the lines.

She ran or rather teetered towards him, arms spread wide,
eyes shining with pleasure and when she kissed him on either
cheek he noticed how radiantly healthy she looked and what
an expensive perfume she was using and how altogether different and more sophisticated she was from the Olga he had
parted from three months before.

"Oh, Martin, it's so good to see you!" she said, breathlessly,
"but don't tell me you're on your way up to town just as
we're coming home. We left the boat nine days before the
end of the voyage so as to get home quicker by overland

route from Marseilles. Andy, darling, he's here!" as the man in the panama hat approached and stood waiting to be introduced. "This is him! This is Martin-Sebastian! Isn't it a shame? He's going up to London on the train we've just left."

The man lifted his hat and smiled but did not seem to be overwhelmed by the coincidence.

"I told you we should have wired, girl," he said, with not much more than a hint of an accent, and to Sebastian: "You aim to be away long, Mr. Sermon? Business trip, maybe?"

"I . . . er . . . I'm not sure," said Sebastian, wishing heartily that he had not drawn attention to himself, and thankful that the reunion was strictly limited by the time factor. "I'm afraid I have to go up, Olga, it's very important but maybe it's lucky we met. Here's your key and you'll find everything okay because Mrs. Gibson came in at midday and promised to clean up while I was away. Look out . . . they're going to shunt!" and he hopped back into his carriage followed by Olga who shouted to Andrew, "It's all right! Our train doesn't go until after his. Be a darling and get the luggage in. I'll travel round and hop out when she's hooked up," and she bounced down on the seat opposite Sebastian, caught up both his hands and gazed at him with the expression of a nice-mannered little girl who had just opened her Christmas present.

"Oh, Martin dear!" she said, breathlessly, "I simply had to get rid of him, if only for two minutes. So much to tell you! So much has happened! But how can I possibly tell you in such a little time? Don't bother about the key, dear, we'll be staying at the Frobisher until Wednesday and anyway the house is officially yours until the end of August, isn't it? Oh dear, how can I begin? I didn't want it to be like this, all gabbled and breathless, but perhaps it's as well . . . you see, Martin . . . !"

"You're getting married," he said helpfully. "You're marrying Andrew, the publisher, and you don't have to break it gently or apologise, Olga!"

She stared at him with such astonishment that he laughed.

"You *knew*? But *how* did you know? Did somebody write? Somebody on the boat . . . ?"

"No, Olga, you told me yourself in your letters. Damn it,

I've been a schoolmaster for twenty-five years and I'm an expert at reading between lines. Boys use words to screen a blank mind and you used them to cover up the truth. In any case I would have known the moment I looked at you."

"Oh dear, does it show that obviously?"

"Yes, it does, you might as well be shedding confetti all over the carriage! When is it to be? On Wednesday you say?"

"Oh no, not that soon, we're just going up to town on Wednesday. Andy's got business with publishers and I've promised myself a terrific shopping spree! We hope to marry very soon tho' and go back to the Continent for the honeymoon, Paris first, then Switzerland . . . but look here, we've only a minute left, how about you? What's been happening while I've been away? I got both your letters but they were terribly disappointing! I don't think I should have accepted Andy if they'd been the kind of letters I thought I might get!"

"Hoped you might get, Olga?"

She stopped smiling and looked confused.

"No, Martin, not really! We don't have to pretend with one another do we? You're still in love with your wife. I always knew that in my heart and I'm sure I did the right thing for both of us. *You* think so now, don't you? Say you do, anyway! Oh, God!" as the coach struck the buffers of the express and almost precipitated her into his lap, "here we are and so much still to be said. Have you really got to go to London? Can't you come back with us and go up next week?"

"No, Olga, I can't," he said, "and you'd better get out before Andy thinks you're having second thoughts. Here," as he opened the door and helped her down, "I'll get in touch soon, early next week perhaps and before you come up to town."

The guard checked the door and blew his whistle. Sebastian could see Andy standing uncertainly beside the Kingsbay train but Olga seemed reluctant to release his hand and only did so when the guard said, "Stand clear, Madam, if you please!"

"Martin," she cried, as the train began to move, "there's something I've simply got to know!"

"What is it, Olga?"

"Will you be staying in Kingsbay?"

"Yes, I will, Kingsbay or district, why?"

She was almost running alongside now and he feared for her safety.

"Would you like to buy the house? Cheap?" she screamed. "What furniture you want and I'll leave a mortgage on . . . !"

The hiss of escaping steam would have drowned any word he uttered but in fact he made no reply because he was too stunned by her question to think of one, even a noncommittal one. He leaned far out of the window as the train gathered speed and caught a last glimpse of her in a swirl of smoke, a bright, eager little figure still teetering along but slowing down as she yielded the race and still, as far as he could determine, screaming that she would sell the house cheaply and leave a mortgage if wanted!

He hoisted the window and returned to his corner wondering how a cruise had transformed a shy and rather lovable little woman into the chirrupy, breathless opportunist he had left behind at Haversham. For an hour or so he sat thinking, and it was contemplation of Olga's offer about the house that switched his thoughts on to an unexplored path. Olga had asked him to buy the house and all the furnishings, things that had comprised her home for years and, until his arrival in Kingsbay, had constituted her major interest in life. Her offer to sell implied a determination on her part to make an absolutely clean break with the past, to put Kingsbay and everything it signified behind her and make a new beginning, probably as far away as Boston, Massachusetts. Could Sybil be induced to do a thing like that? Did she value her marriage highly enough to turn her back on every single thing in her life except a husband who had already deserted her? Apparently not, for she had already expressed her views in this respect, once when she had visited him and again over the telephone when he told her about the Barrowdene offer. But suppose he could find some means of forcing the issue? Suppose he could present her with a reasonable alternative, a pleasantly-situated house of the size and style to which she was accustomed and not a teacher's cottage on a moor? Then, as he pondered this possibility, he had a dazzling inspiration. He remembered that he was the legal owner of the house in Wyckman Rise. Both Sybil and her father had insisted on this when they had bought it twelve years ago.

He thought with excitement, 'Great God, I can sell the damned house from under her and she couldn't do a thing to stop me and neither could her father, for all his cleverness! I could sell it and buy Olga's house and we could live there until I get a housemastership at Barrowdene!' His thoughts raced along keeping pace with the express. Sybil had declared that she couldn't live in Kingsbay but he didn't take this very seriously for, in some ways, Kingsbay could offer the social life that she seemed to find so important to her happiness in suburbia. It had a large number of residents that Sybil would have to admit were 'good-class' and it had a thriving Dramatic Society and a number of excellent shops. Once the initial break was made she would be very much at home in a place like Kingsbay and for the time being he could travel to and from Barrowdene each day. As the pattern of their lives began to emerge he was impressed by its symmetry. All that was missing was the centrepiece and at the back of his mind Sebastian still had a hidden reserve of confidence regarding his power to jolt her into conjugal obedience. He thought: 'By God, it's the answer! What can I lose? If it succeeds I'm home and dry and if it fails we might just as well separate and I'll forget about Barrowdene and go in with Tapper Sugg!' and so satisfied did he feel with his decision that he put up his legs on the opposite seat, folded his arms and dropped off to sleep, lulled by the steady clack of wheels, a sound that had always given him pleasure.

.   .   .   .   .

He did not go straight to Wyckham Rise in the hope of forestalling the report of Scott-James. By now he had dismissed Scott-James from his calculations for without photographic evidence the man was harmless and in any case he would be unlikely to tell the inglorious truth about his encounter at the love-nest. Instead he booked in at a medium-priced hotel and at once telephoned Olga's hotel in Kingsbay, asking her to hold the offer open until he returned early the following week.

After that he was able to put Olga out of mind. She now belonged to the past, as surely so as Napier Hall and the Reverend Victor Hawley, and the thought of his former

Headmaster awakened a sense of mischief in him so that he dialled the school number, asking the secretary to put him through to the Reverend Hawley but neglecting to identify himself or state his business. The Headmaster came to the 'phone and Sebastian could hear him wheezing into the receiver.

"Yes? Who is it? Hawley here!"

"It's Sermon," said Sebastian, feeling waggish, "surely you recall my voice, Headmaster?"

He heard the old man gasp and then begin to gobble with excitement.

"Sermon! My dear fellow! I'm delighted to hear from you, delighted! *Where* are you? In London? At home? Are you coming over? Are you coming back to us?

"You still want me back?" said Sebastian, winking at a sparrow on the bedroom window-sill. "Oh, come now, Headmaster, surely not after what I tried to do to Lane-Perkins last April!"

"Nonsense!" said Hawley, "think no more about it, Sermon. That turned out most unexpectedly and I would have written you about it if I'd known your address. As it was I telephoned your wife, asking her to explain." He did not wait to discover whether Sybil had relayed his message but went on: "The truth is, Lane-Perkins' father came round the following day and asked for you! No, he wasn't angry, all he wanted to do was shake your hand and tell you to repeat the dose once a week! He said he'd never known the boy so tractable and had since taken to walloping him regularly whenever merited and with excellent effect! But look here, Sermon old man, don't let's waste time, I'd begun to think you weren't rejoining us after all and I'm interviewing a replacement."

'You fearful old liar,' thought Sebastian, 'do you imagine that I don't know you're at your wits-end to find somebody to work half as conscientiously as I did at your drivelling little establishment,' but he said, soberly: "Well, as a matter of fact, Headmaster, I can't return to Napier Hall. I appreciate you keeping the job open for me all this time but I've accepted a post at a big school in the West."

"Really?" ('He sounds amazed, damn him!' thought Sebastian) "Might I know which school it is?"

"Certainly," said Sebastian. "It's Barrowdene."

"Barrowdene!" Clearly the Reverend Hawley was impressed. "Well . . . er . . . congratulations my dear chap, that's . . . er . . . splendid, quite splendid! I didn't think we should keep you very long," he went on, forgetting that Sermon had served fifteen years on his staff, "but I . . . er . . . I do hope we shall see something of you before term opens?"

"Perhaps," said Sebastian, suddenly losing interest in the Reverend Hawley, "I'll write you after I get settled."

"By the way, how are you, old man? In good health, I trust?"

"In excellent health," said Sebastian, gravely, and then, as a parting shot, "I think you can safely assume that I'm over the menopause, Headmaster!" and he rang off before he could decide how the Reverend Hawley had reacted to this rather unsporting remark.

He then asked the operator to get him a personal call to his mother-in-law at Beckenham, telling the man that when the caller asked to know who was ringing he was to say 'an old friend' and plug the call through to his room. He did not, on any account, want to converse with his father-in-law, feeling that his advantage lay in keping his presence in London a secret from Sybil.

When the old lady heard his voice she seemed excited.

"Sebastian? It's really you? You're in London? You've gone back to Sybil?"

"No, mother, I haven't but I intend to on certain conditions. Is Sybil's father there? I want very much to talk to you but I don't want him interfering at the moment."

There was a pause, then she said: "No, he's not here, he's gone over to the Conservative Club and won't be back until after eleven. Why don't you come straight over? You could be here and gone before he shows up." Her voice became earnest, "I'd like you to do that Sebastian. I've discussed this silly business with Sybil and I want very much to talk to you before either of you do anything stupid. Will you come? Will you come straight away?"

"Yes," he said gratefully, "I'll get a car and come right away, so long as you're sure he won't be there to confuse the issue."

"He won't be, I promise you!" she said and rang off.

He asked the head porter to get a hire car and while he

waited for it he thought with affection of the shrivelled little woman in the old-fashioned villa at Beckenham. Although it had been Sybil's father who had encouraged his suit he had always much preferred Mrs. Rudge, a simple but intelligent woman who let her husband's bluster flow over her like the cries of a child at play, but one, he suspected, who had always respected him and had been immensely relieved when he stepped in and snatched her daughter from under the noses of the flighty young men who surrounded her.

The car took him over Vauxhall Bridge and through the congested districts of New Cross, Catford and Ladywell and as they passed between rows of yellow-brick houses and shops, with hardly a hint of tree or bush, he wondered why his parents-in-law had never moved further out to a suburb where it was at least possible to draw breath without the taint of petrol fumes and sweating tarmac. Perhaps their roots went down too far in this asphalt and chalk of London so that they found security in this wilderness of brick and grime and perhaps a little of their Cockney prejudice had rubbed off on their daughter who clung to the outer rim of the city as tenaciously as they clung to the inner.

"Turn left here and then second right," he told the driver and the car stopped outside the hideous Edwardian house with its sooty flower beds and mottled laurels.

The old lady met him in the hall and shook hands. She was never one for kissing thought Sebastian as he followed her into the room she still thought of as 'the parlour'. There was a bottle and one small glass on the bamboo fern-table and she said: "You'll have a glass, Sebastian, the same old brew!" and without waiting for an answer she poured a glass of her homemade raisin wine and sat on a high-backed chair opposite, her hands folded on her lap, her beady little eyes regarding him with a mixture of affection and curiosity.

"Now then, let me hear your side of it, I've already heard hers," she said and waited.

He told her his side of it and she listened without a single query or interruption, until he reminded her that he was still technical owner of the Wyckman Rise house and could use his ownership to force Sybil's hand.

"That's a real sensible move," she said approvingly, "providing you'll follow it up, of course!"

"Follow it up with what, Mother?"

"How would I know that? It depends how sure you are of yourself. Anyway, if you do sell the house you'd best sell it to me."

"To you?"

"It's the only way you can do it quickly and without a lot of talk and a lot of time wasted. I know Sybil; she's not a bad girl and never was really but she's lazy, real lazy I mean, not about cooking and keeping the house clean but about making up her mind on everything that matters. Giving that money to her was the worst turn her father could have done the girl. With that sort of money you don't have to think, bank managers and such-like do it for you, you follow me? Yes, you'd better sell me the house at cost. Then I'll make a profit on it and that'll stop Albert putting his oar in! He never could resist a profit, no matter how he come by it!"

The clarity and cunning with which the old lady approached the problem made Sebastian's head spin but he did not doubt her judgement or suspect for one moment that she might have an ulterior motive. She had never been greedy for money and she was right of course about the necessity for taking action before Sybil could make trouble one way or another.

"How could it be done?" he asked, "how could we put it into effect at once?"

"Easy," she said, "you write me a letter in reply to one I write you, stating price and completion date. Write it tonight with yesterday's date and I'll take it over to the lawyer's and get it drawn up as soon as it arrives."

"But you haven't written me a letter yet," Sebastian protested, smiling and thinking how Tapper Sugg would have enjoyed his mother-in-law.

"I'll send one on," she said impatiently, "but it'll have last Monday's date on it! What did you pay for the place? Three-five wasn't it?"

"Three seven-fifty but it's worth double that now," he told her.

"So much the better," she said, "I won't spend any of it and it's all coming to you an' Sybil an' the kids anyway. The kids don't touch none of it until they're twenty-five though, I put that in the will and I'd have made it thirty if the lawyer had let me!"

"Well," he said admiringly, "that seems to be that, so long as you're sure it's legal."

"It will be by the time she gets to looking into it," replied the old woman grimly, "but the house is not all that important, Sebastian, and selling it won't do no good unless you stand up to her and show her who's really boss. I don't mean just a lot o' bluster like my Albert, I mean that streak you've got in you that you've never let out, not for her to see anyway! I reckon I knew it was there years ago and when I heard you'd run off I was glad at first because I reckoned it would bring her up short and so it did. Then she goes and makes a muck of it, or you do, or you both do, so now you got to set to and start all over again!"

She was silent for a moment but Sebastian waited, knowing she had not finished her summing up.

"This other flibberty-gibbet, not the one who's found herself a man but the other one—you aren't really struck on her are you? If you are you might as well call it a day and let my girl stew in her own juice and I can't say as I'd blame you. I wouldn't have any part in making you go back if you hadn't a mind to go."

Sebastian decided to meet honesty with honesty.

"No," he said deliberately, "I'm not in love with Rachel and she's aware of that but I've been to bed with her. Once. Today, as a matter of fact because I was half-crazy with rage over Sybil taking that damned photographer into her confidence."

The old lady gave no sign that she was shocked or displeased.

"Well, I suppose that's your affair," she said, "but don't be such a fool as to tell Sybil about it. She'd sooner not know anyway—most women would sooner not know but you men will start confessing the minute you get worked up! You keep that bit of the tale to yourself and take the initiative from the minute you come out in the open about selling the house over her head. She'll storm back o' course, but that's your cue and don't muff it a second time, you understand?"

"No, I don't, not altogether," admitted Sebastian, "you mean that's my cue for insisting she starts packing and coming back to Kingsbay with me?"

The old lady looked exasperated.

"You seem to stow away any. amount o' book learning son," she said, "but you don't seem to have learned much about my girl all the time you've been living with her. You been insisting she comes where your job is, haven't you, and where's it got you so far? You're still down there and she's still up here and now the pair of you are getting cluttered up with other people! If she stays high and mighty when you tell her you've sold the house and bought another for her then I reckon she'll deserve all that's coming to her and you'll have to fall back on the rough stuff, same as she told me you started to before you left."

"Rough stuff?" protested Sebastian, "oh but look here, Mother, that's what began it all! You can treat some women that way but not Sybil, she isn't that sort at all!"

The old woman looked at him pityingly.

"Isn't she? It's like I said, you're bright about some things but you got a lot to learn about Sybil. *All* those stuck-up women are 'that sort' as you call it! All of 'em, take it from me, and she's no exception. They need to have it slapped out of 'em and if I'd had my way I'd have done it for you when she still wore plaits!"

She looked so small and fragile sitting there in her old-fashioned black dress with her hands folded on her lap that Sebastian found it impossible to picture her chastening a strapping girl like Sybil, yet there was about her an air of authority that told him both Sybil and her father would have gone some distance out of their way before crossing the old lady when she was roused. He said, half-jokingly, "That's old fashioned stuff, Mother and I don't suppose you gave her more than a clout or two!"

The old lady smiled, very grimly, he thought, and her eye seemed to kindle. "Her father was on the road in those days," she said, "and I had the bringing up of her. She'd have been different I can tell you if he'd stayed a commercial traveller! She tried to put it over of course but we didn't have no more than half a dozen set-to's. That was plenty!" and she nodded sharply, as though to drive the point home.

"What did you quarrel about?" he asked curiously.

"The usual things, putting all that stuff on her face too soon, staying out, answering back, the usual. The first couple o' times I did clout her and send her upstairs but after that I showed more sense. I took a stick to her and made sure

I caught her in the bathroom when she had nothing between her and the stick. Twice I did it and the second time she had her breakfast standing! We didn't have no more hanky-panky after that, not until her father come home for good and set about ruining her. Came closer to doing it properly that one time, he did, he could never get over her being so pretty an' popular with the boys."

The old lady's narrowed expression told him that she had used the verb 'ruin' in the final and Victorian sense and that she meant a great deal more than 'spoil'. He said:

"How do you mean, 'that one time'? When?"

Mrs. Rudge seemed to retreat into herself for a few moments, almost as though she was on the point of dropping off to sleep and then like the sudden switching on of two tiny masked lamps, her boot-button eyes twinkled and a half-smile creased the line of her tightly-folded lips.

"Ah, then you didn't know about it after all? I never thought you did, not really, and naturally I never said nothing and never would have, not even now if I didn't think it might jolt you into going about it in the right way! You remember that kid she had, the one who come before its time soon after you was married?"

"The first one? The one we lost at six months?"

"It wouldn't have been yours if it had lived, it would have been that young scallywag's—what was his name?—the one who nipped off abroad!"

"Norman Stephenson? That boy with the sports car that woke up the neighbourhood? Sybil and *him!*" and he jumped up, staring down on her with stark amazement on his face. "Are you sure of that? Are you absolutely sure?"

"Yes, I am sure but don't you ever let her know it was me who told you," she said sullenly. "If you want my advice, and after all that's what made you come here, you'll keep it to yourself same as I have all these years but you'll act on it none the less. Remember it, just so long as she holds out and then forget it again!"

"How could I do that?" he stuttered.

"Sit down again and don't fly off the handle like one o' them actors who give me the gripes on the telly!" she said imperturbably. "It all happened twenty years ago and she's never let you down since, I can swear to that! But she was very gone on that young waster, tho' I could see what he was worth from the start and so could she as soon as she told him she was expecting. He did just what anyone might have expected him to do, took to his heels and didn't stop until he fetched up in China, or Africa, or some outlandish place! Then she pulled herself together and as it was things worked out pretty well all round. Until now, that is, when most couples have got through the worst of it and have grown up like you and Sybil never have!"

He was listening but less than half her words registered, perhaps because he was searching and searching for all the odd pieces of the picture that made up the tableaux set in this house all those years ago; himself with a bunch of freesias calling on Sybil one mild autumn evening about the time everybody was chattering about Hitler and Czechoslovakia and Chamberlain's piece of paper and Sybil, pale and preoccupied, then bursting into tears and throwing herself in his arms and saying something about her having been a beast to him and that Norman Stephenson had treated her so badly going off like that when they were practically engaged. Then the old man, her father, had come into the room and administered little pats on his shoulder and gurgles of comfort for Sybil, and all the time this sharp-eyed old woman had remained silent in the background, watching all three of them with eyes that missed nothing and a mouth closed like a sprung trap. Well, he had been fooled all right, just like a character in one of those television plays the old lady despised but what difference did it make after all these years, after they had bred two not-so-brilliant children of their own and had lived through a world war and its aftermath? The knowledge that she had married him on the rebound did not make him feel resentful. Instead, he felt for her a kind of pity that she had been so shamefully humiliated and with sympathy came pride and wonder that she had recognised him as a man who could give her back her pride and self-respect, and as he thought this he began to see aspects of their early married life that had escaped him or that he had taken for granted or forgotten or mislaid in the weekly wash of married life. He remembered, for instance, Sybil's long silences and troubled looks that he had thought indicated that she was not yet over the Norman Stephenson affair and this of course was true but with a difference, for she had not been thinking of Stephenson, in Malaya, but of his child and whether it could pass as her husband's! He had read of such subterfuges and seen them in films and plays, and inwardly he had always scoffed at them, but now he realised that they were not so implausible after all for until this moment he had never doubted the paternity of that stillborn child and even now he found it almost impossible to accept that what the old lady said was true. Then he remembered something else about that first year of marriage, something that took place soon after Sybil's return from the nursing home. There had been no more silences and no more troubled looks, and it had seemed to him then that he had at last succeeded in banishing the spectre of young Stephenson and his ear-splitting sports car. He had found in her, for a spell at least, a response that had lifted him to the heights and kindled in him ambition that had flared up like a rocket and then gone out, not to be lit again for twenty years. He remembered too, her almost frantic insistence that they should have another child at once and that when he cautioned delay on grounds of her health, she had pooh-poohed the risk and proved her point by having Jonquil with the greatest ease less than a year after she had lost her first child.

It all came back and every piece fitted into place so that after all there was no doubting it and, strangely, he did not want to doubt it, for it answered so many questions about their lives and not least among them the question as to why he had never succeeded in inspiring her apart from those first few weeks when she could look at him with a reasonably clear conscience. He thought: 'I suppose it would be fatally easy to go out by the exit labelled self-pity, to persuade myself that she had made a complete fool of me and had never really cared a jot about me one way or the other, but this isn't so and I know it isn't so! She gave me the chance at that time and I didn't take it! Why didn't I take it? Because I thought so little of myself that I could never get close enough to her to treat her as a woman. I always stood off, wondering at my incredible luck, and asking myself how long it would last and somehow this self-doubt must have communicated itself to her so that her good intentions went soggy and at length she began to see me as the person I saw myself. I'm as much to blame for everything as she is and perhaps rather more, because she began by being grateful and was eager to let gratitude develop into something more positive.'

He came out of his reverie to find the old lady still looking at him and behind her mask of impatient asperity there was sympathy and concern.

"You aren't that upset by it, are you son? You don't have to be, she thinks a deal more of you now than she did then for all her tomfoolery. You do like I say and you'll see for yourself, I swear it, you hear me? I knew her from the very beginning and people don't change much, take it from me! Like they are when they come that way they stay for the most part!"

They heard a spluttering cough on the path and then the gate clicked and she jumped up and threw open the door.

"It's Albert!" she said, "and he'll spoil everything if he sees you. Nip out of the back and round the side, quick!"

He allowed himself to be hustled to the back door and into the sooty garden and as she opened the gate into the passage she said, "Don't forget that letter! Write it as soon as you get back! Where are you staying?"

"The New Continental."

"Right, off with you son and good luck," and she shut the side gate and shot the bolt.

He went down between the garden fences to the street and found his car at the corner. As he crossed to it the once familiar sound of the suburb's summer-evening litany reached him, the low hum of traffic along the Surrey Road, the whirr of hand-mower and the cries of children playing on the pavements as the sun went down. It brought the past into such sharp focus that he could only nod and turn his head away when the driver asked: "Back to the hotel, sir?"

.   .   .   .   .

He wrote and posted the letter that same night and then sent a telegram to Olga accepting her offer of the house in The Coombe. The next morning when the girl brought in his tea, he saw that it was going to be another fine day but much hotter, 'a proper scorcher' as the Cockneys say, for although it was barely eight o'clock the sun blazed in a clear blue sky and dust motes danced above a patch of carpet quartered by the sunbeams. He sipped his tea, planning his day like a general preparing for battle. He knew that today would be Rubicon day, that if he returned to this fusty little room tonight with the situation unresolved then he would never see Sybil again, except perhaps over some impersonal solicitor's table. The reflection projected him from bed and into the tiny tiled bathroom where he looked closely into the mirror for signs of strain but found none, noting only that weeks in the open on Kingsbay promenade had given him a healthy tan and also that he badly needed a hair cut.

After breakfast he went out and walked along the sunny streets to Regent Street, one hand in his jacket pocket fondling the banded roll of notes he had taken from his hoard. There were over three hundred there, all in soiled fivers and the touch of them gave him a degree of confidence never conjured from a cheque-book. He went into Hope Brothers and climbed the stairs where a young man gave him some patterns to inspect. He took his time, finally choosing a dark grey mixture and then submitted to the mild indignity of being measured for a new suit, quoted at thirty-four pounds ten. It would be ready for a fitting, they told him, in about a fortnight and he gave a banker's reference and Barrowdene as his address. It was an act of faith in the outcome of the day.

Then, on impulse, he bought a ready-made suit, a charcoal material with a faint stripe and when he had put it on and had the clothes he was wearing parcelled, he bought two expensive shirts, a light blue tie, a pair of shoes and finally, three pairs of summer socks. The bill, apart from the made-to-measure suit, totalled fifty-seven pounds. Never in his life had he spent more than half this amount during a call at an outfitter's.

He went out into the sunshine feeling extraordinarily pleased with himself. For once he felt he belonged here among smart cars and hooting taxis and making his way down towards Trafalgar Square he turned in at a hairdresser's and asked for a trim, short back and sides but not much off the top. Relaxed in the comfortable leather chair he decided to have the whole treatment and ordered a rum shampoo, a face massage and a manicure. He thought, as he watched the pretty girl pare his fingernails: 'Why didn't I behave

like this long ago? Why did I always creep along the back-
streets of life? Was it because I hated spending Sybil's money and never earned enough myself to buy good clothes and
all the trimmings?' The man held the hand-mirror and he
replaced his glasses to inspect the result. "That's splendid!"
he said and gave man and girl half-crown tips. It was, he
reflected, very cheap at the price, for never had he seen himself looking so suave and well-groomed.

On the way back to his hotel he stopped and bought a
small suitcase and upstairs in his room he packed his old
clothes and collected the rest of his things. When he came to
his knapsack he hesitated. Was this the time to strike his
colours and surrender his standard of the future? He made a
sudden decision and stuffed the knapsack into the inadequate
wastepaper basket, a solemn act of defiance and renunciation.
Then, donning a new shirt, new tie and new shoes he rang
for the porter and ordered a hire car, giving instructions for it
to call for him as soon as he had finished lunch.

His route south-east took him over familiar ground, out
through the maze of streets he had traversed the previous
evening and then beyond them through the outer suburbs
spaced by allotments and half-developed sites. He had seen
this part of London change, for when his mother had first
brought him here as a boy it had been almost rural, with
rows of mid-Victorian houses set well back among clumps of
chestnut trees loaded with conkers, with here and there a
few fields enclosed by hawthorn hedges. Birds had sung in
blackberry thickets and there were still country lanes to be
found where cow-parsley sagged under a sprinkling of white
dust but now this had been transformed into a network of
crescents and avenues composed of houses that all looked the
same, flat pink and white boxes, with tiny lawns and tidy
flower-beds sprouting identical-looking flowers and anaemic
shrubs. As they reached the Wyckham Rise crossroads, he
said to his driver: "Very well, drop me here, I'll walk over
the hill!" and he paid the fare and set off through the sparse
coppice that straggled up to the plateau overlooking the new
suburb.

The place seemed to him smaller and more concentrated,
the effect perhaps of having widened his own horizons and
he topped the rise rather breathlessly for it was now four

o'clock and the glare of the sun drove him to seek shade under the birches. Here, however, walking was more difficult and his new shoes pinched, so that he had to sit down for a moment on the seat he had occupied the day he ran away from Napier Hall. Recognising it he realised he had completed a full circle and that his purpose here today was to begin describing another and wider one with Sybil in tow. For the first time since he had set out from Kingsbay his courage faltered but he rallied almost at once, encouraged by all that had happened since the day he had sat down on this very seat four months ago. It was not only memories that stiffened him but material evidence of his success in the outside world, the suit he was wearing and the roll of notes in his pocket. Up to yesterday the knapsack had been his talisman but now it was his wad of fivers and before he went on he did a little sum, calculating that he was now worth more than twice the amount he had been when he set out and that this in itself was a source of reassurance. He went on down the southern side of the slope and entered his avenue, also strangely shrunken, and at the entrance of the drive he drew a deep breath and walked in.

Two cars were parked in the half-moon outside the terrace but neither car was Sybil's. At the sight of them he instinctively sought the cover of the rhododendrons and then inched his way round to the end of the verandah where he could look directly into the big living-room without much chance of being seen.

His fears were confirmed. Sybil was presiding over one of her casting committees and he recognised every person in the room. They were seated three on each side of the reproduction refectory table, two men and four women, with Sybil at the far end facing his way. The men were Aubrey Marcheson, the bank cashier and Cyril Endsleigh, an older man whom he remembered as the O.C. scenery at all Sybil's productions. The women were Endsleigh's rat-toothed wife, Naomi, their daughter, a willowy and rather desiccated girl unaccountably known as 'Bubbles', Mrs. Beckett, who sometimes co-produced and finally the Club Secretary, Miss Teake.

He gave the group a careful scrutiny before dismissing them and concentrating upon his wife. She was looking very smart indeed in a black two-piece that trumpeted haute-couture, but his general impression was that she was not her usual self for her expression was bored, almost petulant, and always on these occasions she had looked serene and genuinely interested in all that was said. She was a little thinner, he thought, than when he last saw her but her face was more handsome than he ever remembered.

At that moment, and without knowing why, he thought of Norman Stephenson again and the conviction grew in his mind that this was exactly how she had looked all those years ago when she had told the young bounder that she was pregnant and had listened to him playing for time to get on a steamship for Malaya. The pity he had felt for her when her mother had told him the story returned as he watched her glance shift from one speaker to another and with a sudden rush of protectiveness he wanted to stride clear of cover and walk through the window, but at this moment he heard a step on the gravel and saw the figure of Mrs. Balcombe, Sybil's mid-week daily, waddle through the kitchen door and walk towards the side gate. He called to her softly and she looked up with surprise.

"You sir? I thought you was still away like the kids . . . !"

His mind jumped ahead at once. "Kids? Jonquil and Keith? They're . . . not back yet?"

"Why no, not till Saturday, sir. The boy stayed on in camp an extra week so Mrs. Sermon 'phoned Portsmouth and said Miss Jonquil could stay with her aunt if she'd a mind to, but she didn't tell me about you coming home!"

"No," said Sebastian, slowly, "she . . . er . . . she didn't know for certain. Have you been paid, Mrs. Balcombe?"

"It don't matter until Wednesday," she told him, "I'm leavin' an hour early today and would have told Mrs. Sermon but I didn't like to bust in because she don't like me to, so I left a note."

Mr. Sermon, disconcerted by the unexpected presence of six of Sybil's intimates, now began to feel that the cards were falling his way. "I'll give Mrs. Sermon the message, Mrs. Balcombe—here," and he handed her a pound note.

"I got no change," she told him, "it's on'y fifteen bob this week, five hours instead o' six on account o' me having to see me sister-in-law in hospital."

"Well, we certainly can't penalise you for that," said Sebastian gaily, "keep the change!"

"Well, thank you sir," she said, but he had already slipped round the side of the house and entered the kitchen, taking Mrs. Balcombe's note and stuffing it into his pocket. Jonquil and Keith away and Mrs. Balcombe gone an hour before her time! This was surely advance information he could turn to account and he stood thinking for a moment before crossing the hall, softly opening the front door and stepping outside. He pressed the bell twice and waited, hearing Sybil shout for Mrs. Balcombe and then, after a pause, somebody got up and opened the garden-room door. Stepping inside he said, loudly, "Thank you, Mrs. Balcombe!" and returned to the hall where he suddenly came face to face with Miss Teake, the Club Secretary.

The sight of him stopped her dead and Sebastian realised at once that she was privy to the secret that lay behind his prolonged absence. He thought, spitefully, 'I wonder if she knows about Scott-James and his photographic trap?' but he beamed at her and said, "Is my wife there, Miss Teake? I've just arrived," and walked swiftly past her into the room. They must have heard his voice in the hall for everyone was looking towards him with interest as he strode in with apologetic breeziness and then came to a sudden stop.

"I say, I'm sorry, I didn't know you were in session! Why on earth didn't you warn me, Sybil? I could easily have caught a later train." Sybil was by no means an easy person to astonish but he congratulated himself that she was astonished now, not only by his appearance but more, he thought, by his perfidy. He noticed also that each member of the committee instinctively shifted their glance from him to her and that under their collective scrutiny colour flooded into her face, giving him the opportunity to walk the length of the table and plant a resounding kiss on her cheek.

"Look here," he said generously, "I'll make myself scarce! You won't be very long will you? I've had rather a long journey and I could do with a wash and brush up, it was insufferably hot in the train!" and he smiled thinly at them so that first Endsleigh, then his wife and then young Marcheson shuffled to their feet and Endsleigh murmured: "We . . . er . . . we were pretty well through, Sermon; you'll want a . . . a meal, I dare say and we could adjourn until Wednesday, couldn't we?" and he appealed rather pathetically to his rat-toothed wife who was now looking at Sybil for an explanation.

'God damn them, they all know what's happened!' thought
Sebastian, 'and they didn't learn it from Sybil but from
putting their long noses together and sniggering across the
tables at Martyr Café coffee sessions!' and he felt glad that he
had adopted this particular strategy and given them all something to discuss on the way down there for tea, a tea, he
reflected, that they would otherwise have enjoyed right here
at Sybil's expense.

As Sybil said nothing, Mrs. Endsleigh spoke. "Thursday
would have been better after all dear," and said it in a slightly
aggrieved tone. "Of course, there is still the matter of the
junior lead for the April play but there's no real rush about
that!" and with a loud sniff she walked deliberately out of
the French window.

Sybil lost her rigidity. "Wait Vera!" she said, reaching out
her hand but Vera Endsleigh had gone, having contrived to
leave behind her the impression that she had suffered a grave
indignity. Her husband, shuffling a little, said: "Don't worry
my dear, I . . . er . . . I imagine you have things to discuss.
Any afternoon next week will do. Well . . . er . . . !" and he
trailed off, nodding towards Sebastian and hurrying after his
wife. Aubrey Marcheson's exit had slightly more dignity for
he paused to kiss Sybil's hand and Sebastian thought he had
never seen a more affected gesture performed inside an
English house. Then 'Bubbles' Endsleigh went out and after
her Mrs. Beckett and last of all a flustered Miss Teake, who
made a kind of half-curtsy to Sybil and dropped some papers
in her confusion. For the space of about three seconds they
were alone with a line of blotters and ashtrays and then,
moving like a mechanical doll, Sybil went after them without
a glance in his direction.

He heard a good deal of muttering and whispering and
then the cars moved off almost simultaneously and Sybil
returned to the room, her features very composed and holding
herself very erect. He said, quietly, "I'm sorry, Sybil, but I
had to get rid of them! What I had to say is important and
they aren't, believe me!"

Sybil gave no sign of having heard but swept past him into
the hall. He heard her rustle swiftly upstairs and then, faintly,
the bang of the bedroom door. The sound roused him and he
thought, 'If she's reverting to those tactics again she's got a

shock coming to her. The time I let a ninepenny bolt and socket stand between me and my future is past,' but for a few moments he did not move but stood with hands deep in his trouser pockets staring into the garden, forcing himself to review the situation calmly and carefully.

Keith was in camp and Jonquil was in Portsmouth. Mrs. Balcombe had left but Sybil did not yet know they were alone in the house, for the daily usually stayed on another hour. It was Monday, not a gardener's day, and it was unlikely at this hour that a tradesman would call. Thinking it over he realised that he could not have improved his chances if he had planned it this way.

He shut the French windows and returned to the kitchen, locking the door and putting the key on the shelf over the stove. He returned to the hall, slipped the yale catch of the front door and lifted the telephone receiver from the hook. Then, treading softly, he went upstairs and along the corridor to their room.

The door was not locked as he had expected it to be and when he entered she was gathering clothes and putting them into a suitcase that lay open on the bed. She did not look up but went on opening drawers and selecting toilet accessories and items of clothing. He noticed that her lip quivered and that her hands, usually so deliberate in their movements, were clumsy handling small objects. He said, standing by the door, "Where are you off to now, Sybil?"

She paused in the act of crossing from dressing-table to bed. "I'm going to Dora's at Portsmouth and there's absolutely no point at all in your following me or making any more trouble Sebastian! I haven't the least idea what prompted you to behave like that or why, in fact, you came back here at all!"

"I can tell you that, Sybil," he said, doggedly, "I'm here to make an end of this nonsense and take you back with me to Kingsbay. I've learned rather more than how to supervise a foreshore since I've been away! I've learned, for instance, that I'm still very much in love with you!"

Her head came round and for a split second their eyes met, then she threw up her chin as though checking an impulse and said, primly: "I can't accept that, Sebastian! You behaved intolerably when you went away, you've remained away all this time, and when you eventually return the first thing you do is to humiliate me in front of my friends. All that doesn't add up to love or even good manners. In fact, I don't know what it does demonstrate, except perhaps a childish kind of spite and obstinacy."

"You wouldn't admit to obstinacy yourself, Sybil, not even as a basis of discussion?"

She flung the garment she was holding on the bed and whipped round, facing him squarely.

"How dare you say that? What have I done but wait here for you to come to your senses and court fresh humiliation by coming all the way to Devon? Do you expect me to go on pleading with you to come home and accept a normal husband's responsibilities?"

"I haven't any responsibilities here," he said, slowly, "and now I realise that I never did have any. It was lack of them that sent me away."

A little of her self-possession left her.

"You never told me you were unhappy or upset! You never gave me the slightest sign . . . !"

"Yes, I did, the night I left but you wouldn't unbend for a second, or have you forgotten already?"

"No, I haven't forgotten," she said, breathing hard, "and if you hadn't been in such a crazy hurry I . . . !"

She stopped, biting back an admission of what had occurred that evening immediately after he had presented his ultimatum and walked out into the night. Even at this distance she could still recall the humiliation of standing almost naked at the landing window and watching his shadow pass under the street lamp.

"Well," he said, coming into the room and sitting on the bed, "we shan't get very far discussing the past, Sybil. Right now I'm interested in our future and if you say we haven't got one as man and wife I won't accept that. In fact, that's why I took the bull by the horns and sold the house!"

"The house? *This* house?"

He saw that he had shocked her out of her defensive sulkiness and went on, "This house, and I've bought another in Kingsbay! I mean to take that job at Barrowdene because I shall never have a chance like that again and I'm taking you back with me, if necessary, tonight! There's no immediate hurry, however, and you can leave your packing for a moment."

He saw her eyes dart to the door as though she feared a repetition of the scene enacted here the last time they were together in this room but he was not bothered. They were secure from interruption and his easy victory downstairs had restored his confidence in the powers of reason.

"It was the only way to make sure that you gave it a trial," he went on. "This house has become a sort of status symbol to you and as long as you remain here those bloody amateurs will always have far more of you than me!"

She was looking at him in a way that she had never done before, not even when he had emerged, crowned with his yachting cap, from the beleaguered ladies' lavatory.

"You . . . you *can't* have sold the house," she said, at last, "it isn't yours to sell! You *know* it isn't yours to sell! I . . . I could prosecute you for even advertising it!"

"Legally it's mine," he said, "and the deal has already been approved by a solicitor. There's no question of money involved because I've already made the other house over to you. As a matter of fact there's a small profit and I'll put that to your account."

"But I don't want to sell!" she screamed, advancing on him and waving her hands as though she itched to box his ears. "How *dare* you go behind my back and do a thing like that! How dare you take advantage of my generosity in putting the house in your name all those years ago. It's the most despicable trick I've ever heard of!"

"Talking of despicable tricks," he said, calmly, "what's happened to Scott-James, the Private Eye? Has he reported yet?"

"Don't try and sidetrack me!" she snapped, "this house . . ."

"Oh damn the house!" he cut in, irritated by the implication that she cared more for bricks and mortar than what happened to their marriage. "What the devil possessed you to send a man like Scott-James to spy on me? How could you be such a fool, Sybil?"

"So that's why you're here, that's why you're acting like a criminal lunatic? If Kelvin did pay a call on you I expect he told you what action I've decided to take."

"He didn't have time," said Sebastian, grinning, "because I knocked him down and smashed his camera! Somehow I didn't think he'd be in a great hurry to report what happened!"

"It's no good," she said, "I've been a fool to go on hoping you'd come to your senses. I'm not going to try any more and we can continue this discussion in front of a solicitor!" and she suddenly turned away and walked towards the door.

Her withdrawal caught him at a disadvantage. For one thing he had not been expecting it and for another he was sitting and she was standing between him and the bathroom. It was not that he was afraid of the bathroom bolt but he realised that if she did get inside and lock it against him she could get to the telephone before he could stop her and in her present state of excitement she was capable of shouting for help. He leaped up and was just in time to seize her by the shoulder, spinning her round and holding her in the narrow angle of the door and window. It was the first time he had touched her in months and it had a surprising effect upon him for as she shrank under the pressure of his fingers all the resentment and temper left him.

"Look here, Sybil, let's stop behaving like a couple in a music-hall sketch! I love you and I need you more than ever! The kids have grown away from us and whatever the people round here mean to you I can replace them. We could be very happy down there and make a fresh start and that's something we could never do in this district. Let's give it a six-months' trial anyway!"

As he faced her, detaining her by the shoulder, he yearned to be done with pleading and persuasion and break the deadlock between them by an embrace, by touching her lips and her hair. Suddenly he felt so much older and wiser than her, old enough and wise enough to lose face or appear to lose it. Because she made no attempt to break free he sensed the same will to compromise and extended his hold by dropping his right hand to her waist and throwing his left arm round her neck. Then, as he was on the point of kissing her, he felt a stab of acute pain in his right hand and leaped back with a yell, whipping his hand to his mouth then lowering it and staring at a puncture that was already welling blood.

"Good God!" he shouted, looking from the wound to the point of the nail scissors that she now held like an offered dagger, "why did you have to do that?" and when she continued to stare at him he threw aside reason and patience,

surrendering to rage and frustration generated not only by
pain but by all the disappointments that had emanated from
this woman over twenty years, hurts that seemed now to find
their vent through the bleeding stab in his hand. With a yell
of wrath he swept her up and dragged her away from the
window, collapsing on the littered bed with Sybil thrust sideways on top of him. In his fury he did not notice that she
made almost no resistance, that immediately after seizing the
scissors and striking them downward into his hand she had
remained rigid, staring not at him but at the trickle of blood
on his knuckles. He shouted:

"You act like a child and by God I'll treat you as one!"
and holding her firmly with his bleeding hand he used the
other to jerk at the waist-band of her skirt, ripping it almost
free of her with a single tug and proceeding straight away to
follow her mother's advice.

"Stop it, Sebastian . . . I'm sorry . . . sorry!" she cried,
becoming a child again in the shrillness of her plea and a
wild flailing of the legs, but he was resolved to trade smart
for smart and in another second the black silk petticoat had
followed the skirt, both garments becoming entangled in her
high heels and reducing her cover to a pair of nylon briefs.
For a fraction of a second he thought of following the old
lady's example literally but with his injured hand he was
finding it difficult to maintain his grip and in any case the
briefs were totally inadequate protection as her yell testified
the moment his hand descended. She gave a series of ineffectual heaves and her initial shout must have carried down the
long garden and across the tennis-courts in Cedarwood Close
but, far from deterring him, her shout and struggles gave him
the greatest satisfaction and five more times his hand came
down before it brushed against a heaven-sent instrument of
correction, a substantial rosewood hairbrush that was among
the accessories she had thrown on the bed. He seized this
with a fierce joy, renewing his grip and shifting his target
and whacking away at her squirming bottom as though it had
been a carpet on a line. At the fourth blow the brush snapped
in two parts so he hurled the handle to the floor, intending
to resume the work by hand and seemingly bent on continuing indefinitely, but suddenly he realised that her struggles
and outcry had almost ceased and with a sharp sense of

revulsion he loosed his hold so that she slid forward and rolled clear, finishing half-kneeling with her face pressed to the bed, one hand thrown forward, the other spread protectively behind her.

Crouched there it was impossible to see her as a woman of almost forty, her hair and clothes disordered, her kneeling pose that of a scared adolescent caught out in some lie or piece of naughtiness. The illusion was so striking that he reached out and touched her hair, saying, "I'm sorry, but honestly . . . honestly . . . Sybil, you asked for it, you really asked for it," and he fumbled in his breast pocket, taking out a handkerchief and wrapping it round his hand which was now bleeding freely, soiling his new suit, the bedspread and the carpet.

"You hurt me, Sebastian," she said, slowly, "you hurt me dreadfully!"

He did not recognise a subtle change in her voice, its sharpness blunted, all its petulance and condescension drained away. There was no element of complaint in it. The words were said almost wonderingly, as though by someone who had been considerably astonished. He did not notice this because he was bowed under the weight of defeat.

It seemed to him then that they had blundered from mistake to mistake, piling one upon the other until what little prospect there had ever been of a reconciliation was crushed flat under an accumulation of wrongs and grudges. What had begun so well had ended like the last act of a tasteless French farce, with him bleeding all over the carpet and her standing there rubbing her sore behind. What dignity had ever attached itself to their marriage had gone, punctured by nail scissors, drummed out by a hairbrush. He got up and smoothed his jacket.

"I dare say it did hurt," he said glumly, "but so did the scissors! You're quite right, Sybil, there's absolutely no sense in going on like this, we should probably end up by killing one another. I'm sorry I walloped you and I dare say you'll come round to being sorry about my hand. We'd best call it a day but you don't have to trail off to Portsmouth, I'll go back to the hotel and get a train to Kingsbay in the morning."

"Let me look at your hand," she said briefly and without waiting for him to offer it she lifted it from his knee and unwrapped the handkerchief. It was not very much of a cut and had now stopped bleeding but the point of the scissors had penetrated a quarter-inch and it still throbbed painfully. "Wait, I'll get something for it!" and she kicked off her shoes, miraculously still on her feet and went into the bathroom, returning a moment later with some powdered alum and a tin of Elastoplast. She applied the astringent and he pulled a wry face at the smart.

"Hi, that stings like hell!" he protested and this time she smiled openly.

"So does my bottom but alum won't do it any good!" She pretended not to notice his look of amazement and stuck the plaster in place. "I forgot you were left-handed," she said, lightly, "I ought to have put that one out of action!"

For a moment he was too astonished to shake himself free of gloom but watched her in silence as she moved about the room, straightening things, putting bottles and cartons back on the dressing table, picking up the two pieces of the hairbrush and inspecting them with interest. Finally he said: "You mean you don't want me to go? You don't care whether I stay?"

"Yes, I care," she said, frankly, "I care very much whether you go!" She stopped tidying and stood in front of him. "I'm sorry I did such a stupid thing, Sebastian, genuinely sorry, but you don't have to be! I don't know of any other action on your part that would have shocked me into being sorry before it was too late, or before we enlarged our folly. I don't want us to part, God knows I don't and never did! I'm not making any excuses for jabbing the scissors into you but I think I've got a good one for treating you the way I have lately."

"You don't have to bother with excuses," he began, joyfully.

"Yes, I do, Sebastian," she went on, cutting him short with a gesture, "because it's part of the whole pattern of our marriage. I wasn't in love with you when it began and I wasn't when we had the children. I don't think I even started being until you walked out of the house and stayed away all that time but I am now and in a way I find it difficult to tell you because you aren't the same man any more. You aren't the man I cheated by marrying on the rebound and you aren't the Sebastian Sermon who went away from here in the spring. I suppose that man would have satisfied most women but he didn't mean a great deal to me. Well, I've learned something too in the last few months, not so much as you perhaps but something, and because of that I at least owe you the truth, even if it costs all that's left to us now! That first child I had wasn't yours, it was Norman's, Norman Stephenson's, so you can guess how badly I needed a first reserve!"

She paused, awaiting his reaction but there was so little that lack of it made her falter for a moment.

She said, dismally, "I don't suppose you even remember Norman?"

"Yes," he said quietly, "I remember him very well but I don't know why you should want to rake up ancient history at this particular moment." He thought a white lie would do no harm, so he added, "I was never sure whose child it was but I knew well it wasn't mine and I took you on the rebound terms anyway, so why should I be indignant about it after twenty years?"

She looked wonderingly at him and he noticed with a start that her eyes were wet and reached out, taking her by the hand.

She sat down on the bed beside him, twisting her body round and laying both hands on his knee. "You . . . you don't care? You aren't upset by knowing?"

"I don't give a damn," he said cheerfully, "that is—not if you meant what you said just now about being in love with me. That's something I didn't know and something I was resigned to doing without!" and with a sudden movement he threw his sound arm round her, pulled her to him and kissed her on the mouth.

Then he had another surprise, a far bigger one than that administered by her confession, for it was clear to him from the moment their lips touched that for some moments now she had been impatiently waiting some manifestation from him that did not involve excuses, explanations or even protestations. She not only returned his kiss in a way that had never happened before but launched herself at him with a lustiness that almost frightened him.

They were still lying there when the heat went out of the evening sun and twilight hovered over the broken line of roofs in Cedarwood Close. He was sleeping but she was wide awake, musing with his head on her shoulder, his injured hand flung across her breast, and she thought as she listened to his regular breathing: 'Dear God, what fun we've been missing, the pair of us all these years! How long have we got to catch up? He's forty-nine and I'm only ten years younger but can you measure vitality by a calendar? He's got plenty it seems and me? I've got far more than I thought I had that night he came in here rampaging after banging that boy's head against the water-pipes!' and then, as he stirred slightly, and she flexed her hand to rid it of pins and needles, she thought, 'What an odd sequel this is to having one's behind tanned by one's husband! Where did he learn to be so different? Selling antiques? Supervising beach amusements? Or at this new school he thinks so much about?' None seemed to her a likely source and she wondered if there had been a woman somewhere, the girl at the zoo, or someone she didn't know about? If there was she didn't care a hoot. She was as sure of him as any woman can be sure of any man.

She turned her head slightly and looked down at him, noting the deep sun tan on his skin and his general fitness. He had changed physically as well. He not only seemed broader and taller but carried himself differently. His taste in clothes had improved and there was about him an air of decision that had eluded him all his life.

Her left arm was numb and at last she was obliged to withdraw it so that he stirred and opened his eyes. She said, "One thing will have to be changed Sebastian, and that's it—the name—Sebastian. Maybe that was part of the trouble. Didn't anyone ever give you a nickname? Most schoolmasters get one, don't they?"

He said with mild surprise, "Didn't you ever know what the boys called me?"

"No, what was it?"

" 'Preacher'."

She laughed, "Well, it'll do I suppose . . . 'Preacher' . . . Preacher Sermon!" and she savoured it in silence for a moment.

"What time is it?" he asked, presently.

"About nine I should think but we aren't going anywhere, not until morning anyway."

"I'm damned hungry," he said and she laughed again so that he noted how seldom he had heard her laugh in the past.

"I'm not in the least surprised," she said. "Me too! Could you do with cold chicken, ham and salad?"

"By George I could! Then we'll make an early night of it," and he kissed her lightly on the ear.

She got up, stretching, and as she glanced round the dis-ordered room it struck him that a completely new and richly rewarding relationship had been bestowed upon them as though by magic, that this was precisely how he had always thought of marriage, an easy rhythm of passionate possession and relaxed companionship, with free and easy access between two minds and bodies. She went into the bathroom and he heard her humming. The sound, he thought, was as pleasant as her laughter.

He sat up and climbed off the bed, giving himself a covert glance in the long mirror and at that moment she came back into the room.

"That suit!" she said. "It's in a dreadful state and it's brand new, isn't it? Give it to me and I'll hang it up. Why on earth didn't you take it off?"

"You didn't give me time," he said, grinning, and slowly peeled off the jacket.

He watched her smooth the pocket flaps and hang the coat on a hanger thinking that never before had he seen her so tousled or relaxed or at ease with him. As she crossed back in front of the window the last flush of the sunset struck her bare shoulders and seemed to linger a moment in the short hair on her neck. Satiated he still thought of her as the most desirable woman he had ever seen or imagined and said: "You're beautiful, Sybil, far more so than when you were a girl!" She sat down at the dressing table stool and smiled at him in the tilted mirror.

"You've already told me that half a dozen times this evening but I can take any amount of encores at my age— Preacher!" and she began to dress her hair, raising both hands so that golden light ran across her shoulders.

"Come over here again!" he said, but she laughed, spilling a hairpin from her mouth and said, "No, not until we've eaten, but tell me something else. What is it you find so special about this particular school? It isn't status, I know you better than that."

"You'd have to be there for some time and it'll grow on you," he told her. "I'm banking on that but the school is only a part of it, quite a small part."

"It's everything that's happened to you lately!"

"Yes. You notice the difference?"

"Indeed I do, you impressed it on me!" and she stopped arranging her hair and sat sideways on the bed, looking down at him with a curious teasing light in her eyes that was as strange to him as everything else about her since she had dressed the wound on his hand.

He said: "Self-doubt is a worse handicap than a physical disability. A man can get by with one leg or one arm but he's in a strait jacket for life if he learns to think of himself as a non-starter by the time he's twenty! That's what happened to me and it wasn't until I got right away that time that I got one arm free and discovered I was as effective with that as most men are with two! But it wasn't just a case of learning to believe in myself, it was the attitude of other people the moment I made the effort. The first day away I earned twenty pounds on a deal, bamboozled one of the toughest operators in The Trade and was the life and soul of a party at a pub! In the weeks that followed I drove a passenger coach through a storm over some of the worst roads in the country and rescued a child from drowning in front of a hundred people. I also discovered that I could exercise effective authority over men and women as well as boys!"

She was propped up on one elbow looking down at him and the smile, half affectionate, half teasing, was still playing about her lips.

"Anything else? Any more conquered worlds Alexander?"

He paused a moment and then, deliberately, added: "Two women fell in love with me or thought they did! I suppose that helped as much as the other conquests."

"Yes, it would," she said, "I can imagine that. Am I going to hear about them?"

"No, you're not," he said, "at all events not yet!" and he made a grab at her and pulled her down so that their lips met and freshly applied lipstick transferred itself to his chin. "Oh God, Sybil!" he said, the banter leaving his voice, "I need you and want you so terribly! I said I got one hand free but the other never was, not until now! It would have been like winning a fortune and not being allowed to do more than count it every night! I can't believe it's happened the way it has, I need to keep reassuring myself!" and he let his hands

slip down over her shoulders and half-raised himself to kiss
her softly on each breast.

She got up and said, lightly, "You need a shave. I'll call
up when supper's ready," and she slipped into her dressing-
gown and went out.

He got up and went into the bathroom to look for a spare
razor he knew was there and as he ran water he heard her
moving about in the kitchen immediately below. He did not
believe in miracles but here was one, the kind of wife he had
always wanted emerging as from a magic bottle or an Olym-
pian cloud, a gay, tolerant woman who not only welcomed
his affection but had suddenly learned to bask in it and then
feed it back to him with prodigal generosity, a woman with
whom he felt completely at ease as though this fusion of
personalities was the result of years and years of adjustment
and shared experience. He did not believe that a single
dominant act on his part could have brought about such a
change but was inclined to think that the mere act of spanking her at a moment when she was shocked at the sight of
the blood she had drawn had completed a corrosive process,
something that had begun as long ago as last spring when she
had first found herself alone. It must, he thought, have something to do with her physical needs and had she been a
different kind of woman he might well have lost her altogether but she was not a woman who could find satisfaction
in promiscuous relationships. She was Sybil Sermon, the
woman whose apparent need to be surrounded by admirers
and queen of her immediate circle was nothing but a tiresome
substitute for the demands of a single, virile male, someone
who knew what he wanted and how to go about getting it.
His mistake had been in not making those demands long ago,
in not elbowing the troubled memory of Norman Stephenson
and of other men she had known out of the way, and he
realised now that he could have done this from the very
beginning had he possessed one-tenth of the confidence in
himself that he possessed now.

Well, he was extraordinarily lucky that it was not too late,
that they could begin again at a couple of minutes to midnight and as he puckered his lip to scrape away at his beard
with a blade that she had been misusing in his absence, he
was conscious of a great, warm rush of affection for her that

caught at his heart like a chord of organ music and filled him with a sense of joy and well-being so intense that his hand trembled and he had to lay the razor aside and steady himself for a moment.

CHAPTER ELEVEN

For Those Who
Insist on Looking
Round Corners

ON the morning of his fiftieth birthday, a Saturday early in April, Mr. Sermon took advantage of a free period and went across the quad and up the long slope of the sports field to the chestnut tree where the cricket roller was parked.

Sebastian had been doing house-duty for Bennett who was sick and had remained at school overnight so he paused outside the library wondering whether he should phone Sybil but decided against it. When he left her the previous day she had seemed to him to be enjoying the very best of health and was probably at this moment helping Mrs. Baxter, her daily, turn out one of the rooms. Sybil had been doing a great deal of turning out lately and when he had commented upon it she had told him that it was a compulsion that often accompanied pregnancy. He thought, as he walked along the rim of the staked-out running track, 'Great Scot, I'm fifty today and on the point of becoming a father again! If someone had prophesied this a year ago I should have considered them indecent!'

He took a seat on the huge roller and lit a cigarette, considering whether he wanted Sybil's child to be male or female and decided, quite definitely, that it ought to be male. The boy would come here, he supposed but by that time he himself would be getting on for retirement and Sybil would be in her middle fifties. It was rather sad, he thought, that the child should have such elderly parents but that was something that couldn't be helped. The astonishing thing was that it should exist at all and his mind travelled back over the pleasant, almost uneventful months to the day the child had been conceived after that fantastic climax to his seventeen-week odyssey.

The sun was very warm up here, beating on his face through a gap in the larch plantation and he wondered if it was shining on Rachel Grey and if the snows had melted in Ontario. Had she found what she was looking for out there he wondered, or had she abandoned veterinary work in favour of some fresh enthusiasm? He had no way of knowing for sure, she had written once to him and twice to her father but she was not much of a correspondent and never told you anything important. Not like Olga, for instance, now settled in Boston and more American than the Americans if her opinions on the latest world crisis were any guide.

He rummaged in his pocket wondering if he still had Olga's last letter but it was not there and among the various papers and reminder notes he found one bearing a telephone number. For a moment or so it meant absolutely nothing to him and then he remembered, it was a number that Tapper Sugg had urged him to call and make an appointment to see some gilt cupids and oak panelling. He still executed commissions for Tapper and found most of them profitable. He knew now that he would never forsake teaching, would never contemplate exchanging Barrowdene for another school not even if they offered him a Headship but it was pleasant to feel that if ever he needed an alternative means of livelihood there was one waiting for him round the corner. He folded the slip of paper and carefully replaced it in his wallet.

The five-minute bell clanged across the big field and Sebastian saw the crane-like figure of the Headmaster coast round the corner of the chapel and make his way along the cloister to the seat under the fives court, now occupied by a solitary boy.

'That's odd,' he said to himself, 'I wondered why young Kibbins was moping there. Rowlandson can't have sent him

out of class because Rowlandson never sends anyone out!"
and he watched the boy stand up as the Headmaster approached and remain in conversation with him for a moment.
Presently the boy pointed up towards the plantation and the
Head began to stride in Sebastian's direction. 'He wants me
for something,' Sebastian told himself, 'and I imagine it's to
ask about the journey-money cheque.'

"Hullo there!" Grey called when he was about fifty yards
off. "I was looking for you, Sermon."

"I thought you were and I cashed the cheque and gave the
money to the Bursar," Sebastian told him.

"You did what? Oh yes . . . yes, yes, but it wasn't about
that!" He stopped, rubbing his long nose. "Hanged if I can
remember what I did want you for now Sermon, but come,
take a turn with me! Lovely morning . . . I like the smell of
a morning like this, it reduces me to round about forty
again!"

"Delighted to hear it, Headmaster," said Sebastian, "I'm
fifty today!"

"You are? Splendid, splendid, you don't look it my dear
fellow," and the Head took his arm in a familiar fashion and
propelled Sebastian down the gentle slope.

"Have you remembered what you wanted to see me about?"
asked Sebastian, as they approached the war memorial.

"Yes, I have," it's Kibbins," said the Head, "he's going
through a bad time, Sermon. Parents got themselves divorced
last week and the wretched little toad doesn't even know
where he's going when we break up tomorrow week!"

"I'm sorry to hear that," said Sebastian. "He's in Bennett's
house isn't he? Can't Mrs. Bennett take him on for a week
or so?"

"No, she can't," said Grey, "because Bennett's going into
hospital for his operation on Saturday," and he paused,
regarding Mr. Sermon speculatively from under hedgelike
brows. "Fact is, Kibbins' father can't pick him up for a fortnight. He rang me this morning about it and I've just told the
boy. He took it pretty badly," and again he waited, still
looking hard at Sebastian.

"Well, I don't know . . ." began Mr. Sermon, hesitantly and
then, with a glance over his shoulder at the distant figure on
the fives court seat, he made a decision. Without knowing

why he felt a sudden kinship with the boy and it occurred to him that by the end of term Sybil would almost certainly have entered the nursing home. He knew Kibbins but slightly, remembering him as a studious type who kept to himself, read a good deal and was a duffer at games.

"You were saying?" said the Head, hopefully.

"He can stay with me if he doesn't mind pigging it," said Sebastian. "The baby is due any day and when Sybil goes into the nursing home I shall be looking after myself. Would Kibbins care to share my chores until his father calls for him?"

Fred Grey beamed and thumped Sebastian's shoulder. "I'm quite sure he would," he said enthusiastically and then, as though confiding a great secret, "As a matter of fact, Sermon, I was rather hoping you'd offer but I knew your wife's time was near and I didn't like to ask."

"You almost did ask," said Mr. Sermon with a grin.

"Yes, I did, didn't I?" admitted Grey blandly. "He could stay on at school of course, but this is a depressing place when the boys have gone and frankly, Kibbins needs a friend! Not me, I'm far too talkative! Do you know, Sermon, more than half the trouble here can be traced back to the divorce courts!"

"Yes, I've already noticed that," said Sebastian and suddenly he saw the source of his kinship with Kibbins and understood why he had offered to take the boy in. Not long ago he himself had been teetering on the edge of a divorce and he realised, looking back, that he had been very upset about it. Somehow, because of this, he felt that he owed Kibbins a slice of comradeship.

"I'll have a chat to the lad after lunch," he said, "but in the meantime I'd better ring my wife and ask her to arrange for our daily woman to stay on. Was there anything else, Headmaster?"

Grey looked puzzled, clapping a hand to his highest tuft. "Was there? Oh yes, there was! I'm glad you're taking Kibbins, Sermon, because he'll be in your house!" and he gave Sebastian a sly but painful nudge.

"My house? *Bennett's house?* But Bennett isn't retiring for another four years . . ."

"He's changed his mind," said Grey calmly, "or his wife

has changed it for him! This last illness of his has put the
wind up her and she's persuaded him to go at the end of
summer term." He gave Sebastian a long, shrewd glance.
"You won your battle over getting your wife to Kingsbay;
do you think she'd take kindly to moving all over again in
September?"

Mr. Sermon was too stunned to reply. A house! Bennett's
house! Something that he had considered no more than remote
possibility! He wondered how other masters might react to a
man getting a house after less than a year on the staff and
then he remembered that Fred Grey's policy had been to
build up a cadre of very young masters and that all the
elderly men had houses of their own. He said, deliberately,
"I should have to discuss this with Sybil over the week-end.
I think she might come round to the idea but things aren't
quite as simple as they were. The idea of this baby terrified
me at first but now I've got thoroughly used to it and in a
way it's been a Godsend, it has given her so much to think
about!"

"Well, you can both think about it over the Easter
holidays," said Grey, "and don't worry about internal jealousies because there's no one else at all suitable and in any
case I've told Bennett to keep quiet about it for the time
being. Where is your next period?"

"The Lower Third," Sebastian told him.

"I'll keep 'em quiet while you phone your wife now," said
Grey, "for it's obvious you're fidgeting to call her up!" and
he turned abruptly on his heel and strode back towards the
school buildings where mobs of boys were milling to and
fro during the break period.

Sebastian made his way to the library block where there
was a telephone in a room adjoining the bursar's office. No
one was there so he shut the door on the strident chorus
arising from the quadrangle and cloister and asked the operator for his home number.

Sybil answered the call almost at once. "How are you
feeling?" he asked anxiously for he thought she sounded
breathless.

"Elephantine!" she replied cheerfully, "I wasn't half this
size with either of the others and I think we must have
miscounted!"

"Not on your life," he said, "that's one date I'm sure about! You're quite sure you'll be okay until I get back tonight?"

"Quite sure, and don't fuss! Oh, Bignall the Town Clerk has been here. He's invited us both to the Civic dinner on Wednesday. I told him you'd go but it's a case of Miss Otis regrets as far as I'm concerned and he only had to look at me to agree!"

For perhaps the thousandth time since their fight in the bedroom he marvelled at the astounding revolution in her outlook and approach to life, and to him. 'Elephantine', 'Don't fuss', 'Miss Otis regrets . . . !' quips at the expense of her own swelling figure and his old-maidish concern for her, a woman who seemingly had nothing in common with the majestic Sybil Sermon who had queened it over the Wyckham Rise Amateurs for so many years. He said, with some misgiving, "I've . . . er . . . some more news, Sybil! Grey has just offered me Bennett's house, when he retires in July. How do you feel about accepting? It'll mean selling up and moving again."

Five seconds passed, then she said, very clearly:

"Is Bennett's house part of the original building in that wing covered with virginia creeper?"

"Yes, the block nearest the plantation. It's pretty primitive I believe but I dare say Grey will make them renovate here and there before anyone new takes over."

"Tell him you'll take it," she said.

"Oh look, you can't decide that quickly Sybil, you'll have the baby to cope with . . . and anyway we haven't got to decide right now, Bennett's retirement isn't official for months!"

"You want it, don't you?"

"Yes, I do, I want it very much indeed but that isn't the point, Sybil. You gave way over coming down here last year and I'd be more than willing to give way over this and wait for another house to come up."

"How long would that be?"

"Two or three years, maybe."

"We might all be dead by then; take it!"

He let ten or twelve seconds tick by. Then she went on, "This isn't something we need to think about, Sebastian, because there's no longer anyone else to consider! Jonquil looks like being married in a year, and Keith is happy

enough messing about at that Hounslow filling-station. Whatever you want I'll settle for, and if the house needs new
plumbing and a coat of paint we can pay for it ourselves. Tell
the Head that you've spoken to me and I've advised you to
accept it. Tell him that having started a family again at
forty I've decided to go in for mothering in a big way! How
many boys are there in Bennett's house?"

"About fifty," he said smiling. "The youngest is thirteen
plus thank God, but Sybil . . . wait . . . don't ring off!"

"I'm still here."

"Then, thank you dear, and I love you very much. I
can't tell you how much over the bursar's telephone but it's a
very impressive total!"

"Thank *you*," she said, "I'll take you up on that when I'm
in a less interesting condition!" and he heard her laugh as she
rang off.

He went to the window that looked over the steep roofs to
the dark green line of the plantation. From here he could see
the frontage of the old wing, with its twisted Tudor chimney-
pots and creeper-fringed windows reflecting the eleven o'clock
sun. He stood there for a few minutes, appreciation of life
rising in him like sap until his throat contracted and tears
broke thorough and his sense of well-being sprang partly
from contemplation of Bennett's creeper-clad house, soon to
be his house and empire, but far more so from the memory
of Sybil's voice and the communicated comradeship it had
conveyed to him. What chemistry, he wondered, had wrought
such a change in her? They were lovers now in a sense that
they had never been before, not in the very earliest days of
their marriage but there was more to it than that for in the
last six months they seemed to have generated a current of
sympathy, trust and understanding that crackled so fiercely
and continuously that it boosted them clear of the hazards
that menaced couples of their age and temperament. Yet her
acceptance of his news about the house, her readiness to
pack up and move all over again so soon after pulling up
roots astonished him as nothing had since her surrender the
night he returned home. As he thought about it his love for
her engulfed him, so that he wanted most desperately to
express it in deeds he could never achieve and sonnets he
could never write, for today, almost exactly one year after the

first onrush of his Spring madness, Mr. Sermon felt very humble again. The difference was, however, that he now knew humility, while a virtue, required watching as carefully as a secret vice.

78062

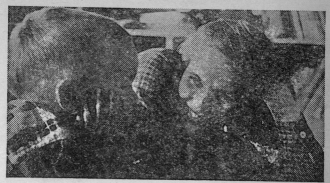

Today they're playing word games.
Before he's five, he can be reading 150 words a minute.

HOW TO GIVE YOUR CHILD A SUPERIOR MIND

A remarkable new book tells how you, yourself—at home—with no special training can actually add as much as thirty points to your child's effective I.Q....how you can help him move ahead quickly in school and enable him to be more successful in an education-conscious world.

Best of all, your child can achieve this early success without being pushed and without interference with a happy, normal, well-adjusted childhood.

GIVE YOUR CHILD A SUPERIOR MIND provides a planned program of home instruction that any parent can start using immediately. *You will learn:*

1. How to awaken your child's inborn desire to learn.
2. How to teach your child to read.
3. How to help your child streak ahead in math.
4. How to give your child the power of abstract reasoning.
5. How to increase your child's effective I.Q.

At all bookstores, or mail coupon today.➤

78062